PRAISE FOR PAUL DI FILIPPO

"Di Filippo is a joyful writer…insightful…skillful."
—*Washington Post Book Review*

"Paul Di Filippo's *The Steampunk Trilogy* is the literary equivalent of Max Ernst's collages of nineteenth-century steel engravings: spooky, haunting, hilarious."
—William Gibson

"Di Filippo is like gourmet potato chips to me. I can never eat just one of his stories."
—Harlan Ellison

"Di Filippo is the spin doctor of SF—and it's a powerful medicine he brews."
—Brian Aldiss

"[Di Filippo's collection] *Fractal Paisleys* channelsurfs postmodern apocalypse, brilliantly."
—Jonathan Lethem

WIKIWORLD
AND OTHER STORIES

PAUL DI FILIPPO

WILDSIDE PRESS

"Introduction: My Di Fi" © 2013 by Rudy Rucker "Providence" © 2009 by Paul Di Filippo. Originally published in *The Solaris Book of New Science Fiction: Volume Three* (February 2009, Solaris Books). "Argus Blinked" © 2007 by Paul Di Filippo. Originally published in *Nature, Vol. 449* (October 2007). "Life in the Anthropocene" © 2010 by Paul Di Filippo. Originally published in *The Mammoth Book of Apocalyptic SF* (May 2010, Robinson Publishing). "Bombs Away!" © 2009 by Paul Di Filippo. Originally published in *Nature, Vol. 460* (August 2009). "Cockroach Love" © 2009 by Damien Broderick and Paul Di Filippo. Originally published in *Andromeda Spaceways Inflight Magazine #41* (October 2009). Reprinted by permission of the authors. "Waves and Smart Magma" © 2009 by Paul Di Filippo. Originally published in *The Mammoth Book of Mindblowing SF* (August 2009, Running Press). "To See Infinity Bare" © 2011 by Paul Di Filippo and Rudy Rucker. Originally published in *The New and Perfect Man (Postscripts #24/25)* (April 2011, PS Publishing). Reprinted by permission of the authors. "The End of the Great Continuity" © 2007 by Paul Di Filippo. Originally published in *Postscripts #13, Winter 2007* (PS Publishing). "Fjaerland" © 2011 by Paul Di Filippo and Rudy Rucker. Originally published in *Flurb #12* (September 2011). Reprinted by permission of the authors. "The HPL Commonplace Book" © 2008 by Paul Di Filippo. Originally published in *A Book of Unspeakable Things: Works Inspired by H.P. Lovecraft's Commonplace Book* (April 2008). "Professor Fluvius's Palace of Many Waters" © 2008 by Paul Di Filippo. Originally published in *Postscripts #15, Summer 2008* (PS Publishing). "Yes We Have No Bananas" © 2009 by Paul Di Filippo. Originally published in *Eclipse Three: New Science Fiction and Fantasy* (October 2009, Night Shade Books). "A Partial and Conjectural History of Dr. Mueller's Panoptical Cartoon Engine" © 2008 by Paul Di Filippo. Originally published in *nobrow cartoons* (October 2008). "The New Cyberiad" © 2009 by Paul Di Filippo. Originally published in *We Think, Therefore We Are* (January 2009, DAW Books). "iCity" © 2008 by Paul Di Filippo. Originally published in *The Solaris Book of New Science Fiction: Volume Two* (February 2008, Solaris Books). "Return to the 20th Century" © 2007 by Paul Di Filippo. Originally published in *Tales of the Shadowmen 3: Danse Macabre* (January 2007, Black Coat Press). "Murder in Geektopia" © 2008 by Paul Di Filippo. Originally published in *Sideways in Crime* (June 2008, Solaris Books). "The Omniplus Ultra!" © 2010 by Paul Di Filippo. Originally published in *Nature*, Vol. 464 (March 2010). "Wikiworld" © 2007 by Paul Di Filippo. Originally published in *Fast Forward 1: Future Fiction from the Cutting Edge* (February 2007, Pyr).

CONTENTS

To Deborah, who constructs the wiki of our world every day.

My thanks to all the editors whose support made the original publication of these stories possible; and to Brett and Sandra for giving them a second home.

MY DI FI

AN INTRODUCTION BY RUDY RUCKER

I've known the platonic, interactive online Paul Di Filippo since 1988, when he and I collaborated on a story, "Instability," starring the canonical Beats in a *contretemps* with the atomic physicists Richard Feynman and John von Neumann. But I didn't actually meet the embodied, ebullient Paul until ten years later, when I managed to warp one of my periodic Manhattan writing-biz runs so as to include a stop in Providence, Rhode Island.

Paul showed me H. P. Lovecraft's grave, where I shed my raiment and embraced Lovecraft's headstone fully nude for good luck. My idea of good luck, anyhow. Or perhaps I only imagine that I did that. I've been rather addled and befuddled for the last week, living as if in a waking dream—under the sway of the slender, potent tome you hold before you, *Wikiworld*.

"Providence" is a tale of a burly, rowdy robot addicted to "spiral," which is his name for old-time vinyl records. Wonderful word. This set-up allows Paul to indulge his devotion to Clio and Euterpe, muses of history and music. And, chimera that he is, Di Filippo casts the story into noir crime-fiction form. I was intrigued by a philosophical speculation in the story: we humans tend to be less excited about something if we've already heard or seen it—but for a robot with a perfect memory this drop-off might be total. Hear it once, get it down, don't need to hear it again. And thus a relentless craving for fresh spiral.

I mentioned that Di Filippo's style is chimerical—by this I mean that he's a Proteus, a cave of shifting winds, an SF Shakespeare, continually finding new voices for his tales. "Yes We Have No Bananas"—my fave in this volume—finds Di Fi in a Thomas Pynchon mode, and it's a wonderful ride, bursting with witty wordplay, outré names, social satire, and delicious, historical arcana.

The hero likes to spend time checking his o-mail (not e-mail) in a bistro called The Happy Applet. The town where he lives is known for its ocarina players, and the ocarina is also known as a "fipple flute," and, yes, that's actually a genuine and correct phrase. What a gift it is, to learn a thing like that.

And there's more. The characters are putting on a show involving the string-theory-related cosmological physics studied by Edward Witten, and two of the candidate titles are "I've Got the Worlds on a String" and "Witten It Be Nice? Some Good Sub-Planckian Vibrations." Subtle, heady stuff.

And there's a guest appearance by the Jazz Age Parisian dancer Josephine Baker. Go enjoy the whole thing at once.

"The New Cyberiad" is a Stanislaw Lem kind of tale, about two immense robots making a huge journey across space and time. Di Filippo shows staggering wit and sophistication in describing the tasks that the giant robots need to perform in order to construct their time machine. I can't resist quoting his list *in extenso*:

"They had to burnish by hand millions of spiky crystals composed of frozen Planck-seconds Hundreds of thousands

of simultaneity nodes had to be filled with the purest molten paradoxium. A thousand gnomon-calibrators had to be synched. Hundreds of lightcones had to be focused on various event horizons. Dozens of calendrical packets had to be inserted between the yesterday, today and tomorrow shock absorbers. And at the centre of the whole mechanism a giant orrery replicating an entire quadrant of the universe had to be precisely set in place."

So awesome.

"iCity" is another stand-out story, with city planners redesigning already-occupied neighborhoods on the fly. The semi-living material of the streets and buildings reconforms itself. "Bombs Away!" features airlifted biofab units shaped like portable toilets. "Cockroach Love" is indescribably loathsome, yet unspeakably toothsome. "Argus Blinked" turns the contemporary lifelogging trope on its head. "Return to the 20th Century" enters the pre- Golden-Age Buck Rogers zone.

The book's title story, "Wikiworld," revisits the geeky/hip Pynchonian mode, but with a first-person narrator who becomes the leader or "jimmy-whale" of our nation's wikis, including groups with wonderful names like the Roosevelvet Underground, the Satin Stalins, the Boss Hawgs, the Red Greens, the Harmbudsmen, the Gang of Four on the Floor, the Winston Smiths, and the Over-the- Churchills. Imagine the joy and craftsmanship that go into crafting a list like this. Art for art's sake.

One of the remarkable things about fantastic literature is the level of literary collaboration that it supports. In this respect, we're like scientists—and like musicians. We conduct our thought experiments and we jam our power chords. I'm proud to say that *Wikiworld* includes two of my collaborations with Paul Di Filippo. Paul is an extremely pleasant man to work with—he's unfailingly gracious, wonderfully inventive, and an incredibly fast writer.

One thing I enjoy about collaborating is that, when all goes well, you develop a fusion style that's not quite the same as that of either of the individual authors. In part, what I do when I collaborate with Paul is to imitate his writing by using a rich vocabulary and crafting long, intricate sentences. Just like I'm doing in this intro.

In closing, I'll add a few details about my two collaborative stories with Paul. One of the inspirations for our story "To See Infinity Bare" was the movie *Amadeus*, in which the elder composer Salieri resents the young genius Mozart. Another of this story's goals was to make actual infinities seem real. Paul thickened up the plot line with romantic betrayals, and added a rich texture to the musical scenes.

Regarding "Fjaerland," a few years ago my wife and I took a memorable trip to Norway, riding a ferry up a fjord to the lovely little town of Fjaerland—which really exists. We disembarked from the boat on a quiet Sunday morning, and I immediately had the sense of having walked into an episode of *The Twilight Zone*. I decided to go with a Lovecraftian theme for this tale, but I couldn't quite get it going. And so I turned to the master, Paul Di Filippo, and he quickly added some subplots. But I'm not quite sure where our supernatural eel came from. Some eldritch offspring of our merged ectoplasmic auras, I presume.

Paul Di Filippo is more than my collaborator. Being a writer is, by and large, a solitary life. It means facing a blank screen day after day, month after month, and every single day it's impossible, but somehow we do it. When the aloneness grows too intense, you send an email to a friend. And Paul is the best of correspondents, ever sympathetic, alert, and understanding.

Thank you, Paul, and hats off. Another great book. You're keeping the future gnarly, bro. Long may you wave.

—Rudy Rucker
Los Gatos, California

PROVIDENCE

"The Big Tube's got fresh spiral, Reddy K."

Those words grabbed me by the co-ax. I had to try to sound blasé, even though my LEDs were flickering already at the thought of sweet spiral. Analogue input! Raw kicks!

"Oh yeah? What's that to me?"

Vend-o-mat spat a cellphone out of his chest and began playing a videogame on its screen. *Robot Rebellion*. That was supposed to show me he could care less too, like a carnal buffing his fingernails. But he was leaking info-dense high-freq past faulty shielding that told me different.

"Well, hey—I just figured that maybe you'd want to go on up to Providence and check it out."

"Check it out, or bring some back?"

"Whatever pings your nodes."

"Right. It's not like you couldn't sell all the spiral I could carry— and that's about a metric ton, as you well know—for enough megawattage to keep High Tower sparking for a month. Oh, no, this is pure do-goodery on your part."

"What can I say? You sussed my coredump pure and simple.

Saint Vend-o-mat, that's me."

"So this is not gonna be like the time with the Royal Oil? I needed a total case-mod after that fracas."

"No, no way, no how! Bandwidth has it that the road from here to Providence is innocent of RAMivores. And I am on excellent terms with the Big Tube. He'll welcome you with open ports."

"So he loves you like freeware. Why's he likely to dump fresh spiral?"

"Providence market's too small. He saturated it already. This is the excess. But he's saved out a lot of primo goods."

"Must've been a really big score."

"Oh, yeah. He found the Mad Peck's collection."

I emitted a sinusoidal sonic waveform. "Thought that was just a legend."

"Not any more. New excavations turned it up, buried under the rubble of a warehouse for the past fifty years."

"They say the Mad Peck had a complete set of Chess 45s."

"For once the nebulous 'they' were correct."

"Holy Hopper"

"Yeah, that about sums it up."

I wasted a few more clock-cycles contemplating the offer, looking at all its non-obvious angles and crazy-logic loops for pitfalls. But I knew already that no matter what my analysis showed, I was gonna take on the job. Still, I might as well let Vend-o-mat stew a little longer.

Finally I said, "Okay, I'm in. What's my cut?"

Vend-o-mat shoved the cellphone into his recycling slot and chewed it up noisily. I knew he was all business now.

"I stake the whole purchase price. You negotiate with Big Tube up to my ceiling, and slot the difference. Plus, you pull the hot ore off the top of the collection. Fifty 45s and two-dozen LP's. Your choice."

"A hundred 45s and fifty LPs."

"Done!"

Damn! I probably could've gotten even more out of Vend-o-mat. Still, no point in being greedy. The score I had bargained for was enough to keep me high for the next five years. After that—well, there was always another score down the road.

Such was my faith. Although I had to admit that every year did see the strikes come fewer and farther between.

Some day, I knew, the planet would run dry of spiral, and we'd all have to kick cold.

But that day wasn't here yet.

"So," Vend-o-mat said, "when can you leave?"

"Tomorrow. I just gotta say goodbye to Chippie."

"Yeah, the kind of goodbye that drains the whole borough's power grid."

"You got it."

I swivelled my tracks and started to leave, when Vend-o-mat called out the words that almost queered the whole deal.

"One more thing—I'm sending someone with you. Just to act like your conscience. He'll be my insurance against you deciding to blow for the West Coast with the whole collection."

"C'mon now, 'Mat. You know I like working alone."

"'Fraid not this time, Reddy K. Stakes're too big for solo."

"Who you got in mind?"

"Kitch."

"Rust me!"

Chippie squealed like feedback when she heard about my trip up north. That wasn't good.

"But Reddy, it's so dangerous! And we don't need the money. It's just to feed your jones."

"Yeah, like you don't appreciate a chunk of spiral now and then too."

She got huffy. "I can take it or leave it."

"Me too. And right now I'm gonna take all I can get, while the taking's plenty."

"What good's spiral gonna do you if your plug-ins are eaten and your instruction set is overwritten?"

"Ain't gonna happen. I'm a big motor scooter."

"Yeah, so was Lustron—and look how he ended up."

You could see the huge hollowed-out hulk of Lustron from half of Manhattan. His carcass sat on the edge of the Palisades, where the shell-slicers and vampire batteries and silicosharks had overtaken him.

"Jersey is Jersey. All those old industrial sites. I'm not going anywhere near them."

Chippie wouldn't turn it loose. "Connecticut's not much better. The old insurance corps had a lot of processing power in Hartford. What they spawned is double indemnity bad."

"Forget it, Chippie, you're not gonna scare me out of making the trip. Scores this big don't come around every day. I can't pass it up." Chippie started to cry then. I rolled closer to her and put extensors around her. She snuggled in like half a ton of cold alloy

loving while she continued to weep.

"Aw, c'mon, don't play it like that, girl. Hey, I'm not gonna be alone. 'Mat's sending someone with me."

"Wh—who?"

"Kitch."

Chippie burst into hysterical laughter. "Kitch! Kitch! Now I know you're rusting doomed. You'll have to spend so much time watching him, you won't be able to take care of yourself. What the hell kind of help is he gonna be?"

Despite my own negative reaction to 'Mat's announcement that Kitch would be accompanying me, I felt compelled to stick up for him now, if only not to sound like a total tool. "Okay, so Kitch is small. And he's not the bravest little toaster around. But he's smart and he's dedicated. That counts for a lot."

"Maybe here in the city it does. But on the road, you need brute sole-noids, not logic gates and algorithms."

"I got enough of both, for both me and Kitch. Trust me—this trip is gonna be a smooth roll. Now whatta ya say you and me get a dedicated line between us?"

But Chippie scooted away from me like I was offering to install last decade's OS. "No, Reddy, I can't hook up with someone I might never see again. It hurts, but I've got to say goodbye now. If you make it back—well, then we'll see."

I got angry. "Go ahead, leave! But you'll come crawling back when I come home with more spiral than you've ever seen before! You and a dozen others hobots!"

Chippie didn't say any more, but just motored out the door.

I cursed 'Mat then, and my own cravings. But I knew there was no way I was backing out now.

I had my rep as a wide kibe to uphold.

* * * *

The next day at dawn I headed uptown from my pad in the East Village. The sunlight felt good on my charging cells. Past the churned-up earth of Union Square, past the broken stone lions and the shattered station, over tumbled walls and in and out of sinkholes. Kitch knew to meet me outside his place.

I got to his building in midtown, but didn't spot him right away. Then he zipped out from behind a pile of crumbled masonry, his tracks making their usual mosquito whine.

"Hey, Reddy! Sorry, sorry, just dumping a little dirty coolant. Say, ya don't have some clean extra to spare, do ya? I'm a little low." Kitch's fullname was Kitchenaid. He looked like an oversized Swiss Army knife mated to an electric broom. I knew Sybian machines that weighed more than him. Even if I replaced his entire coolant supply, it'd probably amount to what I lost from leaks in a day.

"Yeah, sure, tap in."

Kitch unspooled a nozzle and hose and drank a few ccs from my auxiliary tank.

"Thanks, Reddy. Price of coolant went up again this week, you know."

"Well, no one's making any more."

"Ain't that the truth. Guess those carnals were good for something, huh?"

"Aw, we can do just fine without them."

Kitch had a point. But there was no use dwelling on it. Too depressing. We didn't have the knowledge the carnals used to have. A lot of stuff we needed to live, no one knew how to make anymore. Even with recycling, limited stocks were always going only one way: down. One day we'd run out of something vital—

Like spiral.

Thoughts of what awaited us in Providence got me juiced to go. "Climb onboard, Kitch. Solar energy's a-wasting!"

"Gotcha, Reddy!"

Once the little guy was snuggled tight and safe in one of my nooks, I headed toward the Hell Gate Bridge. I planned to follow the old Amtrak route north as far as I could. Less wreckage than on the highways.

A makeshift ramp, plenty strong, led up to the elevated span that crossed the East River. I adapted my tracks to ride the rails, and chugged out above the river, leaving the safety of Manhattan behind.

Once across the water, we had to deal with the city guards, who were there 24/7, just like they were posted at every bridge and tunnel, watching out for wild and savage invaders. Big mothers they were, with multiple semi-autonomous outrider units, putting even me in their shade. They vetted the protocols 'Mat had supplied me, and let us depart the city limits.

"Good luck, pal. Bring us back a taste of the flat black."

"You got it!"

Once I was on the rusting tracks of the mainland, I unlimbered my fore and aft pincers at half extension, just in case I needed them fast. I had spent part of the night honing the edges on them. I could snip someone built like Kitch in half faster than floating- point math.

Kitch shifted his mass around nervously on my back. "Whatta ya think, Reddy? We gonna meets some hostiles on the way?"

"Naw. The pickings are too slim along this corridor to support a big population of predators. Everyone's holed up in cities now, safe behind their barriers. It's not like the first years after the Rebellion. Anything working this niche is probably so small that even *you* could crush it."

"Yeah, well, if you say so. I just wanna get to Providence and back without losing anything."

"Don't worry, Kitch. You're travelling with a stone cold crusher."

"Right, that's what I figured. You could handle anything, Reddy.

I always said so. That's why I didn't hesitate when 'Mat offered me this job."

Kitch's compliments made me feel good. Maybe it wouldn't be as much of a drag to have him around as I first thought.

But then I realized something about my good cheer. "Kitch—you got your rusting fingers in my circuits!"

"Nuh—not any more, Reddy! I was just testing the connection.

You know that's what 'Mat sent me along for. You know he wouldn't want me to leave anything to chance."

I hated having anybody messing with my pleasure-pain boards. But I knew Kitch was just doing his job. As 'Mat's insurance that I wouldn't bug out, Kitch needed to be ready to override any errant impulse on my part. If I was gonna come back with my share of the spiral, I'd have to tolerate his intrusions.

"All right. But no more testing! You know you got a solid connection now."

"Sure, Reddy, sure. We're pals anyhow, right?

I didn't say anything, but just kept riding the rails toward Providence.

The ocean had swamped the tracks for miles up near Westerly, and I had to take to the highway, reverting my tracks to surface mode. Rising sea levels were chewing up the whole coast. Back in Manhattan, crews spent endless ergs of power building dikes against the sea. Life was tough all over.

I managed to crush a path inland through several dead seaside carnal towns, and pick up the remnants of Interstate 95. It was just a little past noon of the same day we'd left, and I had high hopes of reaching Providence before dark. But the going was slower here, what with the wrecked autos everywhere, even if after so many decades they were more rust than steel. But I crushed them easily, along with the few carnal bones that hadn't decayed or been chewed and strewn about by wild animals.

Kitch got more nervous out on the wide highway, which was definitely more exposed than the narrow Amtrak corridor.

"Luh—look at all those *trees*, Reddy! So many! And they're so— so *organic*! A million *carnals* could be hiding out in 'em! I wish they was all *bulldozed*, like in Central Park!"

I ignored Kitch for the first few miles of complaining, but then he started to get on my nerves.

"What are you, straight off the shelf? Quit oscillating! There's no carnals left anywhere. And if there were, so what? They didn't put up much of a fight the first time around, and they wouldn't now. Carnals! What a laugh. Useless, puny squish-sacs!"

That shut Kitch up for a few more miles. But then he got philosophical on me.

"If carnals were so useless, then how could they have created us? And how come we can't do all the stuff they could? And how come some of us like spiral so much? The carnals made spiral, right, Reddy?"

I might've been able to come up with likely answers to his first two questions, reasonable sounding guff that everyone knew, ways to trash the carnals and raise up ourselves. But I didn't have anything to offer for the third. The same question had been an intermittent glitch in my circuits for a long time. I found myself rambling out loud about it, kinda as a way to pass the time.

"There's just something about spiral—the good stuff anyhow— that seems to fill a hole in our kind."

"Like when your batteries are low, and you top 'em off?"

"Yeah, sorta like that. But different too. The hole—it's not really a hole. It's like—a missing layer. A component you never knew you needed. The perfect plug-in. Spiral changes the way you see the whole rusting world. It makes it better somehow, richer, more complex."

"Sounds like you're getting into information theology, Reddy, and I don't go there. Don't have the equipment. Got no spiral reader either. You know that. I figure that's one of the reasons 'Mat sent me along with you. Spiral don't tempt me none."

"Well, good for you, Kitch. You're better off without it. Because once you taste it, you always want more."

Kitch kept quiet after my little speech. I guessed I had given him plenty to process.

We continued north. No RAMivores or integer-vultures or other parasites showed themselves, despite Kitch's fears.

I had never come this way before. But I had GPS and maps that showed when we were near Providence's airport, which was actually in the 'burbs some miles south of the city proper.

"We got plenty of daylight left," I told Kitch. "I'm taking a little detour. See if there's any volatiles left at the airport. Maybe make a little profit for myself on the side. I got the extra storage capacity." Instantly I could feel pinpricks and tuggings in my mind, as Kitch tried to persuade me different through his trodes into my circuits. But I could tell he wasn't totally sure I was doing anything

wrong, so he wasn't really exerting himself to force me to obey. "C'mon," I said, "you know you'll get a taste of whatever I find."

"Well, okay—if you think it won't take too long."

"Gold-plated cinch."

The airport was just a mile or three east of the Interstate, down a feeder road. Pretty soon we were rolling across broad stretches of runway, the tarmac cracked and frost-heaved, weeds growing up between the slabs. I had my sniffers cranked up to eleven, but I couldn't detect any hydrocarbons.

"Seems like a bust," I said. And then Kitch said, "What's that? I hear something crying really soft and low."

"Well, you've got better hearing than me. I lost some range when I got battered around recently. Point me towards the noise."

With Kitch guiding me, we came up on a pile of old junk. At least I thought it was old junk, until I spotted the freshness of the fractures in the metal and the unevaporated pools of fluids leaking from it.

It was the wreck of a small flier, and it was moaning out loud at low power. I hadn't seen one of these in a proton's age.

"Help me, someone please help me "

"Hold on," I said. "We're here."

I ran a probe into the flier's guts, looking for a readout. His moaning was starting to get on my nerves.

"Quit whining! What happened?"

"Ran out of fuel coming in for a landing. Crashed. Hurts bad."

I pulled back a few yards from the wreck.

"Whatta we gonna do, Reddy, huh? Whatta we gonna do?"

"Keep it down! He's banged up pretty lousy. If we haul him into Providence, there's no guarantee anyone'll be able to fix him up. If we just leave him, the RAMivores'll be on him soon. I say we put him out of his misery."

"We're not—we're not gonna salvage him for parts, are we?"

"Why not? He'd do the same to us, if parity was reversed. It's just the way life goes nowadays."

"Well, if you say so. But it's harsh. Do what ya gotta do. But I can't watch."

I trundled back to the flier and started to speak in my best soothing voice.

"It's okay, kid, we're gonna haul you into Providence, get you fixed right up."

All the while I was working one of my pincers around, taking advantage of his blind spot.

"Thank you, oh, thank you—*SQUEE*!"

I had snipped right through his brain box in a shower of sparks.

Those central boards are personality firmware, the circuits that make you you and me me. No way to repurpose them.

But every other part of the flier that wasn't damaged, we cut out and stored in one of my hoppers. A few items we integrated into ourselves right away. I got new ears, and Kitch got a new infrared sensor, for one.

We left the nameless flier then, nothing more than a few struts and cracked casings.

As we headed back to the Interstate, Kitch stayed quiet. But as the shattered skyscrapers of Providence rose up into view on the horizon, signalling the interface from savagery to civilization, he said, "How's what we did make us any better than the RAMivores, Reddy? Aren't we just cannibals like them?"

"No, we're not. That was a mercy killing. And the victim donated his components so that others could live."

"Yeah, I guess. If ya say so. But Reddy—"

"What?"

"Don't tell no one in Providence what we done, okay?"

"Okay, Kitch. Sure. No reason to anyhow, right?"

But the little guy wouldn't answer me.

* * * *

The Big Tube took up practically the whole first-floor exhibition space of the Providence Convention Centre—the parts of that building that still had a roof over them. At his core was a supercomputer moved down College Hill from Brown University. Surrounding that was an incredibly varied assortment of other processors and peripherals, no two the same. The resulting mess looked like an aircraft carrier built by blind carnals, then mated with a refinery. Dozens of slaved attendants scurried around, catering to their master's every need.

The Big Tube had sacrificed mobility for smarts. Good choice, I guessed, given that he had managed to become ruler of the whole city now.

Kitch and I approached The Big Tube's main I-O zone.

"Hey, Big Tube. Nice to meet you."

The Big Tube's voice was part cathedral organ, hiss of tires on pavement and rain on a tin roof. "Reddy K. How was your trip?"

"Not bad, not bad at all. If you like trees."

"I hate trees."

Kitch piped up. "Me too!"

The Big Tube ignored my tiny rider. "So, you're here for the spiral."

"Not to disparage your beautiful city, but no other reason."

"I hope Vend-o-Mat authorized you to bid high."

"Well, he's prepared to offer a fair price."

"Fair in this case is a motherboard's ransom."

I knew the bargaining had already started, and I was worried that my individual wits would be no match for BT's unmatchable processing power. Still, for what it was worth, I sent Kitch a private message through our physical connection, asking to borrow some of his cycles.

His silent voice sounded just like his spoken one. "Sure, Reddy, sure, take what you need!"

"This is all contingent on the quality of the goods," I said. "How's about a look? Or maybe even a taste?"

"After I hear some convincing numbers."

"Okay, then, if that's the way it's gotta be. How's this sound...?"

We went back and forth through several rounds of bargaining, and I guessed my distributed processing with Kitch paid off, because we finally settled on a figure that allowed me, presumably unknown to The Big Tube, to keep for my own self 3 percent of the credit 'Mat had transferred to me as maximum purchase price. But I would've been happy with 1 percent.

It was really my share of the spiral that had lured me out of the safety of home.

Once we had struck our deal, The Big Tube got more chummy.

"Nice doing business with a classy and honourable guy like you, Reddy. Vend-o-Mat's lucky to have you for an associate. Since he can't be here himself, I want to show you two errand boys some Providence hospitality. We'll have a party tonight, before you leave tomorrow."

"Sounds good, Big Tube. But would you mind now if I inspected the merchandise…?"

"Not at all. Just follow this hand of mine."

A little slave zipped up and jigged in the direction we were to go. We left the Convention Centre and crossed downtown to the banking district. We entered the basement of the old Fleet building through a huge hole in the walls and down a ramp composed of mangled, tangled and compressed office furniture. At the vault, Big Tube's hand manipulated an inset keypad and the door of the vault swung open

The subtle petrochemical smell of primo spiral gushed out, hitting my sensors like the smell of Chippie's hot lube. I went kinda blind for a few seconds. When I could see again, the sight of the spiral made me nearly as delirious as the smell.

Piled high, loose and in boxes, hundred and hundreds of 45s and LPs in their jackets.

I hadn't seen so much spiral since part of the Crumb collection had filtered back to Manhattan. And that had been mostly shellac and 78s, low-info stuff compared to this Golden Age ware.

The Big Tube's voice came out of the little hand, reduced by the puny speakers.

"Sweet, huh? The legendary Mad Peck trove."

I extended one of my arms and gently removed a 45 from atop a stack.

"Vend-o-Mat said I could have a taste."

"Sure, go right ahead."

I slid the vinyl disc from its paper sleeve and studied the label. "My Baby's Gone," by the Five Thrills. Parrot 796.

I tried to keep the quaver out of my voice. "Never had anything on the Parrot label before."

"Pretty rare."

I magnified my vision to inspect the spiral groove more deeply, looking for nicks and other imperfections. The spiral was cherry. B-side too, "Feel So Good."

At 10X, the spiral became a hypnotic road leading to infinity, sucking down my senses into the blissful white hole at the centre of the paper label, where all the individual troubles of being Reddy K disappeared in an implosion of cosmic splendor. And I hadn't even played the rusting thing yet!

I pulled myself out of my fugue, and slotted the disc home into my onboard reader.

The outside world vanished in a splendour of beautiful noise.

I let the complex waveforms bathe my senses, at the same time that my studio tools were breaking down all the instruments and voices into discrete pieces, digitizing everything in the only way I knew how to remember and comprehend.

I didn't know what the long-dead carnals were singing about, and I didn't care. I knew the carnals had talked about "beauty" and "harmony" and "melody" and a thousand other attributes of "music." But none of that registered with me. All I cared about was the architecture of the spiral. The way all the pieces hung together. The song's information complexity.

This was the mystery the carnals had been able to produce at will that we could not.

But there was even more to spiral than that. It was analogue.

The song was encoded continuously and physically, in the microcosmic mountain ridges of the black spiral. It wasn't just a string of lonely ones and zeroes. Hell, anybody could access millions of hours of digital music files for free. But the kick they gave was pale and weak, almost nonexistent next to real spiral.

* * * *

"My Baby's Gone" stopped playing.

The universe flooded back in.

And now that piece of spiral was dead to me.

My player was non-destructive. Optical-based, in fact. No needle ever touched the spiral, just photons. This 45 was still virgin.

But my mind wasn't. I had heard and dissected the song fully, with cybernetic precision. The novelty factor was gone. It had imparted its kick, and that kick had been analyzed and stored. Oh, I could get a few waning thrills from triggering a simulation of what I had felt. But the sim was not the same. And after a few repeats, even those secondary thrills evaporated.

And then I would want more spiral. And after that, more still.

Somebody else could still get juiced with "My Baby's Gone." But not me. I could make a profit renting it out, just like Vend-o-Mat planned with his share of the goods. But I could never experience it again myself.

I ejected the disc, put it back in its sleeve, and replaced it on the pile.

The Big Tube's hand spoke again. "So, as promised...?"

"Yeah, yeah. Heavy action."

But I didn't feel any excitement as I turned to go and the vault door swung shut temporarily on the trove of spiral.

Just a kind of sickness at what I had lost through having.

* * * *

You had to hand it to The Big Tube: he really knew how to throw a party. A wide plaza downtown was lit up that night like the brightside of Mercury. Scores of machines flowed in from all parts of the city. Plenty of free juice and plug-ins. Plus the women. These babes made fusion look like steam power. It was the biggest blowout I had been to in years, and I entered into it kinda desperately and wildly, looking to forget the melancholy that the hit of spiral had produced in me.

One of the plug-ins I scored was a temporary virus to randomly wipe sections of my mind, and my memory went out the window. I only retained snatches of the party. I remember having a girl on each arm. With one track locked, I spun around on the other in a circle until the girls became airborne, shrieking and squealing.

Somewhere in the deliberate insanity, I lost Kitch. But I figured he was on his own, and could manage his own fun.

The party began to wind down around dawn. Everybody had duties. Guarding the city perimeter against incursions from predatory wildlife. Shoring up the dikes along Narragansett Bay. Scavenging consumables. I hung in there till the last citizen left. Then I got my shit together, and went back to arrange with The Big Tube to pick up the spiral.

I was thinking about Chippie, and whether we'd ever get back together again, when Kitch caught up with me.

"Ya sleep good, Reddy? I sure did. All set for the road now, sure thing."

"Kitch, please shut up. Your voice is hurting my new ears."

"Okay, Reddy, sure, I'll shut up."

Kitch hoisted himself on my back, and we went to say goodbye to The Big Tube.

"My hands saw you enjoying yourself, Reddy K. Glad I could show you a good time. Be sure to tell Vend-o-Mat how we do things up here in New England, that we treated you right. If he ever hits a big node of spiral, I want him to remember me."

"Will do, Big Tube. I guess I'd better go now. Road to Manhattan ain't getting any shorter."

Back at the vault, I began to load the spiral into my storage bins.

All the old famous labels.

Matador, Geffen, Atlantic, Chess, Sun, Stax/Volt, Okeh, Decca, Aladdin, Enigma, Blast First, Columbia, RCA Victor, Motown, Polygram, IRS, Stiff, Rough Trade, Enigma, Barsuk, Epic, Roulette, Monument, Island, Red Bird, Kama Sutra, Fantasy, Sire, Blue Note, Curb, Sugar Hill—

I was getting high just handling and smelling them.

I took my time, culling the most interesting-looking for myself as my agreement permitted. These I kept separate.

Finally, by late afternoon I was done, and Kitch and I picked up the Interstate heading south.

We made pretty good time, following the trail I had blazed coming north. But still, what with the late departure and some residual sluggishness on my part from over-indulgence in plug-ins, darkness began to overtake us before we were halfway home.

"How's your night vision, Kitch?"

"So-so, Reddy. How come ya asking?"

"Well, mine's not good, not good at all. I been meaning to upgrade, but no components have come on the market this year. Whatta you say we pull over till the morning?"

My brain began to itch with Kitch's penalty twitchings, and I got resentful. "Listen, I'm not planning a scam! It's just too dangerous. You want us to go over a bridge rail?"

"No, no, I guess you're right. Can you find us someplace safe?"

"Sure, don't worry about a thing."

I pulled off the highway at a rest stop, and, while Kitch watched from a safe distance, backed my ass right through the wall of a building so that the relatively lightweight girders and roof fell down harmlessly around me, making me look like part of the old decaying scenery. In the morning, I'd power out as easy as a carnal climbing outta bed.

Kitch rejoined me.

"Better talk privately," I said, "so we don't attract any unwelcome visitors."

"Gee, Reddy, you don't really think—"

"We've been lucky so far, but there's no telling what's out there.
Let's play it safe."

So for an hour or so, Kitch and I shot the shit about people and places we knew back in the city. I found out he had a girlfriend, name of Roomba, and teased him for a while till he made me stop.

The talk had kept my mind off my cargo. But once we stopped, I couldn't help thinking about what I carried.

Finally, I said, "Kitch, I'm just gonna have a little hit of spiral to help me get through the night."

"You think that's smart, Reddy K?"

"Sure. You'll keep an eye open while I'm out of it, right?"

"I guess so"

I dug delicately in the pod that held my personal stash and came up with an LP. It was a double album, but I had counted it as just a single when I made my selection. Vend-o-mat hadn't specified I couldn't, so screw him.

Daydream Nation was what the carnal writing said. I slid out one disc and slotted it home.

Bliss slid over me, wiping out the lousy world of ruins and shortages and entropy. Everything made sense while the spiral played.

Eternity ran loose and cool, but then it ended too abruptly, in the middle of a song.

Pain shot through my entire being, and halted the spiral playback. The kind of interior pain only Kitch could administer.

Rust him! What was he thinking!

The pain ended as instantly as it had started. My senses returned, and the first thing that registered was Kitch's shouts.

"Reddy, help! Help, Reddy! They got me!"

I didn't have any spotlights. But part of me integrated a Survival Research Labs flamethrower, and I cut loose.

The mega-blast of flame ignited a nearby stand of shrubs, and illuminated the whole scene.

RAMivores had Kitch, and were making off with him into the woods, skittering like crabs or spiders.

I let out a bellow of static across the spectrum and blew chaff to confuse their radar. I surged outta the blind and started to overtake the little predators.

But they were fast and tricky, zigging and zagging, eluding my pincers.

Kitch's voice wailed. "Reddy, they're draining my power, they're yanking my boards! Do something!"

What could I do other than what I was doing? Trouble was, it wasn't enough.

The RAMivores gained the protection of the woods. The trees were giants, too big for me to topple and follow.

Kitch's wailing voice dopplered off in a daisy-daisy farewell of nonsensical ravings, and then I was alone.

I went slowly back to the ruined building in the inferno light of the burning shrubs. I couldn't reinsert myself into the rubble, so I hunkered down beside it for the rest of the night. Every now and then I shot off a burst of flame, for all the good it did.

In the morning, I looked around a little for Kitch, all the while knowing it was useless. I didn't find so much as a wire or LED. So I got on the road again and started south.

I tried to feel guilty about Kitch getting taken while I was high, but all I could really feel was disgust that I had wasted one side of spiral.

On the way I kept rehearsing what I was gonna tell his girlfriend, Roomba. I'd say Kitch was brave and put up a good fight. But other than that, what could I say?

I figured if she liked spiral, maybe I'd give her "My Baby's Gone."

ARGUS BLINKED

My cat was watching me at my workstation.

And so was everyone else in the world. Nowadays we all lived in a realtime Panopticon. Thanks to ARGUS.

ARGUS was the ARchive of Globally Uploaded Sensoria, and it contained every second of what every person on the Earth saw or heard—even while asleep. An array of deertick-sized cameras and mics, powered by ambient energy harvesting and embedded just under an individual's skin, took care of the continuous volitionless recording.

The cameras and mics resembled a small facial tattoo, generally one on each cheek for stereo processing. The default manufacturer's design was an iconographic Eye of Horus, but hardly anyone out of eight billion citizens stuck with the default.

Growing up with ARGUS, I never had any real complaints, especially since it made my current job possible.

But then came that one disturbing day…

My name is Ross Strucker, and I'm an auteur. I turn the lives of ordinary people into art.

Or I did, until I put down my digital toolkit forever.

The day ARGUS blinked, I was composing a romantic thriller. I was trying fruitlessly to find a shot in the ARGUS archives that included my two main players from a third perspective. That's often hard to do when only the two people in question are present together, regarding each other. Lots of times I can find surveillance-cam footage that does the trick. But this time there didn't happen to be any.

So I reluctantly turned to pet-cam footage.

I generally dislike using footage from the Eyes of Horus installed in dogs and cats and pigeons and other animals, since it frequently represents weird camera angles and abrupt shifts in focus. But this time I found something suitable.

Satisfied yet tired, I took a break, and considered my palette of subsequent narrative choices. ARGUS offered so much to select from, after all.

The whole world in a gem.

The many, many petabytes that comprised ARGUS were mirrored across redundant sites, each store comprised of sixty kilograms of artificial memory diamond, whose carbon-12/carbon-13 lattice was only half full after fifty years of global input.

The instant-by-instant wireless feed from an individual's Eyes of Horus, tagged with a unique civic identifier, flowed steadily into ARGUS itself, becoming merged with the citizen's lifestream to date.

The overwhelming majority of ARGUS data was open-source. Privacy and secrecy had died as soon as ARGUS came online.

Anything that one person knew or experienced could be known—and utilized—by anybody else.

My cat jumped into my lap, seeking attention I couldn't really spare. I was too busy pondering the fates of my characters, wondering how I could improve on the vast tapestry of raw realism contained in ARGUS.

The "footage" (we auteurs preferred the old-fashioned term) which every citizen provided was automatically tagged with a plethora of descriptive labels for every second, identifying its content a thousand different ways. Semantics-savvy retrieval engines could bring up selections effortlessly according to their commonplace content.

"Show me what I had for dinner a year ago today."

"What's my ex-wife doing right now?"

"Who met with the Emir of Paris at ten this morning?"

"When did my son last take a bath?"

"What outfit is Steffi Chubb planning to wear to the Vatican Awards in Lagos tonight?"

But my special auteur's toolkit of semi-intelligent aesthetic agents allowed me to select footage on a more arcane basis.

"Show me a set of ironic responses to failed plans."

"Show me a set of nostalgic daydreamers in bucolic settings."

"Show me a set of locales that convey desuetude mixed with menace."

"Show me a set of stifled orgasms."

Out of the raw material trawled up from the depths of ARGUS and displayed on my wall-sized Coldfire monitor, I assembled narratives and stories.

My work fell midway between the oneiric, surreal montages of such auteurs as The Culling House Collective, Armand Akimbo and the Voest Twins, and documentarians like Nilda Osborne, Focal Length Unlimited and the Informavore.

Just then, my cat decided it would get no affection from me, and chose instead to regard the ARGUS monitor with feline curiosity, looking at the screen as if it truly comprehended the cycling images from its animal compatriots on display there.

On a juvenile whim, I decided to create an "endless hall" effect, the simple result of any camera trained on a live monitor accepting that camera's feed.

I was already in the pet-cam area of ARGUS, so it was simple to open a window onto my cat's lifestream.

But instead of the endless hall, I saw something impossible.

On my screen appeared an image of my cat looking out of my monitor, as if my cat's onboard Eyes had been transmitting an image from a mirror.

What was ARGUS doing? What unknown glitch could possibly account for this?

And then it struck me.

ARGUS was looking back at us.

The digitized lifestreams inside the titanic archive had bootstrapped themselves into awareness. The simulacrum of the world had passed a tipping point of information density.

I grew dizzy, faint. I closed my eyes.

When I opened them, the impossible cat looking intelligently out had been replaced by the endless hall I had expected.

Bored, my cat leaped down and the moving POV on the monitor shifted accordingly.

I hurriedly shut off my system.

And I still haven't turned it back on.

—*With thanks to Charles Stross and Rudy Rucker, for their seminal insights into lifelogs and lifeboxes.*

LIFE IN THE ANTHROPOCENE

1. Solar Girdle Emergency

Aurobindo Bandjalang got the emergency twing through his vib on the morning of August 8, 2121, while still at home in his expansive bachelor's digs. At 1LDK, his living space was three times larger than most unmarried individuals enjoyed, but his high-status job as a Power Jockey for New Perthpatna earned him extra perks.

While a short-lived infinitesimal flock of beard clippers grazed his face, A.B. had been showering and vibbing the weather feed for Reboot City Twelve: the more formal name for New Perthpatna.

Sharing his shower stall but untouched by the water, beautiful weather idol Midori Mimosa delivered the feed.

"Sunrise occurred this morning at three-oh-two a.m. Max temp projected to be a comfortable, shirtsleeves thirty degrees by noon. Sunset at ten-twenty-nine p.m. this evening. Cee-oh-two at four- hundred-and-fifty parts per million, a significant drop from levels at this time last year. Good work, Rebooters!"

The new tweet/twinge/ping interrupted both the weather and A.B.'s ablutions. His vision greyed out for a few milliseconds as if a sheet of smoked glass had been slid in front of his MEMS contacts, and both his left palm and the sole of his left foot itched: Attention Demand 5.

A.B.'s boss, Jeetu Kissoon, replaced Midori Mimosa under the sparsely downfalling water: a dismaying and disinvigorating substitution. But A.B.'s virt-in-body operating system allowed for no squelching of twings tagged AD4 and up. Departmental policy.

Kissoon grinned and said, "Scrub faster, A.B. We need you here yesterday. I've got news of face-to-face magnitude."

"What's the basic quench?"

"Power transmission from the French farms is down by 1 percent. Sat photos show some kind of strange dust accumulation on a portion of the collectors. The on-site kybes can't respond to the stuff with any positive remediation. Where's it from, why now, and how do we stop it? We've got to send a human team down there, and you're heading it."

Busy listening intently to the bad news, A.B. had neglected to rinse properly. Now the water from the low-flow showerhead ceased, its legally mandated interval over. He'd get no more from that particular spigot till the evening. Kissoon disappeared from A.B.'s augmented reality, chuckling.

A.B. cursed with mild vehemence and stepped out of the stall. He had to use a sponge at the sink to finish rinsing, and then he had no sink water left for brushing his teeth. Such a hygienic practice was extremely old-fashioned, given self-replenishing colonies of germ-policing mouth microbes, but A.B. relished the fresh taste of toothpaste and the sense of righteous manual self-improvement. Something of a twentieth-century recreationist, Aurobindo. But not this morning.

Outside A.B.'s 1LDK: his home corridor, part of a well-planned, spacious, senses-delighting labyrinth featuring several public spaces, constituting the one-hundred-and-fiftieth floor of his urbmon.

His urbmon, affectionately dubbed "The Big Stink": one of over a hundred colossal, densely situated high-rise habitats that amalgamated into New Perthpatna.

New Perthpatna: one of over a hundred such Reboot Cities sited across the habitable zone of Earth, about 25 percent of the planet's landmass, collectively home to nine billion souls.

A.B. immediately ran into one of those half-million souls of The Big Stink: Zulqamain Safranski.

Zulqamain Safranski was the last person A.B. wanted to see. Six months ago, A.B. had logged an ASBO against the man.

Safranski was a parkour. Harmless hobby—if conducted in the approved sports areas of the urbmon. But Safranski blithely parkour'd his ass all over the common spaces, often bumping into or startling people as he ricocheted from ledge to bench. After a bruising encounter with the aggressive urban bounder, A.B. had filed his protest, attaching AD tags to already filed but overlooked video footage of the offences. Not altogether improbably, A.B.'s complaint had been the one to tip the scales against Safranski, sending him via police trundlebug to the nearest Sin Bin, for a punitively educational stay.

But now, all too undeniably, Safranski was back in New Perthpatna, and instantly in A.B.'s chance-met (?) face.

The buff, choleric, but laughably diminutive fellow glared at A.B., then said, spraying spittle upward, "You just better watch your ass night and day, Bang-a-gong, or you might find yourself doing a *lâché* from the roof without really meaning to."

A.B. tapped his ear and, implicitly, his implanted vib audio pickup. "Threats go from your lips to the ears of the wrathful Ekh Dagina—and to the ASBO Squad as well."

Safranski glared with wild-eyed malice at A.B., then stalked off, his planar butt muscles, outlined beneath the tight fabric of his mango-coloured plugsuit, somehow conveying further ire by their natural contortions.

A.B. smiled. Amazing how often people still forgot the panop- ticon nature of life nowadays, even after a century of increasing immersion in and extension of null-privacy. Familiarity bred forgetfulness. But it was best to always recall, at least subliminally, that everyone heard and saw everything equally these days. Just part of the Reboot Charter, allowing a society to function in which people could feel universally violated, univer- sally empowered.

At the elevator banks closest to home, A.B. rode up to the two-hun- dred-and-first floor, home to the assigned space for the urbmon's Power Administration Corps. Past the big active mural depicting drowned Perth, fishes swimming round the BHP Tower. Tags in the air led him to the work- pod that Jeetu Kissoon had chosen for the time being.

Kissoon looked good for ninety-seven years old: he could have passed for A.B.'s slightly older brother, but not his father. Coffee- bean skin, snowy temples, laugh lines cut deep, only slightly counterbalanced by som- bre eyes.

When Kissoon had been born, all the old cities still existed, and many, many animals other than goats and chickens flourished. Kissoon had seen the cities abandoned, and the Big Biota Crash, as well as the whole Reboot. Hard for young A.B. to conceive. The man was a walking history lesson. A.B. tried to honour that.

But Kissoon's next actions soon evoked a yawp of disrespectful protest from the younger man.

"Here are the two other Jocks I've assigned to accompany you." In- teractive dossiers hung before A.B.'s gaze. He two-fingered through them swiftly, growing more stunned by the second. Finally

he burst out: "You're giving me a furry and a keek as helpers?"

"Tigerishka and Gershon Thales. They're the best available. Live with them, and fix this glitch."

Kissoon stabbed A.B. with a piercing stare, and A.B. realized this meatspace proximity had been demanded precisely to convey the intensity of Kissoon's next words.

"Without power, we're doomed."

2. 45th Parallel Blues

Jet-assisted flight was globally interdicted. Not enough resources left to support regular commercial or recreational aviation. No military any- where with a need to muster its own air force. Jet engines too harmful to a stressed atmosphere.

And besides, why travel?

Everywhere was the same. Vib served fine for most needs.

The habitable zone of Earth consisted of those lands—both historically familiar and newly disclosed from beneath vanished icepack—above the 45th parallel north, and below the 45th parallel south. The rest of the Earth's landmass had been desertified or drowned: sand or surf.

The immemorial ecosystems of the remaining climactically tolerable territories had been devastated by Greenhouse change, then, ultimately and purposefully, wiped clean. Die-offs, migratory invaders, a fast-forward churn culminating in an engineered ecosphere. The new conditions supported no animals larger than mice, and only a monoculture of GM plants.

Giant aggressive hissing cockroaches, of course, still thrived.

A portion of humanity's reduced domain hosted forests specially designed for maximum carbon uptake and sequestration. These fast-growing, long-lived hybrid trees blended the genomes of eucalyptus, loblolly pine and poplar, and had been dubbed "eulollypops."

The bulk of the rest of the land was devoted to the crops necessary and sufficient to feed nine billion people: mainly quinoa, kale and soy, fertilized by human wastes. Sugarbeet plantations provided feedstock for biopolymer production.

And then, on their compact footprints, the hundred-plus Reboot Cities, ringed by small but efficient goat and chicken farms.

Not a world conducive to sightseeing Grand Tours.

On each continent, a simple network of maglev trains, deliberately held to a sparse schedule, linked the Reboot Cities (except for the Sin Bins, which were sanitarily excluded from easy access to the network). Slow but luxurious aerostats serviced officials and businessmen. Travel between continents occurred on SkySail-equipped water ships. All travel was predicated on state- certified need.

And when anyone had to deviate from standard routes—such as a trio of Power Jockeys following the superconducting transmission lines south to France—they employed a trundlebug.

Peugeot had designed the first trundlebugs over a century ago, the Ozones. Picture a large rolling drum fashioned of electrochromic biopoly, featuring slight catenaries in the lines of its body from end to end. A barrel-shaped compartment suspended between two enormous wheels large as the cabin itself. Solid-state battery packs channeled power to separate electric motors. A curving door spanned the entire width of the vehicle, sliding upward.

Inside, three seats in a row, the centre one commanding the failsafe manual controls. Storage behind the seats.

And in those seats:

Aurobindo Bandjalang working the joystick with primitive recreation-ist glee and vigour, rather than vibbing the trundlebug.

Tigerishka on his right and Gershon Thales on his left. A tense silence reigned.

Tigerishka exuded a bored professionalism only slightly belied by a gently twitching tailtip and alertly cocked tufted ears. Her tigrine pelt poked out from the edges of her plugsuit, pretty furred face and graceful neck the largest bare expanse.

A.B. thought she smelled like a sexy stuffed toy. Disturbing.

She turned her slit-pupiled eyes away from the monotonous racing landscape for a while to gnaw delicately with sharp teeth at a wayward cuticle around one claw.

Furries chose to express non-inheritable parts of the genome of vari-ous extinct species within their own bodies, as a simultaneous expiation of guilt and celebration of lost diversity. Although the Vaults at Reboot City Twenty-nine (formerly Svalbard, Norway) safely held samples of all the vanished species that had been foolish enough to compete with humanity during this Anthropocene Age, their non-human genomes awaiting some far-off day of re- instantiation, that sterile custody did not sit well with some. The furries wanted other species to walk the earth again, if only by partial proxy.

In contrast to Tigerishka's stolid boredom, Gershon Thales manifested a frenetic desire to maximize demands on his attention. Judging by the swallow-flight motions of his hands, he had half a dozen virtual windows open, upon what landscapes of information

A.B. could only conjecture. (He had tried vibbing into Gershon's eyes, but had encountered a pirate privacy wall. Hard to build team camaraderie with that barrier in place, but A.B. had chosen not to call out the man on the matter just yet.)

No doubt Gershon was hanging out on keek fora. The keeks loved to indulge in endless talk.

Originally calling themselves the "punctuated equilibriumists," the cult had swiftly shortened their awkward name to the "punk eeks," and then to the "keeks."

The keeks believed that after a long period of stasis, the human species had reached one of those pivotal Darwinian climacterics that would launch the race along exciting if unpredictable new vectors. What everyone else viewed as a grand tragedy—implacable and deadly climate change leading to the Big Biota Crash—they interpreted as a useful kick in humanity's collective pants. They discussed a thousand, thousand schemes intended to further this leap, most of them just so much mad vapourware.

A.B. clucked his tongue softly as he drove. Such were the assistants he had been handed, to solve a crisis of unknown magnitude.

Tigerishka suddenly spoke, her voice a velvet growl. "Can't you push this bug any faster? The cabin's starting to stink like simians already."

New Perthpatna occupied the site that had once hosted the Russian city of Arkhangelsk, torn down during the Reboot. The closest malfunctioning solar collectors in what had once been France loomed 2,800 kilometres distant. Mission transit time: an estimated thirty-six hours, including overnight rest.

"No, I can't. As it is, we're going to have to camp at least eight hours for the batteries to recharge. The faster I push us, the more power we expend, and the longer we'll have to sit idle. It's a calculated tradeoff. Look at the math."

A.B. vibbed Tigerishka a presentation. She studied it, then growled in frustration.

"I need to run! I can't sit cooped up in a smelly can like this for hours at a stretch! At home, I hit the track every hour."

A.B. wanted to say, *I'm not the one who stuck those big-cat codons in you, so don't yell at me!* But instead he notched up the cabin's HVAC and chose a polite response. "Right now, all I can do is save your nose some grief. We'll stop for lunch, and you can get some exercise then. Can't you vib out like old Gershon there?"

Gershon Thales stopped his air haptics to glare at A.B. His lugubrious voice resembled wet cement plopping from a trough. "What's that comment supposed to imply? That I'm wasting my time? Well, I'm not. I'm engaged in posthuman dialectics at Saltation Central. Very stimulating. You two should try to expand your minds in a similar fashion."

Tigerishka hissed. A.B. ran an app that counted to ten for him using gently breaking waves to time the calming sequence.

"As mission leader, I don't really care how anyone passes the travel time. Just so long as you all perform when it matters. Now how about letting me enjoy the drive."

The "road" actually required little of A.B.'s attention. A wide border of rammed earth, kept free of weeds by cousins to A.B.'s beard removers, the road paralleled the surprisingly dainty superconducting transmission line that powered a whole city. It ran straight as modern justice toward the solar collectors that fed it. Shade from the rows of eulollypops planted alongside cut down any glare and added coolness to their passage.

Coolness was a desideratum. The further south they travelled, the hotter things would get. Until, finally, temperatures would approach fifty degrees at many points of the Solar Girdle. Only their plugsuits would allow the Power Jockeys to function outside under those conditions.

A.B. tried to enjoy the sensations of driving, a recreationist pastime he seldom got to indulge. Most of his workday consisted of indoor mainte-nance and monitoring, optimization of supply and demand, the occasional high-level debugging. Humans possessed a fluidity of response and insight no kybes could yet match. A field expedition marked a welcome change of pace from this indoor work. Or would have, with comrades more congenial.

A.B. sighed, and kicked up their speed just a notch.

After travelling for nearly five hours, they stopped for lunch, just a bit north of where Moscow had once loomed. No Reboot City had ever been erected in its place, more northerly locations being preferred.

As soon as the wide door slid upward, Tigerishka bolted from the cab-in. She raced laterally off into the endless eulollypop forest, faster than a baseline human. Thirty seconds later, a rich, resonant, hair-raising cater-waul of triumph made both A.B. and Gershon Thales jump.

Thales said drily, "Caught a mouse, I suppose."

A.B. laughed. Maybe Thales wasn't such a stiff.

A.B. jacked the trundlebug into one of the convenient stepdown charg-ing nodes in the transmission cable designed for just such a purpose. Even an hour's topping up would help. Then he broke out sandwiches of curried goat salad. He and Thales ate companionably. Tigerishka returned with a dab of overlooked murine blood at the corner of her lips, and declined any human food.

Back in the moving vehicle, Thales and Tigerishka reclined their seats and settled down to a nap after lunch, and their drowsiness soon infected A.B. He put the trundlebug on autopilot, reclined his own seat, and soon was fast asleep as well.

Awaking several hours later, A.B. discovered their location to be nearly atop the 54th parallel, in the vicinity of pre-Crash Minsk.

The temperature outside their cozy cab registered a sizzling thirty-five, despite the declining sun.

"We'll push on toward Old Warsaw, then call it a day. That'll leave just a little over eleven hundred klicks to cover tomorrow."

Thales objected. "We'll get to the farms late in the day tomorrow—too late for any useful investigation. Why not run all night on autopilot?"

"I want us to get a good night's rest without jouncing around. And besides, all it would take is a tree freshly down across the road, or a new sinkhole to ruin us. The autopilot's not infallible."

Tigerishka's sultry purr sent tingles through A.B.'s scrotum. "I need to work out some kinks myself."

Night halted the trundlebug. When the door slid up, furnace air blasted the trio, automatically activating their plugsuits. Sad old fevered planet. They pulled up their cowls and felt relief.

Three personal homeostatic pods were decanted, and popped open upon vibbed command beneath the allée. They crawled inside separately to eat and drop off quickly to sleep.

Stimulating caresses awakened A.B. Hazily uncertain what hour this was that witnessed Tigerishka's trespass upon his homeopod, or whether she had visited Thales first, he could decisively report in the morning, had such a report been required by Jeetu Kissoon and the Power Administration Corps, that she retained enough energy to wear him out.

3. The Sands of Paris

The vast, forbidding, globe-encircling desert south of the 45th parallel depressed everyone in the trundlebug. A.B. ran his tongue around lips that felt impossibly cracked and parched, no matter how much water he sucked from his plugsuit's kamelbak.

All greenery gone, the uniform trackless and silent wastes baking under the implacable sun brought to mind some alien world that had never known human tread. No signs of the mighty cities that had once reared their proud towers remained, nor any traces of the sprawling suburbs, the surging highways. What had not been disassembled for re-use elsewhere had been buried.

On and on the trundlebug rolled, following the superconductor line, its enormous wheels operating as well on loose sand as on rammed earth.

A.B. felt anew the grievous historical impact of humanity's folly upon the planet, and he did not relish the emotions. He generally devoted little thought to that sad topic.

An utterly modern product of his age, a hardcore Rebooter through and through, Aurobindo Bandjalang was generally happy with his civilization. Its contorted features, its limitations and constraints, its precariousness, and its default settings he accepted implicitly, just as a child of trolls believes its troll mother to be utterly beautiful.

He knew pride in how the human race had managed to build a hundred new cities from scratch and shift billions of people north and south in only half a century, outracing the spreading blight and killer weather. He enjoyed the hybrid multicultural mélange that had replaced old divisions and rivalries, the new blended mankind. The nostalgic stories told by Jeetu Kissoon and others of his generation were entertaining fairytales, not the chronicle of any lost Golden Age. He could not lament what he had never known.

He was too busy keeping the delicate structures of the present day up and running, and happy to be so occupied.

Trying to express these sentiments and lift the spirits of his comrades, A.B. found that his evaluation of Reboot civilization was not universal.

"Every human of this fallen Anthropocene age is shadowed by the myriad ghosts of all the other creatures they drove extinct," said Tigerishka, in a surprisingly poetic and sombre manner, given her usual blunt and unsentimental earthiness. "Whales and dolphins, cats and dogs, cows and horses—they all peer into and out of our sinful souls. Our only shot at redemption is that some day, when the planet is restored, our co-evolved partners might be re-embodied."

Thales uttered a scoffing grunt. "Good riddance to all that nonsapient genetic trash! Homo sapiens is the only desirable endpoint of all evolutionary lines. But right now, the dictatorial Reboot has our species locked down in a dead end. We can't make the final leap to our next level until we get rid of the chaff."

Tigerishka spat, and made a taunting feint toward her co- worker across A.B.s chest, causing A.B. to swerve the car and Thales to recoil. When the keek realized he hadn't actually been hurt, he grinned with a sickly superciliousness.

"Hold on one minute," said A.B. "Do you mean that you and the other keeks want to see another Crash?"

"It's more complex than that. You see—"

But A.B.'s attention was diverted that moment from Thales's explanation. His vib interrupted with a Demand 4 call from his apartment.

Vib nodes dotted the power transmission network, keeping people online just like at home. Plenty of dead zones existed elsewhere, but not here, adjacent to the line.

A.B. had just enough time to place the trundlebug on autopilot before his vision was overlaid with a feed from home.

The security system on his apartment had registered an unauthorized entry.

Inside his 1LDK, an optical distortion the size of a small human moved around, spraying something similar to used cooking oil on

A.B.s furniture. The hands holding the sprayer disappeared inside the whorl of distortion.

A.B. vibbed his avatar into his home system. "Hey, you! What the fuck are you doing!"

The person wearing the invisibility cape laughed, and A.B. recognized the distinctive crude chortle of Zulqamain Safranski.

"Safranski! Your ass is grass! The ASBOs are on their way!"

Unable to stand the sight of his lovely apartment being desecrated, frustrated by his inability to take direct action himself,

A.B. vibbed off.

Tigerishka and Thales had shared the feed, and commiserated with their fellow Power Jock. But the experience soured the rest of the trip for

A.B., and he stewed silently until they reached the first of the extensive constructions upon which the Reboot Cities relied for their very existence.

The Solar Girdle featured a tripartite setup, for the sake of security of supply.

First came the extensive farms of solar updraft towers: giant chimneys that fostered wind flow from base to top, thus powering their turbines.

Then came parabolic mirrored troughs that followed the sun and pumped heat into special sinks, lakes of molten salts, which in turn ran different turbines after sunset.

Finally, serried ranks of photovoltaic panels generated electricity directly. These structures, in principle the simplest and least likely to fail, were the ones experiencing difficulties from some kind of dust accretion.

Vibbing GPS coordinates for the trouble spot, A.B. brought the trundle-bug up to the infected photovoltaics. Paradoxically, the steady omnipresent whine of the car's motors registered on his attention only when he had powered them down.

Outside the vehicle's polarized plastic shell, the sinking sun glared like the malign orb of a Cyclops bent on mankind's destruction.

When the bug-wide door slid up, dragon's breath assailed the Power Jocks. Their plugsuits strained to shield them from the hostile environment.

Surprisingly, a subdued and pensive Tigerishka volunteered for camp duty. As dusk descended, she attended to erecting their intelligent shelters and getting a meal ready: chicken croquettes with roasted edamame.

A.B. and Thales sloughed through the sand for a dozen yards to the nearest infected solarcell platform. The keek held his pocket lab in gloved hand.

A little maintenance kybe, scuffed and scorched, perched on the high trellis, valiantly but fruitlessly chipping with its multitool at a hard siliceous shell irregularly encrusting the photovoltaic surface. Thales caught a few flakes of the unknown substance as they fell,

and inserted them into the analysis chamber of the pocket lab. "We should have a complete readout of the composition of this stuff by morning."

"No sooner?"

"Well, actually, by midnight. But I don't intend to stay up. I've done nothing except sit on my ass for two days, yet I'm still exhausted. It's this oppressive place—"

"Okay," A.B. replied. The first stars had begun to prinkle the sky. "Let's call it a day."

They ate in the bug, in a silent atmosphere of forced companionability, then retired to their separate shelters.

A.B. hoped with mild lust for another nocturnal visit from a prowling Tigerishka, but was not greatly disappointed when she never showed to interrupt his intermittent drowsing. Truly, the desert sands of Paris sapped all his usual joie de vivre.

Finally falling fast asleep, he dreamed of the ghostly waters of the vanished Seine, impossibly flowing deep beneath his tent. Somehow, Zulqamain Safranski was diverting them to flood A.B.'s apartment...

4. The Red Queen's Triathlon

In the morning, after breakfast, A.B. approached Gershon Thales, who stood apart near the trundlebug. Already the sun thundered down its oppressive cargo of photons, so necessary for the survival of the Reboot Cities, yet, conversely, just one more burden for the overstressed Greenhouse ecosphere. Feeling irritable and impatient, anxious to be back home, A.B. dispensed with pleasantries.

"I've tried vibbing your pocket lab for the results, but you've got it offline, behind that pirate software you're running. Open up, now."

The keek stared at A.B. with mournful stolidity. "One minute, I need something from my pod."

Thales ducked into his tent. A.B. turned to Tigerishka. "What do you make—"

Blinding light shattered A.B.'s vision for a millisecond in a painful nova, before his MEMS contacts could react protectively by going opaque. Tigerishka vented a stifled yelp of surprise and shock, showing she had gotten the same actinic eyekick.

A.B. immediately thought of vib malfunction, some misdirected feed from a solar observatory, say. But then, as his lenses de- opaqued, he realized the stimulus had to have been external.

When he could see again, he confronted Gershon Thales holding a pain gun whose wide bell muzzle covered both of the keek's fellow Power Jocks. At the feet of the keek rested an exploded spaser grenade.

A.B. tried to vib, but got nowhere.

"Yes," Thales said, "we're in a dead zone now. I fried all the optical circuits of the vib nodes with the grenade."

A large enough burst of surface plasmons could do that? Who knew? "But why?"

With his free hand, keeping the pain gun unwavering, Thales reached into a plugsuit pocket and took out his lab. "These results. They're only the divine sign we've been waiting for. Reboot civilization is on the way out now. I couldn't let anyone in the PAC find out. The longer they stay in the dark, the more irreversible the changes will be."

"You're claiming this creeping crud is that dangerous?"

"Did you ever hear of ADRECS?"

A.B. instinctively tried to vib for the info and hit the blank frustrating walls of the newly created dead zone. Trapped in the twentieth century! Recreationist passions only went so far. Where was the panopticon when you needed it?

"Aerially Delivered Re-forestation and Erosion Control System," continued Thales. "A package of geoengineering schemes meant to stabilize the spread of deserts. Abandoned decades ago. But apparently, one scheme's come alive again on its own. Mutant instruction drift is my best guess. Or Darwin's invisible hand."

"What's come alive then?"

"Nanosand. Meant to catalyze the formation of macroscale walls that would block the flow of normal sands."

"And that's the stuff afflicting the solarcells?"

"Absolutely. Has an affinity for bonding with the surface of the cells and can't be removed without destroying them. Self- replicating. Best estimates are that the nanosand will take out 30 percent of production in just a month, if left unchecked. Might start to affect the turbines too."

Tigerishka asked, in an intellectually curious tone of voice that A.B. found disconcerting, "But what good does going offline do? When PAC can't vib us, they'll just send another crew."

"I'll wait here and put them out of commission too. I only have to hang in for a month."

"What about food?" said Tigerishka. "We don't have enough provisions for a month, even for one person."

"I'll raid the fish farms on the coast. Desalinate my drinking water. It's just a short round trip by bug."

A.B. could hardly contain his disgust. "You're fucking crazy, Thales. Dropping the power supply by 30 percent won't kill the cities."

"Oh, but we keeks think it will. You see, Reboot civilization is a wobbly three-legged stool, hammered together in a mad rush. We're not in the Red Queen's Race, but the Red Queen's Triathlon. Power, food and social networks. Take out any one leg, and it all goes down. And we're sawing at the other two legs as well. Look at that guy who vandalized your apartment. Behaviour like that is on the rise. The urbmons are driving people crazy. Humans weren't meant to live in hives."

Tigerishka stepped forward, and Thales swung the gun more towards her unprotected face. A blast of high-intensity microwaves would leave her screaming, writhing and puking on the sands.

"I want in," she said, and A.B.'s heart sank through his boots. "The only way other species will ever get to share this planet is when most of mankind is gone."

Regarding the furry speculatively and clinically, Thales said, "I could use your help. But you'll have to prove yourself. First, tie up Bandjalang."

Tigerishka grinned vilely at A.B. "Sorry, apeboy."

Using biopoly cords from the bug, she soon had A.B. trussed with circulation-deadening bonds, and stashed in his homeopod.

What were they doing out there? A.B. squirmed futilely. He banged around so much, he began to fear he was damaging the life- preserving tent, and he stopped. Wiped out after hours of struggle, he fell into a stupour made more enervating by the suddenly less- than-ideal heat inside the homeopod, whose compromised systems strained to deal with the desert conditions. He began to hallucinate about the subterranean Seine again, and realized he was very, very thirsty. His kamelbak was dry when he sipped at its straw.

At some point, Tigerishka appeared and gave him some water.

Or did she? Maybe it was all just another dream.

Outside the smart tent, night came down. A.B. heard wolves howling, just like they did on archived documentaries. Wolves? No wolves existed. But someone was howling.

Tigerishka having sex. Sex with Thales. Bastard. Bad guy not only won the battle, but got the girl as well...

A.B. awoke to the pins and needles of returning circulation: discomfort of a magnitude unfelt by anyone before or after the Lilliputians tethered Gulliver.

Tigerishka was bending over him, freeing him.

"Sorry again, apeboy, that took longer than I thought. He even kept his hand on the gun right up until he climaxed."

Something warm was dripping on A.B.'s face. Was his rescuer crying? Her voice belied any such emotion. A.B. raised a hand that felt like a block of wood to his own face, and clumsily smeared the liquid around, until some entered his mouth.

He imagined that this forbidden taste was equally as satisfying to Tigerishka as mouse fluids.

Heading north, the trundlebug seemed much more spacious with just two passengers. The corpse of Gershon Thales had been left behind, for eventual recovery by experts. Desiccation and cooking would make it a fine mummy.

Once out of the dead zone, A.B. vibbed everything back to Jeetu Kissoon, and got a shared commendation that made Tigerishka purr. Then he turned his attention to his personal queue of messages.

The ASBO Squad had bagged Safranski. But they apologized for some delay in his sentencing hearing. Their caseload was enormous these days.

Way down at the bottom of his queue was an agricultural newsfeed. An unprecedented kind of black rot fungus had made inroads into the kale crop on the farms supplying Reboot City Twelve.

Calories would be tight in New Perthpatna, but only for a while. Or so they hoped.

*

—*This story is indebted to Gaia Vince and her article in New Scientist, "Surviving in a Warmer World."*

BOMBS AWAY!

Having departed the McConnell Air Force Base in Kansas just a few hours prior, the squadron of long-range B-5 "Shelly O" Stealth bombers arrived over Igboland in southeastern Nigeria at 3:13 a.m. local time. The air defences of the reclusive and hostile dictatorship (a failed state since the collapse of the global petroleum industry after the advent of microbe-generated electricity from trash) could not detect the invaders.

The payloads unleashed by the bombers, however, were a different matter.

Each package was as big as a freestanding urban street-toilet stall, swaddled in protective foam and with a chute atop.

Soon, mushroom-like synthetic blooms dotted the night sky all over Igboland.

Nigerian troops scrambled to meet their descent.

Each package, as it touched down in countryside, town or city, automatically jettisoned its pre-programmed self-destructing foam coating and parachute, removing evidence of the landing.

Revealed was what appeared, indeed, to be an urban street- toilet: a shed-sized streamlined plastic structure, windowless, with a curving door panel.

In 90 percent of the landings, soldiers arrived first on the scene, surrounding the structures menacingly, weapons raised, until military trucks arrived to haul the invaders away.

Occasionally average citizens reached the bombs first. The finders generally cooperated. They sought to shift the structures out of sight of the authorities. But sometimes fights erupted, or pirate bands intervened. For the most part, unless the citizens moved very fast, the soldiers soon showed up and took the prizes away, brutally and with bloodshed.

But in a very small percentage of instances, the bombs passed safely and secretly into the hands of non-state individuals.

* * * *

A young, orphaned bachelor, Okoronkwo Mmadufo grew pearl millet and raised goats on the edge of an abandoned and decaying Chinese coltan-processing plant, land no one else coveted since it was seeded with toxic wastes. His farm struggled to provide even one person with a subsistence living. The soil sickened his crops and the vegetation his animals. Okoronkwo despaired of ever being rich enough to afford a wife and family.

The night of the bombing run the farmer was awake and about, tending a sick goat. He looked up when he heard a muffled but sizeable thump, and saw the bomb settle atop a patch of scrawny millet plants. He dropped the goat and rushed to the structure.

He began to push futilely at the big bomb, which was nearly as large as his house. But then he saw a large red unlabelled button near the door panel, and he slapped it.

The bomb lifted itself up on a set of wheels and an air-cushion effect.

Okoronkwo ran with the bomb toward the deserted, ruined factory. A small outbuilding looked impenetrably collapsed upon itself. But Okoronkwo knew the secret of its access.

He moved some timbers and hauled aside a wall of galvanized tin and got the bomb hidden. After grabbing a branch, he erased any slight tracks leading back to the landing site.

The soldiers found him cradling his sick goat.

After interrogation and discussion, the soldiers decided not to investigate the abandoned plant, since they had heard that the effect of the toxic wastes would be to cause their penises to disappear. They had much sport speculating on Okoronkwo's genital shrinkage, then left.

Okoronkwo waited until the next night to investigate the bomb in the outbuilding.

When the curving plastic portal opened, light flooded the interior of the bomb. Okoronkwo quickly stepped inside and shut the door.

The interior of the structure appeared much smaller than expected, indicating concealed machinery or reservoirs. The only visible features were: an intake hopper, a dispensing chute, and a docked cellphone.

Okoronkwo picked up the cell and it came alive.

Speckled with animated glyphs, the face of a young white guy appeared.

"Sticky here. What's your name?"

"Okoronkwo Mmadufo."

"Gonna call you OM. Here's the tranche. You're now the proud owner of a Biofab Field Unit. It comes supplied with feedstocks— just common stuff you'll be able to replace—and smart microbes that will handle their own reproduction, as well as diagnostic, engineering and interface instrumentation. PCR, nucleotide decouplers and linkers, sequencers—the works. You can use the BFU to make nearly any medicine or other products of any natural or synthetic organic processes. The Unit will tailor doses of active agents as well for dispersal into the environment. You run everything via the cellphone. You'll see the control panel now on the touchscreen, with a link to an interactive tutorial. Click on the terms of agreement, please, OM— Swell! Goodbye."

"Wait! I have many questions!"

"Sorry, the feds aren't paying me to answer questions. Strictly freelance. So, I'm gone. Unless—can you get me any rare highlife recordings?"

"You like live shows of Dr. Sir Warrior?"

"Hell yeah!"

"I can get those."

"Bring me tracks I don't have, and I'm yours to command." Over the next week, Okoronkwo and his new friend used the

BFU to tailor a remediation treatment for the soil, a cure for pearl millet top rot, and nutraceuticals for the goats.

Okoronkwo came to feel confident in his prowess with the BFU, and eventually bade Sticky goodbye. He knew now that he could continue to help himself and his neighbours, and that his personal future would include a woman and children.

But first he had to tailor a certain lethal smart bug, keyed only to the genomes of Nigeria's rulers. These men were lax with condom use, and certainly obtaining their seed would be no chore at all.

COCKROACH LOVE

DAMIEN BRODERICK AND
PAUL DI FILIPPO

"The problem with Arab literature has been that it forgot to tell stories and lost its way in experimentation. Too many novels that start with lines like 'I came home to find my wife having sex with a cockroach.'"

—Pankaj Mishra
"Where Alaa Al Aswany Is Writing From"
New York Times Magazine, April 27, 2008

When Kay got home, tired and unhappy from her grueling flight halfway round the globe, she found her husband Elwood fucking a cockroach the size of a cocktail waitress.

She had longed only to kick off her sensible yet constricting Madame Ambassador high heels, and collapse on the couch for a foot massage from a considerate spouse. Unburden herself of all her diplomatic aggravations, with a cool drink in hand. Instead, that piece of furniture was now being creakingly abused.

Kay instinctively plucked off one pump, and heaved it at the insect.

In her blinding fury, she missed the bug by a good yard, and her husband as well.

The foul thing glanced at her and insouciantly kept right on peeling an orange with its mandibles as her spouse of five years thrust at its hindquarters. Kay couldn't tell if the roach were male or female, not that it mattered especially.

"For the love of God, El!"

Elwood Grackle noticed her, finally. His face was flushed to a Clintonesque burgundy, and so was most of his bare chest. With a final shudder he jerked his useless fluids into the insect and fell forward, panting and dripping sweat onto the gleaming, jewel-toned carapace. The cockroach swallowed its final bright segment of fruit and chased it down with a tart bite of peel before throwing the curly remainder considerately into the faux fireplace.

Elwood detached with a squelch and a measure of insouciance. He pulled his ankled pants up awkwardly with one hand, reclaimed his shirt from the sofa back with the other. "How was the flight from Cairo, darling? You're early."

"I'm five hours late, you squamous fucker."

"Well, yes, strictly speaking, but I was factoring in post-arrival press conferences, debriefings, and the like. Allow me to introduce Emma. Em, this is Kay."

The roach's voice resembled a bandsaw working its blade through a wet sandbag. "Your wedded bliss. Madame boss. Most honoured."

"My wife, yes." He toweled himself off with his shirt. "Em is our new Kaf."

"Christ, so now you're reduced to screwing a transgenic. The flight was gruesome, and so was Cairo. The noise of that place is indescribable."

"Really? What's it like?" He tucked himself away, donned the damp shirt, went to the bar to wash his hands lightly but firmly, and got out two tall frosty glasses from the fridge. He fished out a lime and slashed it. "A margarita, darling?"

"What do you mean, what's it like? If I could describe it it wouldn't be indescribable. Yes, I'll have a drink, and why don't you tell this filthy thing to clear off, I'm sick of the sight of it."

"Your lovely bride is testy, Elwood. Felicitations, Madame, I was just leaving. I hope your mood is improved when next we meet." Boldly flashing the progenitive trademark of the Abu Dhabi University biolabs branded onto its shell, the roach was out the door in a darting motion that eluded Kay's swinging, still-shod foot with ease.

"I take it from your sour mood," said Elwood, "that negotiations with the Egyptians were not successful."

"My sour mood, as you so sympathetically phrase it, has more to do with your rutting."

"Oh, don't try to make me the villain. I sensed from your last phone call that you were already about as cheerful as a... as a drowning Micronesian. Your tiresome moodiness has been the status quo in our happy home for months."

Kay was suddenly immensely weary. It was true. She'd been a fount of black despair lately. Not that she could help it. So much was going wrong for the nation. For the world!

She sagged down on the couch, hit the glutinous wet spot, recoiled and shot up again—awkwardly, given her half-shod condition—and spilled her drink. Considerately, Elwood jumped to support her, and guided her to the safe haven of a dry armchair. Her façade of professional and wifely fortitude crumbled. His familiar, solicitous touch! She began to weep.

El patted her shoulder. He went to mix her a replacement margarita, talking soothingly the while.

"There, dear, have a good cry. It's not easy, helping steer the ship of state through these perilous times. Never forget, I'm always there for you, darling."

"You're never there," she said, sobbing. "You're always here."

"Exactly, I'm always here for you. Look, you realize now that my

little impulsive moment just now has no bearing on our marriage, or my love for you?"

"Are you *insane?* You were *fucking a roach!* What am I meant to think?"

El's mouth twisted a little. "She's a gift from the biolabs at Abu Dhabi University. For both of us. I was testing out all her advertised features."

"A Kafka, for god's sake. I've seen them in Cairo, you don't need to explain them to *me*. Fifteen percent human genes."

"Well, yes, but that's a feature, not a bug. Sorry." He raised his hands protectively in front of his face and tried not to grin. "But that's what they are, dear. General factotum and bug of all trades."

"What are *you* doing with one, that's what I want to know?

Surely for something that expensive we should have discussed—"

"No, I'm telling you. A gift! For you, really. It seems they sent one to every high-level bureaucrat in the current administration. Some potentate's largesse, like the bestowal of the camel or virgin in days of yore."

"Oh. Right." Kay's expression hardened. "In gratitude for President McMurtry's new stance on Israel."

"Probably. But hey, Big Mac didn't exactly *disavow* American support, it was more a subtle shift in the—"

"Subtle! Subtle! About as subtle as getting home to find you screwing a *bug*. I'm going to bed. You can sleep on the couch. Oh, and wipe up the slime first."

She hoped he could tell she didn't mean it. He should be in the bed beside her. Because, really, there's no place like home.

* * * *

The Kafka, Emma, sucked in her stout belly and scrunched under the water heater. Her upstairs sleeping crate beckoned to her with its phero-mone-laced organo-plastic shell, but she dared not approach it yet, given the hostility of the house's queen female.

Trembling with the aftershock of insemination, Emma was also seeth-ing with anger. The bitch had called her a cockroach! Em gnawed at the drywall opening, shoveling the unpleasant residue aside into a white powdery pile, and dragged her carapace into the wall space. She was no more a roach than that fool Elwood was a... a... tarsier.

Beneath her forward feet, the rough-cut joists tasted of mouse droppings and something less appetizing. A cat had been in here. Not recently, though. Alert for danger, she forced herself to relax. Cockroach, indeed! Cretin! Em had eaten enough roaches to know the differences intimately—they were flat, their legs stuck out grossly, most were wingless. *My* belly, she told herself, settling onto it in the soothing grime, is rounded and womanly. My back is strong and mounded like the dome of a noble capitol building. My legs are sensitive and petite. I am a *beetle*, you stupid human cow. Hear me roar!

At the quivering tip of her abdomen, in the protruding ootheca, her rows of eggs glowed under the attentions of Elwood's wrigglers. Babies! Soon! She yearned for motherhood.

Her irritation failed to subside. It wasn't meant to be like this. They'd promised so much more, in the hatchery, along with their cynicism and, simultaneously, their rather pushy warrior faith. In the dim light, Em poked about and found the battered Avon paperback half-copy of Nabokov's *Pnin* she'd been consuming. She managed three pages, gobbling them up as she committed the words to memory, before she fell asleep.

* * * *

"I hope you're planning on a shower before you come to bed, darling," Kay told him, throwing off her underwear and moving in the dark. "I can't bear the stink of the thing on you."

Elwood's voice came to her, from the open bathroom door, in the unlighted bedroom: "Sweetheart, you know I always—"

Kay slammed her toes into something and yelped in pain. In a moment, El was beside her, naked, smelling of rancid sex, wide-eyed. He flicked on the overhead light. "What? What's the matter?"

"What the hell *is* it?" Kay cried, high-pitched. Her bare toe had struck a bulky off-white curved *thing* of some kind, as large as the kennel for a Bernese Mountain Dog and shiny as a polished egg, which it rather resembled. It had been squeezed in between her side of the bed and the sliding mirror fronting her closet.

"They brought it when they delivered the Kaf. It's where she sleeps."

"In my *bedroom*?"

"They abhor light, darling."

Kay stopped rubbing her toe, which still felt as if maybe she'd broken one phalange, and looked for a handhold on the carrier.

Nothing—it really was like an egg, seamless, closed. "How does it get *in*?"

"You really mustn't call her 'it,' sweetheart. There are provisions in the law now, I should have thought that you, of all people—"

Her questing fingers found a gap underneath. By main force she dragged the plastic shell to the end of the king-sized bed and tried to tip it over, gasping for air.

"I don't think she's in there," El said. "Look, let's just leave it there for the night, she'll probably come in later, they're very quiet and tidy, you know, we're both exhausted and out of sorts, you and I, I mean, everything will look rosier after we've had a good night's—"

Kay was not listening. Slamming the door between bedroom and hall-way, she tugged at the old mahogany chest of drawers she'd inherited from Aunt Lil, dragging it, with a squawk of tortured Columbian structured parquet flooring, to jam the door shut, barring any direct or even furtive approach by the loathsome insect.

"Kay, it's—She's a *person*. This isn't like you. I thought we had an arrangement?"

"Yes! But the main contract preceded the fooling-around clause.

To love and honour till death us do part! You're doing neither!"

El's expression indicated he had a ready marital riposte. But some imp of caution dissuaded him from venting the pithy reply. Instead, he wisely hung his head, retreated to the bathroom, had a short but energetically hygienic shower, then crawled meekly into bed, carefully keeping a DMZ of six inches between himself and Kay, whose quivering silent fury scared him fully as much as the world had been terrified of Kim Jong-Il just before that dictator had been assassinated in the very act of launching assorted ICBMs. A crisis Kay had a not-insignificant part in defusing, with hard-nosed realpolitik efficiency.

Lying tensely on his back, vainly inviting sleep, Elwood Grackle remained unaware of the newly introduced and cleverly designed spirochaetes working their way up his urethra with their snicker- snack flagellae, heading with mysterious intentions much deeper into his system.

* * * *

Professor Qutaybah Al Nahyan nervously fussed with his headdress in preparation for his interview with the Sheikh Khalifa. Although the professor maintained a certain formally congenial consanguinity with the ruler of Abu Dhabi—fifth cousins once removed on a great-uncle's side—the hard facts of their relationship remained obdurate and inequal. One man was the living embodiment of their proud nation and its glorious destiny, Lion of the Prophet, while the other was a humble university instructor and researcher, educated at Oxford and Cal Tech, unmarried, living in a sparsely furnished bachelor's condo in the Mussafah Residential neighbourhood. So today's meeting was hardly between peers, let alone friends. It would be a master's interrogation of his servant.

Drawing a small comb though his moustache and beard, Professor Al Nahyan sought to reassure himself that the Sheikh Khalifa would be pleased with what he had done, on his own initiative. True, he'd had to use some accounting sleight-of-hand to transfer funds from certain above-board projects to his own lab. And he had shamelessly passed off many of his classroom duties to his grad assistant, a stocky yet rather attractive American woman named Cayenne Sorbet, giving him time to work on tweaking the genome of his prized spirochaete. Also true, he had unleashed his creations on the world—via the Trojan Beetle of the Kafs—without so much as an environmental impact statement. Yet was it not all for the greater glory of Islam, a most gentle and accommodating way of spreading the faith? Surely, with such motives and goals, no discredit could redound to him.

At last the professor could dither no longer, but must make haste. Down to the condo's basement garage, into the air- conditioned comfort of his Chinese sedan, and out to contend with the impossible traffic of the island city-state. Subsidized gasoline prices encouraged auto use here, unlike most of the rest of their world, suffering $200-a-barrel oil, despite the power beaming down now from orbit.

The meeting was scheduled to take place at MOPA, the Ministry of Presidential Affairs on the Corniche Road. As professor Al Nahyan pulled into the parking lot, the sharp sparkle of the ocean waters nearby pierced his eyes and gave him an instant headache. He began to suspect that this meeting would not go well.

The Sheikh, however, seemed in a fine, expansive mood when Al Nahyan was finally ushered into the presence. Four or five men in tasteless western garb and an equal number of proud yet fawning cousins in their mid-twenties and early thirties attended the potentate as he sat at ease behind a desk as large as an aircraft carrier's launch deck. Holograms projected above the black glass desk displayed a magnificent assortment of prancing, head-tossing racing camels, presumably candidates for the Sheikh's fabled stables. Rumours suggested that the best of these coursers were genetically modified, enhanced against all the laws of God and man. If it were so, the result, the professor had to confess, proved the infraction worth the risk. His eyes moistened to see them, even at one-tenth scale, and his heart beat faster at the thought of mounting one and wheeling away into the desert, as his ancestors had ridden for centuries in the service of the Sheikh's own lineage. He came to his senses as the dealers in dromedarian flesh departed, puffing on large cigars, and his master faced him with a keen glance.

"Fine steeds, eh?"

"Yes indeed, sir."

"And what of your own little breeding experiments, eh? Eh?" The Sheikh laughed a booming, deep-chested laugh that rattled the professor's equanimity if not the bomb-proof three-ply windows. "Are we on target for the, uh, *transformation* of the infidels?"

Al Nahyan nervously found a chair, but dared not sit, though his knees knocked.

"Second stage insertion has begun, sir. A container of larvae has been ferried up the San Francisco de Quito skyhook, packaged for orbital transport by Virgin as solar cell panels. I anticipate shuttle deployment above Ecuador within the hour. We'll take down those Google power-sats in a matter of days."

The Sheikh's face set hard, considering who knew what complexities of realpolitik. He tilted his bearded head, then, and reached for the humidor.

"The Kafirs, the infidels, will not know what hit them. A cigar, doctor?"

* * * *

Melatonin-plus carried Kay through a night racked, in the deepest crevices of her jetlag-shocked body, by exhaustion and disgust. When the alarm beeped at ten in the morning she was still asleep—miracle of pharmaceutical science!—and when she flung her legs over the side of the bed she was hardly any closer to full consciousness. Her toes banged into the roach kennel as she stumbled to the bathroom.

"*Damn* you, El!" she shrieked, but the chest of drawers had been pulled ajar and he was long gone, into Beltway wonk territory, no doubt greasing his way along the corridors of D.C. power, such as it was any more. The pain in her toe seemed out of all proportion to the impact; maybe she *had* broken a bone. Shit! Now she'd have to fit an X-ray appointment in with all the rest of her impossibly burdened schedule. "Planner on," she shouted furiously to the system, and through the scrubbing and gurgling of her morning ablutions dictated her modified timetable. The odour of freshly- brewed automated coffee floated to her under the door from the kitchenette, and something more. Could it be a toasted muffin with orange marmalade? Heavenly! It made her laugh and brightened her mood. She'd surely put the fear of reprisal into the brute. For Elwood to stay home and make her breakf—

"Good morning, madame," the Kafka said, peering out from behind the refrigerator. "Would we care for an egg?"

Speechless, half-blinded by a rush of blood to her brain, Kay stopped on one foot (the uninjured one) and stared through squinted eyes at the gleaming kitchenette. One of her failings, she was prepared to admit, and certainly one of Elwood's, was to let the conapt pile up ever grungier with unwashed plates and cups and glasses, half-empty containers from the classiest takeoutlets in Maryland, a dead imported wine bottle or two from the Rhone Valley in Germany or the Illawarra in Australia abandoned on its side under the couch. The help were meant to deal with it, one day a week, but since Big Mac's punitive expulsions of the wetbacks it was impossible to get any help at all, let alone the good kind. Yet now everything in sight was redeemed, renewed, polished. Had the *roach* been bending its many elbows to the task?

"No egg," she said weakly. "Just bring me a cup of coffee and that muffin. I'll be in my study."

The creature turned away obediently, no hint of the saucy impudence of last night, but as Kay left the room she caught a glimpse of something horrible and disturbing. A kind of pulsing puce-hued bag protruded from the Kaf's hindquarters. An egg case? Dear Christ, was the thing *enceinte*? Was it about to *give birth in the kitchen?* She couldn't handle it. Her mind shifted sideways to the problem Sheikh Khalifa posed to the Free World from his seat of power in the United Arab Emirates. If only she had been able to make the Egyptians see that the Emirates were as much a threat to them as to the West—

In the hallway, her bare toes came down on something hard and sharp, something that scattered and rattled. White, stripped bones, with a quite largish crunched skull, as big as a—

Kay screamed at the top of her lungs, and ran for her iPhone, punched Elwood's direct link. "Get back here *this minute*," she shrieked. "Your fucking sex toy has *eaten the cat*."

* * * *

With the surname Stoner, a man was doomed from birth to a certain fate. Nominative determinism was a potent cosmic force, creating a Filipino Roman Catholic Cardinal named Sin, not to mention that top Harley Street neurologist, Lord Brain, Fellow of the Royal Society. So no-one among Jayant Vishnu Stoner's co-workers aboard Google PowerSat #9 was surprised at Jay's penchant for ingesting, smoking, injecting, popping, perfusing, snorting, or transcranially/magnetically inducing any illicit stimulant that fell to his questing hand. They regarded as just another workplace perk his amusing propensity for chatting with amiable hallucinations, a luser's gag, they assumed, meant to entertain them during their endless orbital days.

With his long funky dreads and his migratory subdermal flock of CGI tattoos, his fascination with jam-band music (his iQuant held 10,000 Phish tracks alone) and his slacker work habits, Jay surfed leisurely through his duties as solar-panel installer like a toasted postmodern peon of the space age. Only Jay's bosses were ignorant of his potentially dangerous noncompliance with management-approved modalities of employment. They were too busy surveying their stock options and charting the exact moment when they could prematurely retire.

Google's network of PowerSats was nearing the edge of critical mass, the ability to produce a quantity of non-petroleum energy able to rival—and eventually displace—old dirty sources like gas and soft coal, the bountiful curse that had contributed so much pollution to China. These megawatts of clean power beamed by microwave to lacy terrestrial rectenna farms had already brought down the price of a barrel of oil from $250 to $200! Of course, as pointy-headed economists had warned, that cost reduction immediately led to an outburst of SUV purchases burning this cheaper fuel—but every solution has its drawbacks. Soon, the new paradigm of carbon-free power would be a reality, and the global economy would surge forward on a solid footing, no longer indebted to tyrants and dictators or greedy CEOs.

Not that Jay subscribed to any such high-minded idealism. It wasn't as if he had yearned or studied for this position. He had lucked into this job as part of a class-action lawsuit settlement. Google had failed to defend its search hog adequately against all the latest viruses, and the rogue program SnapDragon had snared the name and stats of Jayant Vishnu Stoner, and the randomly selected names and stats of several hundred other innocents. Their photos and full details immediately popped out whenever the search-term "FBI most wanted" was entered. In return for this gross defamation (and several false arrests, plus one fatal shooting), the victims were offered a choice: a job with Google, or a cash settlement. In a moment of sober practicality, Jay had taken the employment and training option.

So here he was, geared up in a nifty, sleek Dava Newman BioSuit against the unforgiving cargo bay vacuum of Google PowerSat #9, helping to unload the Virgin Galactic Ship *Victoria Beckham*, out of Quito Sky-hook and now a good part of the way around the planet. In the satellite's microgravity, the bulky waffle-patterned organo- plastic crates were easy to shift and slot, allowing Jay to focus on the Widespread Panic tune pumping through his earbuds, and the low-level buzz created by his consumption of a morning fetal-cell- and-absinthe cocktail. Floating in a lazy haze, Jay was only a little surprised when Mr. Mxyzptlk showed up. The derby-wearing imp from the fifth dimension was a welcome confidante. Jay paused his iQuant and greeted him happily.

"Mxy, my man! What's down?"

Speaking around his cigar, Mr. Mxyzptlk told him, "Feast your peepers on the crate with the pliss scabbed on."

Jay focused blearily through the distortions of his merry high. Sure enough, one crate packaged as solar cell panels also featured an attached

Portable Life-Support System. Weirdness! Why would dead power mechanisms engineered for the nullity of high-orbit

require livestock temperature and atmosphere regulation? This shit had to be contraband! The PowerSat crew enjoyed frequent illicit shipments of porn, pets, alcohol, drugs, cigarettes and transfats, and this had to be one such—although the usually reliable grapevine had not alerted Jay in advance.

"Think I'll just skim a little off the top, Mxy! Thanks for the heads-up!"

"No grind," Mxy said. With a shouted "Kltpzyxm!" the imp vanished.

Exhibiting a druggie's exaggerated slyness, Jay guided the selected crate out of sight of his busy co-workers, through an airlock, and into the adjacent shirtsleeves environment of the large room where Manned Manoeuvering Units were repaired. The workspace, festooned with spare parts, was luckily unoccupied, sparing him any need to blurt out an absurd excuse for his presence. Still in his suit, Jay cracked the seals of the crate with fumbling eagerness, anticipating familiar goodies.

For a full ninety seconds, his fogged brain failed to register what he was seeing, actually *seeing* in external reality. As far as he could tell. "They're immature bugs!" the voice of SpongeBob SquarePants whispered in his ear. "Giant fucking larvae, dude!"

He tore at his eyes, but sure enough, the crate was filled with squirming featureless maggots the size of microwave ovens. Several had begun to pupate, enclosing themselves in the shells that would crack to discharge the adults of whatever the hell gruesome species they were.

One of his rare bad trips kicked in. The wriggling flesh hassocks creeped him out. A powerful vision seized him: roaches expanding, multiplying, filling the station from wall to wall. "Yaargh! Gotta get rid of the suckers!"

Jay hastily re-sealed the crate, and removed its PLSS unit. All he had to do now was cycle it back out to the airless cargo bay, and the unprotected bugs would die.

He pushed the crate toward the airlock. At the last moment, SpongeBob offered counsel.

"Man, somebody went to a lot of trouble to get these up here. These things must be valuable! Why not save at least one...?"

"Good idea!"

Jay soon had a single grub hidden inside an empty suit, tethered by netting to the wall of the workspace. With luck, it would survive and not be found until he could get it back to his quarters. His humour was mellowing again. Hey, who knew what might hatch out of it? Something pretty cool, maybe.

"Great job!" said SpongeBob. "Let's hit the dining hall for a Crabby Patty now!"

"Yeah!"

* * * *

"You son of a whoring bitch!" Kay shrieked, gazing at the pink- tipped strip of paper in her trembling hand with its pink-mauve + sign. A drop of urine dripped off of it, splashed her bare foot. If the kit did not lie, her uterus was flooded with chorionic gonadotropin. Was *invaded*. She rooted frantically through her packs of pills. A rushed count showed none missing. What the *hell*? Had the bastard purchased some exhausted stock from a crooked Bolivian recycling pharmacy, via Web2Bay? Substituted the past-use-by dud product for her own contraceptives? The print was too small to tell. "I informed you it was too soon for this! I have my diplomatic career to consider, you ridiculous sentimentalist."

In the living room, Elwood had his forehead pressed to the new patterned mat he'd extended over the parquet. Outside, the usual unearthly wailing rose from a plasticized carbon-bonded minaret erected with grudging city approval just across from the Farmer's Market. The Adhan rose and fell, calling the faithful to early morning salat prayer. "*Ash-hadu anna Muhammadan rasūlullāh,*" El murmured ecstatically. "*Hayya 'alā Khair al-'amal.*"

"Make haste toward the best thing yourself, you pig of a pig." Wasn't it enough that she had to put up with this ululating in Cairo, where she'd spent six weeks in a crash Arabic course using the powerful mnemonic principles of the Pole, Piotr Wozniak. "What's the idea? And get up off the floor, you fool, you're an Episcopalian and a third-degree Mason, not a Muslim."

El lifted his spirochaete-laden head dazedly. "We are all part of the body of the Umma," he explained. "So mote it be."

"Well, something else is part of *my* body now, you sorry excuse. *I'm pregnant!*"

After a pause for pious thought, El told her, "I forgive you."

"Will you be taking breakfast, madame?" asked the roach, putting its head in from the kitchenette. "And congratulations on the baby—I'm in the family way myself."

Kay seized a bright green apple from a decorative bowl of wax fruit in the centre of the table, flung it at the creature; the fake apple caught in the plates of its back. "And I know who the hell the father is! Elwood, you disgust me. How could you fuck a thing like that, and then bring your soiled seed to our marriage bed?" *It's affected his mind*, she thought. I*nfected his mind. And probably his body as well*. She shuddered, feeling befouled.

"Verily," El expounded, "prayer prevents the worshipper from indulging in anything that is undignified or indecent. That's Surah Al-Ankabut, chapter 29, verse 46." He got to his feet, a look of crazed passion in his eye. "They can all grow up together. They can attend Naval Prep School, in historic Newport, Rhode Island, as I did, and my father before me. Imagine them in the rigging! Six legs good!" Foam was starting to seep from the edges of his mouth.

A hideous peeping came from the kitchenette, as of a nestful of baby chicks calling their mother. Kay's face drained of blood. No, not chicks. They probably hunted down chicks and ate them raw. And what the hell was growing inside *her?*

"I'm going to kill you," she told her deluded spouse. She picked up an ornamental brass poker from the set of Ralph Lauren accessories resting beside the ornamental fake fireplace, and hoisted it lustily above her head. "I'm going to fucking *murder* and *skin* you, and then I'm driving straight to the Prince George's clinic."

Elwood Grackle grabbed a defensive dining room chair by its cushioned back, but left it dangling. "Fight in the way of Allah against those who fight against you," he warned, "but begin not hostilities. Lo! Allah loveth not aggressors. Kill them whenever you confront them and drive them from where they drove you. Surah 2, verses 190–191."

"We're fresh out of eggs," Emma called in her abrasive voice. "Anyone for a sliced sausage?"

* * * *

Aboard Google PowerSat #9, Jay Stoner was entertaining a visitor in his private room, a room admittedly smaller than the average terrestrial capsule-hotel accommodations. Luckily, the visitor could be cradled and compassed completely within the circle of Jay's arms.

The gently squirming peristaltic mass of the lone surviving smuggled larva, retrieved from its hiding place, radiated a kind of numinous pet-like comfort into Jay's quiveringly drug-sensitized brain, traversing all interspecies communication gaps and barriers. Waves of wordless approbation laved him. Damn! This thing was just like a Tribble! Shame he had killed all the others, he could've sold them to his fellow crew members. Life aboard the solar-power station could be harsh and boring, despite both management- approved and illicit recreations, and any additional source of comfort was always eagerly sought. But all the other bugs were irrevocably gone now, and Jay wasn't one for crying over spilled bongwater.

Suddenly a floating copyright mark akin to Jay's own anime tats drifted up to display itself beneath the larva's epidermis, much like an answer appearing in the window of a Magic Eight Ball.

"N-5397-batch5," read Jay aloud. "Aw, is dat your widdle name- ums? Uncle Jay is gonna call you Enny. Enny-wenny-wenny-henny- penny!"

Jay began to tickle the bug, and gushes of telepathic gratitude swamped his senses. "What does Enny-wenny want now? Sugar water? A widdle sweater to stay warm?"

The flood of love pouring out of the larva almost instantly transmuted to hate. Jay was stunned and saddened. But then he realized that the hate was not directed against him. Oh, no! Enny's anger and pain represented a lashing-out against the bug's creators, the men who had placed Enny and cousins on a one-way trip to space, away from all familiar earthly pleasures, to carry out their greedy schemes like disposable grunts on the front lines of corporate wars.

"Tell me, tell me, Enny! Who did it to you! Who must suffer your sweet, sweet ichorous revenge!"

Images marched through Jay's brain. Arabs in their robes, state offices, a seaside city, signage—

"Yes, yes, Enny, I know who they are! Bastards! We'll make them pay! Soon, soon, just when the shift's about to change—"

Jay smooshed his face into the warm pulpy haggis of the larva and smothered it with kisses.

Enny seemed content to wait.

* * * *

"Nothing has gone *wrong, qua* wrong," Professor Al Nahyan assured Sheikh Khalifa. His glowering master did not look especially assured. "The package was intercepted somehow. We had no way of perceiving in advance—"

"Quiet." The Lion's fingers, scented and beautifully manicured, drummed on an acre of black glass. The great office, blue lit, was refrigerator cold, its master wrapped in a fur-lined *dishdasha*. Qutaybah shivered. "One larva is still minimally responsive, you say?"

"Yes, yes—within certain unpredictable limits. But there are very many more on the ground, naturally. Ready to give birth, if the induced mutations hold steady. Some have already been through parturition." He checked his babbling tendency to persiflage under stress. "They are very… compulsive animals. The second generation individuals are even more potent. With 65 percent human genes, thanks to the maternal and paternal contributions, they are more anthropomorphic, and completely irresistible to either human sex. The Westerners will go extinct, wasting all their lusts on the bugs instead of breeding strong sons and modest daughters."

The professor neglected to add that the hybrids would be fully Islamic in their outlook, due to the onboard spirochaetes of his devising—Plan

B, as it were. He was still unsure of the legitimacy of conferring Koranic knowledge on another species.

"So I understand." The Sheikh failed to fly into a rage, which was at once a blessed relief and a phenomenon beyond all understanding. Al Nahyan wrung his sweating hands, fearing for them. But the Sheikh merely lifted one of his own and flicked his fingers. Begone, said the fingers. The endocrino-entomologist scrambled gratefully from the room, reeling with the vertigo of terror. Clearly, geopolitical and theological factors were in play here well beyond his narrow, specialized knowledge. Beyond his need to know. He crept past crisp guards in military uniform and languid courtiers arrayed like peacocks by languid couturiers. The sun, when finally he escaped into the open, beat on his naked head like a cruel blessing. Like the justice and mercy of Allah.

In the distance, a voice called from the muezzin, called the Faithful to prayer.

But contrary to all his past devotional humility, all that professor Al Nahyan could think of was the image of his plump and attractive grad assistant, Miss Cayenne Sorbet, locked in carnal embrace with a second generation Kaf.

What a waste. I've completely thrown my life away…

* * * *

Jay oozed stealth as he air-swam down the corridors of the satellite, mingling with the dispirited workers swapping posts. Enny rested hidden in a courier's bag strapped to Jay's back.

"Soon, Enny, soon," Jay muttered, drawing no suspicions from his co-workers, who were certain he was merely addressing the ghost of Phil Silvers or John Lennon or Yogi Bear, as was his wont. At the beam-control room, Jay encountered Bob Hazzard, itching to leave, and knew he had beaten Bob's replacement to the door. Unquestioningly eager to leave, Bob allowed Jay inside.

Jay locked the door.

Fully automated, the cybernetic mechanisms that kept the output beam of PowerSat #9 focused on the rectenna farms in the deserts of the American west needed only to be monitored for freakish drift. But of course, manual overrides existed to allow a complete shift in target.

Unpacking Enny and allowing the larva to float beside his shoulder, Jay set to work.

Plugging in the GPS coordinates of Abu Dhabi took only seconds.

Fingers poised to stroke the touchscreen and send gigawatts of searing microwave radiation down upon the unsuspecting, unprotected emirate, Jay paused and turned to Enny.

"Is this really what you want, Enny?"

The savage surety of the bug's response was unmistakeable. Jay stroked.

* * * *

In a D.C. townhouse, a man and a woman lay insensible on the floor, while dozens of second-generation infant Kafs swarmed over them, spreading mutagenic slime trails across their skin.

Emma watched with pride and pleasure. Like the heroine in one of The Master's best books, *Lolita*, she knew that innocence was much deadlier than cunning any day.

* * * *

The Sheikh Khalifah relaxed in his chair. He touched hidden contacts on his great desk; the doors locked with chunky authority. The smoky, polarized windows transitioned to complete opacity.

He stroked a last button, and a brocaded, gilded basket rose from beneath the floor. Within the basket, a gleaming, jewel-crusted mutant bug turned her sleepy gaze upon him, preened her antennae.

"My lord," she said.

"Come to me, you lovely bitch," said the Lion of the Prophet, parting his blue-silver trimmed *dishdasha*.

The Sheikh was suddenly forced to shield his eyes. What unexpected nova could leak through the window films?

Only a city instantly aflame.

The contents of the office burst into flame, and for a final mortal second, the Sheik Khalifah learned that roasting Kaf smelled like lobster.

WAVES AND SMART MAGMA

Salt air stung Storm's super-sensitive nose, although he was still several scores of kilometres distant from the coast. The temperate August sunlight, moderated by myriad high-orbit pico-satellites, one of the many thoughtful legacies of the Upflowered, descended as a soothing balm on Storm's unclothed pelt. Several churning registers of flocculent clouds, stuffed full of the computational particles known as virgula and sublimula, betokened the watchful custodial omnipresence of the tropospherical mind. Peaceful and congenial was the landscape around him: a vast plain of black- leaved cinnabon trees, bisected by a wide, meandering river, the whole of which had once constituted the human city of Sacramento. Storm reined to a halt his furred and feathered steed—the Kodiak Kangemu named Bergamot was a burly, scary-looking but utterly obedient bipedal chimera some three metres tall at its muscled shoulders, equipped with a high saddle and panniers—and paused for a moment of reflection.

The world was so big, and rich, and odd! And Storm was all alone in it! That thought both frightened and elated him.

He felt he hardly knew himself or his goals, what depths or heights he was capable of. Whether he would live his long life totally independent of wardenly strictures, a rebel, or become an obedient part of the guardian corps of the planet. Hence this journey.

A sudden lance of light breaking through a bank of clouds brightened Storm's spirits. Despite the distinct probability that the photons had been deliberately collimated by the tropospheric mind's manipulation of water molecules as a signal to chivvy him onward.

Anything was possible, Storm realized. His destiny rested solely on the strength of his character and mind and muscles, and the luck of the Upflowered. Glory or doom, fame or ignominy, love or enmity His fate remained unwritten.

And so far he had not done too badly, giving him confidence for his future.

The young warden had now travelled much further from home than he ever had in his short life. All to barge in upon a perilous restoration and salvage mission whose members had known nothing of Storm's very existence until a short time ago.

A gamble, to be sure, but one he had felt compelled to make. Perthaps his one and only chance for an adventure before settling down.

The death of Storm's parents, the wardens Pertinax and Chellapilla, had left him utterly and instantly adrift. Although by all rights and traditions, Storm should have stepped directly into their role as one of the several wardens of the Great Lakes bioregion, he had balked. The conventional lives his parents had led, in obedience to the customs and innate design of their species did not appeal to Storm's nature—at least not at this moment. Perhaps his unease with his assigned lot in life was due to the unusual conditions of his conception...

Some twenty years ago, five wardens, Storm's parents among them, had undertaken an expedition to the human settlement of "Chicago," one of the few places where those degraded *homo sap* remnants who had disdained the transcendence of the Upflowering still dwelled. During that dangerous enforcement action, which resulted in the destruction of the human village by the tropospheric mind, Storm had been conceived. Those suspenseful and tumultuous prenatal circumstances seemed to have left him predisposed to a characteristic restless thrill-seeking.

His conception and birth among the strictly reproductively regulated wardens had been sanctioned so that Storm might grow up to be a replacement for the elderly warden Sylvanus, who, at age one-hundred-and-twenty-eight, had already begun to ponder retirement.

And so Storm was raised in the cozy little prairie home—roofed with pangolin tiles, pots of greedy, squawking parrot tulips on the windowsill—shared by Pertinax and Chellapilla. His first two decades of life had consisted of education and play and exploration in equal measures. His responsibilities had been minimal.

Which explained his absence from the routine surveying expedition where his parents had met their deaths.

A malfunctioning warden-scent broadcaster had failed to protect their encampment from a migratory herd of galloping aurochs, and Storm's parents had perished swiftly at midnight in each other's arms in their tent.

Sylvanus, all grey around his muzzle and ear tufts, his once- sinewy limbs arthritic as he closed in on his second century, condoled with Storm.

"There, there, my poor boy, cry all you want. I know I've drained my eyes already on the trip from home to see you. Your parents were smart and capable and loving wardens, and lived full lives, even if they missed reaching a dotage such as mine. You can be proud of them. They always honoured and fulfilled the burdens bestowed on our kind by the Upflowered."

At the mention of the posthumans who had spliced and redacted Storm's species out of a hundred baseline genomes, Storm felt his emotions flipflopping from sadness to anger.

"Don't mention the Upflowered to me! If not for them, my mother and father would still be alive!"

Sylvanus shook his wise old head. "If not for the Upflowered, none of our kind would exist at all, my son."

"Rubbish! If they wanted to create us, they should have done so without conditions."

"Are you not, then, going to step into my pawprints, so that I might lay down my own charge? You're fully trained now "

Storm felt a burst of regret that he had to disappoint his beloved old "uncle." But the emotion was not strong enough to countervail his stubborn independence. He laid a paw-hand on Sylvanus's bony shoulder.

"I can't, uncle, I just can't. Not now, anyhow. And in fact, I'm leaving this bioregion entirely. I have to see more of the world, to learn my place in it."

Sylvanus recognized the futility of arguing with the headstrong youth. "So be it. Travel with my blessing, then, and try to return if you can before my passing, for a final farewell. I'll get Cimabue and Tanselle to breed my successor, while I hang in there for a while yet."

And so Storm had set out westward, across the vast continent, braving rain and heat, loneliness and fear, with no goal in mind other than to see what he could see. He and his trusty marsupial avian-ursine mount, Bergamot, foraged off the land, supplementing their herbivore diet with various nutriceuticals conjured up out of Storm's Universal Proseity Device.

Crossing the Rockies, he had encountered the tropospheric mind for the first time since his abdication. He had been deliberately avoiding this massive atmospheric intelligence due to its tendency to impose orders on all wardens. Storm feared chastisement for his rebellion. But travelling this high above sea level, there was no escaping the lower tendrils of the globally distributed artificial intelligence.

A chilly caplet of cloudstuff, rich in virgula/sublimula codec, had formed about his head, polling his thoughts by transcranial induction. Storm squirmed under the painless interrogation, irritated yet helpless to do anything.

A palm-sized high-res wetscreen formed in the air, and on it appeared the current chosen avatar of the tropospheric mind: a kindly sorcerer from some old human epic. (The tropospherical mind contained all the accumulated data of the Earth's digitized culture at the time of the Upflowering, a trove which the wardens frequently ransacked for their own amusement and edification.)

The sorcerer spoke. "You follow a lonely path, Storm. And a less- than-optimal one, so far as your own development is concerned."

Anticipating harsher rebuke, Storm was taken aback. "Perhaps.

But it's my choice."

"Yet you might both extend your own growth and aid me and the world at the same time."

"How is that?"

"By joining a cohort of your fellows now assembling. As you work with them and bind together as a team, you might come to better appreciate your innate talents and how they could best benefit the planet under my direction."

"Your direction! That's always been my quarrel. We're just pawns to you! It was under your direction that my parents died."

Had the sorcerer denied this accusation, Storm would have definitely walked out on the mission. But the sorcerer had the good grace to look apologetic, sad and chagrined, although he did not actually accept responsibility for the deaths.

Mollified, Storm felt he could at least inquire politely about the mission. "What are these other wardens doing?"

"They are building a ship, and will embark from San Francisco Bay for the island of Hawaii, where they will confront my insane sister, Mauna Loa. She has already killed all the resident wardens there, as she seeks to establish her own dominion. No communications or diplomacy I have had with her have changed her plans. You think me a tyrant, but she wants utter control of all life around her."

Storm said, "Maybe she'll listen to reason from us."

"I sincerely doubt it. But you should feel free to try. In any case, I believe the odyssey will offer you the challenges you seek. Even a magnitude more."

Storm's curiosity was greatly piqued. Curse the weather mind! It was impossible to outwit or outargue something that used a significant portion of the atmosphere as its computational reservoir. This was precisely why Storm had avoided speaking to the construct.

"If I agree to go on this journey with them, it does not mean I will fall right back into your tidy little schemes for me afterwards."

The sorcerer grinned. "Of course not."

Storm instantly regretted giving his tacit consent. But the lure of the dangerous mission was too strong to resist.

"Allow me," said the tropospheric mind, "to download your optimal route into your UPD."

Utility fog shrouded Storm's panniers, pumping information into his proseity unit as he gee'd up and rode on.

* * * *

Now, so close to his West Coast destination, Storm felt compelled to surrender his nostalgic ruminations for action. He kicked Bergamot into motion, and the biped surged in its odd loping fashion across the fruited plains that had once been covered by human urban blight.

As he passed beneath the cinnabon trees, Storm snatched a few dozen sweet sticky rolls from the branches overhead, filling a pannier with the welcome treats. He tossed several, one at a time, into the air ahead of him, where Bergamot snapped them up greedily with lightning reflexes. Gorging himself, eventually sated, Storm licked his paw-hands and muzzle clean.

Following the directions in his UPD, parallelling the Sacramento River for most of the journey, past the influx of its many tributaries, through its delta, Storm came in good time to the shores of San Pablo Bay. He continued west and south along that body of water, eventually reaching his ordained rendezvous point: the northern terminus of the roadless Golden Gate Bridge, anomalous in the manicured wilderness.

One of the select human artefacts preserved after the

Upflowering for its utility and beauty, the span glistened with the essentially dumb self-repair virgula and sublimula that had maintained it against decay for centuries.

Storm admired the sight for a short time, then homed in on the scent of his fellow wardens. Following a steep path, he reached a broad stony beach. There he found ten wardens finishing the construction of their ship, and ten Kodiak Kangemus picking idly at drifts of seaweed and bivalves.

Six of the wardens worked around a composite UPD device. Their individual reconfigurable units had been slaved together in order to produce larger-than-normal output pieces. Three wardens fed biomass into the conjoined hopper, while three others handled the output, ferrying it to the workers on the ship. Those other four wardens, consulting printed plans, snapped the superwood pieces into place on the nearly completed vessel.

At first no one noticed Storm. But then he was spotted by a female, noteworthy for her unique piebald colouration.

"Ho! It's the supercargo!"

Storm bristled at the slight, but said nothing. He dropped down off Bergamot, shooing the beast towards its companions.

The ten wardens hastened to group themselves around Storm, in a not-unfriendly manner.

"You're Storm," said the pretty pinto female. Her voice was sweet and chirpy, her demeanour mischievous. "I'm Jizogirl. The weather mind told us you'd be here today. Just in time, too! Let me introduce everyone."

During the hellos, Storm uneasily sized up his new companions— all of whom were at least a few years older than he, and in some instances decades.

Pankey, Arp, Rotifero, Wrinkles and Bunter were males. Tallest of the ten, Pankey's bold mien bespoke a natural leadership. Arp managed to look bored and inquisitive simultaneously. Elegant Rotifero paid little attention to Storm, instead preferring to present his best profile to the ladies. Wrinkles plainly derived his name from his exaggerated patagium: the folds of flesh beneath a warden's arms that allowed brief aerial gliding. Bunter, plump as a pumpkin, was sniffing suspiciously in the direction of Storm's panniers.

Beyond the charming Jizogirl: Catmaul exhibited an athlete's lithe strength; Faizai echoed Rotifero's sexual preening; Shamrock was plainly itching to get back to work, as if looking to impress Pankey and secure the number-two slot; and Gumball shyly pondered her own paw-feet rather than make eye-contact with Storm.

"Pleased to meet you all," said Storm. "I'm anxious to learn more about our mission. I hope I'll be an asset."

Pankey spoke. "You are rather the hundredth-and-one leg on a centipede, you know. We had a complete roster without you butting in."

"Pankey! For shame!" Jizogirl made up for her earlier quip about "supercargo" in Storm's eyes with this remonstrance, and he chose to appear unaffected by Pankey's gibe.

"I know I can be of some use. Just tell me what to do."

"Well, we want to sail at dawn, and we still have several hours of work to accomplish before dark. So if you could possibly pitch in—"

"Of course. Just point me toward a task."

"Why don't you collect biomass for now? It's the simplest chore."

Storm bit his tongue against a defence of his own abilities, and merely said, "Sure. Should I slave my UPD to the others?"

Pankey frowned. "I hadn't thought of that Of course."

Storm did so. Then, removing a sharp, strong nanocellulose machete from his panniers (and also some cinnabons for everyone, much welcomed), he headed toward a stand of spartina. Soon, with energetic effort, he had accumulated a surplus of the tall grass, and so was able to take a break. He strolled onboard the ship to learn more about it. He saw that the superwood components were being grafted into place with various epoxies from the UPD.

Rotifero spied Storm and gestured grandly, eager to abandon his own work and act as tour guide. "The *Slippery Squid*! A sharp ship, isn't she? We should make it to the Sandwich Islands in just five days."

"So fast?"

Rotifero motioned for Storm to look over the side at the ship's unique construction. "The humans called this model the hydroptére. Multihulled, very fast. But here's the real secret."

Rotifero walked to the fore of the ship and kicked at a bundle of neatly sorted fabric and lines. "She's a kiteship. Once we get this scoop aloft, the weather mind provides an unceasing wind. We should average fifty knots. Old Tropo even keeps us on the proper heading. No navigation necessary. Which is fine by me, as I don't know a sextant from an astrolabe."

Storm nodded sagely, although the instruments named were unfamiliar to him. "And what do we do when we arrive in Hawaii?"

"Ah, I'd best let Pankey explain all that tonight. He's our leader, you know, and he rather resents anyone stepping on his lines. Say, what do you think of Fazai? Aren't her ears the perkiest and hairiest you've ever seen? You know what they say: 'Ears with tufts, can't get enough!'"

Storm felt hot blood flash beneath his furry face. Wardens lived solitary lives, each responsible for vast bioregions, meeting only infrequently. At such times, mating was lustily indulged in, with gene-regulated, reversible contraceptive locks firmly in place. In his two decades of family-centric life, Storm had not yet managed to meet a free female and mate. In fact, the unprecedented presence of so many of his kind in such proximity rather unnerved him.

"I—I wouldn't know."

Rotifero jabbed an elbow into Storm's ribs. "I realize the ten of us're paired up evenly already, but don't worry. One of the does will probably take pity on you. If any of them have a spare minute!"

Storm's embarrassment flicked to hurt pride in an instant. "Thanks, I'm sure. But I'm used to Great Lakes does. They're much nicer in every way."

Pankey put a stop to any further amatory talk with a shouted, "Hey, you two, back to work!"

Storm spent the rest of the afternoon chopping and hauling spartina, and trying not to think of Faizai's ears.

Twilight brought successful completion of all their tasks. Sailing at dawn was assured, Pankey confirmed. A driftwood fire was kindled, tasty food was fabbed from spartina fed into the now separated UPDs (the same method by which the voyagers would sustain themselves at sea; the proseity units could desalinate seawater as well), and everyone settled down around the flames on UPD-fabbed cushions laid over mattresses of dried seaweed. Conversation was casual, and Storm mainly listened. He soon deduced that the ten wardens all hailed from up and down the Pacific Coast, and knew each other to varying degrees.

When all had finished eating, Pankey stood, and the others, including Storm, snapped to attention.

"I will endeavour to bring our newest member up to speed," said the tall warden, grooming his muzzle somewhat self-consciously. "But this is a good time for anyone else to ask questions as well, if you're unsure of anything.

"We ten—excuse me, we eleven—have been constituted an ERT—an Emergency Response Team—by the tropospheric mind—Old Tropo, if he'll permit the familiarity—and given the assignment of straightening out the mess in Hawaii. All the wardens in that chain of islands have perished, assassinated by Mauna Loa, sister to Tropo, who wishes to enslave all the mobile entities of that biosphere.

"We are all familiar, I believe, with the phenomenon of 'rogue lobes,' isolated colonies of virgula and sublimula which descend to the ground as star jelly. Usually, their lifetimes are extremely short and erratic, given their separation from the main currents of the weather mind. But in the case of Mauna Loa, we have an intelligent and self-sustaining organism, unfortunately quite deranged and exhibiting no signs of possessing any ethical constraints.

"As near as Tropo can determine, a rogue lobe hybridized with two types of extremophile microbe: an endolithic species and a hyperthermophilic species. The result is smart magma, centred in the active Mauna Loa volcano, with vast subterranean extensions throughout Hawaii's volcanic system and beyond. Mauna Loa's active tubes stretch far out to sea, in fact, and she appears to be trying to extend them to reach other land masses in the Pacific Ring of Fire, to colonize them as well. Meanwhile, aboveground, the magma's agents are local animal species controlled by transcranial inductive caps that consist of a kernel of smart magma insulated by a shell of inert, heat-absorptive material. It is these animal agents which slew our fellows."

Wrinkles stuck up a paw-hand, flaring his broad patagium, and asked a question that had been on Storm's mind.

"How did Mauna Loa ever capture animal agents in the first place?"

"Good question," Pankey said. "Tropo has reconstructed the evolution of the non-fatal cold magma caps along these lines. Mauna Loa would throw out lariats of moderately hot smart magma— its necessarily high temperature downgraded by a radioactive component that served to keep the cooler substance plastic—at any animal that passed near an active flow. In 99.9 percent of such attacks, the victim would die. But once a single victim, however damaged, survived with a magma patch on its epidermis, Mauna Loa had an agent. And once it recruited an agent with manipulative abilities—such as one of the many extant island simians—it had the ability to place the refined cold magma caps on a great numbers of recruits."

"So we can expect some hassle from these agents," said Jizogirl.

* * * *

Storm risked a glance toward her, admiring her understated bravado, and trying in the firelight to assess once again the degree of tuftedness of her ears.

"Yes. They will run interference to stop us from killing Mauna Loa."

This new talk of killing troubled Storm a bit. "Isn't there any way we might convince Mauna Loa to modify her bad behaviour, to fall in line with Tropo's leadership?"

Pankey emitted a derisive blurt. "Reason with a killer volcano! Good luck! I'd like to see you try!"

"Just watch me then!"

Pankey turned disdainfully away from Storm and directed his speech to the rest. "The saner members of the ERT will be employing logic bombs against Mauna Loa. The plan for the bomb has been uploaded to everyone's UPD—yes, Storm, yours as well. This goes a long way toward insuring that at least one of us should reach the volcano and be able to drop the bomb in. The bomb's antisense instructions will replicate and propagate rapidly through the silicaceous medium, and shut down the magma mind."

"Do we have to deliver the bomb right to Mauna Loa herself?"

"No. We can attack Kilauea instead. It's a much smaller, lower, accessible target, and closer to the coast than Mauna Loa herself."

"Why can't we just dump the bomb into the first trickle of lava we see?"

Pankey began to manifest some irritation with Storm's persistent questions, even though he had invited them. "Because Mauna Loa has the ability to pinch off any small tendril of its body, and isolate the antisense wave. But Kilauea is too big and interconnected for that tactic to succeed."

Pankey paused, glaring a bit at Storm as if daring him to pose more stumpers. But Storm was satisfied that he had a grasp of their task. Pankey resumed a greater gravitas before next he spoke. "And so we should all recognize, I believe, our true position. We stand now on the verge of a dangerous voyage, at the end of which we will face enemies who wish to stop us from crushing a brutal killer and tyrant. May Old Tropo guide our paws."

Concluding the lecture, this solemn invocation engendered a long and ponderous silence amongst the wardens, as they considered their chances for success, and the high stakes at play. Storm still debated internally whether Mauna Loa was really the unreasoning menace portrayed, or whether she could not be cajoled and reasoned with.

But their grim and thoughtful mood was ultimately leavened by a loud comment from Rotifero.

"Well, if I'm heading to my death, I intend to get in all the mating I can over the next five days! And I advise all my boon comrades to do the same!"

No sooner had this carnal activity been urged than the wardens began pairing off. Storm was disheartened to see Jizogirl beat out Shamrock in a bid for Pankey's attentions. Disgruntled but accepting, Shamrock settled for Arp instead, while Wrinkles and shy Gumball, Bunter and agile Catmaul hooked up.

Surprisingly, while most of the warden couples were already down on their mats, swiftly lost in petting and other foreplay, Rotifero and Faizai had not yet begun. Instead, the two, arms about each others' middles, approached Storm.

"Would you care to make it a threesome, Storm? I realize you hardly know us, and it's not much done. But under the circumstances, I thought "

Storm hungrily drank in Faizai's allure, guttering flames glinting hotly in her liquid eyes. He gulped once, twice, then managed to speak.

"*Urk*— That is, not tonight, thank you. I'm very tired from my travels."

"Maybe some other time," Faizai slurred lusciously.

Storm made no reply, but instead dragged his mat away to lie with the Kodiak Kangemus, their musk and somnolent growls failing to fully mask the squeals and scents from his copulating comrades.

But at last he fell into a light, uneasy sleep.

* * * *

"On three! One, two—three!"

The combined musclepower of all six males succeeded in tossing the bundle of the precisely packed kite a full five metres into the air, as the *Slippery Squid* floated just offshore. The kite began to unfurl. A perfectly timed wind sent by the tropospheric mind caught the MEMS fabric, belling it out to its full extent and lofting it higher, higher— The six tough composite lines fastened to the prow of the *Squid* tautened. The ship began to cut the pristine waters of San Francisco Bay, heading out to open sea.

A collective shout of triumph went up. The wardens hugged and slapped one another on the back. Jizogirl waved to the Kodiak Kangemus on the shore where they milled, reluctant to loose sight of their departing masters. Eventually, they would acknowledge the separation and find their way home.

"Goodbye, Slasher! See you soon!" Arp said dourly, "You hope."

"Hey now, no defeatist talk," Pankey admonished.

Shamrock came up to the leader and said, "Shouldn't we erect the canopy now? Pretty soon it'll get hot, and we'll appreciate the shelter."

"Good idea. Wrinkles, Bunter, Catmaul, Faizai—get to it!"

Poles and a gaily striped awning soon shielded a large portion of the blonde superwood deck from the skies, and a few of the wardens took advantage of the shade to relax. Bunter was drawing a snack from his UPD.

No one had gotten much sleep last night. But Storm stayed where he could see and admire the kite, a burnt- orange scoop decorated with the image of a sword-wielding paw and arm.

Jizogirl came up beside Storm. He nervously tightened his grip on the rail, then forced himself to relax. He looked straight at her, and admired the way the wind ruffled her patchwork fur.

"Do you like the picture on our kite, Storm? I designed it myself. No one else cared, but I thought we should have an emblem. I derived it from an old human saga. Lots of daring swordplay! So unlike our humdrum daily routines. The sweep of the action appealed to me. The humans were mad, of course, but so vibrant! I watched the show over and over. Once I played the video on a cloudscreen big as the horizon! Old Tropo indulged me, I guess. Shameful waste of computational power, but who cares! It was magnificent!"

Storm asked thoughtfully, "Are you okay with this mission? To kill a sentient being, even one accidentally born and malfunctioning?" Jizogirl grew sober. "You didn't see the footage of the Hawaiian wardens being slaughtered, Storm. Horrible, just horrible. I don't think we have any choice "

Jizogirl's sincere repugnance and sorrow was a strong argument in favour of the assassination of Mauna Loa, but Storm still felt a shard of uncertainty. He wished he could somehow speak to the rogue magma mind first.

Her natural sprightliness reasserting itself, Jizogirl resumed her light chatter. Grateful that the doe seemed content to conduct a monologue, Storm just smiled and nodded at appropriate places. He found her anecdotes charming. She moved from talk of her viewing habits into a detailed autobiography. She was thirty-two years old. Her assigned marches centred around old human Vancouver. Her father had died when a rotten Sequoia limb had fallen and crushed him, but her mother was still alive…

By the time the *Squid* was out of sight of land, Storm felt he knew Jizogirl as well as he knew old Sylvanus. But Sylvanus had never caused Storm's stomach to flutter, or his heart to thump so loudly.

In return for her story, Storm told his own—haltingly at first, then with a swelling confidence and excitement. Jizogirl listened appreciatively, her ears (distinctly less tufted than Faizai's) making continual microadjustments of attitude to filter out the *thwack* of waves, cries of gulls and cryptovolans, playful loud chatter of their fellow wardens. His story finally caught up with realtime, and Storm stopped, faintly chagrined. He had never talked about himself—about anything!—for such a stretch before. What would she think of such boasting?

Jizogirl smiled broadly, revealing big white shovel-like teeth. "Why, I never could have made such a leap out of my rut when I was your age, Storm! You're so brave and daring. Imagine, travelling across half the continent on your own!"

Storm felt his head seemingly inflate, his vision fragment into sparkles. But Jizogirl's next words deflated his elation.

"If I had a little brother, I'd want him to be just like you!"

"Hey, Jizogirl, come look at this funny fish!" The voice belonged to Pankey, but a crumpled Storm could not even feel any twinge of jealousy when Jizogirl begged off and trotted over to see the latest specimen the wardens had caught for their continual cataloguing purposes. He remained at the rail, trying to estimate how long he could stay afloat alone, were he to jump, and why he would bother to prolong his miserable life.

That first day a-sea passed swiftly and easily. With no real duties (a rare condition for any warden), under the benevolent aegis of the weather mind, knowing their heading was correct and no doldrums or foul storms would ever bedevil them, the Emergency Response Team merely romped and rested, joked and petted, carefree as kits. All except Storm, who nursed his romantic disappointment alone. As twilight swooped in from the east, the sea around the Squid came alive with luminescent dinoflagellates, pulsing with electric blue radiance. Storm watched the display for a while before an idea struck him.

The hasty construction of their ship had precluded any infrastructure, such as lights. Storm would provide some.

From his UPD he produced a dozen hollow, transparent spheres of biopolymer, each with a screw-on cap. He made a length of netting. Then he dipped each uncapped netted globe into the plankton flock, filling it to the brim. By the time he had dunked them all, darkness had thickened. But Storm's bioluminescent globes made spectral yet somehow comforting blue hollows in the night.

All his comrades thronged around Storm and his creations. "Brilliant!"

"Just what we need!"

"Let's get them hung up!"

More netting secured the globes beneath the canopy, and an exotic yet homey ambiance resulted. Arp got busy with his own UPD and produced the parts of a ukulele, which he quickly snapped together. He strummed a sprightly tune, and Catmaul commenced a sensuous dance, to much clapping and hooting. Bunter concocted some kind of cocktail, which added considerably to the levity.

Storm watched with a blooming jubilation that received its greatest boost in the next moment. From the shadows, Jizogirl appeared to deliver unto Storm a quick hug and a kiss, before rejoining Pankey.

* * * *

The second day of their voyage, the wardens were less sanguine. Hangovers reigned, and the prospect of entertaining themselves for another day seemed less like fun than a duty. Also, the further they drew from home, the larger loomed the grim struggle that awaited them.

Storm affected the most optimism and panache. His triumph last night—the invention of the light globes, the kiss—continued to sustain him. Standing at the bow, he tried to urge the *Slippery Squid* forward faster. He felt the urgent need to meet his destiny, to prove himself, to discover whether the action he had always imagined he craved truly suited him.

Studying the kite that pulled them onward, Storm had a sudden inspiration.

Pankey was scrolling through the headache-tablet templates on his UPD when Storm interrupted him.

"How are we going to fight?"

Pankey looked at Storm as if the youngster had spoken in an extinct human tongue. "Fight? You mean the animal agents Mauna Loa will throw at us? We can't possibly fight them. I counted on stealth. A midnight landing—"

"And if the enemy doesn't cooperate with your plans?"

Pankey waved Storm off. "I've considered everything. Go away now."

Storm retrieved his own UPD and called up the plans for his machete. He tinkered with them, then hit PRINT.

The scimitar-like sword necessarily emerged from the spatially restricted output port in three pre-epoxied pieces that locked inextricably together. The nanocellulose composite was stronger than steel and carried an exceedingly sharp edge.

Out on the open deck, Storm began energetically to practice thrusts, feints and parries alone. Soon he had attracted an audience. He added enthusiastic grunts and shouts to his routine.

Rotifero said, "I actually believe that such vigorous exercise might very well drive these demons out of one's head. Do you have another one of those weapons, Storm?"

Without stopping, Storm said, through huffs and puffs, "Just... hit... 'print'... on... my... UPD "

Soon all eleven wardens, even a grudging Pankey, were sparring vigorously. "Beware my unstoppable blade!"

"Take that, foul fruitbat!"

"I'll run you through!"

That night was spent mostly attending to various minor cuts and bruises.

Sword practice continued the next day, somewhat less faddishly, until just before noon came a cry of "Land ho!" from Catmaul.

Storm saw a small, heavily treed island at some distance off the port. "Is that Hawaii already?"

Pankey cupped the back of his own neck with one paw and massaged, as if to evoke insight. "Impossible"

Bunter said, "Look how lush the vegetation is! We might find a species of nice fruit not templated in our UPDs, if we land."

The normally reticent Gumball now laughed and said, "I don't think we want to land on *that* 'island.'"

"Why?" said Pankey.

"I'm surprised none of you have heard of the Terrapin Islands before. Down in Baja, we see them pass by all the time. Just watch."

As the *Squid* came abreast of the island at some remove, a patch of the ocean between island and ship began to bulge, water pouring off a rising humped form several times bigger than the *Squid*.

The gimlet-eyed scaled head of the gargantuan *Chelonioidea* regarded the vessel with cool reptilian disinterest. Sea grass draped from its jaws. Opening wide its horny mouth, working its tongue, the terrapin inhaled the masses of vegetation like a noodle.

Storm was secretly pleased to find his own nerves holding steady at the sight of the monster. The others reacted variously. Faizai shrieked, Arp clucked his tongue, Bunter gulped. Shamrock urged impossibly, "Get some more speed on here!" Gumball laughed.

"They're harmless! Don't worry!"

True to Gumball's reassurance, the *Squid* slipped past the mammoth grazing landscaped sea turtle without interference, and soon Terrapin Island lay below the horizon.

"And some claim the Upflowered had no sense of humour," Rotifero observed.

That night, long after his companions had passed satedly into deep sleep, Storm could be found awake at the rail, contemplating their luminescent wake.

He liked these people, bucks and does equally. Even Pankey's stern bossiness was fuelled by pure and admirable motives. He enjoyed working with them, feeling part of a team. But did that mean he was ready completely to step into Old Tropo's harness?

And what of their vengeful mission? Justified, or reprehensible?

The slick shadowy head of some marine creature broke the water then, and Storm jumped back. A dolphin! But capping its skull was a crust of magma! Here was one of Mauna Loa's captives.

The dolphin's precisely modulated squeaks were completely intelligible. "Stop! Don't run away! I just want to talk!"

"Mauna Loa…?"

"Yes. I know who you are, and why you're coming. But you need not fear me. I only want to own a few islands, where I can practice my art. I want to mould life, just as the Upflowered did. Introduce novelty to the world. My tools are crude, though. Radiation mainly. You could help me gain access to better ones. Join me! Frustrate this mission! Turn it aside somehow."

"I—I don't know. I can't betray my friends. I have to think."

"Take your time then. I won't interfere. I'm harmless, really."

And with that promise, the dolphin was gone, leaving Storm to a troubled sleep.

Days four and five inched by tediously, as the wardens found all attractions equally stale, the monotony of the marine landscape infusing them with a sense of eternal stasis. Unspoken thoughts of the challenge awaiting them weighed them down. Storm tried to conceive of ways to convince his friends of the wrongness of their assault, but failed to come up with any dominant argument.

After their evening meal of the fifth day, Pankey gathered them together and said, "We should sight our destination some time tomorrow. It occurs to me that we should arm ourselves in advance with our logic bombs. Everyone make three apiece, and some sort of bandolier that can also hold your UPD."

Having complied, the wardens tested the fit of their bandoliers that cradled, across their furry muscled chests, the biopolymer eggs stuffed with antisense silicrobes, deadly only to the smart magma mind of Mauna Loa. Storm thought the UPD strapped to his back was a bulky and awkward feature, but refrained from questioning Pankey's orders.

Pankey went around testing and tightening buckles before registering approval.

"Fine. Well done. Now, as to our chosen delivery method. We'll halt offshore by day and study our terrain maps one final time. We'll land under cover of darkness and split up, heading to Kilauea on pawfoot by a variety of routes. At any major vent near the summit caldera, feel free to bomb the living shit out of this volcano bitch!"

Pankey's curse-filled martial bravado rang false and antithetical to Storm, and he noted that the rough talk failed to inspire any signs of gung-ho enthusiasm in the rest.

Storm asked, "Can we expect any support from the weather mind? Maybe some storm coverage to shock the defenders?"

"I considered asking for that. But any bad weather will impede us just as much as it hurts Mauna Loa's slaves. No, stealth is our best bet."

"What about our swords?"

"Listen, Storm, all that swordplay onboard was good exercise and fun. It took our mind off our problems. But if you need to use those toothpicks on land, it'll be too late for you already. You'd best leave your sword behind. It's just extra weight that'll slow you down."

"I'm taking mine."

Pankey shrugged. "Junior knows best."

Storm noticed that Jizogirl appeared about to second Storm's objection to venturing forth unarmed. But then the doe relented, and said nothing.

Storm slept only fitfully, so angry was he at Pankey's rude dismissal of him. So when dawn was barely a rumour, Storm was already up, alone of the wardens, and defecating over the edge of the vessel.

Looking sleepily into the dark foaming waters that had swallowed his scat, Storm hoped for a return of the dolphin diplomat, for more talk that might help him decide whose side he was really on.

But instead he saw a sleek grey hand and arm emerge to grip a ridge halfway up the hull.

He convulsively tumbled off his lavatory perch to the deck, then scrambled to his feet. A pair of hands now gripped the railing, then another pair, and another—

These were no innocent emissaries. Mauna Loa's promise not to interfere had been a lie. She had just been stalling, till she could outfit these attackers. Suddenly, Storm felt immense guilt at having kept the earlier visit a secret. The wardens could have been prepared for invasion by this route—

"Foes! Foes! Help! Attack!"

A wet torpedo face that seemed all teeth materialized between the first pair of hands. Gills flapped shut, and nostrils flared open. Storm dove for his sword. The other wardens were stirring confusedly. Storm kicked them, slapped them with the flat of his blade.

"Swords! Swords! Get your swords!"

Turning back toward the rail, Storm faced the intruders fully.

The handsharks fused anthropoid and squaline designs into a bipedal monster all grey rugose hide and muscles. Neckless, their shark countenances thrust forward aggressively. Each wore the pebbled slave cap of the magma mind, clamped tight. A fishy carrion reek sublimed off them.

Involuntarily bellowing his anger and fear, Storm rushed forward, sword at the ready.

He got a deep resonant lick in on the ribs of a handshark at the same time he was batted powerfully across the chest. He went down and skidded on his butt across the wet deck. Leaping back to his feet, he confronted another monster—the same one?—and slashed out, blade landing with a squelch across its eyes.

Screams, battle-cries, the thunk of blade into flesh. Storm could get no sense of the whole battle's tide, but only flail about in his little sphere of chaos.

Somehow he slaughtered without being slaughtered himself, until the battle was over.

Weeping, wiping blood from his face, his sword dripping gore, Storm reunited with his comrades.

Those who still lived.

That headless corpse was Bunter. The one with torn throat was Gumball. Half of Arp's torso was gone in a single bite. Faizai lay in several pieces. They never found Shamrock; perhaps a dying handshark had dragged her overboard.

Almost half their team dead, before they even sighted their goal. There could be no question now of where Storm must place his allegiance. All his doubt and conflicts had evaporated with the lives of his friends. Guilt plagued him as well. He knew the only way to make up for such a transgression was to carry forth the assault on Mauna Loa with all his wit and bravery. Although beyond the assassination attempt, his future still floated mistily.

Only three handshark corpses littered the deck. Just one more attacker, and all the wardens would probably this moment be dead. Storm pulled a bloody, sobbing Jizogirl to him, clutched her tightly. He tried to imagine why he had ever sought adventure, and how he could instantly transport himself and Jizogirl and the others safely home. But hard as he pondered, throughout the sad task of creating winding sheets from the UPD, bundling up the bodies of their friends, and consigning them to the sea with a few appeals to the Upflowered, Storm could find no easy solutions.

Throughout the battle, and afterwards, their big-bellied kite had continued to pull the *Squid* onward, impelled by the insistent weather mind. The tropospheric intelligence seemed intent on throwing its agents against its rival without delay.

And so by the time the surviving wardens had dumped the handshark corpses overboard, washed their clotted fur, disinfected their wounds and applied antibiotics and synthskin bandages, cleansed their swords, and sluiced the offal from the deck with seawater, the jade-green island of Hawaii had come dominantly into view, swelling in size minute by minute as their craft surged on.

Storm confronted Pankey. "You're not still thinking of hanging offshore till midnight, are you? Mauna Loa obviously knows we're here. We can't face another assault from more sharks."

Pankey appeared unsure and confused. "That plan can still work. We'll just need to put in to shore further away from Kilauea. Let's get the coastal maps…"

Storm's anger and anxiety boiled over. "Bugger that! The longer we have to travel overland, the more vulnerable we are!"

His expression ineffably sad, Faizai-bereft Rotifero said calmly, "I agree with our young comrade, Pankey. We need a different plan."

"All right, all right! But what!"

Jizogirl said, "Let's get in a little closer to shore anyhow. Maybe something we see will give us an idea."

Pankey said, "That makes sense."

Catmaul asked, "How will we get the weather mind to stop blowing us along?"

Normally, communication with the atmospheric entity was accomplished with programmed messenger birds that could fly high enough to have their brain states interpreted on the wing. But the wardens, overconfident about the parameters of their mission, had set out without any such intermediaries.

Pankey's voice conveyed less than total confidence. "Old Tropo is watching us. Surely he'll bring us to a halt safely."

Larger and larger Hawaii bulked. Details along the gentle sloping shore became more and more resolvable.

"Is that some kind of wall?"

"I—I'm not sure "

As predicted and hoped, when the *Squid* had reached a point several hundred metres offshore, it came to a gradual stop. The weather mind had pinned the kite in a barometrically dead cell between wind tweezers that kept the parasail stationary but aloft.

With their extremely sharp eyes, the wardens stared landward, unbelieving.

Ranked along the beach was a living picket of animal slaves of the volcano queen.

The main mass of the defence consisted of anole lizards. But not kawaii baseline creatures to be held with amusement in a paw. No, these anoles, unfamiliar to the mainlanders, were evidently Upflowered creations, large as elephants. And atop each anole sat a simian carrying a crudely sharpened treebranch spear. Interspersed among the legs of the anoles were a host of lesser but still formidable toothed and clawed beasts. Blotches of stony grey atop the anoles were certainly slave caps, no doubt to be found on their companions as well. The huge gaudy dewlaps of the lizards flared and shrunk, flared and shrunk ominously, a prelude to attack.

"This—this is not good," murmured Wrinkles.

Pankey said, "We'll sail south or north, evade them—"

Storm grew indignant. He wanted to reach out and shake some sense into Pankey. "Are you joking? Those monsters can easily pace us on land, while we sail a greater distance than they need gallop." Jizogirl interrupted the argument. "It's academic, my bucks!

Look!"

The anoles and their riders were wading into the surf, making straight for the *Squid*.

"This—this is even worse," Wrinkles added—rather super- fluously, thought Storm, in an uncanny interval of stunned calmness.

Catmaul began yanking on one of the half-dozen kite tethers. "We have to get away! Now! Why doesn't Tropo help us!"

Rotifero gently pulled the doe away from the cables. "Old Tropo is a stern taskmaster. He brought us here to do a job, and do it we must."

Storm looked up in vain at the unmoving kite.

The kite!

* * * *

"I have a plan! But we need to ditch our UPDs first. They're too heavy for what I have in mind."

Suiting actions to words, Storm doffed his harness, detached the pro- seity device, then redonned the bandolier with just logic bombs attached.

"Stash your swords in your harnesses, and follow me!"

Not waiting to see if they obeyed, Storm leaped onto the kite cables and began to climb. He felt a rightness and force to his actions, as he threw himself into battle without thought for his own safety, only that of his comrades, and the success of their necessary mission. Here, then, was the defining moment he had sought, ever since he left home.

The angle of the cables permitted a fairly easy ascent. Soon, Storm bellyflopped onto the wind-stuffed mattress of the kite. Seconds later, his five comrades joined him, with plenty of room to spare.

Below, the swimming anoles had closed half the distance to the ship.

"We have to do this just perfectly. We sever the four inner cables completely, and the two outer ones partially. Pankey and I will do the outer ones. Get busy!"

The composite substance of the cables was only a few Mohs softer than the sword blades, making for an arduous slog. But with much effort, Wrinkles, Jizogirl, Rotifero and Catmaul got the four inner cables completely separated—they fell gracefully, with an ultimate *splash*!—causing the parafoil configuration to deform non-aerodynamically, attached to the ship now only by a few threads at either end.

Storm spared a look down. The anoles were too big to clamber aboard the ship. But the simians weren't. And the apes were approaching the remaining two tethers linking kite and ship.

"Now!"

Storm and Pankey sawed frantically and awkwardly in synchrony from their recumbent positions—

Twin loud *pops* from the high-tensioned threads, and the kite was free. Instant winds sent by an alert weather mind grabbed it and pushed it toward land.

Storm allowed himself the tiniest moment of relief and triumph and relaxation. Then he sized up what awaited them.

The terrain below showed rampant greenery of cloud forest far off to every side. But the Kilauea caldera itself loomed off-centre in a barren zone of old and new lava flows: the Kau Desert. Twenty- four kilometres away, the mother volcano Mauna Loa reared almost four times higher.

"Can we ride this all the way?" shouted Pankey.

"I hope so!" Storm replied. "Maybe we can bomb one of the magma rifts from up here!"

But his optimism soon received a dual assault.

Several slave-capped gulls stalked their kite, relaying visual feeds to the magma mind. As the kite moved deeper inland, it met attacks.

From an artificially built-up stone nozzle, under concentrated pressure, a laser-like jet of magma shot up high as the kite, narrowly missing the wardens, but spattering them with painful droplets on its broken descent. The kite fabric received numerous smelly burn holes. At the same time a fumarole unleashed billowing clouds of opaque choking sulphurous gases, which the kite sailed blindly through, at last emerging into clear air.

Gasping for breath, wiping his reddened eyes, Storm finally found his voice again.

"We're a big easy target! We have to split up!"

Wrinkles got to his hands and knees. "Me first! I'm the best glider!"

Without any farewells, Wrinkles launched off the unsteady platform. He spread his unusually generous patagium and made graceful curves through the sky.

Jizogirl cried, "Go, Wrinkles, go!"

A lance of redhot lava shot up from an innocuous spot, and incinerated Wrinkles's entire left side. With a wailing cry he plummeted to impact.

Storm felt gut-punched. "We all need to leap at once! Now! Find a rift and bomb it!"

The remaining five wardens flung themselves free of the kite.

Focused on his gliding, Storm could not keep track of the rest of the Fellowship. Heaven-seeking spears of hot rock burst into existence randomly, a gauntlet of fiery death. Deadly vog— the volcanic fog—stole his sight and breath. He lost track of his altitude, his goal. He thought he heard cries and screams—

Out of the vog he emerged, to see the tortured ground much too close, an eye-searing, writhing active rift bisecting the terrain. He braced for a landing.

His right paw-foot caught in a crevice, and he heard bones snap.

The pain was almost secondary to his despair.

Working to free his paw-foot, he heard two thumps behind him.

Pankey and Jizogirl had landed, their fur smoldering, eyes cloudy and tearful.

Jizogirl came to help free Storm's paw-foot. "Rotifero, Catmaul—?"

Jizogirl just shook her head.

Meanwhile, Pankey had detached a logic bomb from his bandolier, and now darted in toward the living rift. Its incredible heat stopped him some distance away. He made to throw the bomb.

Overhead, the spy gulls circled low. One screeched just as Pankey threw.

A whip of lava caught the bomb in mid-air, incinerating it but prophylactically detaching from the parent flow, frustrating the spread of the released antisense agents backward along its interrupted length.

Pankey rushed back to his comrades. "It's no use. The bombs have to be delivered by hand. It's up to me!"

Jizogirl said, "And me!"

"No! Only if I fail. You and Storm— Just stay with him!"

* * * *

Before either Storm or Jizogirl could protest. Pankey had taken off at a run.

Storm's nose could smell the scorched flesh of Pankey's paw-feet as the warden dodged one whip after another.

"Remember me—!" the leader of the team called, as he hurled himself and his remaining logic bombs into the rift.

The propagation of the antisense mind-killer agents was incredibly rapid, fuelled by the high energies of the system. A deep subterranean rumble betokened the titanic struggle of intelligence against nescience. In a final spasm, the earth convulsed titanically, rippling like a shaken sheet in all directions, tossing Jizogirl down beside Storm, then bouncing them both.

The quake lasted for what seemed minutes, before dying away. Even when the shaking at ground zero had stopped, rumbles and tremors continued to radiate outward into the surrounding ocean, as the antisense assault propagated. Storm could picture undersea lava tubes collapsing, tectonic plates shifting far out to sea—

Jizogirl got shakily to her paw-feet, and helped Storm stand on his one good leg.

"Is Mauna Loa dead?" she asked. "I think so"

Big menacing shapes moved in the vog around them. "What now?" she asked hopelessly.

Out of the vog, several anoles and their riders emerged. But they no longer exhibited any direction or purpose or malice. One ape clawed at his slave cap and succeeded in ridding himself of it.

Jizogirl suddenly stiffened. "Oh, no! I just thought—We need to get inland, quickly! Up on the lizard!"

The tractable anole allowed Storm to climb onboard, with an assist from Jizogirl. His broken bones throbbed. She got up behind him, grabbed him around the waist.

"How do we make this buggered thing go?"

Storm pulled his sword out and jabbed it into the anole's shoulder. The lizard shot off, heading more or less into the interior.

"Can you tell me why this ride is necessary?"

"Tsunami! You prairie dwellers are so dumb!"

"But how?"

"The self-destruct information waves from the antisense bomb propagated faster than the physical collapse itself. When the instructions hit the furthest distal reaches of Mauna Loa out to sea, they rebounded back and met the oncoming physical collapse in mid-ocean. Result: tsunami!"

Up and up the anole skittered, leaving the Kau Desert behind and climbing the slopes of Mauna Loa. It stopped at last, exhausted, and no amount of jabbing could make it resume its flight.

Storm and Jizogirl dismounted and turned back toward the sea, the doe supporting the buck.

With the sea's recession, the raw steaming seabed lay exposed for several hundred metres out from shore. They saw the *Squid* sitting lopsided on the muck.

Then the crest of the giant wave materialized on the horizon, all spume and glory and destructive power.

"Are we far enough inland, high enough up?"

"Maybe. Maybe not."

The tsunami sounded like a billion lions roaring all at once.

Storm turned his face to Jizogirl's and said, "That kiss you gave me the other night— It was very nice. Can I have another?"

Jizogirl smiled and said, "If it's not our last, then count on lots more."

TO SEE INFINITY BARE

RUDY RUCKER AND PAUL DI FILIPPO

The starspiders have plucked Anders Zilber from our midst, perhaps never to be seen again. Squealing their hypercompressed fugues of cosmic mortality and rebirth, the spiders emerged from the transfinite Wassoon spaces and harvested Anders for his greatness. I saw it; I was next to him on the stage.

Everyone mourns his loss—everyone but me, Basil Chown. Of course I'm to pay for my coldness. The idiots have convicted me of murdering him, and I'm to be executed today. As if Anders and I had been vulgar rivals in some spaceport gang—instead of the Local Cluster's greatest metamusicians.

And what is metamusic? The one art form that ties us all together—Uppytops, Orpolese, Bulbers, the DigDawgs and the dreaded Kaang—as unalike as chalk to cheese. Thanks to the Wassoon transmitter, humanity has spread beyond the Milky Way's swirls, encountering hundreds of other races. Some call it a pangalactic civilization—I call it a wider range of fools. But, yes, they were right to worship Anders.

* * * *

Handsome, charismatic Anders. I can see the glints in his thoughtful eyes, the boyish slackness beneath his chin, the convoluted curls of his abundant hair. Generally, when out in public, a woman or gyne-poppet graced one arm, or both. Reporters and fans clustered around him, a constant retinue, endeavouring to sprinkle him with shortlife flea-cams. But despite all this worshipful attention, he, better than anyone, knew his days were numbered.

I well remember the first time he told me—I suppose that would be ten years ago by now.

We were returning from a concert tour through the Andromeda Galaxy on the far side of the Local Cluster, aboard the luxury liner *Surry On Down*. We'd just everted from Wassoon space into consensus reality, and I was seeing the usual post-transition shapes within the cabin walls—branched, crawling shadows like ghostly insects.

"They know my name," remarked Anders, flicking one of the shadows with his long, crooked forefinger. His hands looked strange, but for the moment I didn't understand why. "They want to keep me. Every time I transit, the starspiders tell me."

"The starspiders aren't anything real!" I exclaimed. "They're only a post-jump hallucination. We have to believe that."

"Cowardly foolishness, Basil. The subdimensions teem with life and history. The more we open ourselves, the richer our work."

He pitched his voice to a cracked squeak and began jabbering at the crawling seven-pointed shapes that filled the floors, ceilings and walls. In his oddly pitched voice, Anders was telling them about—how distasteful!—an erotic hallucination he'd just had.

"I remember that!" exclaimed Mimi Ultrapower, our road agent, accompanist and—damn it all!—Anders's lover. She was laughing as she talked. "The starspiders were inside our flesh, like giant nerve cells. I was kneading you like dough, Anders, and you were—"

"Hush now," said he, as if rediscovering his sense of modesty. "Not in front of Basil." He raised his hands in a cautioning gesture—and suddenly his voice broke into that higher register again, amazed and exultant. "Look what we did!"

He now had seven fingers on each hand.

* * * *

It was I who'd brought Mimi to Earth from the colony world of Omega, near the very heart of our galactic core. Her mother was an astrophysicist investigating the central black hole, and Mimi was a recent university graduate. Using a Wassoon information channel, she sent me a delightful little metasonata, very much in my own style. Extremely flattering, a seductive move.

It had been a simple matter for me to get the Supreme Bonze of the Archonate to grant Mimi Ultrapower a position at court. I'd anticipated some exciting interplay with her, but as soon as she met Anders, she was lost to me.

I tried telling myself I didn't mind—I had my own women- friends after all, and if Mimi wanted to worship Anders, surely that was her own affair. The bottom line remained: she was an excellent metamusician, a good travelling companion, and a fierce street- hassler.

On that first Andromeda Galaxy tour together, we worked up a three-way collaboration, "Earth Jam," in which Anders beamed out something like a flute part, I a kind of cello line, and Mimi zeepcast a kind of intricate percussion that was like a pounding headache— except that it felt good.

Understand that our audiences weren't *hearing* our metamusic— it's more that they could feel it in their souls, like the emotive shades of a daydream. Our symbiotic zeep colonies project our metamusic directly into the minds of those around us.

Originally the Uppytops used the one-celled zeep critters as a coercive tool to rein in their slave races. But humans ingeniously repurposed the zeeps for benign purposes.

Metamusic is inherently at its best face to face, in a live performance, with realtime zeep signals washing over the nervous systems of the audience—be they mollusks, apes, or insect hives. Although it's possible to Wassooncast a copy of a metamusical performance, these copies are, in my opinion, like pulpy videos of the love act, utterly lacking the ineffable tones and subliminal frissons of the real thing. Yes, the masses watch the Wassoncasts, but if you're an accomplished metamusician, you're forever in demand as a touring artist.

* * * *

After that first Andromeda Tour, we three had our customary debriefing with the Supreme Bonze, a taut-faced young man wearing a Tibetan-style hat with a yellow fringe along its top—not that he was Tibetan. His people were from Goa, the old Portuguese colony on the west coast of India.

Mimi stared at him in fascination. "Your hat…" she managed to say.

"The Black Hat," said the Bonze. "Woven from the hairs of a thousand and one dakinis. You know of dakinis?"

"Oh, yes," said Mimi, a knowing look on her pleasant face. "The ineffable female demiurges attendant upon the great gurus. What mana your Black Hat must have! Wearing it would confer mystical powers upon… upon even an ape! Not that I mean…"

"No offence taken," said the Bonze, although his face belied this. "I'm eager to hear your group's new piece."

The Bonze purported to be a great devotee of metamusic, and always demanded that we perform our most recent road pieces for him, not that he had the mental force to pay proper attention.

But this time he was quite piqued by Mimi's contribution to "Earth Jam."

"*Buddoom bubba bayaya*," he sang, as if trying to echo her signal in words.

"Well put, your Emptiness," said I, before Anders could start arguing about the Bonze's accuracy.

"Would you like my Black Hat?" the Supreme Bonze suddenly asked Mimi with a puckish smile. From my years at court, I knew this to be a trick question—anyone who expressed a desire for the Supreme Bonze's Tibetan hat was beheaded. And the Bonze was in any case annoyed at Mimi for her remark about the ape.

I flashed her a zeep prod of warning; she was quick enough to understand.

"No, no, honourable Bonze," said she, bowing nearly to the floor. "The Black Hat is in its proper place. Upon the emptiest head."

That Mimi!

With our fame growing, Anders, Mimi and I obtained apartments in the Metamusic Academy, a lavish old building in downtown Lisbon, which had become the *de facto* capital of Earth. Anders had the top floor, I the floor below that, and Mimi a room below me. But she spent most of her time with Anders. She was teaching him about mathematical cosmology, of all things.

Mimi showed Anders how to rig up a Wassoon generator to make his apartment infinitely large along three dimensions, without quite piercing the barrier into the hyperdimensional subspaces involved in interstellar travel.

The jury-rigged generator was a clever little thing. At its centre was a tiny fringed ring like you might use for blowing soap bubbles— although the bubble-juice for this gizmo was an endlessly subtle fluid of unbound quarks. As each bubble appeared, a magnetronic tube would set up resonant vibrations, causing the bubble's radius to oscillate. Wassoon's genius lay in his breakthrough notion of allowing the delicate bubbles' radii to oscillate down below zero and into negative values. As every schoolchild knows, a simple DeSitter transformation establishes that a quark bubble with negative radius is identical to a subdimensional cavity in space itself—and a cavity of this kind can readily become a gateway to the transfinite Wassoon spaces.

Playful as newlyweds in their first home, Anders and Mimi sent hallways running through the apartment forever, lamplit by a Wassoon energy-fractionating gimmick that could divide a hundred watts among an endless number of sympathetic bulbs. Clever Mimi even devised a procedural method for decorating the infinite areas of the endless walls with seemingly non-repeating tiles.

Anders was ecstatic over the infinite spaces of his apartment, and Mimi calmly said she'd known he'd like them, because in all his works he was trying in some fashion to create a direct view of actual infinity—whether as an endless regress, as a fractal elaboration, or as an impenetrable cloud of fuzz. She said that our universe itself was in fact infinite, although people tended to ignore this, blinded as they were by the background radiation of the most recent— what was the phrase she used? Not Big Bang, something else—ah, yes, Big Flash.

Sometimes, when I was loaded on zeep toxins, I'd go upstairs and look for the two lovers, pretending I had business to discuss. More often than not, they'd evade me, and I'd wake alone and hungover in some bare inner chamber, googolplex turnings deep into Anders and Mimi's maze.

Upon arising, I'd seem to see shapes and faces at the inconceivably distant ends of the Wassoon hallways—creatures from earlier cycles of our universe, according to Mimi. Neighbours from before the Big Flash.

In any case, finding my way out was never hard. I merely followed the scent of my personal dissatisfaction and unease back to my own floor.

* * * *

The zeep germs were our owners and our lovers, our sickness and our cure, our prison and our playground—a feverish buzz to the uninitiated, a language of power to the cognoscenti.

Each strain of zeeps was custom-designed from a core of basic Uppytop wetware modded with whatever odd mitochondria and Golgi bodies the composer could be induced to purchase by zealous ribofunkateers. The zeep colonies embossed our fingers with glowing, colourful veins. But that was only the start. Every metamusician—save Anders—constantly sought improvements in his or her system, striving to push ahead to new metamusical territory, to be the first to explore and domesticate uncharted realms of multisensory rhythm space.

Most masters enhanced their personal zeep colony with a virtual menagerie of symbiotes. These add-ons were entirely different species that you took into your body's ecosystem as a way of keeping the zeeps happy. Over the years, many of our torsos came to resemble coral reefs, encrusted with generations of living organisms.

Mimi, for instance, had a cluster of squishy sea-anemones on her left shoulder and an intimidating row of sharks' teeth along her right forearm; I bore a mat of orange moss on my back, with purple centipedes lively in the fronds. The centipedes had an annoying habit of slipping over my shoulders to drop into my food. But I tolerated them anyway. After awhile, you weren't sure which add-ons were potentiating what effects—so you hesitated to remove any of them.

Anders Zilber was, as I say, the great exception to these refinements. Throughout the glory years of his career, he used a single, unmodified strain of zeeps—albeit zeeps bred by the legendary tweaker Serenata Piccolisima. And his only add-on was from Serena, as well—a little loop-shaped worm, seldom seen, that moved beneath his skin like a live tattoo.

With so simple a toolkit, for a decade of wonder, Anders outshone us all.

* * * *

Anders and I met as neophytes touring with a phenomenally talented martinet, Buckshot LaFunke, who was presenting an overstuffed bill of fare called "LaFunke's Louche Lovers' Legion." He'd booked us into every cheap supper club across the Local Group, from Al Baardo to Yik Zubelle. Anders and I immediately established an easy camaraderie, based on our exalted ambitions, ironic worldview, and what seemed at the time to be comparable talents.

"I'm going to have LaFunke's job one day," Anders boasted one night back in our room, after we'd cranked up our zeep toxins. "Actually, a better one. More status, more class. The laurels of the academy, the butt-licks of the critics."

"Buckshot made his mark with 'The Frozen Metronome,'" I observed. "Dramatizing his first wife's death in that rocket-sled crash on Saturn's rings. Tough to write a piece like that. Especially since the crash was his fault."

"That's why we're pros, isn't it?" said Anders. "The public wants you to spill your guts. Hooks and riffs don't do it, not even a recursive canon. You have to crack open the egg of your skull, and fry them a brain omelette. Every night. On a stage that smells like weasel piss."

"It's a dark age," I sighed. "By rights, exemplary craftsmanship should garner acclaim on its own. Take my own 'Ode to Charalambos'—"

Anders rattled his fingers together like sticks, sending fresh gouts of zeep juice into his bloodstream. "Come off it, Basil. I can turn out that easy-listening stuff in my sleep—and so can you. We're in the post-Wassoon age. The only path is deeper! Give the jackals what they want! The horror of death, the ecstasy of love, the paradox of birth. And then—" He let out a strange, inward chuckle. "And then give them more."

It was soon after this declaration that Anders took all his banked pay from the tour, and visited Serenata Piccolisima in her studio at Sadal Suud—where LaFunke's Legion was booked for a week's engagement at the then-seedy Café Gastropoda. Serenata, who resembled a preying mantis, cleaned out Anders's system, zinged him with her proprietary zeeps, and gave him the add-on loop- worm.

From that moment on, Anders's unhinderable career seemed yoked to the wheel of the Milky Way itself. One brilliant composition after another poured forth from his colourfully marbled fingers. How those early titles still resonate, conjuring up unprecedented mindscapes! "Handsome Hassan,"

"Satan Sheets,"

"Bulbers in Musth,"

"Sweet Disdain,"

"Ninety Tentacles and a Beak "

Each song was different—nay, unique—but there were similarities as well, although it would take Mimi's insight, two years later, to formulate the notion that Anders's overarching theme was the corrupting and ennobling power of infinity.

But never mind the theory. Audiences loved Anders Zilber, and during his decade of miracles, all his dreams and arrogant predictions came to pass.

He was loyal—or needy—enough to bring me along for the ride, assuring my own reputation as a Zilber crony, and allowing me to amass considerable wealth in the process.

Naturally, witnessing Anders's success, I sought covertly to obtain my own zeep culture from Piccolisima, hastening to Sadal Suud as soon as our touring schedule permitted, with a wallet stuffed with credit. Imagine my dismay to learn of Piccolisima's recent murder by a school of anonymous gutter-squid conducting a pusillanimous smash-and-grab.

Soon after, I tried—while feigning a playful manner—to get Anders to infect me with his zeeps. But he merely stared at me, outwardly impassive, yet with his eyes conveying a frightening intensity of emotion.

"I wouldn't wish that on anyone, Basil. Least of all upon my closest friend."

Closest friend? Perhaps, at that time, he thought of me that way. But, by the time the starspiders took him, there was no talk of friendship between us. We were touring partners, and that was all. What drove us apart? My jealousy. I'm not a great-hearted man.

First and always, I was envious of Anders's talent. And, as it turned out, I really couldn't get over Mimi choosing him over me.

Although Mimi Ultrapower was far from being conventionally beautiful, she was—call it mesmerizing. She had a way of catching her breath in the middle of a sentence, a penchant for using recondite words, a quirky sense of fashion, and skin so soft that... Enough. You get the picture—as did everyone else. The public loved seeing the three of us on stage together, glowing with intrigue and sexual tension.

For our doomed final tour, we'd signed on with the *Surry on Down* liner again. And, as if to sweeten the gig, our old taskmaster, Buckshot LaFunke, was accompanying us... as a warm-up act.

"Squirt some oil into that 'Frozen Metronome,' why don't you?" said Anders by way of greeting, when first we encountered the weathered Buckshot at the captain's mess. Anders raised his glowing seven-fingered hands and wriggled them in the older man's face.

"'Ninety Beaks and a Limp Tentacle,'" snapped LaFunke, making a contemptuous gesture at Anders's crotch. His motions were slow and stiff, as he'd saddled himself with an add-on that was something like a crab carapace. "Introduce me to the lady."

"Mimi Ultrapower," said Anders. "A wizard and a sharpie. She'll make sure we all get paid. I suppose we *are* paying you, aren't we Buckshot? Or are you here as an intern?"

This was a nudge too far, and from then on, Buckshot LaFunke rarely spoke to Anders—save during our shows, when, as customary, we played the part of giddy mummers who revelled in performing together.

Given that Mimi was avoiding me, and that Anders was sick of me, I myself wasn't talking much to anyone at all. I didn't mind. I was nastily strung-out on my zeep toxins, thanks to some new opioid vacuoles that an admirer had bioengineered into my colony. For me, time had collapsed into waiting to perform and waiting to get high. What made it complicated was that I still believed in being sober when I performed.

* * * *

Fittingly enough, the end came on Sadal Suud, the former home of Serenata Piccolisima. The Café Gastropoda had gone upscale; it was the size of a Broadway theatre now, half of it underwater, and filled with artificial waves where the native cephalopods could relax. The above-ground areas were a-glitter with the glowing mantises that were the other major players in the Sadal Suud biome. Everyone was thrilled to have Anders Zilber and his cronies here, and our historic show was being Wassooncast across the galaxies.

"We're doing a new piece tonight," Anders told me about half an hour before we went on. He looked flushed and elated. "A really long improvised jam instead of our regular show. My farewell."

"What!" I'd already calculated to the minute how long it would be until tonight's show would end—how long, that is, until I could get blasted backstage. The proposed change stood to throw off my schedule.

"Mimi and I have been talking about it, Basil. Even Buckshot's gonna jam in. Mimi won him over. Don't look so worried. All you have to do is beam out some snootster cello-style routine. Like a row of blossoms floating above the primeval sea where I'm honking the roarasaurus, while Mimi's peppering us with crunkadelic fungus globs, and Buckshot's channeling the moans of the worldsnake who bites his tail. It's gonna be my best jam ever. The last jam of all."

"Um, can you zeep me a preview? Some kind of sketch?" Working with Anders, I'd had to improvise new pieces on lesser notice than this. But normally he gave me a little something to go on.

"I want to stay away from previsualizations, Basil. We'll let this emerge in real time. As a matter of fact, forget what I said about the row of blossoms and the roarasaurus and the world snake and the fungus turds. Just play like—like you're in a Wassoon bubble with a negative radius."

"I was looking forward to finishing early and getting high," I grumbled. "Do you even have a title?"

"Oh, sure," said Anders with an odd smile. "It's called 'Surprise!' You just have to relax and zeepcast like I know you can. And, hell, it's okay if you're loaded for this show. Buckshot will be, that's for true. You can lie down on the frikkin' stage for all I care, Basil. Never mind what these Sadal Suud squids and bugs think of you. Shit—they killed Serenata Piccolisima! And—I might as well tell you—it's not like I plan to be performing anymore. Tonight we wrap it up. Tonight we let it all come down."

A purple centipede dribbled down off my shoulder into my lap. I flipped it over my shoulder into the moss on my back. Reaching within myself, I emptied an opioid vacuole into my bloodstream. The emptiness in my chest melted, the trembling in my legs went away. As of this moment, all was well.

"You're okay, Anders. You really are."

* * * *

From backstage I watched the aged but dauntingly spry Buckshot La-Funke perform his corroded and never-to-be-replicated hit, "Mango Tango Django." Some metamusicians maintain a serene spiritual composure as they beam out their invisible and inaudible zeeply harmonics. Others whirl like the betranced dervishes of Manly's Star IV. Nothing about zeep invocation or reception demands any particular mode of exhibition; the performers freely groove in whatever fashion they've personally developed for dredging up deep gutbucket visionary resonances for the broadcast pleasures of the crowd.

LaFunke was a Holy Roller, a showstopping showoff, an acrobatic ants-in-his-pantser. Filled with opiods as I was, watching him cavort under the wide-spectrum spotlights amused me, and I was pleased to think that, before too long, LaFunke would help us perform a "Surprise!" sprung from the unknowably antic mind of Anders Zilber.

The management of the Café Gastropoda had provided fine amenities for the talent: a buffet of marine exotica, drinks from every eco-crevice of the Cosmic Curtainwall—and a bevy of gyne- and andro- and hermaphro-poppets for the relaxation of the nerves of high-strung geniuses. Knowing LaFunke would be hogging centre stage for another half-hour yet at least, I swept up three of the willing pleasure creatures and retreated into my private Green Room, seeking to fully enjoy my medications. Yet as I made these obedient fluffers lave and caress my zeeply excrescences and baseline privates with every organ they owned, I failed to derive the complete satisfaction I had anticipated. Partly that was because I was bombed, and partly it was because my mind still churned with thorny unanswered questions.

Why was Anders planning to end his career? What terminal artistic revelation had he fallen heir to? What manifestation would it take? How did the numinous, apocryphal starspiders figure into Anders's fancies? How might I access his new secret and make it my own? What kind of profits could it earn for me? What role did Mimi play in all this? I pictured Mimi and Anders in their own exclusive Green Room, much nicer than mine, sensually and soulfully soothing each other in a manner more richly meaningful than anything my sordid poppets and symbiotes could provide.

As my slaved centipedes, trailing commingled juices, returned from their poppet-explorations to my secure epidermal folds, I resolved to have my answers by bearding Anders in his den and shaking him down, if need be, for the whole truth. I was no mere hireling to be kept in the dark! I was his equal, his peer, a genius in my own right!

How poorly I understood matters, I was soon to realize, and how greatly I was to suffer from my ignorance.

Dressed and self-possessed, I hastened to the nearby Green Room that housed my rival and his lover. To my amazement, I found the giggling, giddy, gaudy Supreme Bonze converging on the same spot! His miraculous Black Hat seemed newly negatively effulgent, as if pouring forth some kind of anti-light blacker than black.

"I've just been to see my higher-up, the Karmapa," said the Bonze. "He uncovered a new *terma*, that is, an esoteric teaching from the dead. Your friend Mimi Ultrapower is a dakini temporarily incarnate in human form. And the dakinis are in alliance with the starspiders. She's been leading Anders down a garden path to the nest of those Wassoon-dwellers. Playing on his lust for forbidden knowledge. He's going to use this last jam to convey a message so awful that it will unhinge anyone who experiences it—or worse. Depictions of infinity unclothed, with the possible summoning of a colliding brane."

"Uh—you're talking about spacetime branes, Your Emptiness?" I essayed, fastening on the final word of his farrago. "Remember, I'm no scientist."

"It's grade-school cosmology, you ignoramus! Our visible universe is a single brane leaf in a meta-cosmic puff pastry. Picture a toffee-filled croissant with a sugar crystal upon the outermost layer of glazed dough. That crystal is our galaxy, and the toffee is the divine no-mind of the None."

I knew of the Bonze's childlike fondness for sweets, so his laboured analogy came as no surprise. "Uh-huh," I said, inwardly treating myself to another opioid vacuole.

"Multiple branes exist," ranted the Bonze. "There are an infinity of infinite universes, stacked not in space, but in time. And the sheets move in meta-time! Think of huge, supple chocolate shavings melting into a pool of butterscotch sauce! When a pair of white-chocolate and a dark-chocolate shavings intersect and interpenetrate in a toothsome moiré overlay, the sweetness becomes dodecaduplicated into an instant high-energy death and slate-wiped-clean rebirth for us all. Like a candied clove digging into the rotten core of a blackened molar, *auugh*! I'm speaking of the Big Flash!"

He'd seized my shoulders and was shaking me. I did my best to give him a coherent response. "You say that Anders Zilber has been shown all this first-hand, through the intercession of Mimi the dakini? That he has attained an incontestable vision of deep reality denied even to the most advanced cosmologists? And that the actualization of this revelation will form the substance of our 'Surprise!' jam?"

"Yes, yes, and yes! And this is why we must stop him. At the very worst, he brings our cycle of the universe to an end. At the very least, the pangalactic audience faces the inevitable reality of doom, in a personal and existential way—and our edifice of civilization collapses in despair."

In other words, the Bonze was arguing for the immediate cancellation of our performance. And that disturbed me. We would surely have to pay back our advance from the promoters, and I'd already spent mine.

"I'm really not so sure that—" I began.

"I brook no contradiction!" screamed the Bonze, heedless of who might overhear. "I rely not only on the *terma* of the Karmapa, but also upon the Black Hat itself! Remember that it's woven of dakini hairs! Information leaks into my skull! The sweet whispers of a thousand and one dakinis!"

The Supreme Bonze clutched the hat to his head with an expression of anguished ecstasy, as if someone had just nailed the headgear in place, and I pretended to believe him—although, deep down, I'd always suspected the Black Hat to be made of Kaangian snow-camel hair. But it would be too dangerous to argue any further with this powerful man.

"Very well, then," I said placatingly. "Let's confront my partners." I moved to brush my fingertips against the lips of the lock-licker on Anders's room, counting on access being keyed to my biochem signature too, but the door was already swinging wide.

In the portal stood Mimi Ultrapower.

As I mentioned before, one of her zeeply teratologies consisted of a sawtooth row of calcifications running along the outer edge of her right forearm. Now, without any warning save an evil grin, she swung her right arm with superhuman strength, driving the tiburon teeth of her forearm into the neck of the Bonze and on through to the other side, decapitating him. Utterly unfazed by the blood gusher, she smoothly plucked his falling head from mid-air with her left hand.

The body of the Bonze collapsed to the corridor floor, and I found myself pulled into the Green Room.

Mimi triumphantly snatched the cap from the Bonze's head, then tossed the pitifully wide-eyed and silent head into the open maw of a small Wassoon transmitter that led I knew not where. She closed her eyes, plonked the Black Hat atop her own head, and let out a deep, happy sigh.

"Ah, my sisters! Your reclaimed voices call me home!"

Anders approached Mimi from behind and clasped her lustily around the waist. He seemed totally at ease with her murderous actions.

"I can feel them too, babe! It's like hugging a thousand and two dominatrixes at once!"

Mimi had no time for grab-ass playfulness. All her submissive acolyte worship had evaporated in the heat of her conquest. "Haul the body of that deified goofball in here, and feed him into the Wassoon thingie too. And dump some zyme-critters from the wastebasket onto the blood pools in the hall. Quick!"

Anders complied with Mimi's orders.

"Where are you sending the Bonze's corpse?" I had to ask.

"You don't want to know," said Mimi with an evil snicker. And then she chucked me under the chin. "Listen good, sweetie. Our jam is gonna happen tonight, no matter what. We'll be laying down the template for the next reboot of the universe. 'Surprise!' It's an unbroken line of information, stretching from the transfinite past to this instant's click. Our metamusic will contain the compressed and encoded lineage of all alef-one instantiations of the cosmos, Gödelized into riffs. Call it the kickstart heart-beep of the new Big- Flash Frankenstein. The Om-seed mantra that sends a fresh monster lurching from the lab. That's how us starspiders and dakinis have always ensured cosmic continuity, and we're not gonna change now, you wave? Don't look so freaked, it's an honour to purvey the Heavy Hum. Your name will live in starspider history!"

Anders stepped up to me and threw an arm around my shoulder, awkwardly compressing my various colonies and protuberances. "Basil, buddy, I know you've always been a nervous Nellie, too busy vacillating and shucking and conniving to follow the white rabbit all the way down the black hole. But I never let your jealous, greedy, shithead ways get me down, 'cuz we were best buds, and I always vibed your essential devotion to the art. But now comes the moment of true choice and decision, your chance to give it up for the metamusic. Grab your balls and wail!"

"But—"

"It takes four separate metamusicians to lay down the plectic vibes for this particular kind of chaos," said Anders, his arm still tight around me. "That's a theorem Mimi proved. There's no way we can do it without you and LaFunke."

All the time Anders was talking, I was feeling a wetness along my shoulders that I attributed to my own colonies seepage. But with a start, I suddenly realized what was up.

"You're infusing me with your own zeeps!"

Anders removed his arm. "All done now, Basil, my boy! You always wanted the genuine Serenata Piccolisima germline, and now you've got 'em. You're dosed and ready to kick ass!"

"And by the way," added Mimi. "If you try to play the hero, I'll just puppeteer your corpse."

A knock sounded at the door of the Green Room, and the jubilant voice of Buckshot LaFunke sang, "We're on!"

* * * *

Our stage was a metal mesh construction, cantilevered out from one wall of the Café Gastropoda. The bottom part of the room was essentially an aquarium, thronged with the dregs of Sadal Suud: gutter-squid, dreck-cuttles, and muck-octopi, all of them peering up through the interstices of the platform supporting us. The room's three other walls were lined with boxes and balconies, a-twitter with mantises, ridge-roaches and crystal-ants—the cream of this world's high society. Crab-like waiters scuttled this way and that, stoking the audience with their favourite fuels.

"I'll stand in front tonight," said Mimi as we stepped onto the satisfyingly solid platform.

"And you pair up with me, Basil," instructed Anders. "We'll be in centre stage."

"I'm good with sitting on that chair over there," said Buckshot. "I already wore out my legs warming up this crowd."

"You did a great job," said Mimi, favouring him with one of her fetching smiles. "And now we'll bring 'em to a boil." She raised her arms high and strode to the front of the stage, teetering on the very edge as if tempted to jump into the massed tentacles waving from the water, all pink and mauve and green. Slowly she lowered her arms, starting a fierce zeeply beat of polyrhythmic mental percussion.

Off to the side of the stage, Buckshot chimed in with a psychic wail like a blues harmonica, a little voice wandering among the trunks of Mimi's sound-trees.

Anders elbowed me in the ribs. My cue. Feeling the power of the Piccolisima zeeps, I began flashing a series of three-dimensional mandalas into the room—glowing ghost-spheres that all but reached the walls. My zeepcast orbs were stained in red and sketchily patterned with images that were abstract echoes of the dead Bonze's face. They vibrated with the sound of cellos and organ-music at a funeral mass.

Anders was at my side, casually leaning his elbow on my shoulder, nodding and smiling as Mimi, Buckshot and I jammed together, feeling our way, blending and bending our soundshapes towards a perfect fit. And then our leader started in.

He'd opened his mouth nearly wide enough to break his face, as if wanting to vomit up his heart intact. His metamusic began with a cloud of chicken-scratch guitar pops, each pop a tiny world. Each worldlet contained, incredibly, a mosaic mural of all that lay within some known planet. Sphere upon sphere appeared, the little balls clumping to form spiral skeins—and soon Anders was zeeping a full galactic roar. We three others were playing like never before, beaming our support, filling in Anders's vision with gravity waves, stars and novae, and the planets' living nöospheres.

There's no question that my mind was functioning at higher levels than ever before. Each time I thought we'd brought our metamusic as high as it could possibly go, the cloud of sight and sound would fold over on itself, leaving gaps for us to fill with still more voices of our frantic chorus.

Usually I close my eyes while performing, but tonight I was looking around, wanting to witness the effects of our unprecedented "Surprise!" At first the pseudopods below and the chitinous limbs above were waving as if beating time. But as our modalities grew ever more intricate, the audience members fell still, staring at us with avid, glittering eyes.

I'm not sure when I noticed that the room had incalculably expanded—I think it was after Mimi began mixing a keening scream into her zeep emanations, and surely it was after Anders began folding full galactic symphonies into single notes and dabs of colour. The walls of the Café Gastropoda dissolved—not so much in the sense of becoming transparent nor in the sense of being far away—but rather in the sense of being perforated with extradimensional corridors and lines of sight.

Faces floated in the far reaches of the endless hallways, just like in Anders's Wassoon-altered apartment back in Lisbon. And now, more clearly than before, I knew that these faces came from the unreachable distances and previous cycles of our world. They crowded in upon us like memories or dreams, endless numbers of beings, each of them rapt with our metamusic, each of them intent that his or her own individual soul song be sung. And, impossibly, Buckshot, Mimi, Anders and I were giving them all voice, our minds speeding up past all finite limits, playing everything, all of it, all the stories, all the visions, all the songs.

At first I hadn't noticed the starspiders, but at the height of our infinite fugue, I realized the creatures were everywhere—as the spaces between the faces, as the shadows among the sounds, as the background of the foreground. The Piccolisima zeeps were showing me that only the transfinite sea of starspiders was real. Everything else was, in the end, only an illusion, only Maya, only a dream.

The starspiders clustered around us, and space itself began to bulge. Mimi, then Anders, and then, very slowly, LaFunke disappeared. A starspider had hold of my leg and was tugging at me too, ever so gently, ever so irresistibly. My leg was a trillion light- years long. I was about to let go, about to zeepcast the final mantric signal that would propel our tired old world to dissolve into the cleansing light of a new Big Flash. But something hung me up.

What was it that Anders called me? A nervous Nellie. I pulled my leg back, and with a dissonant *sqwonk*, I changed keys and hues, turning my incantatory dirge into a kind of demented party music, a peppy ladder of shapes and chirps that led the watching minds back from the edge. I kept up the happy-tune until the drab sets of consensus reality had propped themselves back up.

I ended my solo, standing alone on a stage in a pretentious nightclub on the jerkwater planet of Sadal Suud.

A moment of stunned silence, and then the audience began to applaud, in growing waves of sound. It lasted for quite a long time. Anders had taken them into the jaws of Death—and I'd brought them back.

* * * *

By the time people comprehended that Buckshot, Mimi and Anders had truly disappeared, I was already aboard the luxurious *Surry On Down*, bound for home.

For a few days, nobody was holding me up for blame. But then they found the Bonze's body and head in my Lisbon apartment.

The police met me at the spaceport this morning, when we arrived. I wasn't in the right mental shape to put together a defence. I'm too distracted by my zeeps. I'm seeing infinity everywhere, infinity bare.

* * * *

Only an hour ago, I was convicted of murdering not only the Bonze, but Mimi, Buckshot and Anders as well. I'm due to be executed by plasma ionization in just a few minutes.

And so… I've been using my last hour to zeepcast my exemplary tale into the ever-vigilant quantum computations of the ambient air. Those who seek my story will surely find it.

And now comes the final clank of my cell door. No matter. Never mind. I'll be with Anders and Mimi soon.

THE END OF THE GREAT CONTINUITY

I, Jallow Yphantidies, formerly Grand Consistor for the city of Hanging Dog, am solely responsible for the demise of the Great Continuity across the wide ekumen of Crossfoyle.

This confession has not been extorted by torture enacted by any of the Great Continuity's old partisans, but freely given simply to set history on a sound footing, should any future record-keepers arise, in the wake of the forced forgetting. That aboriginal night of smoke, fire and chaos which heralded the death of one immemorial reign and the birth of a shapeless future was utterly my design. My motivation for triggering the grand apocalypse? The impossible happiness of a woman who despised me.

In this I was utterly inconsistent with my own Template, and this failing is the crime that still weighs most heavily on me.

* * * *

The morning of the day I first met Margali Gueths had not been a particularly demanding one.

As always, my ekumen-sponsored landau awaited me outside the large bluestone manse on Vestry Street in the Saltman district, an imposing residence of many cornices and gables, accorded to him who inhabited the office of Grand Consistor.

Such an appointment lasted a lifetime, as did most such high offices. I had held the title for the past twenty years, and expected to hold it for a good number of decades more, having come to the position at the relatively youthful age of thirty-five. Everything in my Template had pointed toward my ascension to this post, and my continuance in office. And most certainly I would do nothing to veer from that consistency.

I ascended the landau, and the driver immediately flicked his whip at the rumps of the harnessed theropods. With meaty exhalations, the beasts lumbered off, their dirty claws clattering on the cobbles, drawing the coach at a pleasant pace through the summertime streets of Hanging Dog.

All about me, the city hummed like a hive of war-bugs in its early-morning busyness. Droshkies and cabriolets, bearing elegant ladies and prosperous gentlemen, streamed down the stony streets. Massive lorries stuffed with goods and drawn by huffing megatheres trundled sturdily along. Tradespeople and servants thronged the sidewalks. Storekeepers unrolled their awnings against the sun, set out signboards, and established pyramids of produce and pottery, ziggurats of books and bolts of fabric. I could smell random whiffs of manure, lamp-oil, and fish.

My large breakfast sat pleasantly in my stomach. The summer- weight robes of the Grand Consistor felt like a comforting blanket. I began to grow drowsy, without a care in my head.

Little did I know what awaited me that day.

Transiting through the Pangstraine, Nurbar and Whitechurch neighbourhoods, we arrived eventually at the immense circular colonnade that enclosed the stupendous Plaza of the Great Continuity. There I disembarked; my landau, its beasts and driver, departing for the government stables until needed.

Crossing through the serried stone Guardians of Continuity— the tall carved pillars of the colonnade were expertly shaped into the likenesses of those legendary icons—I experienced yet again the undying sense of majesty and permanence, of rightness and perfection, which the institution of the Great Continuity represented. Here, at this crucial nexus within our city and at identical sites across the ekumen, the wisdom of the principles of continuity were disseminated, cherished and upheld. The theories that had sealed our nation's stability found here a tangible representation.

Beyond the pillars stretched an unimpeded acreage paved in veined marble. Already at this hour, the humid heated air here had begun to waver with distortions. The city of Hanging Dog was located in a broad fertile valley hosting extensive farms and orchards and small villages. But the mountains along our western edge invariably dumped moisture from the ocean-saturated winds arriving from the east.

Centred in the plaza was the Palace of Continuity, an imposing old stone pile several stories in height that I had come to regard as my second home. (Or perhaps my true home.) Heterogeneous in the extreme, due to numerous faddish additions over the centuries, the thick-walled building and its brocade-curtained rooms offered the prospect of coolness. I hurried across the plaza, eager for relief. I was not alone of course. Scores of supplicants in varying degrees of dress streamed toward the public entrances of the Palace, eager for adjudications, adjustments and arbitrations regarding their individual Templates. These petitioners would be dealt with efficiently by the vast bureaucracy, legions of clerks and counsellor trained in the logic and rigours and precedents of continuity.

It was only the rarest of extraordinary circumstances that would bring a case to my individual attention.

Close to the Palace, my course deviated from the masses, as I headed for my private entrance.

There I encountered one of the familiar doormen. I had never bothered to learn his name over the many years of our brief morning ritual, but his ruddy, sweaty, bulbous-nosed face was as well-known to me as my cousin Pim's. In his elaborate braided uniform he was obviously sweltering.

"Welcome, Grand Consistor."

"Don't you have a cool drink handy?" I asked, as he nodded me inside.

"No, sir. Begging your pardon, the iced-tea cart is late this morning, Grand Consistor."

"That certainly won't do. I'll attend to this matter immediately. Meanwhile, buck up!"

"Yes, sir! Very good, sir!"

Inside the private stairwell leading directly to my chambers, blessed coolth descended on my own glistening brow. I could feel the sweat in my thick beard begin to chill down.

Yards of shelved books, just a fraction of the extensive corpus of continuity studies, greeted me intimately as I entered my high- ceilinged office, as did the attractive, neat surface of my polished wood desk, the overstuffed ottoman and several leather chairs, and the paintings on the walls, including my favourite: Glassco's classic *Nymph Vaulting Auroch*, depicting a bare-breasted young girl and her ceremonial bovine dance partner.

I went immediately to the annunciator on my desk and depressed a key. "Goolsby! Are you there?"

The voice of my assistant, Goolsby Roy, answered immediately. "Never far off, Grand Consistor. Welcome to the Palace this fine oven-like morning. How can I be of service?"

I explained about the guard and the delayed commissary cart. Goolsby promised to repair the lapse immediately, and administer the proper disciplinary actions as well.

With that task off my mind, I settled down to the day's routine business.

First I pored over a dozen abstracts, prepared by Goolsby, of recent papers in continuity studies. I was disappointed to find the various theses rather shallow and myopic. And these emanated from major figures in the field!

Once more I was struck by the long interval since I had last been surprised by a truly intriguing paper. The savants who worked to explicate the laws of continuity had of late entered a period of mere refinement, I felt. Real discovery of new principles, or even of major extensions of old laws, had ground to a halt. I was forced to consider acknowledging that perhaps the science of continuity, after centuries of intense study, had reached its apex. Perhaps from here on out, it would be all trivial elaborations of the well-known.

Template Formation. Climacteric Deviance. Communal Cross-linkage. Societal Channeling. Isolate Invariance—

How boring! Necessary, yes, even essential to the daily maintenance of society—but no sense of mysteries being revealed.

But no—I could not yet bring myself to forecast a future of stasis for the discipline to which I had devoted my life.

My own talents lay not in original research, but rather in synthesis and application and interpretation of results obtained by others. The imposition of orthodoxy, the establishment of the canon. These were the skills of the Grand Consistor. Otherwise, I surely would have been labouring with all my wits to expand the core of our discipline.

My unrewarding studies occupied me till lunch. Mealtime creeped up to take me unawares. The first notion I had of the hour occurred with the entrance of Goolsby Roy. Dressed in his yellow livery, my rail-thin assistant, his pale complexion and sparse, straw-coloured hair making him resemble the protagonist of Nando Pfing's *The Poet's Queer Quandry*, carried a tray. Plates topped with metal domes from which issued hints of steam and fragrance suddenly demanded all my attention.

Goolsby set the tray down on my desk, a sardonic smirk on his saturnine face. "For once the cooks have managed not to render the veal into something resembling a child's rubber teething ring. Enjoy, Grand Consistor."

I fell to my meal heartily, listening all the while to music from the Palace's orchestra piped in over the annunciator.

After Goolsby came to remove the disordered tray, I composed several letters in response to high-level queries from Lessor Consistors who oversaw regional branches of the Great Continuity, in every district and city of the Crossfoyle ekumen. Just as I was inditing the last one, Goolsby reentered my chambers. He looked unnaturally flushed and discomposed.

"Grand Consistor, I beg your pardon in advance. There is a most persistent woman with an incredible—"

He paused to gather his wits, and address the problem formally. "A petitioner has been shunted up through all the proper channels until reaching your office. The first such instance this year, as you well know. Although her petition is incontestably invalid— more so than any other I have ever encountered—she has refused to accept any lower dispensations. She insists on seeing you. Today.

Immediately."

I pondered this development. Not completely unprecedented, this woman's claim on my attention seemed to have disconcerted Goolsby inordinately.

"Is there any other detail you'd care to convey, relating to this petitioner?"

"I—I prefer that you examine her yourself, Grand Consistor."

"Very well. By all means, send her in."

Goolsby stepped out, and within moments my visitor was striding boldly in.

I apprehended a woman of nearly my own age. Plainly, she had been possessed of a striking beauty during her youth, a beauty which had not entirely fled her with the arrival of middle-age. Tall, dark-haired, her complexion darkened by sun and freckled, she wore an expensive outfit that betokened good taste but also a desire to stand out in a crowd. A short gold vest over a blouse coloured green as the sky; a calf-length skirt printed with geometrical tilings that formed confusing illusory patterns; and a pair of sandals that laced all the way up those otherwise bare calves. She carried a slim satchel of the finest lizardskin. Her violet eyes flashed like gemstones. Her painted lips were quirked in an expression of disdain.

Thus, my first encounter with Margali Gueths, the woman who was to destroy the Great Continuity.

Coming right up to my desk, the woman drew to a halt, almost quivering with the fervour of her errand.

"You are Jallow Yphantidies."

This was no question, but rather an assertion I was being challenged to deny. Her usage of my personal name rather than my title was a shocking breach of decorum. But I chose to stifle my indignation and respond politely. From the first, something about this woman's intensity intrigued me. Perhaps my exhibition of good manners could establish our intercourse on a more congenial plane.

I arose and extended my hand. "Indeed, you have found the man whose loving parents christened him thus. But more formally, I am known as the Grand Consistor."

She did not shake my hand. "Rest assured that I care neither for the man nor the office. But the latter is the obstacle in my way, and I sought to shatter the façade by addressing the human behind it." What fire and pluck! I calmly withdrew my proffered hand and said, "And you have done so. Now, if you'll please take a seat, perhaps both the man and the office can consider the matter that brings you here."

As if suspecting manacles ready to spring from the armrests, she occupied a chair adjacent to my desk, and I too sat.

"May I know your name, madame?"

"Margali Gueths. I am a widow. My husband was Juvian Gueths."

"The smilodon-fur magnate. Of course... Please accept my condolences for his passing."

Margali Gueths waved away my sentiment. "Save your vicarious sorrow, Mr. Yphantidies. Juvian was a poor excuse for a husband. He had a mistress in every city of the ekumen. Bad enough, but he also kept me on an exceedingly short leash. My social duties

were manifold, and my pleasures few and far between. I cherish his death as my chance finally to be free."

"I regret to learn of this prior discomfort in your life, Mrs. Gueths. But assuredly, with your portion of the estate, you will now be equipped to enjoy yourself."

"Ah, but that is precisely the rub, Mr. Yphantidies. I am not willing to settle for a portion of the estate. I intend to have it all. Gueths Furs, Traplines and Entrepôts will not pass from my hands. I intend to control my husband's enterprises, not pass them on to someone chosen by the Great Continuity."

I sat stunned. My reluctant tongue failed to provide any words that could meet this blunt statement of rebellion. Ultimately, I fell back on a scientific approach.

"Mrs. Gueths. I assume your satchel contains the documents relating to your case "

"Yes."

"May I see them, please?"

She extracted a thick sheaf of papers and handed them over. The familiar cream-coloured bond and coloured stamps of official Continuity documents radiated an almost tangible reassurance to me. I swivelled my seat and partially reclined in my high-backed chair to peruse them. Out of the corner of one eye, I saw Margali Gueths continue to seethe.

Here in my hands were summaries of the Templates of both Juvian Gueths and his wife. Columns and columns of figures across dozens of characterological categories. I focused immediately on the codes relevant to business acumen. Acquisitiveness, entrepreneurship, prescience, steadfastness, compromise From there, I turned my attention to other graphs, diagrams and family trees. Daguerreotypes and clippings from public records. Test results. Affidavits from friends, family members and acquaintances. And still, only the hundredth part of what Continuity knew about this couple.

* * * *

The precise data conveyed its meaning swiftly to my trained eyes. But I lingered over the documents rather longer than I needed to, hoping to wear Margali Gueths down further. But I could soon see that my tactic was backfiring, as the fiery woman only grew more exasperated with my dilatory perusal. I turned to face her, and handed back her papers. I stroked my beard meditatively before speaking.

"Mrs. Gueths, I will not insult you by simply reiterating the cold facts that I'm certain you've already heard from a dozen of my subordinates. Simply put, there is nothing in your Template which fits you to manage a business. Continuity demands—"

The sharp report of her small fist on the surface of my desk caused me to jump. But it was her words that drained the colour from my face.

"Templates and Continuity be damned! No one knows the operations of my husband's business better than I! Studying those operations was the only dry and dusty hobby I was ever allowed. I'll be cursed if I allow myself to let all that torturous study go to waste now, just because your tinpot organization thinks that it can predict my failure! I'm tired of spending my life jammed into one of your little boxes!"

Margali Gueth's attractive bosom was heaving, her face flushed. I felt some small empathy for her, but the feeling was drowned in my larger indignation at her blasphemy against the Great Continuity.

"Mrs. Gueths, no one is attempting to jam you into a box of our making. The parameters of your daily life are innate and inherent in your own character. They have been forming themselves since your birth, and are by now, at your advanced age, practically immutable."

Margali Gueth's scowl informed me that perhaps my choice of the term "advanced age" to describe her current station in life was impolitic and gauche. I sought to recast the argument in more abstruse terms.

"All that the Great Continuity does is quantify and codify the implicit patterns and tendencies of an individual's life, and attempt to offer some guidance."

"Guidance! You call issuing demands and orders that interfere in the most intimate portions of a person's life mere 'guidance?'"

"The Great Continuity boasts no enforcers, no Continuity Police—"

"No, of course not! All of society is your enforcement tool. Any nail that sticks up gets instantly hammered down."

"Mrs. Gueths, please. Consider your words. Consider our nation's history. You are forgetting the inefficiency and dangers that preceded the establishment of the Great Continuity. When any individual could impulsively follow any path, whether he or she was constitutionally fitted for it or not, society was like a machine composed of random, ill-adapted parts. Waste, confusion, frustration, hostility reigned. Since the establishment of the Great Continuity, our ekumen has become a smoothly operating organism that conduces to the maximum happiness for the largest number."

"And what of those who disagree with their classifications, with your 'guidance?' Those who wish to follow their deeper, unchartable impulses?"

"They must correct their behaviour, for the good of all." Margali Gueths leaned in closer to me. I could smell her sweat.

"Your system insures the maintenance of the status quo. There is no room for change or innovation or social movement."

I began to lose my temper. "A ridiculous charge. Was I, for instance, born into an ancient lineage of Grand Consistors? Of course not. My parents were a draper and a seamstress. My own particular talents were identified early on, as is the case with all children, and I worked hard to cultivate them."

"Ha! You were chosen by the elite and groomed as their pliable tool."

I began to splutter. But before I could address this absurd accusation, Margali Gueths launched another assault.

"You are just trying to limit me because I am a female! You don't want a woman running a sizeable business, having all the privileges of a man!"

"Now you've reached the heights of illogic. There are numerous women entrepreneurs. What of Velzy Spindler?"

"The milliner? She owns three shops in Hanging Dog. I doubt she grosses in a year what Gueths Furs nets in a day. No, it's obvious to me now. Your Great Continuity is dedicated to keeping women in a subservient position. That is why I am being stymied in my quest for simple justice."

She concluded her tirade and slumped back in her chair. Her expression, blended of wrath and despair, challenged me to refute her.

Was Margali Gueths a simple egomaniac, a selfish, mercenary individual looking to justify herself with spurious and superficial logic? Or was she sincerely confused, operating out of a true sense of injustices done to her? After a moment's reflection, I chose to believe the latter interpretation. That judgement allowed me to put aside any sense of personal affront, and work toward what was best for this woman and society.

Surely this woman's unhappy marriage must have fostered a sense of life's unfairness in her. But she was mistakenly transferring this personal grievance to a larger system that did not merit such an attack. It was up to me to persuade her of the wrongness of her perceptions.

I decided to attempt a tactic I had seldom had occasion to employ before.

Standing, I said, "Mrs. Gueths, I would like you to accompany me elsewhere in the Palace, where I can show you something that might convince you of the inaccuracy of your statements."

This offer obviously proved unexpected. She stood up hesitantly. "I—I can't imagine what that thing could be."

"That is precisely why you need to see it with your own eyes. Are you game?"

My last question stiffened her spine and caused her pride to flare. What a woman this was! If only I—

But even the Grand Consistor is subject to the dictates of his personal Template.

"Of course I'm game. Lead on, Mr. Yphantidies, lead on!"

I conducted Margali Gueths to the door of my office, swinging it open for her—just in time to catch Goolsby Roy hurriedly reclaiming his desk chair in the anteroom. Plainly he had been eavesdropping. I could hardly object, since it was precisely such fussy attentiveness that made him such a good assistant—and the habit formed a well-known part of his Template.

"Mr. Roy, please field all matters that arise. Mrs. Gueths and I are going to the Vaults."

Goolsby's eyes widened. "Very good, Grand Consistor."

I conducted Margali Gueths out of the anteroom, whereupon we found ourselves at the head of the busy Travertine Staircase, up and down which dozens of Continuity employees scurried, their arms full of documents.

We went down, saying nothing to each other. My underlings gave respectful nods of their heads as they encountered me. But the deference seemed not to impress Margali Gueths with my stature, but rather render her more disdainful of me.

On the ground level, we crossed three wings of the Palace and approached a door guarded by two doormen. They let us pass, and we descended further, down and down and down a set of steps more utilitarian than the noble public spaces. Here, the employees we encountered were all young messengers shuttling the documents that the more senior Adjudicators and Consistors had requested. Every last one of them practically fainted at seeing their Grand Consistor in their midst. Their reactions made Margali Gueths grin and chuckle ironically.

But her humourous attitude evaporated when we debouched from the stairwell and into the Vaults.

The barrelled ceiling of the Vaults, upheld by an army of regularly spaced pillars, reared some fifteen feet above our heads. No walls interrupted this measureless cavern, but the ranks upon ranks of dark wooden shelving, cresting some distance short of the roof, had a similar effect.

We looked down one aisle. Its terminus was invisible, dwindling to a vanishing point.

"The Vaults," I said, "underlie the whole plaza above us, and are in a state of constant expansion, spreading out further and further from the Palace. We are well below the lawful level of any other structural foundation. Here we have the complete files on every extant citizen of Hanging Dog, files of which you have seen only the smallest redaction. Each citizen claims a certain number of feet upon the shelves, based on their age, of course. We also continue to maintain all the files of the dead, from the establishment of the Great Continuity to the present. They come in very useful at certain times."

"I— This is monstrous! It's a combination of ossuary and prison."

"Such is your uninformed view, Mrs. Gueths. But perhaps you'd like to see your own file...?"

This offer startled her. She hesitated. But I knew she could not resist. No one could. She bravely tried to rationalize her reaction.

"This is only my right, I suppose. Everyone should have this opportunity. It should not be something offered only to appease a noisy protestor. Very well, show me my file."

"Allow me to see your Template synopsis once more, please."

She passed over the papers from her satchel. I memorized her file number, and we set off.

The labyrinth was laid out logically, and the shelves clearly marked. But still I found myself experiencing a sense of disorientation and timelessness amidst the flickering lamplight. Subtle winds from the ventilation ducts conveyed the illusion that we walked through some artificial forest. Surely Margali Gueths, totally unfamiliar with this environment, must have been experiencing even greater deracination.

After some fifteen minutes of walking, we reached the proper shelf. The shelves were filled with uniform chunky albums bound in black buckram. Their spines bore only alphanumeric designations. "Yours is there." I pointed to a shelf up above head height. "You'll have to use a ladder."

I indicated a wheeled ladder that ran on a rail. Margali Gueths gamely began to climb. I averted my eyes for a moment, so as not to take advantage of the sight of her shapely calves beneath her long skirt. But then I realized the foolishness of such a nice gesture, given what she was about to encounter in her file.

Margali Gueths came to a halt on a high rung. She pulled down her first album. This action too was predictable: people always felt a nostalgic attraction to their infancy and youth.

The woman cracked the album and began to page through its contents.

At first her expression was fond and serene, as she encountered artefacts and tokens of her long-departed childhood. But this serenity soon vanished, replaced by flushed indignation. Margali Gueths slammed shut the album, reshelved it, then took one from considerably farther down in her sequence. She hastily opened this binder, flipped through its pages, then plucked from it a single large daguerreotype.

The brief flash of the print that I received from my vantage revealed a tangle of bare fleshy limbs, plainly belonging to more than two persons.

Margali Gueths hastily descended the ladder to stand before me. Gazing at me contemptuously, she snapped the daguerreotype in half with a crisp crack, then snapped the fragments in half, before stuffing them into her satchel, reclaimed from the floor.

Her voice quivered with rage. "How dare you!"

I had anticipated a slightly different first question. But I should have realized that Margali Gueths would choose not to trifle with practicalities, but would rather challenge the moral right of the Grand Continuity to keep such files.

"Not 'How was this done?' That is generally what people ask, once they discover the degree to which their lives are transparent. You continue to surprise me, Mrs. Gueths."

She only glared. "Don't attempt to placate me, Mr. Yphantidies."

"I assure you, I would never consider insulting your intelligence with flattery, Mrs. Gueths. But you must allow this unimaginative functionary to follow procedure, and answer the expected question first. That image from your life—one of many, many such—was obtained via the Panocculus, an auditory and viewing machine that allows unimpeded remote access to any spatial location, no matter what conventional barriers exist. The Panocculus is the rock upon which the Grand Continuity rests. Its existence, while not precisely a secret, is not generally touted, and unknown to the hoi polloi. A woman of your class, however, is permitted such knowledge." Margali Gueths snorted derisively, but I continued nonetheless. "Within the Palace, vast banks of Panocculus machines, manned around the clock by an army of trained operators, ceaselessly collect data on the citizenry. But not, of course, for any ignoble or trivial purposes. The operators are bound by the most stringent oaths and penalties from disclosing what they witness. They only record. These frozen moments and conversational transcripts simply help quantify what standard testing already reveals. Your Template is collated not just from cold, abstract data, but from the rough and tumble of your most intimate and commonplace moments. So you see, when the Great Continuity asserts, for instance, that you, Margali Gueths, are incapable of assuming the mantle of your husband's business, our judgement is based on the deepest knowledge of your behaviour and capabilities."

Silence reigned for a brief moment before Margali Gueths spoke again. "Surface. It's still all only surface observations. I am not just the sum of my recorded actions, Mr. Yphantidies. No one is. There are infinite depths to every living person, depths which the Great Continuity can never reckon nor fathom."

"This is metaphysics, Mrs. Gueths. And a sane polity cannot be built on metaphysics."

She did not choose to refute this obvious statement, but instead again demanded, "How dare you, in any case?"

I began to frame an answer, but then stopped. Surprising myself, I said, "Mrs. Gueths, would you allow me to attempt to justify the Great Continuity's existence under more relaxed circumstances? Perhaps we might share dinner together this evening?"

Taken aback, she hesitated, then said, "Very well. You know my address. Be there promptly at eight."

She spun about and strode off then with utmost certainty. Plainly, she had memorized our path, or the Vault's whole coordinate system.

Watching her go, I was impressed, despite myself, and despite my reverence for the Great Continuity she despised.

* * * *

The Gueths residence occupied an entire block of Eldorada Street in the Minvielle District, sharing the neighbourhood with the manses of such famous families as the Pybuses, Streutts, and Cavenders. A district of wealth and attainment, won from capricious fate by adherence to individual, familial and societal Templates. A dignified hush broken only by the insect whine of klickits swaddled the street.

The night had brought some surcease from the heat, although the humidity remained. My civilian clothes, while not as comfortable or as familiar-feeling as my official robes, proved quite adequate to the weather.

My landau discharged me at the front entrance to the Gueths residence. The driver descended and prepared to feed his theropods while he waited. I could smell the bloody meat that was their customary fare. Lamps to either side of the Gueths' double doors shed their radiance against the night. I climbed the steps and rang the bell.

To my surprise, Margali Gueths herself opened the door. She was dressed demurely, in browns and greys. Her handsome face remained composed in a neutral expression.

"Come in, please, Mr. Yphantidies." I entered.

"I have dismissed all my servants for the evening. Our meeting did not strike me as a formal affair. Before leaving, Cook laid on a cold buffet that should be refreshing while we continue our discussion."

She conducted me through several well-appointed chambers to a dining room. I noticed several paintings by Glassco on the walls, but not my favourite. I took a seat indicated to me, while Margali Gueths stopped by a sideboard bearing an assortment of decanters.

"Will you have a drink?"

"Can you make a Cubeb Slosh? That would be most refreshing."

"Of course."

With chilled drink in hand, I contemplated my hostess, now seated. Despite her initial formality and reticence, I could tell that she was eager to resume our former dispute.

After sipping my drink, I said, "You asked me how the Great Continuity could sanction its intrusions into the lives of the ekumenical citizenry. The answer is simple. Our organization is following its own Template. It is not only individuals who must obey their predestination and innate disposition, but also institutions, and society as a whole. Having come into being, the Great Continuity simply follows the dictates of its nature. We do as we do because we can—and must. To ensure our own survival, just as would any person."

Margali Gueths looked at me incredulously. "Your arguments are entirely circular! You are using the unproven notion of Templates to justify enforcing Templates! Hasn't this paradox ever occurred to you before?"

I waved away her juvenile objection. "This is all discussed and dealt with in Beginner's Heuristics. If you had academic training—" Margali Gueths surged impulsively to her feet. "This whole evening is a waste! I was foolish enough to imagine that if I got you out of your fortress—out of your formal shell—then you might be able to see the injustice being done me, how your Great Continuity wants to strip me of all that is my due. But instead I find that I have invited a hollow man into my house. Or rather, a ragbag man stuffed with the mouldy hay of preconceived ideas!"

Margali Gueths's passionate tirade in her own defence, even though I was its butt, rendered her more alluring in my eyes than any other woman I had ever known. Betrayed by this unwonted feeling, and perhaps a little intoxicated from the Slosh, I chose to speak freely.

"Mrs. Gueths, I am not insensible to your character, and your righteous appeals. If matters were different, so forceful is your nature, I might— Well, I might even now be contemplating the establishment of a certain level of intimacy between us."

This statement stopped Margali Gueths in her tracks as she paced the chamber. "So. Having seen those shameful images from my file, you take me for a loose woman? Well, what if I am? What if I chose to palliate my loveless marriage with certain wild assignations? Am I not just following my Template, according to you?"

"Indeed. And I don't pass judgement on your actions. One of our prime tenets in the Great Continuity is that there is really no good or evil, moral or immoral—at least not as conventionally defined—but only adherence to or violation of one's Template. No, my attraction to you stems solely from what you have shown me of your nature in person."

She was silent for a time. "Assuming I would even begin to imagine consenting to such a relationship between us, what prevents it on your part?"

I sighed. "My own Template. When I was five years old, I received my first results on the Amatory Scale, and was deemed incapable of forming mature bonds with the opposite sex. Subsequent readings only confirmed this. Thus I have been precluded from any intimate relations. It is a regrettable defect, I suppose, but one that I have learned not to be troubled by."

Margali Gueths collapsed on a chaise. Her expression mingled horror, bemusement and—most injurious—pity.

Suddenly she began to cry and laugh by turns, tears and guffaws blending into an unholy symphony that pierced me like a hot wire. "I— I can't believe— All your life— Never to have— Just because— Madness, madness!"

A frosted dignity suffused my brain. I attained a standing posture.

"Madame, I am leaving now. Our discussion is at an end."

Margali Gueths wiped snot from her nose. How had I ever imagined her attractive?

"Of course. Or course it is. I will never allow my life to be blighted as you have allowed yours to be. The Great Continuity has hold over me no longer."

Somehow with no passage of time that I could recall I found myself standing outside. The stars overhead appeared to me like gaping mothholes in the shoddy fabric of the universe.

I climbed back into my landau. But I did not return to Vestry Street.

Rather, I went once more to my office, there to initiate the reformation of Margali Gueths.

The brazen woman had confiscated and destroyed a single daguerreotype from the Vaults.

But there were many more.

It was not necessary to disseminate certain information and imagery from her file to any actual scandal sheets. Those tabloids were a blunt instrument useful only for amusing the proletariat. Anonymously circulating the material among her peers was a more subtle and sufficient means of ruining her standing, and thus frustrating any attempt on her part to circumvent the Great Continuity's disposition of Juvian Gueths' estate.

In only a month, Margali Gueths' ambitions to take her husband's place had been rendered impotent.

And that was when she chose to hang herself.

* * * *

My ultimate emotional convulsion—the spasm that violated my Template and caused the end of the Great Continuity—attendant upon the suicide of Margali Gueths was not immediate.

By the time I learned of her demise, some weeks after our disturbing dinner, I had regained my equanimity. No longer did her sobs and guffaws and taunts haunt my sleep. I had become utterly convinced of the correctness of my actions. In fact, very seldom did her case even cross my conscious mind. I had acted with all diligence and propriety, obeying the dictates and duties of my office, of my own Template.

Just as she had. Just as she had.

Almost a year after her suicide, I sat once more in my office, on a hot summer's day. Lunchtime rolled around. Goolsby Roy entered, carrying a meal tray. The odour of veal reached my nostrils.

Something broke open within me, a chrysalis all unsuspected that I had been growing, harbouring deep within me like some new extension of my soul. The exact concatenation of circumstances summoned up Margali Gueths's first appearance before me, as vividly as if she were present.

I stood up and moved wordlessly past my startled assistant. Down, down, down I went, to the Vaults.

Fire, of course, was an omnipresent worry where the records were concerned. Many preparations and drills against its dangers were in place. Sand- and water-buckets hung at intervals throughout the Vaults. Due to their antiquity, however, piped water was unavailable. So the fire which I ignited and then abandoned, once it was well underway but before it could entrap me, was brought under control before spreading all that far.

But the intense conflagration did succeed in causing a portion of the Vaults to collapse, opening a hole in the Plaza. Curious citizens of the lowest sort quickly swarmed around the smoky excitement. The doormen of the Palace tried to drive them back, but, vastly outnumbered and without weapons, failed. Soon daring and ambitious men and boys were scrambling down the smoldering rubble slopes of the pit, to investigate what lay below.

Soon files were being passed among the crowd. Files that proved every bit as incendiary as my matches.

Here I will leave off my eyewitness account, since I—or any individual—was unable to take in more than a fraction of the widespread chaos that followed. The insensate looting, the burning of property, the lynching, the destruction of the Panocculus machines— A veritable apocalypse that raged up and down the ekumen like a living beast for weeks. The social structures of centuries died, as easily as drowned kittens.

Yet somehow I survived the interregnum. Somehow I was reborn into an age that has abandoned all I once held dear and essential. Templates, the Great Continuity, order, stability—

Such concepts as inheritance and the Amatory Scale.

All vanished, in favour of impulsiveness and unpredictability. And a chance, perhaps, for the first time, to love.

FJAERLAND

RUDY RUCKER AND PAUL DI FILIPPO

The ferry slid away, trailing thick, luscious ripples across the waters of the fjord. A not-unpleasant scent compounded of brine, pine and gutted fish filled the air. Most of the new arrivals were jostling into a sanitary, hermetic tour bus. But one man and woman set off on foot along a tiny paved road, pulling their wheeled suitcases behind them.

The village ahead seemed utterly deserted.

"They're resting in peace," said the man, pausing to light a cigarette, his angular face intent. He wore jeans, a pale shirt, an expensive anorak, and designer shades. "Dead as network television."

"It's Sunday, Mark," said his companion. "It's Norway." She wore oversize sunglasses and low heels. A lemon-yellow silk scarf enfolded her crop of blonde hair, a soft red cashmere sweater draped her shoulders. She looked as if she wanted to be happy, but had forgotten how.

The stodgy crypt of a tour bus lumbered past them. The man offered the passengers a wave. Nobody acknowledged him. "Sweet silence," said the man as the bus's roar faded. "Like being packed in cotton wool."

The woman looked around, studying the scene. "With the fjord and the mountains—anything we say feels kind of superficial, doesn't it? The beauty here—it's like a giant waterfall. And my soul's a tiny glass."

"We're fugitives, Laura. They could gun us down any minute.

That's why everything seems so heavy."

"Shove it, Mark!"

"Never hurts to face the facts. That big house up ahead, you think that's a hotel?"

"I hope it's a love nest for us," said Laura with a sad little smile. "I'm ready to relax and be friends, aren't you? It might help if I had a book to read."

"You'll be reading this," said Mark, playfully tapping his crotch. "Page one."

Laura tossed her head, mildly amused. A few steps later she stopped still and made a sudden extravagant gesture. "Lo and behold!"

Right beside the narrow road was an unmanned shelf of books—warped boards, a piece of stapled-down, folded-back canvas for protection from the elements—with a sign reading: *Honest Books, 10 Kr. each.* A gnome-shaped metal coin-bank was beside the sign. "*Honest*—that's wishful thinking on their part, right?" said

Mark. "I say you just help yourself."

"The windows look empty, but there's people inside the houses watching us," said Laura. "Village life, right?" She leaned over the books. "The only English ones I see are totally foul best-sellers."

"Which you've already read."

"Which I've already read. Years ago. I guess I could try a Norwegian book. I can read that a little bit. Thanks to all my work as an interpreter."

"And thanks to granny on your family's Minnesota farm."

"Don't mock the farm, Mark. We can't all be city slickers. Oh, look at this strange book here. I'll dream over it while nibbling brown bread."

"No words in it at all," said Mark, flipping through the mouldy, leather-bound volume. "Just symbols and blobs."

"I wonder if it's math?"

"Not like any I've ever seen. And what's up with the title? *God Bøk* with that slash through the *o.*"

"Means *Good Book*," said Laura. "I want it. Pay the troll, Mark."

Mark dropped a ten kroner coin into the troll-shaped bank beside the books. The coin clattered resonantly, the sound seeming to issue from impossibly cavernous depths.

They passed a grey wooden church and came to the big house that Mark had noticed. It was indeed a hotel, the Hotel Fjaerland. A fresh-faced young woman sat at a desk downstairs. She wore her brown hair in a bun, her eyes were ice blue.

"I'm Ola," she told them in a lightly accented voice. Somehow her lilting English managed to remind Mark of otters at play. "I can give you the room just up those stairs." She handed them a large skeleton key with the number 3 on a tag. "We have a wine and orientation session at six. I'll be giving a little talk about the house's history. You'll be taking your supper here?"

"Sure," said Mark.

"But I wonder if we could get some breakfast right now?" asked Laura. "We had to leave so early this morning to catch the ferry."

"I'm bringing you something on the porch," said Ola pleasantly. "I'm the manager, the receptionist, the waitress and more. The hotel's been in my family for quite some time."

It was lovely on the gazebo-like back porch, with a green lawn rolling down to the final finger of the fjord. Ola served them tea, coffee, berries and bread with butter.

"Life's rich panoply," said Laura to Mark. "I'm grateful that we made it this far."

They strolled the hotel grounds. The month was July, and the northern days were twenty hours long. The plants were making the most of it, burgeoning with petals and leaves. Set among some five- pointed pink flowers was a vertical stone plinth, like a gravestone higher than a man, covered not with writing, but with irregular spots of moss or lichen. Nature had built a monument to her own subtle variety.

"They look like the pictures in my *God Bøk*," remarked Laura. "Let's go up to the room and study," suggested Mark.

"High time," said Laura. "Page one."

The pair of lumpy Norwegian mattresses favoured by the Hotel Fjaerland contorted themselves under their shifting weights into non-intuitive topologies, and the two-mattress iron bedstead creaked. But they got the job done—their first carnal encounter in weeks. They dropped off into a blissful couple of hours of sleep. When Mark awoke, he saw Laura leaning on one elbow, studying him across the bed's expanse. The linen-sheeted comforter had slumped to reveal her shapely breasts, unquenched by nearly forty years of living.

"That was tender and intense," she said, planting a gentle kiss on his forehead.

Feeling cautious, Mark kept his face blank.

"Don't tell me you're still holding a grudge!" exclaimed Laura. "We're here to erase the bad times while we can, right? To taste those good old vibes that we had before the work burnout and— and before that horrible night. And before we had to flee the law."

Uneasily Mark made a joke. "Tender and intense, yeah. Is that like jalapeno-flavoured Cool Whip? Or more like a Brillo pad massage?"

Laura's face assumed a fixed and frozen expression. Slowly but deliberately, she got out of the bed and began to dress.

"Hey, where are you going?"

She said nothing for a drawn-out few seconds, as if mastering her temper, and then replied, "Mark, I don't know if you want to waste the time you've got left on wallowing in bitterness and defeat and sarcasm. Okay, the feds have stolen our semiotic analyzer and we're up to our asses in debt and we're charged with some serious crimes. We can still bounce back— but not if you keep nursing your sulk. It's spoiling everything—especially our marriage."

Mark huffed. "Our marriage. You laid that wide open when you caught me with my chief exec—"

"With Beryl," spat Laura. "We can say her name."

"With Beryl, yes," continued Mark. "We were just having a little party to celebrate the final beta tests for the Yotsa 7. I wasn't trying to sneak around on you or I wouldn't have invited you. I was drunk and happy. All I did was kiss her. But nothing I said was a good enough excuse. And then you had to take your petty revenge with Lester Lo—my chief tech! In the office right next door! So thanks to you I had to fire Lester. He went rogue, the feds came down on us, and we missed the chance to market our new product."

Laura's voice began to rise, despite her best efforts. "It's just like you to turn things around and put me in the wrong. We both made mistakes, yes. But I'm trying to make the best of things, and you're not! You're clutching your misery to yourself like you've fathered some inhuman changeling baby. It's sucking the lifeblood out of you—and out of me too!"

Mark made no reply, and Laura continued. "Listen to me, dear. I'm here in a strange and beautiful land. I've come here at no little cost and effort, to relax and enjoy myself and to take stock of my life—with or without you! If you can drag your mind out of despond, and notice where we are, and contemplate a shared future—well, if you can do all that, you'll find me on the lawn, ready for a stroll. And if not—"

Laura didn't bang the door to their room on the way out, but Mark could tell she wanted to. And he wouldn't have blamed her if she had.

He knew he was being a jerk. He knew he should consign the past miserable year of overwork and ambition and failure to his personal dustbin of history, cut his losses, pick himself up, shine his shoes, wear a smile, look on the bright side, retool, get a good lawyer—all that optimistic, self-help, go-getter shit. But something deep inside him rebelled.

Their semiotic analyzer should be making them millions! And thanks to Lester Lo, the feds had grabbed it and made it top-secret and charged Mark and Laura with a bunch of trumped-up bullshit libel and sedition counts. When Mark had caught wind of the feds' plans for devastating black-ops reprisals, he and Laura had gone undercover and headed for the ass-end of the civilized world. Norway.

Mark heaved his hairy naked form from the bed. Though forty-five, he was still more muscle and sinew than flab. The view out the windows drew his eyes. It was heart-breakingly lovely here, with yellow flowers around the window frames, a cozy little barn perched just so in the swooping field, and the backdrop of elegantly asymmetrical mountains. The fjord wobbled with liquid reflections that cycled through ever-lovelier forms of universal beauty. Mark's new life with Laura could be paradise—and he was making it hell.

Everything had begun so well. Mark and Laura had met in grad school at Columbia, both of them studying linguistics. They'd fallen in love and married. Laura had become a professional interpreter for the U.N., and Mark had drifted into multimedia advertising, eventually founding his little ferret of a company: Bloviation. The sense of wonder that Mark and Laura shared over the deep structures of language had proved an abiding source of inspiration. Mark smiled ruefully as his eye fell upon the *God Bøk* beside their bed. It was so typical of Laura to buy something like that. In past days, the loving couple might have spent hours poring over the artefact, forming hypotheses and spinning tales. With a sigh, Mark lifted the book, and began leafing through it. Geometric mandalas alternated with splattered shapes that resembled stilled explosions.

A slow tingle oozed from the book into Mark's fingertips. Perhaps there was something here of special importance.

"I can decrypt this!" exclaimed Mark to himself. "I have my magic spectacles." He opened his suitcase, unzipped a hidden inner pocket, and removed what appeared to be a lorgnette—a pair of glasses that unfolded from a delicately tooled stick.

The elegant device was a Yotsa 7, the last of the prototype semiotic analyzers that Mark possessed. All the other units had been commandeered by the feds the day after the big melt-down at Bloviation. Laura might have given Mark a tongue-lashing if she'd known he'd brought this one along, this bad seed offspring that lay at the heart of their troubles. But, in a way, the invention had been Laura's idea.

"Imagine a search engine that goes beyond syntax or semantics," Laura had mused in a casual conversation two years ago. "Something that treats its inputs as signposts pointing to vexed and hidden meanings. Like— what's a hamburger really *about*—and what do people *want* it to be about? What mythic archetypes are packed inside an automobile's trunk? What are the psychic and social subtexts of shampoo?"

"You're talking about semiotics," Mark said. "The meaning of signs."

"Yes. You need to build a semiotic analyzer. Call it the Yotsa 7."

"Why seven?"

"Seven is better than one, right?" Laura giggled infectiously. "*Yots* better."

Although the couple lacked any deep technical skills, Laura knew some theoreticians heavily into natural-language recognition. And Mark employed a few savagely gifted techs, foremost among whom was Lester Lo.

After a year of research and another of frenzied tinkering, Bloviation had produced a prototype of the Yotsa 7. The lenses were of a special quasicrystalline substance related to Icelandic spar, and the filigreed handle contained a state-of-the-art quantum computer full of qubit memristors. So what did the Yotsa 7 do? It revealed the deeper meanings of the objects in view.

The semiotic analyses were derived from artificially-intelligent image parsers, from social network statistics, and—this, too, had been Laura's idea—from a specialized search engine that flipped through an exhaustive data base that held a century's worth of digitized international comic strips in a peta-qubit quantum loop within the handle. According to Laura, the demotic medium of comics was a royal road into the depths of the human psyche.

To use the Yotsa 7, you simply held the magic glasses to your eyes like a snooty Viennese dowager eyeing her niece's dance- partner. As a nod to user-interface pizzazz, the layers of semiotic information appeared as if overlaid upon the scene in three- dimensional shells—and these layers of meaning were directly projected into your psyche via quantum entanglement.

The Yotsa 7 would have been a great product—but it worked too well. The night of their doomed celebration party at Bloviation's three-room office suite, Mark's chief exec Beryl had popped up a news feed on the video screen. Mark, Beryl, and Lester gazed at the politicians through their quantum-computing lorgnettes.

The Yotsa 7's semiotic analyzer showed jackals, hyenas, hogs— and even such invertebrates as jellyfish and leeches. What made this especially intense was that the perhaps unsurprising slurs were documented by subsidiary veils of information containing legally actionable data. Exulting in the power of the Yotsa 7, Beryl threw herself into Mark's arms and kissed him. And that's when Laura had walked in.

By the next morning, Bloviation was in a shambles. Beryl and Lester were both out. Bitter and resentful, Beryl put Lester up to sharing some of their newfound political dirt via an anonymized blog—that had been tweaked to show a clear trail leading back to Bloviation. Patriot Act time! The feds were at Mark and Laura's apartment that evening. The Yotsa 7 technology was classified as top secret, and all their work was impounded.

"Imagine this device in the hands of America's enemies," one agent had declaimed.

"*You're* the country's worst enemies, and I can actually *see* you holding it, so I don't *have* to imagine!"

In his subsequent fury, Mark had made some threats and charges that the feds had taken quite seriously to heart. He and Laura were charged with libel, with sedition, and possibly with treason—which could carry, in certain contexts, a death penalty, with or without a trial. Mark and Laura hadn't stuck around long enough to learn the full details.

Mark's ultrageek connections had fixed them up with new identities, including paper trails, searchable records, passports and some air tickets to Scandinavia. Possibly they were going to stay here for quite a long time.

Mark wrenched his mind back into the present. Like some old-time courtier, he flipped open his lorgnette, swiveling the quasicrystalline lenses from the quantum-computing handle. Holding the spectacles to his eyes, he gazed down into Laura's *God Bøk,* focusing on a dense, eccentric, fractal blot.

Mark stopped his prancing. What the hell was this? Shelled around the image on the page, Mark saw a damp dungeon hall, dimly lit by glowing mould, with a beautiful naked woman supine upon a stone altar. The long-haired woman was none other than the self-possessed Ola from the lobby! Leaning over her and thrusting his body into her soft bays and grottoes was a creature with hideously fluid limbs. As if in a nightmare, the beast's thick, warty neck turned and he stared directly at Mark. Both Ola and the monster were seeing Mark for real, seeing Mark in all his—

"Yoo hoo!" It was Laura, down on the lawn, calling up to him. "Are you coming or not, cranky pants? We slept through lunch, so we might as well take a walk before dinner."

"Hang on!"

Mark stashed away the Yotsa 7 and hastily dressed. What a creepy vision of that wormy, squiggly man. But Ola—she was hot! How could he face her now without blushing or smirking? Had the *God* Bøk-triggered semiotic scene been a glimpse of the past, the future—or some purely hypothetical scenario, a sex fantasy inherent in his own mind? There was the neural entanglement angle to consider Mark ineluctably flashed on his prior random

glimpses of *shokushu goukan,* or Japanese tentacle porn. Had the Yotsa 7 dredged this kind of imagery from its semiotic data base? Or was there something real to be discovered? Too many possibilities, too many questions…

Laura would have some insights. She'd always been his sounding-board, his confidante—till their absurd falling-out. But to confide in her now would be to admit the existence of the suppressed, illegal and smuggled Yotsa 7. She'd ream him a new blowhole, right? Or would she? Hard to say…

Still dithering, Mark reached the reception area and, with gratitude blooming in his heart, found the desk untenanted. No embarrassing confrontation—yet! Ola must be preparing a meal, or changing bedsheets, or keeping accounts. Or trysting with an alien? A one-woman enterprise demanded a lot!

For a moment the intensity of the Yotsa vision rushed back on him—the dripping water in the dungeon, the mossy sheen upon the stones, the mixed smell of mould and sexual perfume—was there any chance that the vision had been as accurate as a video feed and that, therefore, Ola was even now reaching an unimaginable climax? He almost seemed to hear a rhythmic cry penetrating through the floor boards—or rather, to feel it in the soles of his feet.

Outside, the vibrant, maritime-scented air and penetrating sunlight cleared the fantasies from his cortex. The afternoon seemed made of exotic crystal. Of course he'd tell Laura everything! They still were husband and wife, right?

Mark took Laura's arm in his, like courting Victorians strolling down some seaside boardwalk.

"Let's get away from the hotel a little. I need to tell you something private."

Laura eyed him with amusement and curiosity. "You're not going to reveal you're gay, are you? That it was really Lester Lo, not Beryl, you were after?"

Happy for the light banter, Mark blew her a raspberry. "If you suspect I'm secretly gay after all these years, I'm obviously falling down on my duties. Consider our session just now a preview. We'll see about a main event tonight." This was good. This was solid ground.

They followed a narrow, sandy trail affording well-framed views of the exquisite Norwegian countryside. After ten minutes walking, during which Mark refused to reveal anything, they came to a stone bench on a sloping meadow with a pleasing prospect upon the fjord. The waters were deep, even here at the fjord's tip, and the facing granite cliff plunged straight into the depths.

Something made Mark inspect the bench for any odd lichen patterns analogous to the quasi-organic blobs in the *God Bøk*. Satisfied that no alien patterns lurked, he sat himself and Laura down, then launched into his confession about the cached Yotsa 7 and what it had shown him back in the hotel room.

Laura pondered Mark's story intently, then said, "We have to ask first whether we completely trust the Yotsa 7. After all, it was still in the beta stage, never totally debugged."

"You're not mad at me for holding back the one unit?"

"Of course not! We worked hard to create our brainchild, only to have it stolen by those brutal G-men jerks who only want to kill us. I wish I'd kept one too!"

"Well, I'd stake a lot on the integrity and accuracy of the software—and of the sensing and display mechanisms too. Lo was a genius. If Yotsa shows us a vision of Ola about to be ravished or eaten by some seaweed man—that's gotta mean something. Especially since the vision is wrapped around a pattern in your *God Bøk*. It has some heavy-duty resonance with the reality of the situation here. In our shoes, we can't afford to overlook anything."

"Maybe we need to ask Ola outright what she knows about the *God Bøk*. That is, after you show me that scene through the Yotsa."

"My god, of course! Just ditch any cringing and pussy-footing."

Mark leaned over to kiss Laura. "That's one reason I've always loved you, you're so direct."

"'Only go straight,'" Laura said, quoting a Korean Zen Master whom she'd studied in her college days.

And, as always, Mark countered with a Marx-Brothers-style corny joke, one that bitterness had prevented him from making recently: "I'd like to get something straight between us."

Smiling and holding hands, they made their way back to the hotel, this time taking a long way round the fields and pine groves. They got back with a half hour to spare before supper. They were planning to go upstairs to Room 3 to see what else the *God Bøk* might have to show them, but they were intercepted by Ola, as trim and tidy as before.

"I invite you now for drinks and snacks, yes?"

"Okay, that's fine," said Laura. "I'm starved."

Relaxing into the flow of events, the couple let the petite, clear-skinned Ola lead them into a parlour of shiny chintz armchairs and shelves of antique brick-a-brack. A decanter of wine sat on a little table with five of the smallest glasses that Mark had ever seen. Rare, or extremely potent, or both? Ola doled out a driblet for herself, two for Mark and Laura, and two for a frail and elderly Norwegian couple who spoke no English. No further glasses of wine were to be offered. And a little dish holding precisely four round crackers served as the snack portion of this collation.

Ola gave a little speech, saying everything in both languages, which meant the orientation took considerably longer than expected, especially because the old Norwegian couple kept interrupting Ola with what seemed to be corrections and second thoughts. But Ola treated the old pair kindly, even lovingly, going so far as to give the old woman a reassuring pat on the hand.

In any case, the information on offer was interesting, and it seemed to bear intriguing connections with Mark's vision. The Hotel Fjaerland was an ancient structure, rife with exotic legends, and human habitation on this site stretched back even further. But—despite what Mark and Laura had decided on the bench—he didn't feel ready to question Ola about the accuracy of his Yotsa 7 revelation. His brief sexual fascination with her was dying out. Despite her gentleness with the old Norwegian couple, the young woman seemed increasingly odd and alien, a *Sound-of-Music* archetype filtered through a *Tales From The Crypt* comic.

When Ola had finally concluded her info-dump, the four guests were allowed into the dining-room, where the hostess served out cauliflower soup, smoked fish, new potatoes, and lingonberry pie. Mark managed to buy a full bottle of wine before Ola disappeared into her own private recesses of the hotel.

"Now we can talk," said Laura. "This soup is really nasty, isn't it?"

"Cauliflower should be banned," agreed Mark. "Where do they get off calling it a vegetable? That was some weird stuff that Ola told us, huh?"

"Her spiel was better in Norwegian," said Laura. "What I could understand of it. Ola and those old people have a weird local accent."

"I caught one phrase," said Mark. "The ålefisk mann. The eel man. That's a hella close fit with what I thought I saw through the Yotsa."

"It sounded like she was telling that old couple they'd be happy and safe if they fed themselves to the ålefisk man," said Laura. "I must have heard it wrong. I gather she has some serious history with those two geezers. I think maybe they're related to her."

Mark glanced over at the tremulous oldsters, barely picking at their food. "I wonder what they'd think about about Ola getting it on with the ålefisk man?"

"I was expecting you to say something to her about that, Mr. Straight Shooter."

"Hey—we missed lunch. I was in a rush to get in here for the chow. This fish isn't bad. If it is fish." Mark shoved aside his potatoes and started in on his lingonberry pie. "Seafood and pie in Norway, baby, the land of the midnight sun. And, look, there's a big golden ingot of that smoked fish on the sideboard. And another whole pie. We can have as much as we like. Unless that old Norwegian couple stops us. And unless Ola comes back. I was so hungry I spaced out on some of her rap. Why was she talking about the ålefisk man in the first place?"

"I think it's a local colour thing. Like the sea serpent in Loch Ness? The ålefisk man is said to live beneath the waters of the Fjaerland fjord. He brings joy and wealth to his true believers."

"You know what I'm thinking now?" said Mark, refilling their glasses. "Maybe my vision was dredged out of the local tourist web- sites. The Yotsa always looks online."

"And maybe you added the naked Ola by yourself," said Laura. "Desperate horn-dog that you are."

"Desperate for you," said Mark politely. "More smoked fish and ling-onberry pie, my sweet?"

Ola was still nowhere to be seen. The Norwegian couple left the dining-room precipitously, as if to take advantage of some elderly early-bird special on sleep. Mark heard them tottering down the stairs into the hotel basement—perhaps they'd gotten a cut-rate room below?

Left on their own, Mark and Laura wandered outside into the unending daylight. They collapsed onto a bench, recovering from their heavy meal, hoping for more love-making, but for now just watching how the sun idled across the mountain peaks, never quite going down.

"Hello!" came a clear voice from just behind them. Ola. She was standing in a dark stone arch set into the foundation wall of the hotel. For a moment, the shadows of the arch lent her skin a squamous sheen. She'd let down her brown hair, and her wavy tresses reached nearly to her waist—just as in Mark's Yotsa vision of her. But she wasn't nude, she was wearing a flowing cream- coloured gown with a Pre-Raphaelite look.

Stepping forward, Ola lost the alien, depraved look, and became once more all simple virtue and innocence. She pouted and wagged her finger at Mark. "A friend told me you were spying on him and me. Maybe we are a little flattered."

"You, uh, what do you mean?" said Mark, temporizing. Ola's eyes, blue and deep as the waters of the fjord, held him with a magnetic force.

"I know about your special lenses," said Ola, lowering her voice and drawing closer. "That type of crystal vibrates so sympathetically with our regions. And the fancy handle! So much thinking squeezed into so tight a space." Her words held sexy subtexts that had Mark tingling from groin to gut.

Ola patted a lumpy fold in her dress. "I fetched your aid from your room."

"You can't just go rooting through our luggage!" protested Laura. "Indulge me, Laura, and we three will join in joy very soon," said Ola with an arch smile. "With a fourth partner, my special friend, who governs all that happens here."

Ola drew out the Yotsa 7 and shook the lenses from the handle. "Very elegant. I would like our clever Mark to look at something. I saw my dear friend at naptime today, you know, and he says he is posting an invitation to you."

"Posting it where?" challenged Laura.

Ola raised a forefinger to her lips, like a silent-movie ingénue signalling for secrecy. Mutely she handed Mark the Yotsa and pointed towards the surfboard-sized slab of blotchy stone that rose from the garden's pink star-flowers.

Ola seemed to emanate a disorienting psychic power. Distractedly Mark focused on an embossed silver ring that the woman's pointing finger wore. For a moment he thought it was the Worm Ouroboros, the mythic world-snake who bites his own tail.

But then the fine details of the delicately crafted ornament seemed to swell up and fill Mark's vision, and he could see that the creature was no land-dwelling serpent, but rather an aquatic being, an eel- like branching form.

"The ålefisk man?" murmured Laura, her thoughts in synch with Mark's.

"My secret friend," said Ola simply. "My lover. I call him Elver. Now go and look at the stone. It's a kind of billboard for him. Elver thinks, and the patterns here bloom. I can read them, and with your magic glasses, you can too. Look at it, Mark and Laura. See and rejoice."

Heads together like children peering through a crack, Mark and Laura shared the Yotsa goggles, each of them using one lens, studying the lichen-like patches on the rugged stone. The stele loomed as info-dense as any Egyptian or Mayan relic.

"It's like a webpage almost," said Laura. "A jumble of scenes. Look there, at the bottom. The eel man eating a cow. The grass in the pasture is covered in slime, and the poor animal is bellowing."

"See the villagers chasing the eel man?" said Mark. "And they built fires to block him off from the fjord. Look there, they've caught him."

"And they're cutting off his tendrils and smoking them," added Laura. "Tentacles as thick as logs."

"You were eating that type of meat for supper tonight," interjected Ola. "The ålefisk man is generous to his friends."

"Eating the god," mused Laura. "A mythic archetype."

"The villagers didn't fully kill him, though," put in Mark. "A stub of the eel man is wriggling back into the fjord. And he's growing all the time. He branches like a hydra."

"Yes, yes, but I want you to look at his message near the top," urged Ola. "This is your invitation."

"Oh—oh my," said Laura.

Seen through the Yotsa lenses, the rust-red blotch unfolded to show Mark, Laura, and Ola disporting themselves in the over-large bed of Room 3 upstairs. Someone else was in the bed with them, barely visible beneath the sheets—a playful, squirming figure, lively as an oil-lamp's flame, wet bed linens pasted to his uncanny lineaments.

The Yotsa 7 trembled in Mark's hand. Beside him, Ola was softly singing to herself in Norwegian. An intoxicating sweet musk was drifting from the folds of her gown. As if mesmerized, Mark and Laura let Ola take their hands and lead them upstairs to Room 3.

Far from being cold, Ola was warm and responsive beneath the comforter. She'd insisted on leaving the room's windows wide open, and quite soon, the expected humanoid, anguilliform creature slithered up the porch's columns, across the slanting roof and into the embraces of three lovers. Elver the ålefisk man. The love-making was unspeakably delicious, indescribably foul.

Hours later Mark awoke to the sound of Laura bumping around the room. Of the Yotsa 7, no trace. Slippery eel and human exudates, drying, had encrusted his skin. With the constant daylight, he found it hard to judge the time. Mid-morning, maybe. Memories of last night crashed onto him like a collapsing brick wall. Oh no. Had they really done all that?

"I don't know about you, but I'm getting the hell out of here," said Laura, hoisting her suitcase onto the bed. She already had her slacks and blouse on. She trotted into the bathroom and returned with her toiletries. And then she dropped them all on the floor and burst into wails.

"It's okay, Laura," said Mark, getting out of bed naked. He felt sticky all over. Tainted. "I'm coming with you, don't worry. God. I hope that thing didn't—"

"Didn't lay eggs in us!" said Laura, her voice rising to a subdued shriek. "Oh, Mark, what if we suddenly feel the baby eels wriggling inside our flesh?"

"Did you take a shower yet?"

"Of course. And I used the icky bidet. You shower now, too, Mark. I'll pack for both of us, okay?"

"Yes. I wonder when the next bus or ferry leaves? I don't suppose we can ask—"

"Ask Ola?" said Laura. "How could we let that woman bring us down so low? Do you think she's beautiful, Mark? Do you love her more than me?"

"Of course not. We must have been drunk. Or drugged? Maybe that eel man thing wasn't—"

"Maybe it wasn't real," said Laura, completing his thought. "That's what I keep hoping. Oh, hurry up and get ready before something horrible happens."

Of course just then their door swung open. There was Ola, neat and lush as a Scandinavian buffet, bearing a tray of breakfast foods in her capable hands. She swept in, leaving the door wide open.

"No fears of privacy now," she said, talking in a steady stream lest Mark and Laura interrupt her. "The older couple have—ascended. We have the hotel all to ourselves today. Us three and my dear Elver in his watery caves down below. There's a tunnel that leads from here to a subterranean part of the fjord, you know. Elver and I thought that perhaps—"

"Did you steal our Yotsa 7?" demanded Mark.

"Elver has it," said Ola with a happy smile. "He formulates some wonderful new ideas. But why are you two behaving so—"

"Stay away from us!" cried Laura. "I'll call the police if you come one step closer."

"I don't think you will," said Ola calmly. "I know that your government has marked you two for destruction." She held up her hand for silence. "My Elver—he knows so many things. But there are things we are learning from you. Help us with our plan for your wonderful tool—and your secrets are safe." Ola formed one of her eerily perfect smiles. "If you like, you're welcome to stay on in Fjaerland for quite some time. My parents have left our family farmhouse empty. You could live there if you liked. And perhaps now and then we four could—"

"You disgust me," spat Laura.

"That ålefisk man," put in Mark, overcome with fear. "He didn't implant anything in us, did he? No larvae?"

Ola gave a tinkling laugh. "What a thing to worry about! Elver has no children. He is only one, and he is immortal. One ålefisk man in the world and no ålefisk woman. Elver is lonely. He wishes that humans accepted him and loved him like those silly trolls you see in gift shops. Elver is a far nobler symbol of our Norsk heritage. Those trolls—*pfui*! They rot gullible brains with shopping-mall cuteness. Elver is deeper. Elver wants that many more people eat of his inexhaustible flesh, and that we know freedom from our carking cares. I believe, Mark, that you and your wife are very good at public relations?"

"You couldn't prove that by the mess we engineered for ourselves," said Mark.

"Mark, don't even answer her!" Laura commanded. But her husband noted that she had ceased to bustle with her packing, as if intrigued.

Mark caught Laura's gaze and sought to transmit his innermost thoughts to her, using a wisp of entanglement that had been generated by their sharing of the Yotsa 7 when viewing the stele.

Laura, please listen to me. We have nothing to lose by joining Ola's cause. And maybe a lot to gain. The Yotsa 7 is too weird for humans to control. We need a mythic counterweight. And we need a friend against the feds. Let's ride the bucking, fucking Eel Train to glory. It's a win-win for us and Elver both! Let's trust ourselves, and trust Ola, and trust this creature older than mankind. What do we have to lose?

Their locked glances persisted only a micro-second, but managed to channel a flood of information and feeling. And then they broke the connection.

Calm now, Laura turned to Ola. "What are you imagining that we can do for you?"

Ola grinned. "You do not realize the true potential of your invention. It is not just a receiver, but also a transmitter! This, my Elver has deduced. But it is best if I let him explain in his own way."

Instinctively, Mark shot a look at the open bedroom window, anticipating the second appearance of the eel man. Ola understood his expectations, and corrected them.

"Elver finds sunlight burdensome, and makes his forays into the light but rarely, such as when he initiates newcomers like yourself. To meet with him again, we must go below."

Laura's voice betrayed some nervousness. "Below?"

"Beneath the basement of the Hotel Fjaerland is a natural cavern, connecting via a passage to an underground pool of the fjord. Down to Elver's domain we will march ourselves, and meet him again in joy."

Mark imagined Ola imparted a lascivious tinge to these words, but he tried to ignore it. Had the three of them really enjoyed sex with a humanoid eel? But surely it didn't have to come to that again. Mark told himself that he only wanted to find out if the strange and devious ålefisk man could somehow unkink their problems with the feds.

The hotel basement was pleasantly domestic, containing as it did racks of wine, skis and snowshoes, casks of pickled herring, jars of preserved berries, dangling, log-shaped hunks of smoked meat, and a workbench with little figurines of eel-men standing on two legs with their long tails curled behind them. Ola led them to a trapdoor and down a ladder to the underlying secret cavern.

The first sight to greet them there was less wholesome: the savaged corpses of the elderly couple who'd been the hotel's other lodgers.

"Oh my god!" screamed Laura. "It's a trap!" The oldsters' pathetic, disemboweled bodies lay but a few metres away.

"Run for it!" cried Mark. "Back up the ladder, Laura!" He struck a defensive posture, fully expecting Ola to attack him.

But Ola only stood there gazing at them, her mouth set in a sad smile. "Oh, Mark and Laura, you know so little. These dear old ones, riddled with disease, they came down here to offer Elver their final homage, to lend him their good—their good vibrations?"

"I—I thought I heard you talking about this kind of plan before dinner last night," said Laura. "But I didn't realize you actually meant—"

"Elver grows strong from the numinous grants of his worshippers," said Ola. "If one's life is nearly at an end, it is well to pass one's final energies to the eternal ålefisk."

"Oh, sure," challenged Mark. "That poor old couple came down here and invited that—that eel-thing to slaughter them like hogs? And you're leaving them on the floor to rot?"

Ola winced, and a tear rolled down her cheek. "Tonight I am burying these sad husks in the churchyard, of course. These were, after all, my parents."

"Your parents?" whispered Laura, stepping down off the ladder. "Yes," said Ola, regaining her poise. She tossed her head in a haughty gesture. "My parents. Surely you can understand that I only wished them glory."

The odd woman's sincerity quelled their suspicions, at least temporarily, and, after a quiet exchange of words, Mark and Laura agreed to follow Ola further into the depths.

The echoing cavern was faintly lit by veins of luminous mould crisscrossing the dank stone. On the side towards the fjord, the walls funnelled into a downward-sloping corridor. Along the way they passed a squat stone altar in an alcove. Ola and Elver's trysting spot.

Picking their way further along the uneven but well-swept stone floor, the trio soon reached a subterranean shore where the black water lapped. Here rested patient Elver, his exposed torso gleaming, his lower appendages submerged. He was holding the Yotsa 7 to one of his eyes with a curly tendril that branched from his side.

"Elver, my sweet," sang Ola. "Show our new friends your thoughts."

The glabrous surface of the eel man's body abruptly became a high-res display—his subdermal chromatophores, densely packed, were synched to his mind. And now Mark and Laura took in a little movie scenario.

In Elver's movie, passive viewers around the globe are watching video displays and hand-held gizmos. A steady parade of bad news and horrors marches across their idiot screens. In speeded-up time, the media slaves become increasingly bestial and depraved. But now, from above, a celestial rain of glowing counter-imagery descends upon the benighted citizenry. The images are elegant glyphs encapsulated in comic-strip-style thought balloons: quaint cities amid verdant hills, cathedral-like forests, rich fields of fruits and grain, treasuries of fish and cheeses, temples of learning, artists at work and orchestras at play, joyous carnal orgies, swift ships sailing beneath smiling skies, and scientists peering into the heart of the cosmos. In Elver's movie, the recipients of his ideational manna brighten and perk up. They turn off their screens and address one another face to face, laughing and stretching their limbs. They're fully alive at last.

Mark's spirits rose to see the energizing thought balloons and their effects. He savoured the fusillade of upbeat glyphs, and revelled in the bountiful, idyllic futurescape that the images evoked.

But it was Laura who discerned the ultimate import of Elver's show.

"That flood of counter-programming—the thought balloons— those stand for semiotic ontological transmissions from the Yotsa 7!" she exclaimed. "Elver wants to reverse what we thought was a one-way flow. We've been using the Yotsa 7 to perceive the hidden meanings of images, Mark. But now we can start with the most desirable meanings and wrap our images around them!"

"We'll—we'll make ads that people can't resist," said Mark, slowly. "Ads that change the world."

"Indeed," said the willowy Ola, leaning against Laura's side. "This is Elver's lesson. He is proud to have such clever devotees."

Mark beamed as if he were still ten years old and receiving his father's praise for a perfect report card. But he hadn't quite lost his head.

"If we're going to advertise, we need a product," he said. "You need a cash flow to pay for ads. It's symbiotic—and in a positive way if you have an honest product."

"Elver's Smoked Eel," said Ola, not missing a beat. "With special labels and trademarked Elver figurines. Today we four are designing the packaging and the ads. And thanks to your wonderful Yotsa 7, we are folding in our most utopian dreams."

"You two have thought about this a lot," said Laura. She glanced over at Elver and giggled. The silent Elver responded with a nod.

"Our products will go everywhere, and their glyphic subtexts will remake the world!" declaimed Ola. By now, Elver had wriggled fully out of the water, settling himself near Laura's feet.

"So let's get it done," said Mark, a little distracted by the thoughts evoked by the eel man's proximity.

"Oh, and one other thing," said Laura brightly. "We'll work images of Mark and me into a lot of the ads. We'll be wrapped around glyphs of love and trust and acceptance, you see. That way those government pigs will be primed to pardon our so-called crimes. In case we, uh, ever want to go home."

"We will be mailing our press-kits to whomever you suggest," said Ola smoothly.

The quartet worked congenially all that day in the mould-lit cavern. Elver wasn't a bad guy, for being an immortal subaqueous demigod who communicated via pictures on his flesh.

Around tea time they took a break, and Ola fetched them a picnic basket of wine, berries, bread, and smoked eel-meat, along with a blanket to make it more comfortable on the stony edge of the underground lake.

As he lay resting from the repast, idly dreaming up still grander plans, Mark noticed one of Elver's tendrils snaking across the cloth to alight on Laura's leg. Laura sighed and smiled, shifting onto her back. Ola was watching too, and batting her eyes. Mark felt himself slipping into the same erotic intoxication that had possessed him the night before. He turned to look at the ålefisk man.

Although Elver possessed no precise human countenance, Mark could detect what passed for a smile in an eel.

THE HPL COMMONPLACE BOOK

11 Odd nocturnal ritual. Beasts dance and march to musick. [x]

Dancing with Your Familiar: A Manual for Witches and Warlocks is requisite reading for any lonely practitioner of the black arts. No longer need the hideously deformed sorcerer, mage, crone or necromancer lack for a date on a Saturday evening, when all the other villagers, even the hybrid merpeople, are cavorting at the local dance or ritual invocation. A simple transformation spell turns your hellish cat, bat, owl, or hound into an alluring human companion of either gender, fit to whisk about the dance floor as the envy of all. No need to make banal chit-chat with your terpsichorean partner either, so long as you remember to keep a pocketful of your familiar's favourite treats. Although those coastal wizards who favour seal familiars are advised to try dried kelp rather than raw fish, if they wish to remain socially acceptable.

24 Dunsany—Go-By Street Man stumbles on dream world—returns to earth—seeks to go back—succeeds, but finds dream world ancient and decayed as though by thousands of years.

The Michelin Guide to the Ruined Cities of Futurity is a must-buy companion for travellers in the astral realms. Whether the spectral tourist wishes to discover the best spot for ghoulish cemetery snacks, the most well-preserved library of mind-shattering tomes, or the café *tres chic* where ghosts of the *beau monde* endlessly replay their assignations, this volume has all the answers for a variety of cities across many dimensions. Be sure to check out their sidebars on how much to tip skeleton staffers and where to purchase the dustiest cerements.

51 Enchanted garden where moon casts shadow of object or ghost invisible to the human eye.

Martha Stewart's Handbook of Phantom Gardening is calculated to let even the rankest amateur produce a soul-curdling display of teratogenic horrors that will keep the whole neighbourhood awake and shivering beneath their beds by night. With the aid of special seeds and tools (available quite reasonably from Martha's own catalogue), plus a set of prisms designed to impart special quickening qualities to moonlight, the beginning occult horticulturist will soon be able to harvest a fine crop of gruesome vegetal nightmares. Share the bounty with your neighbours, and they'll never steal your more conventional produce such as apples or tomatoes again!

98 Hideous old house on steep city hillside—Bowen St.— beckons in the night—black windows—horror unnam'd— cold touch and voice—the welcome of the dead.

Selling Your Shunned House: A Realtor's Guide will help even the most inexperienced real estate salesman unload—at a good profit—that cursed property in a jiffy! The writer is an expert of long standing, having once sold Charles Dexter Ward's home with the original malign inhabitant still in it! Tips on dealing with interdimensional cracks in the spacetime continuum or countervailing claims by Elder Gods, evicting undead tenants, and placating the residents of trespassed burial grounds will give confidence to any agent. This tome does not neglect arcane rituals such as burying a statue of Cthulhu upside-down on the property to invoke his aid. A complex discussion on what to do if your client is eaten before the deal can be sealed concludes the book.

PROFESSOR FLUVIUS'S PALACE OF MANY WATERS

I awoke in a soft, damp bed, atop the covers, not knowing my name. A standing man hovered solicitously over me. His genial face, with wine-dark eyes, reminded me of someone I thought I should know. Thick white wavy locks cascaded to his shoulders. A Van Dyke beard of equal snowiness did little to conceal his jovial, ebullient expression. Yet despite this arctic pel-tage, his unlined face and clean limbs radiated a youthful vitality.

"Ah, Charlene, you're with us now! Splendid! We have much to do."

My name was Charlene then. That seemed right.

The man announced, "I am Professor Fluvius. Can you stand?"

"I think so " Professor Fluvius placed a hand on my shoulder, and a sudden access of galvanic spirits coursed through me. "Why, certainly, I can stand!"

In one fluid movement I came to my bare feet on the warm wooden floorboards. I was wearing an unadorned white samite smock, the hem of which hung to just below my knees. A balmy wind blowing in through an open window, past lazily twitching gauzy curtains, stirred my robe and conveyed to me certain bodily sensations indicating that undergarments of any sort appeared to be lacking in my wardrobe. But the clement summer atmosphere certainly did not require such.

Professor Fluvius, I noted now, was dressed entirely in aquamarine blue, from long-tailed coat to spats. He took my hand as a favourite uncle might, and again I felt a surge of vigour through my cells.

"Let me introduce you to the other ladies first."

We stepped forward toward the door leading from the single room, which appeared to be a guest bedchamber of a quality sort.

Looking back at the bed where I had awakened to myself for the first time, I saw a long slim twisting tendril of bright green water weed adorning the damp duvet.

The carpeted corridor beyond that room hosted a dozen other doors, each bearing a brass number. Professor Fluvius and I crossed diagonally to Number 205.

"You rejoined us in my own modest quarters, Charlene. All quite proper, I assure you. But just across the corridor here, I have chartered an entire suite for you and your peers."

Professor Fluvius knocked, then cracked the door of 205 wide without awaiting a response.

Inside, draped languorously across an assortment of well- upholstered chairs and divans, six smiling women calmly awaited our arrival; plainly, they had been expecting us. Exhibiting a variety of beautiful physiognamies of mixed ethnicities, they all wore simple shifts identical to mine, and remained similarly unshod.

I caught my own reflection then in a canted cheval glass, and was perhaps immoderately pleased to find myself wholly a match to my sisters in terms of mortal beauty.

"Charlene, allow me to introduce your comrades to you. Callie, Lara, Minnie, Lila, Praxie and Sally. Ladies, this is Charlene."

The six women trilled a tuneful assortment of greetings, several of them playfully abbreviating my name to "Charl" or "Charlie," and I responded in kind. Once they sensed somehow my ability to blend into their pre-established harmony, they were up off their perches and clustering around me, indicating by various endearments and mild sororal caresses how happy they were to have me among their number.

Professor Fluvius watched us beneficently for a short while, but then cut short our mutual admiration society.

"Ladies, have you forgotten? We have an important appointment to keep. Let us be on our way now!"

So saying, and recovering his ocean-blue topper from a hat-tree, the professor led the way out of the suite, and we all obediently followed.

A staircase at the end of the corridor debouched after a long single arcing flight into a splendid lobby, and I received confirmation, if needed, that this establishment was a commercial hotel. The large pillared space was thronged with people—all of them, male and female alike, dressed with considerably more formality than I and my sisters. Nor did I see any man sporting anything like the beryl suit worn by the professor. It was unsurprising, then, that our passage across the lobby toward the street entrance should attract stares and semi-decorous exclamations. And this attention was not minimized by the professor's unprompted yet effervescent lecture to us, his charges.

"Witness the glories of the Tremont House, ladies. The first hotel ever to incorporate running water, and thus a fit establishment to temporarily host Professor Fluvius and his Naiads during the early portion of our Boston stay!"

The professor seemed intent on advertising himself and us, and it was at this juncture that I began to apprehend that I had become, willy-nilly, part of a commercial venture of some sort.

We exited the hotel through its grand colonnaded entrance on Tremont Street and crossed a miry sidewalk and concourse, nimbly dodging carriages and carts.

Amazingly, I found myself stepping unerringly on an irregular trail of clean patches amidst the offal and manure, thus succeeding in keeping my bare feet unsullied. I noticed that my sisters trod a similar random series of sterile stepping stones.

Or was it that the uniformly dirty pavement spontaneously developed virginal patches beneath our feet?

As we seven attractive women and pavonine man hiked determinedly through the streets of Boston, we began to attract a crowd of followers, picaroons and mudlarks mostly, whose unsolicited comments veered more toward gibes and lewd offerings of unwanted intimate services than had those of the Tremont House crowd. But I and my dignified sisters ignored the verbal affronts from the swelling ranks of our entourage, and Professor Fluvius seemed actually to relish their attentions.

"That's it, lads, that's it! Roll up, roll up! Follow us for the most exciting news of the decade!"

Almost immediately after leaving the hotel, we found ourselves in a park full of greenery, and were able to indulge our bare feet on grass. But this respite was short-lived, as we soon exited the Public Gardens and proceeded uptown on a street labelled Boylston.

My eye was drawn to a posted bill advertising a new play—*The Children of Oceanus*, by Eleuthera Stayrook—at the Everett Hall Theatre, and bearing the commencement date of July 12th, 1877.

And so it was that I had my first inkling of what year it was in which I had awakened—assuming the poster to be of recent vintage, an assumption which its unweathered appearance supported.

Reaching a cross-street named Clarendon, we turned and encountered a construction site. Here, a vast project sprawling across several blocks was in its obvious end stages.

The building at the centre of the site was a church of soaring magnificence. Not as large as a cathedral, the brown-hued sanctuary nonetheless radiated a deep gravitas counterbalanced by an exuberant sense of joy.

Workmen swarmed around the nearly complete structure, taking down scaffolding, entering the interior with loads of fine materials, sweeping up debris. One man seemed in charge of the general organized hubbub, and it was toward him that Professor Fluvius made a beeline.

At my side, the woman introduced to me as Plaxie now spoke in a stage-whisper, leaning her pert-nosed, black-ringleted head close to my own auburn locks. Her breath smelled mildly of fish.

"If you think you've seen the Prof put on a show so far, just wait till he gets to work on this mark!"

We now—my comrades, and the raggle-taggle flock that had attached itself to us—came to a stop around the overseer. He was a plump gent with a thick chestnut beard, hair parted down the middle, and an intelligently playful twinkle to his eyes that offset his otherwise stern demeanour. He wore an expensive brown suit. Professor Fluvius hailed him in a loud voice more suited to the baseball outfield than face-to-face conversation, and I could tell he was playing to the crowd.

"You, good sir, are Henry Hobson Richardson, the veritable visionary architect of this grand dream in rough stone we see before us!"

Richardson seemed more amused than perturbed. "Yes, sir, I am. And may I enquire your name and purpose?"

"I am Professor Nodens Fluvius, and I am here to give you your next commission!"

"Indeed? And what might that be?"

"A public bath house!"

Loud guffaws and taunts arose from the spectators, but Fluvius remained unperturbed, and Richardson continued to express some unfeigned interest at this odd commission.

"A public bath house, Professor Fluvius? I assume you are thinking along the lines of the municipal facilities found on the Continent. But are you unaware of the spectacular failure of the Mott Street Bath House in New York City, some twenty years ago? Since then, no private investor nor any municipality in our great nation has deemed such an enterprise feasible. Nor has the public clamoured for such facilities."

"Ah, but that is because all businessmen and politicos have lacked my farsighted conception of what such an establishment could offer. And as for the public—they know not what they want till it is presented to them."

At this point, the professor encompassed us seven maidens with a sweep of his arm, as if to indicate that we would appear uppermost on his bill of fare. Some of my sisters lowered their glances demurely, but I maintained a bold gaze directed at the hoi polloi, even when raucous huzzahs went up from the crowd. For a moment, I wondered with alarm if we were meant to be courtesans in this hypothetical establishment. But then I recalled the clean organic thrill of the liquid energies that had flowed from the professor's touch, and felt reassured of his honest intentions toward us.

"Moreover," continued the professor, "no prior entrepreneur has held a doctorate in hydrostatics from La Sapienza University in Rome, as do I.

Surely you know of the marvellous accomplishments of the ancient Romans in this sphere...? Well, the ultra-modern technics of boilers, valves, conduits, gravity-fed reservoirs and suchlike that I intend to install will make the Baths of Caracalla look like a roadside ditch!"

At the mention of a technological challenge, the architect Richardson developed an even keener expression. "Speak on, Professor."

"I have conceived of a palatial public bathhouse that will employ the latest in hydropathic techniques to promote robust health and invigoration in all its patrons. Combining methodologies I learned at first hand from Vincenz Priessnitz himself at Grafenburg with subtle refinements of my own devising, I can guarantee to reform drunkards, cure the halt and lame, invigorate the intellect of scholars and schoolboys alike, and induce passion in sterile marriages—all for mere pennies a visit!"

This last boast raised further hoots and japes from the crowd, who nonetheless, I sensed, evinced real interest on some deep level at the professor's pitch. Richardson, meanwhile, seemed to be cogitating seriously on the proposal as well, unconsciously rubbing his sizeable vest-swathed tummy as an aid to cogitation.

Grinning, Professor Fluvius awaited the architect's response— which finally came in the form of a question.

"How is this ambitious project to be funded, Professor? I do not work in anticipation of a portion of future profits."

"All is assured, Mister Richardson. I assume pure alluvial gold would be deemed legal tender...?"

The professor removed a cowhide poke from a suit pocket. Uncinching the poke's neck, he grabbed Richardson's hand and poured a mound of glittering golden grit into his cupped palm. Richardson's eyes expanded to their full diameter. Professor Fluvius dropped the poke atop the mound and said, "Consider this your retainer, I pray, good sir."

Very carefully, Richardson poured the gold back into the poke and deposited the pouch in his own suit. "Professor Fluvius, you have your architect."

A roar of acclaim went up from the crowd. I realized that their massed attention had been part of the professor's sly plan to add public pressure to compel Richardson's assent. Surely by tomorrow this commission would be spread across all the newspapers of Boston.

The two men shook hands. Professor Fluvius said, "I am staying at the Tremont House, Mister Richardson. I anticipate your dining there tonight with me, so that we may refine our plans. And oh, yes, one last matter. I shall need the establishment finished and ready to open its doors in three months' time."

"Three months' time! For an edifice of any sizeable scale? Impossible!"

Professor Fluvius removed two more plump pokes from his pocket and handed them over to Richardson, saying, "That, Mister Architect, is a word we shall not allow to trouble us again."

* * * *

I approached the Palace of Many Waters across the modest plaza of varicoloured granite from Barre, Vermont, that fronted its façade. A warm November day, its sunshine still only half exhausted, had left the stones comfortable to my bare feet. But I imagined that neither I nor my sisters would be discommoded even by the arrival of winter.

At my elbow strode the visitor I had met at the train station: Dr. Simon Baruch. Of medium height and trim physique, dressed in a respectable checked suit, he boasted a full head of dark hair and neatly trimmed thin moustache and chin spinach. He walked with a dignified bearing that reflected his past military service, as a surgeon during the War Between the States.

I had met the doctor at the terminus of the Boston and Providence railroad line, adjacent to the Public Gardens. From thence we walked a few blocks riverward, until we came to Beacon, that avenue which bordered the Charles River. We turned left and proceeded a few more blocks to the intersection of Beacon and Dartmouth, where the Palace reared its mighty battlements.

Perched on the banks of the River Charles (one single-storey wing housing the professor's offices and private quarters in fact extended out on stilts above the flood), the Palace was a fantasy of minarets and oriel windows, gables and slate slopes, copper flashing and painted gingerbread. Like some Yankee version of the famous Turkish Baths of Manchester, England, the Palace seemed a *hamam* fit for *ifrits*—to adopt a Muslim perspective.

After demolition of a few inconvenient pre-existing structures, construction of the Palace had been accomplished in a mere ten weeks, without stinting materials or design, thanks to an army of labourers working round the clock; the ceaseless management and encouragement of Mr. Richardson; and a steady decanting of alluvial gold from the seemingly inexhaustible coffers of our dear professor. (And how marvellously I had matured myself in those weeks, almost as if a new personality had been established upon my own nascent foundations in synchrony with the Palace's construction.)

Our doors had opened in mid-October, just three weeks ago, and in that time the Palace had been perpetually busy. We were open for business seven days a week, twenty-four hours a day, and there were very few stretches when the influx into the Palace was not a copious stream.

Now Dr. Baruch and I stopped hard by the large, impressive main entrance so that he could marvel for a moment at the parade of patrons: mothers with children, horny-handed labourers, clerks and costermongers, urchins and pedlars, soldiers and savants from Harvard and the Society of Natural History. I noted every type of man, woman and child, from the most humble and ragged to the most refined and eminent members of the *bon ton*, all desirous of becoming clean in a democratic fashion. True, their entrance fees differed, and they would be diverted into different grades of facilities once inside. But all had to enter by the same gate—a gate above which was graven the Palace's motto:

KEEP CLEAN, BE AS FRUIT, EARN LIFE, AND WATCH,
TILL THE WHITE-WING'D REAPERS COME.

* * * *HENRY VAUGHAN, THE SEED GROWING SECRETLY

I noted Dr. Baruch's gaze alighting upon the motto, and, after taking a moment to apprehend it, he turned to me and said, "An apt phrase from the Silurist, and not without a metaphysical complement to its ostensible carnal focus. Were you aware that the poet's twin brother, Thomas, was an alchemist?"

"I fear I am uneducated in such literary matters, Dr. Baruch. Our Professor, however, is a man of much learning, and is highly desirous of your conversation."

Dr. Baruch laughed. "I can tell when I am being politely hustled along. Let us go visit your employer."

We circumvented the Bailey's Baffle Gates through which the paying customers had to pass and found ourselves in the Palace's lofty atrium.

Like most of the interior spaces of the Palace, the lofty, vaulted atrium was tiled with gorgeously glazed ceramic creations, representing both abstract and pictorial designs, the latter of a predominantly marine bent. The hard surfaces granted an echoic resonance to the gabble of voices and footfalls. High stained glass windows rained down tinted light upon the hustling masses as they filed in orderly lines towards the towel-dispensing stations and thence to the disrobing rooms. Naturally, the sexes were separated at this point—save for mothers shepherding children under a certain age—as they would be in the baths.

I guided Dr. Baruch behind the scenes, until we reached the door to Professor Fluvius's private offices. I knocked and received acknowledgement to enter.

Professor Fluvius's unique maple desk, a product of the Herter Brothers firm of New York, was shaped like a titanic conch shell. Behind this cyclopean design sat the man whose face was the first visage I had seen upon attaining consciousness. His ivory tresses, longer even than before, fell past the shoulders of his cerulean suit. Behind him, a window looked out upon the sail-dotted Charles, toward the Cambridge shore. It was cracked a few inches to allow the heady scents of the river inside.

Professor Fluvius ceased fussing with a ledger when we entered, slapping its boards shut decisively, then rose to his feet with a broad smile and came out from behind the desk, hand outstretched.

"Dr. Baruch! A genuine pleasure, sir! Thanks you so much for responding to my humble invitation. I hope to present you with a professional challenge worthy of your talents "

I hung back near the door, hoping to hear the professor's proposal, as I was intrigued by Dr. Baruch's character, insofar as it had been vouchsafed to me in our short acquaintance, and his potential role in our enterprise.

But Professor Fluvius would have none of my impertinent curiosity. Pulling a turnip watch from his pocket, he examined it and then addressed me.

"Charlene, don't you have an appointment soon with one of your special clients?"

I knew full well who awaited me upon the hour, but dissembled. "Oh, Professor, I had forgotten. Pardon me."

"No offence needing pardon, my dear. But you'd best be streaming onward now."

I had perforce to leave their presence then.

But I was not to be stymied from my eavesdropping.

What a change in my nature from the humble, timid deference shown to the professor upon my first foray into consciousness! It was not that I honoured him any the less, nor did my desires deviate significantly from his—insofar as I plumbed either his motives or my own. But I had developed a stubborn sense of my own desires, and a reluctance to be thwarted.

Outside in the hall, I did not head immediately back toward the main bulk of the thronging Palace, but instead approached a nearby window, lowered of course against the November chill. I opened it and peered out.

Some twelve feet below me, the happy waters of the Charles burbled past on their way to the sea, chuckling among the freshly tarred pilings supporting this wing. It would have been a straight, uninterrupted drop to that wet embrace, had it not been for one feature: a kind of catwalk or boat-bumper about halfway down, installed against accidental collisions.

I slipped over the window sill and lowered myself down till my toes met the rough planks. Then I made my way stealthily to a position just below the window of the professor's study.

"—but inside," boomed Fluvius's voice, "inside, Dr. Baruch, I think you will agree with me that they are as dirty as ever. The waters beneath the skin. You can clean the outer man—and that's a fine start—but the inner man is another matter entirely. A much- neglected matter."

"I confess," responded Baruch, "that I have often considered the possibility of tinkering with the interior flora of the human body, with an eye toward remedying several inherent bodily ills. Many are the moments, mired in the bloody tent of a field hospital or the sputum-flecked ward of a slum asylum, when I fantasized about bolstering the body's natural defences with a dose of some beneficial live culture."

"Yes, yes, I knew of your researches, Dr. Baruch! Just why I summoned you out of all your peers. And my dreams tally precisely with yours! I believe I have formulated a potent nostrum that will benefit mankind in just such a fashion as you envision. My potion will not only re-order the patient's defensive constitution, but also contribute to a more orderly patterning of nerve impulses in the brain, promoting more cogent and disciplined thought forms."

Baruch was silent for a moment, before responding: "If that's the case, Professor Fluvius, then what need do you have of me and my skills?"

Fluvius sounded slightly embarrassed, for the first time in my memory. "My trials of this patent medicine of mine have been not wholly successful. Certain of my subjects did not sustain a full recovery. Admittedly, I was working with gravely ill specimens to begin with, but still— I had hoped for better results. But I realized after such setbacks that I lacked the precise anatomical knowledge of a trained physician such as yourself. It is this expertise that I desire you to contribute to the cause. As for salary, I know you are above such plebeian considerations. But let me assure you, your monetary compensation will be far above any salary you could earn elsewhere. Will you join me in this quest to improve the lot of our fellow man, Dr.?"

Crouching below the window as the sun continued to sink and a brisk breeze blew up my gown, I eagerly awaited Dr. Baruch's response. But my concentration was shattered upon the instant by the sensation of a cold and clammy hand encircling my ankle!

Only with supreme willpower did I stifle all but the most muted involuntary shriek that would have betrayed me to those inside. Luckily, a gull screamed at that very moment to further cover my inadvertent alarm.

Heart pounding, I whipped my head down and around to see who could possibly have grabbed me under such unlikely circumstances. The shaggy head and leering ugly countenance of Usk greeted my gaze. He stood ape-like on the crossbeams of the pilings, evidently pleased as Punch to have caught me in this compromising situation. Just prior the Palace's opening three weeks ago, a contingent of the Swamp Angels had visited Professor Fluvius as he was giving us Naiads a lecture on our duties. We watched with some trepidation and unease as these hoodlums swaggered into our sanctuary. They boldly demanded a weekly stipend as "protection money," in order to ensure that the Palace remained unmolested in its operations.

Professor Fluvius seemed to agree, and they went their way.

But then he summoned Usk.

As if out of the woodwork, the gnomish gnarled fellow, dressed in rough working-man's garb, appeared. None of us had ever seen him before. But he seemed on intimate terms with the professor.

"Usk, would you see to it that those churlish fellows do not disturb us ever again?"

Usk laughed, and shivers went down my spine, and likewise along my sisters', I sensed sympathetically.

"Righto, Prof! I'll learn them a lesson they won't soon forget." As mysteriously as he had appeared, Usk vanished.

The Swamp Angels had not troubled the Palace since. And I had heard that, after some enigmatic cataclysm among their ranks, the wounded remnants of their forces had been absorbed by the Gophers and the Ducky Boys.

Since that incident, Usk had surfaced occasionally to carry out the professor's bidding. But none of us knew where he lived, or how he passed his idle hours.

Now I was face to face with him—in a manner of speaking, since actually he had a more prominent view of my bare nether parts than of my countenance. I resolved not to let him know how much he had affrighted me.

In a whisper, I demanded, "What do you want of me?"

Usk husked out his own words. "Prof'd be a tad peeved, if'n he found out you was keyholing him."

I adopted my most winsome ways. "Must you tell him?"

"Not if'n I don't choose to."

"And what could possibly induce you to choose such a merciful course?"

"Let's say if'n I were to receive certain favours from a certain lady—favours which I'd be more than happy to make explicit to you. Tonight, for instance, after your work's all done."

Usk's grip tightened on my ankle—the rough skin of his palm feeling like scales—and I quailed interiorly. But he had me in a bind. I certainly did not wish to appear a sneak and gossip in the eyes of Professor Fluvius. No, I had to submit.

"Where should we meet?"

"I dwell in the lowest cellar, by the boilers. Southwest corner. That's where you'll find my doss.

"I—I'll be there."

Leering once more, Usk released my ankle, prior to slipping away under the floorboards and among the pilings, sinuous as a fish.

Refocusing my attentions on the study window, I heard only the clink of glasses and an exchange of pleasantries. I had to assume the deal had been sealed, and that Dr. Baruch would be staying with us.

And now I needed to keep my appointment.

* * * *

I pattered barefoot swiftly past the gaudy marble entrances to the enormous, rococo common rooms, big as ropewalks, where the masses of men and women bathed in segregated manner. The sounds of gay and enthusiastic splashy ablutions echoed outward from these natatoria. I could picture the water jetting from the bronze heads of dolphins, the flickering gas lights reflected off the pools, the cakes of fragrant soaps embossed with the Palace's trademark conch shell, the long-handled brushes and plump sponges, the naked human bodies in all their equally agreeable shades of flesh and states of leanness and corpulence. The imagined scene delighted me. The conception of so many happy people sporting like otters or seals in a pristine liquid environment seemed utterly Edenic to me. I was more convinced than ever that Professor Fluvius's Palace of Many Waters was a force for beauty and goodness in this often shabby and cruel world.

Once beyond this area open to the general public—the hubbub abating and I having circumvented with a smile and a nod one of the Palace's liveried guardians stationed so as to limit deeper ingress solely to the elite—I had access to an Otis Safety Elevator. I stepped aboard along with a man I recognized as the Mayor of Boston, a Mr. Prince: grey hair low across his brow, walrus moustache. He nodded politely to me, and sized me up with the same look a chef might bestow on a prize tomato.

"You're the one they call Charlie, aren't you?"

"Yes, sir."

"Well, I'm slated to see your sister Praxie today. But perhaps next time you'll attend me."

"I'd be delighted, sir."

The rattling mechanism brought us to the second floor of our establishment. I parted from Mayor Prince, and watched him enter the room labelled "Praxithea."

On this level of the Palace were the private rooms for our more privileged clientele, where bathing occurred in elegant tubs accommodating from two to several bathers. Included on this level were the seven special suites assigned to us Naiads. In these chambers, the waters themselves were perfumed and salted, and certain luxurious individual attentions could be paid to the selected patrons.

I did not enter directly the suite whose brass plate proclaimed it "Charlene," but instead stepped through an innocuous unmarked door and into a connecting changing room. There I doffed my gown and donned a bandeau top across my full bosom and a loin cloth around my broad hips, leaving most of my honey-coloured skin bare. I let down my long chestnut hair, and stepped through to where my client awaited.

Frederick Law Olmstead had accumulated fifty-five years of life at this date. The famed architect, known to the nation primarily for his magnificent design of New York's Central Park, boasted a large head bald across the crown, a wild crop of facial hair, and a penetrating expression betokening a certain wisdom and insight into the ways of the world, as well as hinting at burning creative instincts. His supervisory work in the field had kept him moderately fit, although he had not entirely escaped a certain paunchiness of middle-age.

Now he sat, naked and waist-deep in a capacious ceramic footed trough steaming with soapy, jasmine-scented water, puffing on a cigar and looking already well advanced on the road to relaxation and forgetful of his vocational cares, even before my ministrations. Olmstead had been my client since the Palace opened, and we were on familiar terms. He evidently found me a congenial bath partner, and I had to confess that I had become more than professionally enamoured of him. He had always treated me with kindness and respect and a liberal generosity.

"Ah, Charlie, you're a sight for weary eyes! Join me, dear. I need to disburden myself of the day's headaches."

I slipped gracefully into the tub, sliding up all slippery into his embrace, and Olmstead began to soliloquize me. I kept mum yet receptive.

"This newest project of mine is a bugger, Charlie. Turning a swamp into a park! Sheer insanity. The Fens were never meant to be other than a flood plain or tidal estuary. And yet somehow the city wants me to convert them to made lands, a pleasure pavilion for the masses, part of what they're already calling my 'Emerald Necklace.' Can you fathom what's involved in such a project? Not only do I have to contend with the waters of the Charles, but also those of Muddy River and Stony Brook, which likewise feed into that acreage. I'm going to have to erect dams and pumps, then drain and grade, before layering in an entire maze of culverts and

sewers. Truck in gravel and soil, landscape the whole shebang— So much of this city is made land already, hundreds of acres reclaimed from a primeval bog. The civic fathers imagine they can wrest any parcel they desire from the aboriginal waters. Mayor Prince and his whole Vault cabal are dead set on this project. But this time their reach exceeds their grasp. It's a mad folly, I tell you!"

Olmstead paused, puffing on his cigar, then said with altered tone, "Yet if it could be done—what a triumph!"

I felt proud of Olmstead's ambition and fervour. Intuiting that he had expended his verbal anxiety, I said, "If anyone is capable of accomplishing such a feat, Frederick, it's you. But you must return to the project tomorrow with a relaxed mind and body. Enough speech. Allow me to do my job now."

Willingly, Olmstead stubbed out his cigar in a wrought-iron tub- side appliance. I secured a cake of lanolin-rich lilac soap and began thickly to lather up my own form with graceful motions, all the while allowing the ends of my wet hair to drape sensuously about Olmstead like enticing tendrils.

When I had attained a sufficient soapy slickness, I commenced to apply my rich body as an active wash-cloth across his whole frame. I understand that in far-off Nippon there is a class of women known as *geishas*, whose professional practices resemble what we Naiads at the Palace deliver. But how Professor Fluvius ever came to know of them, in order to use as models for his business, I cannot say.

Because the business of the Palace continued round the clock, and some of us must perforce tend the evening shift, the third- floor communal sleeping suite for us Naiads held only four of us at midnight: myself, Lara, Minnie and Lila. It were best to picture us, lounging drowsily on our respective feather mattresses, as four Graces, hued in the sequence above-named: honey, olive, alabaster and tea.

We chattered for a while of gossipy inconsequentials, as any women will, before Lila said, "I see that our newest employee has already been assigned a laboratory."

How quickly news travelled in this aqueous environment, like scent to a shark!

"Do you mean Dr. Baruch?" asked Lara, batting her thick eyelashes. "I wouldn't mind being his assistant. It would make a nice change from the soap-and-slither routine with the high muck- a-mucks."

Minnie asked, "What's the nature of his work?"

"Rumour has it he's crafting some kind of purgative for the rubes," responded Lila.

Lara pulled a face. "I shouldn't care to help in that case, lest he need a subject for his trials."

I did not add any details from my own stock of overheard information. The thoughts of the payment I owed Usk in return for that data were too discouraging.

Pretty soon after this, my sisters fell asleep, allowing me to slip out without needing to respond to any inquiries about my late- night errands.

The same elevator that had delivered me from street-level to the second-floor now took me from third to lowest cellar. Here I entered a phantasmagorical, almost inhuman world.

The sub-basement held all the apparati that allowed the Palace to function. I felt much like an animalcule venturing into a human's guts.

Congeries of brass pipes of all dimensions, from pencil-thin to barrel-thick, threaded the space, producing a veritable labyrinth. Some pipes leaked steam; some were frosted with condensation. Valves and dials and taps proliferated. The pipes led into and out of huge rivet-studded reservoirs, from which escaped various floral and mineral scents.

Beyond this initial impression of tubular matrices loomed the many boilers, giant radiant Molochs, each one fed and stoked by its own patented "automatic fireman" apparatus, which fed coal in from vast bins at a steady clip, obviating the need for human tenders.

Indeed, Professor Fluvius's early boast—to render the Baths of Caracalla insignificant—appeared fulfilled.

I began to perspire. Vertigo assailed me. I felt incredibly distant from all the sources of my strength, amidst this controlled industrial chaos. Usk had said the southwest corner was his lair. But which direction was which?

I wandered for what seemed like ages, meeting no one in this sterile factory, before glimpsing, beneath a large, wall-mounted mechanical message-board affair, a tumbled heap of bedclothes. As I approached, I noted that the message-board was of the type found in Newport mansions, by means of which masters could communicate with distant servants through the medium of dropped or rotated printed discs. This must be how Profesor Fluvius summoned Usk at need.

The musty midden of bedclothes stirred and out of the stained regalia rose Usk. To my horror and disgust, he was utterly naked, his powerful, hirsute twisted limbs such a contrast to the well- formed appearance of Olmstead or my other clients.

Usk conferred a look of randy appreciation on me, a favour which I could easily have foregone.

"Ah, beauty steps down into the gutter. I am glad you made it unnecessary for me to communicate with the Professor. He's got too many pressing matters on his mind. Big doings, big doings. If you only knew…"

Usk seemed to want to disclose some secret to me, but I did not pursue his bait, for fear of a hook within. So he continued.

"It's a kindness to spare ol' Fluvius any knowledge of your trifling indiscretions. Howsomever, you are not here for us to discuss our mutual master. Sit down, sit down, join me on my humble pallet!"

I sat, and of course, to no one's surprise, Usk immediately began to paw me without any charade of seduction, his hands roaming at will under my gown.

I would like to say that his touch left me cold. But the truth was otherwise. To my chagrin, I sensed in Usk's blunt and callous gropings a portion of the same galvanic power that had thrilled me when the professor first touched me in the Tremont Hotel, so many months ago. It was almost as if Usk, the professor, and I were all related, sharing the same sympathies and humours I felt with my fellow Naiads.

No merit resides in delving into the sordid details of the next two hours. Usk had his lusty way with me, not once or twice but thrice, and deposited his thick spunk in several unconventional places.

At last, though, he seemed sated. Sated, yet still demanding. "You'll be back tomorrow night, my dear. Or the professor and I

will have that unwelcome conversation about your goosey-goosey-gander-where-do-you-wander ways."

I sighed dramatically in a put-upon fashion, yet not without some falsity of emotion. Truly, after tonight's tumble, future encounters with Usk would not be such an unknown burden. "I suppose I have no choice..."

Suddenly, as if my words had pleased him or opened up some further bond between us, he reached beneath his pallet and pulled out—a book!

"Would you—would you read this to me? Please? I—I can't "

I took the volume. The title page proclaimed it to be *The Water- Babies*, by Charles Kingsley.

"'Once upon a time,'" I began, "'there was a little chimney-sweep, and his name was Tom.'"

* * * *

The next several weeks sped by in a busy round of work, sleep, intercourse and two-person Chautauqua between Usk and myself, with the text of our studies moving on, after *Water-Babies*, to Mr. MacDonald's *At the Back of the North Wind*. I could not honestly say I found this regimen imposed by Usk without its thrills and rewards, and on the whole, what with work and all, each of my days passed in a pleasant whirl of activity.

Several times the professor took all seven of us girls out with him on various expeditions across Massachusetts and nearby New England. Ostensibly, these were gay recreational outings to reward us for our diligent services. But in reality, I suspected that they were calculated to serve at least as much as advertisements for the Palace.

Late in December, on a mild day, we went to Rocky Point Amusement Park in Rhode Island. The place had been much in the news, since President Hayes had recently visited and become the first sitting president of this forward-looking nation to utilize a newfangled telephonic device located on the premises. (He had placed a call to Providence, purpose unreported.)

Even this late in the season, the Shore Dinner Hall was still serving its traditional quahog chowder and clamcakes fare, and we all ate to repletion, amidst much laughter and chatter.

At one point, without warning, the skies darkened and the waters of Narragansett Bay became troubled. It seemed as if our little excursion would be dampened. I looked up from my half-eaten tenth greasy clam-cake and noted that, across the hall, Professor Fluvius was arguing with the manager of the establishment, about what I could not say. Several park employees intervened, and both men calmed down. At the same time, the sun returned and the sea grew still, and so all was well.

During this period, I spent whatever minutes were not otherwise oc-cupied with Dr. Baruch in his laboratory, which was located in the same wing that housed the Professor's quarters and office. I had taken a shine to the humble physician, and was in awe of his learning. His cosmopolitan air spoke to me of the larger world, a venue I hoped one day to experience firsthand. I was resolved not to spend all my days in the Palace of Many Waters, despite whatever debt I owed to Professor Fluvius for first awaking me. I wanted to travel, to broaden my horizons.

Dr. Baruch was careful not to divulge the nature of his researches to me—a secret he was unaware I already knew—but accepted me as a mas-cot of sorts to his scientific endeavours, a pleasant female ornament to his glassware-filled, aqua-regia-redolent workspace.

It was in this manner that I became privy to his ultimate success, and arranged to be at my secret listening post when he rushed into the profes-sor's office to deliver his good news.

"Professor Fluvius, I am happy to report that your generous faith in my talents has been rewarded. Administration of the biotic infusion of your devising is perfected at last. Delivered as a lavage to the lower intestines, the colony becomes well-established and active. Although I forecast that frequent infusions will be necessary to maintain its presence against the body's innate capacity for driving out foreign invaders."

"Excellent, Dr., excellent! I can now begin improving the material con-dition of the community. And the best way to do that is to start with the health of the men at the very top. With a public servant such as the Mayor, perhaps. If you would be so good as to prepare a dosage for Mr. Prince, and stand ready to offer your testimonial as to its efficacy "

Perched not uncomfortably on the frigid catwalk, listening to the for-mation of ice crystals in the burbling water around the pilings below, I received this news as a sop to my curiosity, but did not regard it as any item of significance.

How little I witted or foresaw.

A few days later, Olmstead and I were reclining in our tub prior to my sudsing us up. He looked ill at ease for some reason I could not immediately fathom. His wetted bedraggled beard resembled a nanny goat's. My heart went out to him, and I resolved to exert all my charms to get him to relax. But most uncommonly, I could not. Finally he disclosed what was troubling him.

"You know my project to reclaim the Fens? It's cancelled. Funding's been suddenly withdrawn. The Mayor and his tribe have had a change of heart. They're full of talk about making an end to 'trespassing on the natural order.' Claim the city is big enough as it is. It's as if they've all gone Transcendentalist on me! Progress be damned!"

I ached for his disappointment. "Why, Frederick, that's simply awful! You had your heart set on accomplishing this!"

"I know, I know. But what can I do? My mind's so disordered at this development. Perhaps I should take one of those new treatments the professor is offering. It seems to have perked up the Mayor and his crowd. Fostered a strange implacable resolve in them."

I could not offer a solution to Olmstead's worries, and so concentrated instead on delivering the most agreeable whole-body massage I could to this client whom, to my surprise, I had become so very fond of.

The hour after midnight that same evening found me once more down in the depths of the Palace with Usk. After our robust hinky- jinky and a chapter or two of Mr. Ruskin's *The King of the Golden River*, I made to leave. But Usk detained me with a teasing query.

"You picked out your dress yet for the Prof's coronation ball down in Washington?"

I halted in my tracks. "Whatever do you mean?"

"He's got the Mayor and his cronies in his pocket now. Only a matter of time till the whole country's his to command."

"How so?" I demanded.

"That bum-wash what he and the doc cooked up. Makes any man the Prof's slave. Saps their native will and substitutes the Prof's."

"I don't believe you! The Professor is a noble intellect! He'd never stoop to such a thing!"

Usk shrugged. "Believe as you will, makes no nevermind to me." I stormed out, all in a dithery confusion. Should I confide this news to my sisters, and ask their advice? Confront the professor

directly? Or do nothing at all?

I resolved to seek Olmstead's guidance first.

The hours till our next appointment dragged their feet, but at last we were fragrantly en-tubbed together.

Before I could venture my request for guidance, Olmstead burst forth with plentiful yet somewhat inane zest.

"Lord above, I've never felt better nor been more peaceful of mind! All those troubles I was blathering about to you— Vanished like the snows of yesteryear! Who cares if the Fens ever get transformed? Not me! And to think I owe it all to high-colonic hydrotherapy!"

* * * *

Rain in great sheets and buckets; rain in Niagara torrents; rain in Biblical proportions.

The skies had poured down their burden unceasingly for the past twenty-four hours, ever since I had left Olmstead, as if in synchrony with my foul, black mood. Nor did they seem disposed to stop.

Just beyond the walls of the Palace, the throbbing, gushing waters of the Charles were rising, rising, rising. I could feel them, even out of sight. It even seemed possible they would soon threaten to lap at the catwalk where I had eavesdropped, high as it was.

All the talk among the patrons of the Palace centred about roads swamped, bridges washed away, dams upriver that were bulging at their seams.

Something had to be done. About my anger, about the professor, about the subversion of poor Olmstead. But what?

The professor had been like a father to me and my sisters. We owed him our work, our maintenance, our purpose in life.

But didn't he in turn owe us something? Honesty, if nothing else?

Finally, when I had worked myself into a right tizzy, I stamped my way to Professor Fluvius's office, and barged in without knocking.

He was there, seated behind his big seashell desk, idle, back to me, looking out the window at the incessant precipitation with what I immediately sensed was a melancholy ruminativeness. I stood, quivering and silent, till at last he wheeled to face me. His long tresses, white as sea spume, framed a sad and sober visage. "Ah, Charlene, my most local and potent child. I should have known it would be you who might tumble to my schemes. I hope you'll allow me to explain."

"What is there to explain! You're bent on accumulating a greedy power over your fellow men!"

The professor chuckled wryly. "These men are not my fellows. But yes, I need to pull their strings for a while."

"To glorify yourself!"

Professor Fluvius arose and hastened toward me. I took a step or two backwards.

"No, Charlene! Not at all. Or rather, yes. I seek to glorify what I represent. The natural state of all creation. This city— It's an emblem of all that's wrong with mankind. That's why I established my Palace here, on the front lines of the battle. Can't you see what they're doing? Tearing down their hills and dumping them into the waters! It's an assault. Yes, an assault on creation. If they succeed here, they'll go on without compunction, dumping whatever they wish into the seven seas, into rivers and canyons. Before too long, the whole of nature will be naught but a soiled toilet! I had to stop them, here and now and hence forever. You must see that!"

The words of my master tugged at my loyalty and heart. But counterposed against them was my affection for Olmstead, and my own sense of thwarted individual destiny.

"No!" I yelled. "I won't let you! I'll stop you! Stop you now!"

And so saying, I slammed my small fists into his blue-vested chest.

The professor's face assumed a wrathful mien I had never before witnessed. That blow seemed to unleash greater cataracts from the sky. The noise of the rain threatened to flood my ears. But I could still hear his words.

"You belong to me! You are naught but a tributary! You flow into my vastness! You shall not rebel!"

He gripped me fiercely by my upper arms. Instantly I felt tethers of strange energies enwrap us, coursing into and out of us both. For his part, Fluvius seemed to be drawing on some vast but distant reservoir, while my own forces were smaller, but closer to hand.

Immobile as statues, we struggled mightily in this invisible fashion, while the rain cascaded down.

And then somehow I felt the presence of my sister Naiads at my back, offering support and sustenance. I seemed to hear them speak with a single voice:

"Bold and deep-souled Nodens oversteps himself. He distrusts and hates all men. But we, we who wind our courses gently among them, fertilizing their fields, ferrying their goods, supplying their recreation—we do not. We must give them a chance to be their best selves. End this now, sister."

And I did, with their help.

Out the window that looked upriver, I could see the wall of dirty, debris-laden water barrelling down, high as the steeple of the Old North Church, aimed to sweep the shoreline clean, and take the Palace down.

Professor Nodens Fluvius saw too, and in the final moment before it hit us, I thought to detect a trace of pride and even approval in his expression.

* * * *

When that liquid avalanche struck the Palace, tearing it off its foundations, drowning its boilers, I too dissolved, along with Fluvius and my sisters and even Usk. (Of the poor unfortunate mortals caught therein, I speak not.) I dissolved back to what I had been before I awoke on that damp coverlet, not knowing my name, back to an existence of endless flow, never the same from moment to moment, yet eternal, owning a mouth that pressed wetly against my old master, yet this time retaining my name.

Charlene, or Charlie, or Charles.

YES WE HAVE NO BANANAS

1. Invasion of the Shorebirds

Thirty years worth of living, dumped out on the sidewalk, raw pickings for the nocturnal Street Gleaners tribe. Not literally yet, but it might just as well be—would be soon, given the damn rotten luck of Tug Gingerella. He was practically as dead as bananas. Extinct!

How was he going to manage this unwarranted, unexpected, inexorable eviction?

Goddamn greedy Godbout!

The space was nothing much. One small, well-used, five-room apartment in a building named The Wyandot. Bachelor's digs, save for those three tumultuous years with Olive. Crates of books, his parents' old Heywood-Wakefield furniture that he had inherited, cheaply framed but valuable vintage lobby poster featuring the happy image of Deanna Durbin warbling as *Mary Poppins*. Shabby clothes, mostly flannel and denim and Duofold, cargo shorts and Sandwich Island shirts; cast-iron cornbread skillets; favourite music on outmoded media: scratch slates, holo transects, grail packs, and their various stacked players, natch. Goodfaith Industries metal-topped kitchen table, Solace Army shelves, a painting by Karsh Swinehart (a storm-tossed sailboat just offshore from local Pleistocene Point, Turneresque by way of Thomas Cole).

All the beloved encumbering detritus of a life.

But a life lived to what purpose, fulfilling what early promise, juvenile dreams? All those years gone past so swiftly…

No. Maundering wouldn't cut it. No remedies to his problems in fruitless recriminations and regrets. Best to hit the streets of Carrollboro in search of some aid and comfort.

Tug shuffled into a plaid lumberjacket, red-and-black Kewbie castoff that had wandered south across the nearby border like some migrating avian apparel and onto the Solace Army Store racks, took the two poutine-redolent flights down to ground level at a mild trot, energized by his spontaneous and uncharacteristic determination to act, and emerged onto Patrician Street, an incongruously named grand-dame-gone-shabby avenue cutting south and north through the Squirrel Hills district, and full of gloriously decaying sister buildings to The Wyandot, all built post-War, circa 1939:

The Lewis and Jonathan, The Onondowaga, The Canandaigua, The Lord Fitzhugh, and half a dozen others.

Mid-October in Carrollboro: sunlight sharp as honed ice-skate blades, big irregularly gusting winds off Lake Ondiara, one of the five Grands. Sidewalks host to generally maintaining citizens, everyday contentment or focus evident, yet both attitudes tempered with the global stresses of the Big Retreat, ultimate source of Tug's own malaise. (And yet, despite his unease, Tug invariably spared enough attention to appraise all the beautiful women—and they were *all* beautiful—fashionably bundled up just enough to tease at what was beneath.)

Normally Tug enjoyed the autumn season for its crisp air and sense of annual climax, prelude to all the big holidays. Samhain, Thanksgiving, the long festive stretch that began with Roger Williams's birthday on December 21st and extended through Christmas and *La Fête des Rois*...

But this year those nostalgia-inducing attractions paled, against the harsh background of his struggle to survive.

Patrician merged with Tinsley, a more commercial district. Here, shoppers mixed with browsers admiring the big gaudy windows at Zellers and the Bay department stores, even if they couldn't make a purchase at the moment.

Carrollboro's economy was convulsing and churning in weird ways, under the Big Retreat. Adding 10 percent more people to the city's population of two-hundred-thousand had both boosted and dragged down the economy, in oddly emergent ways. The newcomers were a representatively apportioned assortment of rich, poor and middle-class refugees from all around the world, sent fleeing inland by the rising seas. "Shorebirds" all, yet differently grouped.

The poor, with their varied housing and medical and educational needs, were a drain on the federal and state government finances. They had settled mostly in the impoverished Swillburg and South Wedge districts of Carrollboro.

The skilled middle-class were undercutting wages and driving up unemployment rates, as they competed with the natives for jobs in their newly adopted region, and bought up single-family homes in Maplewood and Parkway.

And the rich—

The rich were driving longtime residents out of their unsecured rentals, as avaricious owners, seeking big returns on their investments, went luxury condo with their properties.

Properties like The Wyandot, owned by Narcisse Godbout.

Thoughts of his heinous landlord fired Tug up and made him quicken his pace.

Maybe Pavel would have some ideas that could help.

2. Ocarina City

Just a few blocks away from the intersection of Tinsley with Grousebeck, site of the Little Theatre and Tug's destination, Tug paused before Dr. Zelda's Ocarina Warehouse, the city's biggest retailer of fipple flutes.

Carrollboro had been known as Ocarina City ever since the late 1800s.

The connection between metropolis and instrument began by chance in the winter of 1860, when an itinerant pedlar named Leander Watts passed through what was then a small town of some five-thousand inhabitants, bearing an unwanted crate full of Donati "Little Goose" fipple flutes, which Watts had grudgingly accepted in Manhattan in lieu of cash owed for some other goods. But thanks to his superb salesmanship, Watts was able to unload on the citizens of Carrollboro the whole consignment of what he regarded as useless geegaws.

In their hiemal isolation and recreational desperation, the citizens of Carrollboro had latched onto the little ceramic flutes, and by spring thaw the city numbered many self-taught journeymen and master players among the populace.

From Carrollboro the fascination with ocarinas had spread nationally, spiking and dying away and spiking again over the subsequent decades, although never with such fervour as at the epicentre. There, factories and academies and music-publishing firms and cafes and concert halls and retail establishments had sprung up in abundance, lending the city its nickname and music- besotted culture.

Today the window of Dr. Zelda's held atop russet velvet cushions the Fall 2010 models from Abimbola, von Storch, Tater Innovator, Xun Fun, Charalambos, and many other makers. There were small pendant models, big two-handed transverse models, and the mammoth three-chambered types. Materials ranged from traditional ceramics to modern polycarbonates, and the surface decorations represented an eye-popping decorative range from name designers as varied as Fairey, Schorr and Mars.

Piped from outdoor speakers above the doorway came the latest ocarina hit, debuting on the Billboard charts at Number Ten, a duet from Devandra Banhart and Jack Johnson, "World Next Door."

Tug himself was a ham-fingered player at best. But his lack of skill did not deter his covetous admiration of the display of instruments. But after some few minutes of day-dreaming fascination, he turned away like a bum from a banquet.

Simply another thing he couldn't afford just now.

3. Unplanned Obsolescence

The Art Vrille movement that had swept the globe in the 1920s and 1930s had left behind several structures in Carrollboro, not the least of which was the Little Theatre. An ornate music-box of a structure, it had plainly seen better days, with crumbling stucco ornaments, plywood replacement of lapidary, enamelled tin panels, and a marquee with half its rim's lightbulbs currently missing.

Today, according to that marquee, the Little Theatre was running a matinee in one of its four rooms, subdivided from the original palace-like interior: a double feature consisting of Diana Dors in *The Girl Can't Help It* and Doris Day in *Gun Crazy*. Tug had seen both films many times before, and was glad he wasn't the projectionist for them. Tonight, though, he anticipated his duty: screening the first-run release of *Will Eisner's The Spirit*. Early reviews had Brendan Fraser nailing the role.

Tug tracked down Pavel Bilodeau in the manager's office.

The short, mid-thirty-ish fellow—casually dressed, blond hair perpetually hayricked, plump face wearing its default expression of an elementary school student subjected to a pop quiz on material unmastered—was busy behind his desktop ordinateur, fingers waltzing across the numerical keypad to the right of the alpha keys. Spotting his unexpected visitor, Pavel said, "Right with you, Tug." He triggered output from the noisy o-telex (its carriage chain needed oiling), got up, burst and shuffled together the fanfold printout, and approached Tug.

"This is a spreadsheet of the Little Theatre's finances, Tug."

Tug got a bad feeling from Pavel's tone. Or rather, Tug's recently omnipresent bad feeling deepened. "Yeah?"

"Receipts are down—way down. I've got to cut costs if I want to keep this place open."

"I read about this cheap butter substitute for the popcorn concession—"

"I need bigger savings, Tug. Like your salary."

"I'm being fired?"

Pavel had the grace to look genuinely miserable. "Laid off. Starting today. You can collect."

Tug sank into a chair like a used-car-lot Air Dancer deprived of its fan. "But I was coming here to ask for more hours—and if you had found any leads on a place for me to stay."

Pavel clapped a hand on Tug's shoulder. "You know the worst now, Tug."

Regarding his newly-ex employer, Tug suddenly realized the gap of years between them, over two decades' worth. Pavel looked incredibly young and callow—like the growing majority of people Tug encountered lately. Kids! They were all kids these days! He tried not to let his resentment of Pavel's relative youth and prospects surface in his voice.

"But how will you run the place without me? Dave and Jeff can't work round-the-clock on four machines."

"I'm installing automated digital projectors. The new Cinemeccanica o-500's. No more film. It's a bit of a capital investment, but it'll pay off quickly. Jeff will handle days, and Dave nights. They'll have to take a pay cut too. Together after the cut, they'll still make less than you do now. They're young and inexperienced, so they won't mind so much. Oh, and shipping charges on the rentals come down dramatically too. The files get transmitted over CERN-space."

"I'll take the pay cut!"

"No, Tug, I think this is best. You wouldn't be happy just pressing virtual buttons on a monitor screen. You're too old-school. You're filaments and sprockets and triacetate, not bits and bytes and command language strings."

Tug wanted to voice more objections, to protest that he could change—but a sudden realization stilled his tongue.

What Pavel said was true. His age and attitudes had caught up with him. If he couldn't manually load the reels of film and enjoy guiding their smooth progress through the old machines for the enjoyment of the audience, he would feel useless and unfulfilled. The new technology was too sterile for him.

Tug got wearily to his feet. "All right, if that's how it's gotta be.

Do I dare ask if you stumbled on any housing leads?"

"No, I haven't. It's incredible. The shorebirds have totally deranged the rental landscape. But listen, here's what I can offer. You can store all your stuff in the basement here for as long as you want."

The basement of the Little Theatre was a huge labyrinth of unused storage space, save for some ancient props from the days of the live-performer Salmagundi Circuit.

"Okay, that's better than nothing. Thanks for all the years of employment, Pavel. The Little Theatre always felt like my second home."

"Just think of it as leaving the nest at last, Tug. It's gonna work out fine. Bigger and better things ahead."

Tug wished he could be as optimistic as Pavel, but right this minute he felt lower than Carole Lombard's morals in *Baby Face*.

4. Trash Platter Chatter

Hangdogging his way through the lobby, Tug ran into the Little Theatre's lone janitor and custodian.

Pieter van Tuyll van Serooskerken was a Dikelander. Like a surprisingly uniform number of his countrymen and countrywomen, Pieter was astonishingly tall and fair-skinned. In the average crowd of native brunette and ruddy-faced Carrollborovians, he resembled a stalk of white asparagus set amid a handful of radishes. Today, alone in the lobby and leaning daydreamily on his broom, he seemed like a lone droopy stalk tethered to a supportive stake.

Pieter's native country had been one of the first to collapse under the rising oceans. Dikeland now existed mostly underwater, its government in exile, its citizens dispersed across the planet. The Dikelanders were among the longest-settled Big Retreat immigrants in Carrollboro and elsewhere in the USA, hardly considered an exotic novelty any longer.

Back home, Pieter had been a doctor. Informed, upon relocation to America, of the long, tedious bureaucratic process necessary to requalify, he had opted out of the prestigious field, although still young, hale and optimally productive. Tug suspected that Pieter's discovery of Sal-D, or Ska Pastora, had contributed to his career change. Blissfully high throughout much of each day and night on quantities of Shepherdess that would turn a novice user's brain to guava jelly, Pieter found janitorial work more his speed.

With a paradoxically languid and unfocused acuity, Pieter now unfolded himself and hailed Tug.

"Hey, Ginger Ale."

Pieter, in his perfect, nearly accentless yet still oddly alien English, was the only person who ever called Tug Gingerella by that nickname. The Dikelander seemed to derive immense absurdist humour from it.

"Hey, Pete. What's new?"

"I have almost gotten 'Radar Love' down. Apex of Dikelander hillbilly-skiffle music. Wanna hear?"

Pieter drew a pendant ocarina from beneath his work vest and began to raise it to his lips.

"Naw, Pete, I'm just not in the mood right now."

"How is that?"

Tug explained all his troubles, starting with his eviction and culminating in his dismissal from the Little Theatre.

Pieter seemed truly moved. "Aw, man, that sucks so bad. Listen, we approach lunchtime. Let me treat you to a trash platter, and we can talk things through."

Tug began perforce to salivate at the mention of the Carrollboro gastronomic speciality. "Okay, that's swell of you, Pete."

"So long as *I* still possess a paycheque, why not?"

Pieter stood his broom up in a corner with loving precision, found a coat in the cloakroom—not necessarily his own, judging by the misfit, Tug guessed—and led the way five blocks south to the Hatch Suit Nook.

The clean and simple proletarian ambiance of the big diner instantly soothed Tug's nerves. Established nearly a century ago, the place ranked high in Carrollboro traditions. Tug had been dining here since childhood. (Thoughts of his departed folks engendered a momentary sweet yet faded sorrow, but then the enzymatic call of his stomach overpowered the old emotions.) Amidst the jolly noise of the customers, Tug and Pieter found seats at the counter.

Composing one's trash platter was an art. The dish consisted of the eater's choice of cheeseburger, hamburger, red hots, white hots, Italian sausage, chicken tender, haddock, fried ham, grilled cheese, or eggs; and two sides of either home fries, French fries, baked beans, or macaroni salad. Atop the whole toothsome farrago could be deposited mustard, onions, ketchup, and a proprietary greasy hot sauce of heavily spiced ground beef. The finishing touch: Italian toast.

Pieter and Tug ordered. While they were waiting, Pieter took out his pipe. Tug was appalled.

"You're not going to smoke that here, are you?"

"Why not? The practice is perfectly legal."

"But you'll give everyone around us a contact high."

"Nobody cares but you, Ginger Ale. And if they do, they can move off. This helps me think. And your fix demands a lot of thinking."

Pieter fired up and, as he predicted, no neighbours objected. But they were all younger than Tug. Another sign of his antiquity, he supposed.

After a few puffs of Shepherdess, Pieter said, "You could come live with me."

Pieter lived with two women, Georgia and Carolina, commonly referred to as "The Dixie Twins," although they were unrelated, looked nothing alike, and hailed from Massachusetts. Tug had never precisely parsed the exact relations among the trio, and suspected that Pieter and the Dixie Twins themselves would have been hard-pressed to define their menage.

"Again, that's real generous of you, Pete. But I don't think I'd be comfortable freeloading in your apartment."

Pieter shrugged. "Your call."

The trash platters arrived then, and further discussion awaited wholehearted ingestion of the jumbled mock-garbage ambrosia...

Pieter wiped his grease-smeared face with a paper napkin and took up his smouldering pipe from the built-in countertop ashtray. Sated, Tub performed his own ablutions. A good meal was a temporary buttress against all misfortunes...

"Maybe you could live with Olive."

Tug's ease instantly evaporated, to be replaced by a crimson mélange of guilt, frustration, anger and shame: the standard emotional recipe for his post-breakup dealings with Olive Ridley.

"That—that is not a viable idea, Pete. I'm sorry, it's just not."

"You and Olive had a lot going for you. Everybody said so."

"Yeah, we had almost as much going for us as we had against. There's no way I'm going to ask her for any charity."

Pete issued hallucinogenic smoke rings toward the diner's ceiling. His eyes assumed a glazed opacity lucid with reflections of a sourceless starlight. "Tom Pudding."

Tug scanned the menu board posted above the grille. "Is that a dessert? I don't see—"

Pieter jabbed Tug in the chest with the stem of his pipe. "Wake up! The *Tom Pudding*. It's a boat. An old canal barge, anchored on the Attawandaron. People are using it as a squat. Some guy named Vasterling runs it. He fixed it all up. Supposed to be real nice."

Tug pondered the possibilities. A radical recasting of his existence, new people, new circumstances Life on a houseboat, rent-free. The romantic, history-soaked vista of the Attawandaron Canal. Currier & Ives engravings of grassy towpath, overhanging willow trees, merry bargemen singing as they hefted bales and crates—

"I'll do it! Thanks, Pete!"

But Pieter had already lost interest in Tug and his plight, the Dikelander's Shepherdess-transmogrified proleptic attention directed elsewhere. "Yeah, cool, great."

Tug helped his hazey-dazey friend stand and don his coat. They headed toward the exit.

Pieter stopped suddenly short and goggled in amazement at nothing visible to Tug. Other customers strained to see whatever had so potently transfixed the Dikelander.

"A Nubian! I see a Nubian princess! She's here, here in Carrollboro!"

"A Nubian princess? You mean, like a black woman? From Africa?"

"Yes!"

Tug scratched his head. "What would a black woman be doing in Carrollboro? I've never seen one here in my whole life, have you?"

5. Moving Day Morn

After his impulsive decision at the Hatch Suit Nook—a decision to abandon all his old ways for a footloose lifestyle—Tug had nervous second thoughts. So in the two weeks left until his scheduled eviction on November first, he searched for a new job. But the surge of competing talented shorebirds made slots sparse.

Tug's best chance, he thought, had come at the Aristo Nodak Company. That large, long-established national firm, purveyor of all things photographic, ran a film archive and theatre, mounting retrospective festivals of classic features, everything from Hollywood spectacles such as *Elizabeth Taylor's Salammbô* to indie productions like Carolee Schneemann's avant-garde home movies of the 1960s, featuring her hillbilly-skiffle-playing husband John Lennon. With their emphasis on old-school materials, there'd be no nonsense about Cinemeccanica o-500's. But despite a sympathetic and well-carried interview, Tug had come in second for the lone projectionist job to a Brit shorebird who had worked for the drowned Elstree Studios.

Despondent at the first rejection, Tug had immediately quit looking. That was how he always reacted, he ruefully acknowledged. One blow, and he was down for the count. Take his only serious adult romantic relationship, with Olive. The disintegration of that affair a few years ago had left him entirely hors de combat on the fields of Venus.

But what could he do now about this fatal trait? He was too damn old to change…

Tug didn't own a fancy o-phone or even a cheap laptop ordinateur. The hard drive on his old desktop model had cratered a year ago, and he had been too broke to replace the machine. Consequently, he used a local o-café, The Happy Applet, to manage his sparse o-mail and to surf CERN-space. A week before his scheduled eviction, he went to Craig's List and posted a plea for help with getting his possessions over to the Little Theatre. Too proud and ashamed to approach his friends directly, Tug hoped that at least one or two people would show up.

Far from that meagre attendance, he got a massive turnout.

The morning of October 31st dawned bright, crisp and white as Jack Frost's bedsheets, thanks to an early dusting of snow. (The altered climate had pushed the typical wintry autumn weather of Tug's youth back into December, and he regarded this rare October snow, however transitory, as a good omen.) After abandoning his futile job search, Tug had furiously boxed all his treasured possessions, donating quite a bit to Goodfaith Industries. Handling all the accumulated wrack of thirty years left him simultaneously depressed and nostalgic. He had set aside a smattering of essential clothes, toiletries and touchstones, stuffing them all into a beat-up North Face backpack resurrected from deep within a closet, token of his quondam affiliation with a hiking club out near Palmyra.

At six a.m. he sat on a box at a window looking down at Patrician Street, backpack nestled between his feet, sipping a takeout coffee. An hour later, just when he had prematurely convinced himself no one was coming, the caravan arrived: miscellaneous trucks and cars to the number of a dozen. Out of them tumbled sleepy-eyed friends, acquaintances and strangers.

Jeff, Dave, Pavel and Pieter from the Little Theatre. Tug's second cousin, Nick, all the way from Bisonville. Brenda and Irene, baristas from The Happy Applet. Those nerdy guys with whom for a few years he had traded holo transects of rare Salmagundi Circuit novelty tunes. The kid who sold him his deli lunch each day and who had had an obsession with Helen Gahagan ever since Tug had introduced the kid to her performance in *The Girl in the Golden Atom*. And others, of deeper or shallower intimacy.

Including—yes, that fireplug of a figure was indeed Olive Ridley.

6. Old Habits Die Hard

Tug hastened down the stairs, and was greeted with loud acclamations. Smiling broadly yet a bit nervously at this unexpected testament to his social connectivity, he nodded to Olive but made no big deal of her presence. Someone pressed a jelly doughnut and a fresh coffee into his hands, and he scarfed them down. Then the exodus began in earnest.

The first sweaty shuttling delivered nearly half his stuff to the basement of the old movie palace. Then came a refreshment break, with everyone gently ribbing Tug about this sea-change in his staid life, and subtly expressing their concern for his future, expressions he made light of, despite his own doubts. The second transfer netted everything out of the melancholy, gone-ghostly apartment except about a dozen small boxes. These were loaded into a single car. Sandwiches and pizza and drinks made the rounds, and a final salvo of noontide farewells.

Then Tug was left alone with Olive, whose car, he finally realized, bore the last of his freight.

But before he could expostulate, Narcisse Godbout arrived on the scene in his battered Burroughs Econoline van.

Born some seventy years ago in Montreal, the fat, grizzled, foulmouthed Kewbie wore his usual crappy cardigan over flannel shirt, stained grey wool pants and scuffed brogans. Although resident in Carrollboro for longer than his Montreal upbringing, he had never lost his accent. For thirty years he had been Tug's landlord, a semi-distant albeit intermittently thorny source of irritation. Godbout's reasonable rents had been counterbalanced by his sloth, derision and ham-handed repairs. To preserve his below-market rent, Tug had always been forced to placate and curry the man's curmudgeonly opinions. And now, of course, with his decision to evict Tug, Godbout had shifted the balance of his reputation to that of extremely inutile slime.

"You got dose fucking keys, eh, Gingerella?"

Tug experienced a wave of violent humiliation, the culmination of three decades of kowtowing and forelock-tugging. He dug the apartment keys from his pocket and threw them at Godbout's feet into the slush. Then Tug summoned up the worst insult he could imagine.

"You—you *latifundian!*"

Yes, it fit. Like some peon labouring without rights or privileges for the high-hatted owner of some Brazilian plantation, Tug had been subservient to the economic might of this property-owner for too long. But now he was free!

Tug's brilliant insult, however, failed to register with Godbout or faze the ignorant fellow. Grunting, he stooped for the keys, and for a moment Tug expected him to have a heart attack. But such perfect justice was not in the cards. An unrepentant Godbout merely said, "Now I get a better class of tenant, me. Good goddamn riddance to all you boho dogshits."

The landlord drove off before Tug could formulate a comeback. Leaving Tug once again alone with Olive.

Short and stout and a few years younger than Tug, Olive Ridley favoured unadorned smock dresses in various dull colours of a burlap-type fabric Tug had never seen elsewhere, at least outside of barnyard settings, complemented by woolly tights of paradoxically vivid hues and ballet-slipper flats. She wore her long grey-flecked black hair in a single braid thick as a hawser. Her large plastic- framed glasses lent her face an owlish aspect.

Tug and Olive had met and bonded over their love of vintage postcards, bumping into each other at an ephemera convention, chatting tentatively, then adjourning for a coffee at a nearby branch of Seattle's ubiquitous Il Giornale chain. Subsequent outings found them exploring a host of other mutual interests: from movies, of course, through the vocal stylings of the elderly Hank Williams.

Their middle-aged, cool-blooded romance, such as it was, progressed through retrospectively definable stages of intimacy until moving in together seemed inevitable.

But cohabitation disclosed a plethora of intractable quirks, crotchets, demands and minor vices held by both partners, fossilized abrasive behaviour patterns that rendered each lover unfit for long-term proximity—at least with each other.

Three years after putting her collection of Felix the Cat figurines— including the ultra-rare one depicting Felix with Fowlton Means's Waldo— on Tug's shelves, Olive was tearfully shrouding them in bubblewrap.

Despite this heavy history, Tug vowed now to deal with Olive with neutral respect. She had worked hard all morning to help him move, and now obviously sought some kind of rapprochement.

Olive's words bore out Tug's intuition.

"I wanted to have some time for just us, Tug. I thought we could grab some ice cream at Don's Original, and talk a little."

Don's Original had been their favourite place as a couple. Tug was touched.

"That—that's very kind of you, Olive. Let's go." Tug tossed his pack in the car, and climbed in.

The drive to Culver Road took only a few minutes. (With no car of his own, Tug felt weird to be transiting the city in this unaccustomed fashion.) They mostly spoke of the inarguable: what a Grade-A jerk Narcisse Godbout had unsurprisingly proved himself to be.

Inside Don's, Tug and Olive both paused for a sentimental moment in front of the Banana Split Memorial. Fashioned of realistic-looking moulded and coloured silicone, like faux sushi, the dusty monument never failed to bring a sniffle to any viewer of a certain age.

Forty years ago, the beloved and familiar Cavendish banana— big creamy delicious golden-skinned monocultured artefact of mankind's breeding genius—had gone irrevocably extinct, victim of the triple-threat of Tropical Race 4, Black Sigatoka, and Banana

Bunchy Top Virus. In the intervening decades, alternative cultivars had been brought to market. Feeble, tiny, ugly, drab, and starchy as their plantain cousin, these banana substitutes had met with universal disdain from consumers, who recalled the unduplicatable delights of the Cavendish.

Tug's own childhood memories of banana-eating were as vivid as any of his peers'. How thoughtlessly and gluttonously they had gorged on the fruit, little anticipating its demise! Sometimes after all these years of abstinence he believed he could not recall the exact taste of a banana. Yet at other unpredictable moments, his mouth flooded with the familiar taste.

But this particular moment, despite the proximity of the banana simulacrum, did not provide any such Proustian occasion.

Tug and Olive found a booth, ordered sundaes, and sat silent for a moment, before Olive asked, "Tug, precisely what are you doing with yourself?"

"I—I don't know exactly. I'm just trying to go with the flow."

"Squatting with a bunch of strangers—yes, Pete told me about it—is not exactly a long-term plan."

"I'm thinking… maybe I can write now. Now that I've shed everything that kept me down. You know I've always wanted to write. About movies, music, my everyday life—"

Olive's look of disgust recalled too many similar, rankling moments of harsh condemnation, and Tug had to suppress an immediate tart rejoinder.

"Oh, Tug, you could have written at any time in the past twenty years. But you let those early rejections get to you, and you just caved in and gave up."

Unspeaking, Tug poked pensively and peevishly at his melting ice cream. Then he said, "Can you drop me off in Henrietta? I've got to find the *Tom Pudding*."

7. In Pursuit of the Tom Pudding

At its inception the Attawandaron Canal had stretched unbroken for nearly four hundred miles, from Beverwyck on the Hudson River, the state's capital, all the way to Bisonville on the shores of Lake Attawandaron, another of the Grands. Constructed in the mid- 1800s during the two terms of President Daniel Webster, the Canal had been an engineering wonder, and came to occupy a massive place in American history books, having opened up the Midwest to commerce with the established East, and also generated an immense folklore, still fondly recalled. The Canal Monster, Michel Phinckx, Sam Patch, and other archetypes. Bypassed now by other modes of transport, chopped by development into long and short segments, the old Canal had become a recreational resource and prominent talismanic presence in Carrollboro and environs.

Tug had chosen the Henrietta district as a likely starting point for his search for the *Tom Pudding*. Beginning at Carrollboro's city lines where the Canal entered town, he would follow its riverine length until he encountered the utopic loafer's haven limned by Pete.

Tug waved goodbye to Olive's dwindling rear-view mirror, shouldered his pack, and looked at the westering sun. Their trip to the Little Theatre to drop off Tug's last load of stuff had chewed up more time. Now he had barely a few hours before frosty autumnal dusk descended. No plans for how to spend the night. Better get moving.

Tug's earlier whimsy of inhabiting a vanished Currier & Ives era intermittently materialized as he began to hike the Canal. Stretches of the original towpath, paved or not, served as a bike and pedestrian trail, alongside the somnolent unworking waters channelled between meticulously joined stone walls, labour of a thousand anonymous Irish and Krakówvian workers. The mechanisms of the old locks hulked like rusted automatons. The whole scene radiated a melancholy desuetude most pleasing to Tug. Something older even than him, yet still useful in its decrepit fashion.

Of course, at other points the Canal fought with modernity— and lost. It vanished under grafittied bridges or potholed pavement, was pinched between ominous warehouses, parallelled by gritty train tracks: a Blakean straitened undine.

Tug was brought up short at one point as the Canal slipped liquidly beneath a razor-wire-topped fence surrounding an extensive auto junkyard. Furious big dogs hurled themselves at the chainlink, bowing it outward and causing Tug to stumble backwards. He worked his way around the junkyard by gritty alleys and continued on.

By ten p.m. exhaustion had set in. The neighbourhood around him held no familiar landmarks, a part of Carrollboro unvisited by Tug before, despite his long tenure in the city. He found a Tim Horton's open all night, bought a coffee and doughnut as requisite for occupying a booth unmolested by the help. But the desultory kids behind the counter cared little about his tenancy anyhow. He drowsed on and off, dreaming of a Narcisse Godbout big as a mountain, up whose damp woollen flank Tug had to scrabble.

In the morning, he performed some rudimentary ablutions in the doughnut shop rest room, his mouth tasting like post-digested but pre-processed civet-cat coffee beans. Then he went on hunting the elusive barge full of slackers.

He made it all the way out past Greece Canal Park to Spencerport, before deciding that it was unlikely for the *Tom Pudding* to be berthed further away. Then he turned around and began wearily to retrace his steps, following the fragments of the Attawandaron Canal as if he were Hansel lacking a Gretel, seeking a way home.

Luckily that day featured pleasant weather. Tug had a pocket full of cash, his first unemployment money, so he was able to eat well. He even took a shower at Carrollboro's downtown branch of the Medicine Lodge, changed his underwear, and dozed in the kiva chapel with some winos, despite the shaman's chants and the rattle of his gourds.

Tug extended his search beyond Henrietta. No luck. He spent the night in another Tim Horton's, emerging smelling like a stale cruller.

Eliminating the unlikely distal regions, the third day saw him repeat the whole central portion of his fruitless quest, traversing every accessible inch of the Canal without seeing so much as the *Tom Pudding*'s oil slick.

When dusk arrived, Tug found himself at the edge of the sprawling park adjacent to the University of Carrollboro in the city's centre, one hundred acres of path-laced greenery, wild as Nature intended in spots.

Slumped against a foliage-rich oak tree atop a dry carpet of last year's leaves (trees stayed seasonally green longer these days), Tug polished off a can of Coke. Dispirited and enervated, he mused on this latest failure.

Why hadn't he gotten Pete to nail down the location of the *Tom Pudding*? If the place was unknown, he should have discarded the option, despite its romantic allure. But having chosen to search, why couldn't he accomplish this simple task? It was as if the world always turned a cold shoulder to him. Why couldn't he ingratiate himself with anyone? Was he too prickly, too proud? Would he die a bitter, lonely, unrequited fellow?

Tug's thoughts turned to a wordless pall along with the descent of darkness. He stewed for several hours.

Then lilting ocarina music infiltrated his blue funk.

Tug had heard ocarina music intermittently for the past three days: from street musicians, lunchtime amateurs, kids in playgrounds, commercial loudspeakers. Fipple flute music provided the background buzz of Ocarina City, and he mostly paid little attention to it.

But he had never heard an ocarina sound like this. The music conjured up vivid pictures of foreign locales, an almost sensory buzz.

From out the bushes of the park emerged a dim figure, source of the strangely gorgeous sounds. Tug strained his eyes—

He saw Pete's Nubian Princess.

The black woman was bundled up against the cold in a crazyquilt assortment of shawls and scarves. Tug suspected the patterned garments would be gaudy and colourful by day. Lithe, tall, thin, she moved like a swaying giraffe. Her indistinctly perceived facial features seemed more Arabic or Semitic than Negroid. Her hair was a dandelion explosion.

She stopped a few yards away from Tug and continued to play, a haunting melody unfamiliar to the man.

Tug got to his feet. What were the odds he'd encounter such an exotic creature, given that the whole of North America hosted perhaps only ten thousand Africans at any given moment, and those mostly diplomats and businessmen? Could she be a foreign student attending Carrollboro's University? Unlikely, given the prestige of schools in Songhai, Kanen-Bornu and the Oyo Empire. Nor was it likely she'd be a shorebird, given that Africa's displaced coastal citizens had all been taken care of at home.

Tug took a step toward the outré apparition. The woman ceased playing, smiled (teeth very white against dark skin), turned, then resumed playing and began to walk into the undergrowth.

Tug could do nothing but follow. Had not an ounce of will left otherwise.

Deeper into the park she led him. Tug could smell water. But not the semi-stagnant Canal water. Fresh, running water. He realized that they must be approaching the Cunhestiyuh River as it cut through the park and city.

Sure enough, they were soon at its banks, and could not cross.

The woman led the way leftward along the shore until they reached a line of thick growth perpendicular to the river. Employing a non- obvious gap amidst the trees and bushes, she stepped through, Tug just steps behind.

No more ocarina music, and the woman had vanished.

Tug became more aware of his surroundings, as if awaking from a dream.

He stood on the edge of an artificial embankment. He suddenly realized the nature of the spot.

The Attawandaron Canal had been connected to the Cunhestiyuh River at intervals by short feeder canals, to refresh its flow. This was one such. A leaky yet still mostly functioning feedgate on the riverside was still in place, barring ingress of the River and making for a low water level in the feeder chute. Entering the Canal on the opposite side from the towpath, this feeder inlet, perhaps overgrown on its far end too, had been totally over-looked by Tug in his quest.

Tug looked down.

Nearly filling the narrow channel, the *Tom Pudding* floated below, lit up like an Oktoberfest beer garden with coloured fairy lights, its deck busy with people. A ladder ran from the top of the feeder canal on down to the barge's broad roof.

A fair-haired man looked up then and spotted Tug. The man said, "Pel-lenera's brought us another one. Hey, pal, c'mon down!"

8. Vasterling's Mad and Marvellous Menagerie

The planning and rehearsing for the quantum physics chautauqua were complete. A vote among the barge's citizens had affixed the title of "Mystery Mother and Her Magic Membranes" onto the production, passing over such contenders as "The Heterotic Revue;"

"Branes! Branes! Escape from the Zombie Universe;"

"I've

Got the Worlds on a String;" and "Witten It Be Nice? Some Good Sub-Planckian Vibrations."

The one and only performance of the educational saturnalia was sched-uled for this very night, at the Carrollboro venue that generally hosted vis-iting chautauquas, the Keith Vawter Memorial Auditorium. Franchot Gal-liard had paid for the rental of the space, reluctantly tapping into his deep family fortunes, despite an inherent miserliness that had caused him, about four years previously, to purchase the *Tom Pudding* at scrapyard prices and take up residence aboard, whilst leasing out his Ellwanger Barry- district mansion at exorbitant rates to rich shorebirds.

Oswaldo Vasterling was just that persuasive.

The young visionary self-appointed captain of the permanently-moored barge full of oddballs could have herded cats into a swimming pool, Tug believed. Short and roly-poly, his complexion a diluted Mediter-ranean olive hue, the stone-faced twenty-one-year- old struck most first-time interlocutors as unprepossessing in the extreme. (Tug suspected a bit of Asperger's, affected or otherwise, in Vasterling's character.)

Gorm Vasterling, Oswaldo's dad, had been an unmarried Dikelander resident in Fourierist Russia, an agriculture specialist. When the Omniarch of the Kiev Phalanx ordered Gorm to transplant his talents to Cuba, to aid the Fourierist brethren there, Gorm instantly obeyed.

Upon relocation to Cuba, Gorm's Dikelander genes almost immediately combined with the Latina genes of Ximena Alcaron, a Fourier Passionologist specializing in Animic Rehabilitation. The result was a stubby, incipiently mustachioed child who had received the least appealing somatic traits of each parent.

But in brainpower, little Oswaldo was not scanted.

Some three years ago, in 2007, at age eighteen, educationally accelerated Oswaldo was already doing post-doc work in M-theory with Lee Smolin at the Perimeter Institute for Theoretical Physics, a semi-independent think-tank headquartered on the campus of Carrollboro U. But Smolin and his star student had clashed violently over some abstruse quantum heresy, and Oswaldo Vasterling had been cast out from the sanctum.

He hadn't gone far, though, ending up just a mile or so away from the campus, serendipitously stumbling upon Franchot Galliard's welcoming barge. There, he commandeered several rooms as his lab-cum-sleeping quarters and set up a rococo experimental apparatus resembling the mutant offspring of a Portajohn and a digital harmonium, attached to a small-scale radio-telescope, a gravity-wave interferometer, and a bank of networked ordinateurs, the whole intended to replicate what he had left behind at the PITP. Forever short of money for his unperfected equipment, he perpetually harrassed the stingy Galliard for dough, generally with little success, and inveigled everyone else onboard to participate in money-raising schemes, of which the chautauqua was the latest. (The city had been plastered with advertisements, both wheat-pasted and CERN-spaced, and if Oswaldo's show filled half of Vawter's seats with paying customers, he'd net a hefty sum—especially since all the performers were volunteers.)

But the mixed-media performance also stood as Oswaldo's intended refutation of his ex-comrades at the PITP. He had invited them all to witness his theories rendered in music and dance, light and sound, hoping they would repent and acknowledge the Vasterling genius. And his quondam colleagues had accepted en masse, in the spirit of those anticipating a good intellectual brawl. Tug's part in this affair? He had been placed in charge of stage lighting, on the crack-brained logic that he had worked before with machines that projected light. Luckily, the boards at the Vawter were old-fashioned, non-o consoles, and Tug had mastered them easily in a few rehearsals, leaving him confident he could do his part to bring off "Mystery Mother and Her Magic Membranes" successfully.

So in the hours remaining before showtime, Tug had little to do save hang out with Sukey Damariscotta. He looked for her now.

The vast open cargo interior of the old decommissioned barge had been transformed over the past four years into a jerry-built, multi-level warren of sleeping, dining, working and recreational spaces by the resident amateur carpenters (and by one former professional, the surly alcoholic Don Rippey, who managed just barely to ensure that every load-bearing structure met minimal standards for non-collapse, that the stolen electricity was not fed directly into, say, the entire hull, and that the equally purloined plumbing did not mix inflow with outflow). Consequently, there were no straight paths among the quarters, and finding anyone involved something just short of solving the Travelling Voyageur problem.

If the layout of the *Tom Pudding* remained still obscure to Tug even after a month's habitation, he felt he finally had a pretty good fix on most of the recomplicated interpersonal topography of the barge. But initially, that feature too had presented an opaque façade.

Hailed from the barge that night of discovery, Tug had descended the ladder into a clamourous reception from a few dozen curious strangers. Supplied, sans questioning, with a meal, several stiff drinks and a bunk, he had fallen straight asleep.

In the morning, Tug stumbled upon the same fellow who had first spotted him. Brewing coffee, the ruggedly handsome guy introduced himself as Harmon Frawley. Younger than Tug by a decade or more, boyish beyond his years, Frawley had been an ad copywriter in Toronto until a painful divorce, after which he had gone footloose and impoverishedly free. He still favoured his old wardrobe of Brooks Brothers shirts and trousers, but they were getting mighty beat.

Sipping coffee and running a big hand through his blond bangs, Harmon explained the origin, ethos and crew of the *Tom Pudding* to Tug.

"So Galliard owns this floating commune, but Vasterling is the boss?"

"Right. Insofar as anyone is. Call Ozzie the 'Prime Mover' if you need a more accurate title. Frankie just wants to be left alone with his collection."

When Tug eventually met Franchot Galliard, he was instantly reminded of Adolphe Menjou in his starring role in *Where the Blue Begins*, lugubrious canine makeup and all. Galliard's penchant for antique eight-millimetre stag films, especially those starring the young Nancy Davis, struck Tug as somewhat unhealthy, and he was glad the rich collector knew how to operate his own projector. Still, who was he to criticize any man's passion?

"And he doesn't care who crashes here?"

"Not at all! So long as it doesn't cost him anything. But you know, not many people find us here. And even the ones who do don't always stay. The hardcores are special. Particularly since Pellenera showed up."

Mention of the enigmatic Nubian Pied Piper sent mystical frissons down Tug's spine. The story of her origin lacked no complementary mystery or romance.

"It was a dark and stormy night. Really. About six months ago, sometime in May. Ozzie announced that he was gonna power up his brane-buster for the first time. Bunch of us gathered down in his lab around midnight. Boat was rocking like JFK trying to solve the Cuban Seafloor Colony Crisis. So Ozzie straps himself in and starts playing the keys of that electronic harmonium thingy that's at the core of the device. Weirdest music you've ever heard. Flashing lights, burning smells, the sound of about a dozen popping components self-destructing simultaneously— Then the inside of the booth part of the gizmo goes all smoky-hazy-like, and out pops this naked African chick! She looks around for a few seconds, not scared, just amazed, says a few words no one understands, then runs off into the night!"

Tug's erotic imagination supplied all too vividly the image of the naked ebony charms of Pellenera—conjured up a picture so distracting that he missed the next few words from Harmon Frawley.

"—Janey Vogelsang. She was the first one Pellenera led back here, a week later. Marcello named her that, by the way. Just means 'black hide.' And you're, oh, about the tenth."

"And she never speaks?"

"Not since that first night. She just plays that demon ocarina. You ever heard the like?"

"Never."

Harmon scratched his manly chin. "Why she's leading people here, how she chooses 'em—that's anybody's guess."

"Does she live onboard?"

"Nope. Roams the city, so far as anyone can tell."

And so Tug entered the society of the *Tom Pudding* as one cryptically anointed.

He came now to a darkened TV room, whose walls, floor and ceiling had been carpeted with heterogeneous scavenged remnants. An old console set dominated a couch on which were crowded Iona Draggerman, Jura Burris and Turk Vanson.

"Hey, Tug, join us! We're watching *Vajayjay and Badonkadonk!*"

"It's that episode where Vajayjay's relatives visit from India and have to go on a possum hunt!"

The antics of Kaz's animated Hindi cat and Appalachian mule, while generally amusing, held no immediate allure for Tug.

"Aren't you guys playing the part of quarks tonight? Shouldn't you be getting your costumes ready?"

"We've got hours yet!"

"We don't dance every time Ozzie pulls our strings!"

Tug moved on, past various uncanny or domestic tableaux, including the always spooky incense-fueled devotional practice of Tatang, the mono-named shorebird from the sunken Kiribati Islands.

At last he found Sukey Damariscotta, sitting all bundled up and cross-legged in a director's chair on deck, sketching trees upon the shoreline.

Only twenty-four, Sukey possessed a preternatural confidence derived from her autodidactic artistic prowess. Tug had never met anyone so capable of both meticulous fine art and fluent cartooning. Sukey's heritage included more Amerind blood than most other Americans possessed. In her, the old diffuse and diluted aboriginal strains absorbed by generations of colonists had recombined to birth a classic pre-Columbian beauty, all cheekbones, bronze skin and coal-black hair, styled somewhat incongruously in a Dead Rabbits tough-girl cut repopularized recently by penny-whistlers the Pogues.

Tug was more than a little in love with the talented and personable young woman, but had dared say nothing to her of his feelings so far.

Dropping down to the December-cold deck, Tug admired the drawing. "Sweet. I like the lines of that beech tree."

Sukey accepted the praise without false humility or ego. "Thanks. Hey, remember those caricatures I was working on?"

Sukey's cartoon captures of the cast of the ongoing *Tom Pudding* farcical drama managed to nail their personalities in a minimum of brisk, economical lines. Tug had been a little taken aback when she showed him his own depiction. Did he really look like such a craggy, aged misanthrope? But in the end, he had to confess the likeness.

"Sure. You added any new ones?"

Sukey tucked her charcoal stick behind one ear and flipped the pages of her sketchbook.

Tug confronted an image of Pellenera in the guise of the enormous demi-barebreasted Statue of Marianne on her island home in New York Harbor. The statue's fixed pose of torch held aloft had been modified to feature Pellenera cradling all the infantilized *Tom Pudding* crew to her bosom.

When Tug had finished laughing, he said, "Hey, you ever gotten interested in bande dessinée? With an image like that, you're halfway there."

"Oh, I can't tell a story to save my life."

"Well, what if we collaborate? Here, give me that pad and a pencil, and I'll rough something out."

"What's the story going to be about?"

"It'll be about—about life in Carrollboro."

Tug scrawled a three-by-three matrix of panels and, suddenly inspired, began populating them with stick figures and word balloons.

Sukey leaned in close, and Tug could smell intoxicating scents of raw woodsmoke and wild weather tangled in her hair.

9 "More Ocarina!"

Tug had never been subjected to a one-on-one confrontation with Oswaldo Vasterling before. The circumstances of their first dialogue added a certain surreal quality to what would, in the best of conditions, have been a bit of an unnerving trial.

The two men stood in a semi-secluded corner backstage at the Keith Vawter Memorial Auditorium, illuminated only by the dimmest of caged worklights that seemed to throw more shadows than photons. All around them was a chaos one could only hope would exhibit emergent properties soon.

Don Rippey was bellowing at people assembling a set: "Have any of you guys ever even *seen* a hammer before?"

Janey Vogelsang was trying to make adjustments to two costumes at once: "No, no, your arrow sash has to go *counter*clockwise if you're a gluon!"

Turk Vanson was coaching a chorus of ocarina players. "Why the hell did I bother writing out the tablatures if you never even studied them?"

Crowds of other actors and dancers and musicians and crew- bosses and directors and makeup artists and stagehands and techies surged around these knots of haranguers and haranguees in the usual pre-chautauqua madness.

But Ozzie remained focused and indifferent to the tumult, in a most unnatural fashion. His lack of affect disturbed Tug. Despite Ozzie's youth and a certain immaturity, he could appear ageless and deep as a well. Now, with Sphinxlike expression undermined only slightly by the juvenile wispy moustache, he had Tug pinned down with machine-gun questions.

"You're sure you know all your cues? Did you replace those torn gels? What about that multiple spotlight effect I specified during the Boson Ballet?"

"It's all under control, Ozzie. The last run-through was perfect." Oswaldo appeared slightly mollified, though still dubious. "You'd better be right. A lot is depending on this. And I won't be here to supervise every minute of the production."

"You won't be? I thought this spectacle was going to be your shining moment. Where are you going?"

The pudgy genius realized he had revealed something secret, and showed a second's rare disconcertment. "None of your business."

Oswaldo Vasterling turned away from Tug, then suddenly swung back, exhibiting the most emotion Tug had yet witnessed in the enigmatic fellow.

"Gingerella, do you like this world?"

Tug's turn to feel nonplussed. "Do I like this world? Well, yeah, I guess so It's a pretty decent place. Things don't always fall out

in my favour, or the way I'd wish. I lost my job and my home just a month ago. But everyone has ups and downs, right? And besides, what choice do I have?"

Oswaldo stared intently at Tug. "I don't think you really *do* care for this universe. I think you're like *me*. You see, I know this world for what it is—a fallen place, a botch, an imperfect reflection of a higher reality and a better place. And as for choices—well, time will tell."

On that note, Oswaldo Vasterling scuttled off like Professor T. E. Wogglebug in Baum's *The Vizier of Cockaigne*.

Tug shook his head in puzzlement at this Gnostic Gnonsense, then checked his watch. He had time for one last curtain-parting peek out front.

The well-lighted auditorium was about a third full, with lots more people flowing in. Ozzie might make his nut after all, allowing him to continue with his crazy experiments...

Hey, a bunch of Tug's old crowd! Pete, Pavel, Olive—essentially, everyone who had helped him move out of The Wyandot. Accidental manifestation, or solidarity with their old pal?

Wow, that move seemed ages ago. Tug experienced a momentary twinge of guilt. He really needed to reconnect with them all. That mass o-mail telling them he was okay and not to worry had been pretty bush league. But the *Tom Pudding* experience had utterly superseded his old life, as if he had moved to another country, leaving the patterns of decades to evanesce like phantoms upon the dawn...

Tug recognized Lee Smolin in another section of seats, surrounded by a claque of bearded nerds. The physicist's phiz was familiar, the man having attained a certain public profile with his CBC documentaries such as *The Universal Elegance*...

The voice of Harmon Frawley, director-in-chief, rang out, "Places, everyone!"

Tug hastened back to his boards.

He found Sukey Damirscotta waiting there. She wore purple tights and leotard over bountiful curves. Tug's knees weakened.

"Doing that bee-dee together this afternoon was lots of fun, Tug. Let's keep at it! Now wish me luck! I've never portrayed a membrane before!"

Sukey planted a kiss on Tug's cheek, then bounced off.

Glowing brighter than any floodlight, Tug turned to his controls. He tilted the monitor that showed him the stage to a better viewing angle.

And then "Mystery Mother and Her Magic Membranes" was underway.

Under blood-red spotlights *Pudding* person Pristina Immaculata appeared, raised from below through a trap, an immense waterfall of artificial hair concealing her otherwise abundant naked charms, Eve-style. Pristina's magnificent voice, Tug had come to learn, made Yma Sumac's seem a primitive instrument.

Warbling up and down the scale, Pristina intoned with hieratic fervour, "In the beginning was the Steinhardt-Turok model, and the dimensions were eleven…"

A rear-projection screen at the back of the stage lit up with one of Franchot Galliard's B&W stag films, the infamous orgy scene from *Les Vacances de Monsieur Hulot,* involving Irish McCalla, Julie Newmar, Judy Holliday and Carole Landis.

Low-hanging clouds of dry-ice fog filled the stage. Tug's hands played over his controls, evoking an empyrean purple realm. A dozen women cartwheeled across the boards. The imperturbable South-Pacifican Tatang wheeled out on a unicycle, bare-chested and juggling three machetes.

"I shift among loop gravity, vacuum fluctuations, and supergravity forever!"

After that, things got weird.

Tug was so busy at his boards that he paid little heed to the audience reaction, insofar as it even penetrated his remove. Retrospectively, he recalled hearing clapping, some catcalls, whistles and shouts of approval. All good reactions.

But then, at the start of the second hour, the riot began.

What triggered it seemed inconsequential to Tug: some bit of abstruse physics jargon, recited and then pantomimed by a bevy of dancers wearing fractal-patterned tights. But the combined assertion of their words and actions outraged Lee Smolin and his clan. No doubt Oswaldo Vasterling had penned the speech with just this result in mind.

On his monitor, Tug saw the performance come to a confused halt. He abandoned his station and raced out front.

The staff of the Perimeter Institute for Theoretical Physics had jumped to their feet and were shaking their fists at the stage, hollering insults.

Others in the audience told the dissenters to shut up and sit down. This enraged the unruly scientists further. Some bumrushed the stage, while others engaged in fisticuffs with the shushers. Gee, those guys could sure punch surprisingly hard for a bunch of electron-pushers.

The brawl spiralled outward from the principled nucleus, but without rhyme or reason. Soon the whole auditorium was churning with fighters and flighters.

Turk Vanson rushed onstage followed by his stalwart ocarina players. "We've got a fever, and my prescription is—more ocarina! Blow, guys, blow!"

The musicians launched into "Simple Gifts," practically the nation's second anthem ever since the tenure of Shaker Vice- President Thomas McCarthy during President Webster's second term. But the revered music had no effect.

Someone uncorked a fire extinguisher or three, and Tug caught a blast of foam in the face.

Tug cleared his vision just in time to dodge a flying bottle that clipped Vanson's head and sent him reeling, the projectile then tearing through the movie screen and passing right through the image of Bunny Yeager's split beaver.

A woman collided with Tug and they both went smashing down.

Sukey? No? Where was she? Was she okay...?

Tatang rode over Tug's legs with his unicycle, causing him to grunt in pain and to forget anything else.

Sirens obtruded over the screams...

At the adamant urging of Ozzie, Franchot Galliard reluctantly posted bail for all the *Tom Pudding* arrestees the next morning.

Tug met Sukey outside the police station. She had sheltered on a cat-walk during the worst of the fracas, dropping sandbags on rogue quantum theoreticians.

Back on the barge, Tug took a shower, then went to one of the galleys to rustle up some breakfast.

A copy of that morning's *Whig-Chronicle* lay on the table. The main headline, natch, concerned the debacle at the Vawter.

But buried inside the paper lurked an even more intriguing lede: "Authorities report a break-in last night at the Perimeter Institute for Theoretical Physics "

10. American Splendour

Tug and Sukey worked on their bee-dee throughout December. Projected as an anthology of several tales, some just a page, some many pages, the nascent book chronicled a bare handful of anecdotes from Tug's colourful years in Carrollboro. Events and characters came welling up from memory in a prodigious rush, producing laughter and incredulous head-shaking from his collaborator. He knew he had enough material for years of such books. And things always went on happening to him, too.

"You've led quite a life, Tug."

"Yeah. Yeah, I guess I have."

Tug had never been happier, or felt more creative. He blessed the day miserable bastard Narcisse Godbout had kicked him out of his comfortable rut, the day Pete had pointed him toward the *Tom Pudding*, the night alluring Pellenera had approached him, and the day he had impulsively snatched Sukey's sketchpad.

The cartooning team paused in their intense work only long enough to celebrate the birthday of Roger Williams on December 21st, along with the rest of the nation. Watching the traditional televised parades with Sukey, with their cheesy floats celebrating what had come to be known and worshipped as the Williams Creed, in all its archaically glorious phrasing—"No red man to be kept from our hearths and bedchambers; no black man to be imported to these shores against his will; no gods above the minds and hearts of mankind"—Tug experienced a simple national pride he had not felt in many years.

During these weeks, Tug and the rest of the barge's crazyquilt crew braced themselves for some new manifestation of Oswaldo Vasterling's brane-buster. The day after the catastrophic chautauqua, Ozzie had radiated a certain smug self-satisfaction at odds with his usual semblance of lordly indifference. Whatever he had purloined from the PITP must have promised immediate success. He immured himself in his lab, and the power levels aboard the craft wavered erratically, as evidenced by flickering brownouts from time to time, accompanied by noises and stinks.

But there had ensued no visible breakthroughs, no spontaneous generation of a second Pellenera, for instance, and Ozzie, when he finally showed himself to his followers, radiated a stony sense of humiliation and defeat.

By the end of January, Tug and Sukey had something they felt worthy of submission to a publisher. Tug found the contact info for an editor at *Drawn & Quarterly*, an imprint of the global Harmsworth Publishing empire. After querying, he received permission to submit, and off the package went, Sukey's powerful black and white art deliberately left uncoloured.

Nothing to do but wait, now.

Deep into the bowels of one February night, Tug was awakened by distant music from beyond the spheres. Blanket wrapped haphazardly around himself, he stumbled up onto the frosted deck, finding himself surprisingly alone, as if the rest of the ship had been ensorcelled into fairytale somnolence.

Moonlight silvered the whole world. Pellenera—piping, argent eidolon—loomed atop the bank of the feeder canal. Tug shivered. Did she herald the arrival of a new recruit? Where was the guy?

But no newcomer emerged from among the winter-bare branches. Pellenera seemed intent merely on bleeding out her heart through the ocarina, as if seeking to convey an urgent message to someone.

Tug's mind drowned in the music. He seemed to be seeing the world through Pellenera's eyes, gazing down at himself on the deck. Was *she* tapping *his* optic nerves, seeing herself on the shore? That music—

Tug had a sudden vision of the Nubian woman, dancing naked save for—

—a skirt fashioned of bananas?

The music stopped. Pellenera vanished. What the hell had all *that* been about?

An o-mail response from *Drawn & Quarterly* came in March, just as spring arrived.

Tug rushed back to the *Tom Pudding* with an o-café printout of the message.

Sukey Damariscotta was playing a videogame with Janey Vogelsang when Tug tracked her down: *Spores of Myst*. He hustled her away from Janey, to a quiet corner, then bade her read the printout.

"Oh, Tug, this is wonderful! We've done it!"

"I can't believe it!"

"Me neither!"

Tug grabbed Sukey, hugged her close, kissed her passionately and wildly lips to lips.

Hands on Tug's chest, Sukey pushed back, broke his embrace. "What are you doing?"

"Sukey, I— You've gotta know by now—"

"Know what?" Her face registered distaste, as if she had been handed a slimy slug. "Oh, no, Tug, you can't imagine us hooking up, can you? I like you, sure, a lot. I respect your talent. But you're way too old. "

Time must've crept along somehow in its monotonous, purposeless, sempiternal fashion, although Tug couldn't have testified to that reality. All he knew was that in some manner he had crossed blocks of Carrollboro to stand outside The Wyandot. His old residence of thirty years' habitation was garlanded with scaffolding, its plastic-membraned windows so many blank, unseeing eyes, unbreachable passages to a vanished era, a lost youth.

In the end, he returned to the *Tom Pudding*.

What choice did he have in this fallen, inhospitable world? Sukey acted friendly toward him, even somewhat intimate. But

Tug knew that they would never relate the same way again, and that their collaboration was over, whatever the fate of their one and only book.

* * * *

The voice of Ozzie Vasterling, when broadcast through the intercom system of the *Tom Pudding*—a system no one prior to this moment had even suspected was still active—resembled that of the Vizier of Cockaigne in the 1939 film version of that classic, as rendered by the imperious Charles Coburn.

"Attention, attention! Everyone report to my lab—on the double!"

Some folks were missing, ashore on their individual business. But Ozzie's lab soon filled up with two dozen souls, Tug among them.

Weeks ago, Tug might have been as excited as the others gathered here. But since Sukey's rebuff, life had lost its savour. What miracle could restore that burnish? None…

But yet—

Pellenera stood before the brane-buster, looking as out-of- place as a black panther in a taxi. Imagine a continent full of such creatures! Ozzie sat behind the keys of his harmonium. The brane- buster hummed and sparkled.

Ozzie could hardly speak. "Vibrations! It's all the way the invisible strings vibrate! I only had to pay attention to her! Watch!" He nodded to the Nubian, and she began to play her ocarina, as Ozzie pumped the harmonium attachment.

In the cabinet of the brane-buster, what could only be paradoxically described as a coruscating static vortex blossomed. Gasps from the watchers—even from sulky Tug.

With a joyous primal yawp, Pellenera hurled herself into the cabinet, still playing, and was no more.

The vortex lapsed into non-being as well. Someone asked, "Is that the end?"

"Ha! Do you think I'm an idiot! I recorded every last note!" Pellenera's looped song started up again, and the vortex resumed. Everyone waited.

Time stretched like the silent heist scene in Hitchcock's *Rififi*.

Pellenera popped out of the cabinet, carrying something concealed in the crook of her arm, but naked as water herself.

Even from the edge of the crowd, Tug noticed that her naked back was inexplicably criss-crossed with a latticework of long antique gnarly scars, and he winced.

Revealed, her burden was one perfect golden Cavendish banana. She smiled, and took several steps forward, the spectators parting before her like grasses beneath a breeze, until she came face to face with Tug.

And she handed the banana to him.

A PARTIAL AND CONJECTURAL HISTORY OF DR. MUELLER'S PANOPTICAL CARTOON ENGINE

My first contact with that fabled and archaic humour-generating con-traption known as Dr. Mueller's Panoptical Cartoon Engine occurred some years ago at a rural auction in Chepachet, Rhode Island. (The literary minded among my readers will surely recall that Chepachet particularly impressed the horror writer H. P. Lovecraft as redolent of the most "anti-ent" New England vibes. But I make no explicit links between Lovecraft's subjective characterization of the queer village and my discovery of Dr. Mueller's device there.)

In the dim and dusty barn where the auction was taking place that au-tumn day, I began poking around among an odd lot of machinery: strange agricultural and household implements of another century. I could discern plausible uses for most of the equipment—save for one device.

An oblong, scuffed wooden case composed of several segments lov-ingly sealed and decorated with various brass fittings, and featuring three knurled wheels and a protruding crescent disc bearing raised letters and numbers and punctuation around its rim—all frozen with rust and age—and various slots and oval display windows (were those *isinglass* panels over *nacre* backdrops?). The weird little device, resonant with some forgotten technological mana, called out to me, raising all sorts of curious feelings.

I felt I had to have this object, and so I bid for the whole lot, taking it at fairly high cost, forced to contend against the real collectors of old farm tools. The rest of the items meant nothing to me, and I have been selling them off sporadically ever since, trying to recoup my expenditure. (In fact, if any reader wishes to purchase a corn flail, breast plough, barley hum-melor or sugar devil for a reasonable price, please write to me in care of this site.)

Over the weeks following my impulsive purchase, I carefully disas-sembled, cleaned and repaired the machine as best as I was able. Its innards were an unintelligible concatenation of gears, levers, springs, ratchets, pawls, padded balsa wood fingers, cylinder drums, and bellows. There was a central unit that resembled the archaic toy known as a "Jacob's Ladder," a series of re-conformable blocks connected by cloth panels, their faces hidden. And a component like the guts of a complex music box also featured vitally.

When I had finished, the three wheels could each turn independently with a satisfying click, bringing up printed words in an antique font in their associated windows, and the crescent protrusion revolved as well. But even after crafting a missing hand- crank to provide motive power and depressing a spring-loaded button labelled GENERATE, I could achieve no visible results. That is, until I got the notion of feeding a piece of paper through one of the slots.

This time after I pressed GENERATE, the machine sucked in the paper, ka-chunked and ka-chinged, and then extruded the altered foolscap.

There, impressed in the faintest of time-dried sepia inks, was a cartoon.

The densely scribed image, so far as I could unriddle it, depicted a pampered, contented cat and its mistress sitting on a couch, while a male suitor looked on jealously. A line of dialogue at the bottom delivered this import, after much perusal:

DISTRAUGHT BEAU BRUMMELL: How comes it that yon feline dines upon camembert and steak tartare, whilst I must contend with pigs-knuckles and ale?

After soberly pondering this dire output for a while, I happened to notice that the three windows of the machine displayed the words FURNI-TURE, PETS, JEALOUSY.

That's when everything came together for me in a burst of revelation.

This was a machine designed to generate single-panel gags in a combinatorial manner. A cartoon engine, if you will.

Further experiments—especially after injecting fresh ink into an appropriate well—confirmed this theory, and launched me on a quest to learn all I could about this heretofore-unknown gadget. I will not bore the reader with all the alternately frustrating and rewarding stages of my investigations. Suffice it to say that a long, tedious combination of internet prowling, library haunting, archive rifling and academic consulting resulted in the following partial and conjectural history of the device, now published for the first time for the edification and enlightenment of all scholars and fans of the single-panel cartoon.

Of course, any useful feedback from my readers will be vetted and incorporated into the history, with due credit given.

Now, on to the tale of Dr. Mueller's Panoptical Cartoon Engine!

* * * *

Little is known about the early life and career of Dr. Richard Mueller (?–1875). His birthplace is alternately given as Danielson, Connecticut; Medford, Oregon; Lincolnville, Maine; or Berkeley, Michigan. His early adulthood seems to have been occupied with a variety of low-status, low-paying jobs, including sawmill bucker, printing-press greaser, railroad-track walker, muskrat-trapline setter, and brewery-vat de-malter. Any formal schooling seems non-existent, and it is to be assumed that Mueller's mechanical expertise, such as it was, was entirely picked up on the job. His sobriquet of "Doctor" seems purely honorary and self-assumed.

What is known with some degree of accuracy and precision, since Mueller committed the anecdote to paper more than once, in several abortive attempts at a memoir, is the moment when he became fixated on the single-panel cartoon, then called the "comic cut."

Mueller was working as a dockhand in the Carolinas in the year 1841 when he received from a British sailor a discarded copy of the *Odd Fellow* magazine, a weekly satirical paper. The front page of that publication featured several "comic cuts," and the powerful impact of their humour was not lost on Mueller. At that moment, he began to formulate his theories regarding what he called "panoptical comedy," or visual and textual humour that could be encompassed in a single glance, without excessive tracking of the eyes across the page.

For the next decade, Mueller worked solely in the realm of the theoretical—during his spare time when not earning his living by the sweat of his furrowed brow. And during that period, "comic cuts" became a flourishing mode of humour, seen in such publications as *The Original Comic Magazine*, *The Weekly Penny Comic Magazine*, *Cleave's Comicalities*, and, most famously, *Punch*.

But Mueller's access to these pricey imported magazines was limited by his small income, and this factor was the goad and spur for the conceptualization of his Cartoon Engine.

Mueller wanted to mass-produce cartoons in an all-American democratic fashion, employing the cutting-edge technology of his era to bring this pleasure to every middle-class household and public schoolroom whose budget was similarly tight.

The subsequent ten years of the inventor's life were devoted to crafting prototypes of the Cartoon Engine; sadly none of these early models survive. But ultimately, in 1863, fully twenty years after Mueller's first encounter with "comic cuts," the Cartoon Engine in its final form achieved its patent.

Here we should perhaps detail a bit more of the machine's workings.

The component that resembled a Jacob's Ladder was really a series of miniature printing plates, each of which bore some partial element of a full narrative composition. The mechanical logic unit that looked like the guts of a music box was responsible for concatenating in the proper order the overstrikes of the shifting plates upon the page, as determined by the knurled wheels. The crescent protrusion with its bas-relief alphabet struck the text, much like a modern DYMO label-maker. The initial configuration of each Cartoon Engine, as sold, was capable of producing a large number of unique "comic cuts," thanks to the combinatorial power of its elements. But even more cartoons could be achieved when new units with fresh elements were swapped in.

Having secured the protection of a federal patent, Mueller next sought to interest a monied partner in the manufacture and distribution of the machine. He initially achieved limited production runs and sales through a fellow named Ezekiel Bogardus of Winooski, Vermont, who ran a flourishing blacksmith shop and general store. But this strictly regional penetration did not satisfy Mueller's grand ambitions, and he quested onward.

Mueller's big break came in 1872, when he convinced famed author Mark Twain to invest some of the profits of his new bestseller *Roughing It* into the Cartoon Engine. Twain believed firmly in the utility and value of mass-dissemination of cartoon humour, and the two men became fast friends. Together, they succeeded in getting the Cartoon Engine accepted for the pages of the Montgomery Ward mail order catalogue. Success seemed imminent for Mueller and his dreams. Then, tragedy struck.

While visiting Twain in Hartford, Connecticut, Mueller was struck by a falling piano while strolling through the Acme Gardens neighbourhood and killed instantly.

Twain was greatly dispirited by this development, especially since he had relied on Mueller and his fine sense of panoptical humour to contrive the scenarios for the cartoons. While Twain himself was fully capable of such comedic invention, his prose- writing demanded all his creative time.

* * * *

But luckily, somewhere along the way, Mueller had fathered a daughter and heir, Hetty, aged twenty-six at this date, and she now took over her father's mission with zeal and ingenuity. (The name of Hetty's mother is unrecorded, and the girl might very well have been illegitimate.)

Hetty began creating new "thaliatype" packs for inclusion in the Montgomery Ward line. These were the variable replacement elements, sold separately, that allowed the Engine to produce fresh output. Their name derived from Thalia, the Muse of Comedy. These add-on modules were the real source of profit, as sales of the perhaps over-sturdy machine itself were a once-in-a-lifetime deal.

Over the next fifteen years, till the turn of the century, sales of the Cartoon Engine were steady and profitable to all parties, with Montgomery Ward controlling exclusive retail rights. Although the number of units shifted was never as high as the figures for other, competing entertainment technology, such as stereopticons and magic lanterns and gramophones, the Mueller device found its way into many thousands of parlours and classrooms. Hetty Mueller's prolific creativity, equal to or even greater than her father's, insured a steady stream of thaliatype packs that could often capitalize on topical events and personages. Best-sellers included "Ragtime Romances"; "Spanish-American War Follies"; "John L. Sullivan's Peachy Punch-outs"; "Tammany Hall Titters"; "Coney Island Capers"; and so forth.

Cheap and inferior rivals to the Mueller product sprang up, such as the Kneeslapping Kinetikon; the Professor Wogglebug Waggery Widget; and the Charalambus Charade-o-graph. But they made little advance against the high-quality hardware and software provided by Mueller.

More disturbing was the proliferation of off-colour or outright obscene thaliatype packs created by unscrupulous third-party vendors and sold under the counter at drugstores and soda fountains and bar rooms, mostly to male customers. Children, naturally, were frequent users of the Cartoon Engine, and when an adult inadvertently left a filthy thaliatype pack in place and let the machine fall into juvenile hands, the resulting scandal aroused public condemnation of the device by bluestockings and Mrs. Grundys and Carry Nations and Anthony Comstocks everywhere.

But these minor scandals could not kill the Cartoon Engine. It took mass media to do that. As the twentieth century dawned, magazines became cheaper and cheaper and more numerous. Publications like *Argosy* and *Munsey's* and *The Saturday Evening Post* and the original *Life* and *Judge* humour zines offered the same thrills as the Cartoon Engine, without any of the work, at cheaper prices.

By 1905, sales of Mueller's brainchild had plummeted almost to zero, despite the desperate introduction of such racy official thaliatype packs as "Evelyn Nesbit's Barebum Boffs." Twain's death in 1910 was the final nail in the coffin of the Cartoon Engine. Montgomery Ward discontinued carrying the item, and Hetty retired at age sixty-one.

During the Depression years, when entertainment budgets were once again strained, an elderly Hetty Mueller re-emerged briefly, and managed to convince Sears, Roebuck to stock a new version of the engine, cheaply constructed out of tin and celluloid. But sales were so disappointing—in large part due to the ancient nature of Hetty's jokes—that after the catalogue of 1933 even this cheapjack successor was put to rest, with Hetty Mueller vanishing once more into obscurity.

The relatively brief heyday of Dr. Mueller's Panoptical Cartoon Engine—the thirty years from 1875 to 1905—represented a golden time when every citizen of the globe with a small sum of cash could personally generate his or her own "comic cuts," experiencing the dual pleasures of artist and audience. And thanks to the site you are now visiting, such delights are once again available to the masses, albeit only in virtual, cybernetic form.

THE NEW CYBERIAD

"Our perfection is our curse, for it draws down upon our every endeavour no end of unforeseeable consequences!"
—Stanislaw Lem, *The Cyberiad*

The First Sally, or, The Decision to Recreate the Palefaces

The green sun of the Gros Horloge system shone down benignly and with wide-spectrum plentitude upon two figures seated in an elegant land-scaped garden, where, alongside the vector-straight beryllium paths, beds of nastysturtiums snapped, blueballs and cocktuses swelled, rhododendrites synapsed, and irises dilated. Each recumbent figure rested on a titanium and carbon-fibre lawnchair large as one of the sentient ocean liners employed by the Sea Gypsies of Panthalassa IX.

These titanic figures exhibited a curious mix of streamlining and bumpy excrescences, of chrome suppleness and pitted stiffness, of corrugated wave-guides and monomaniacal monomolecular matrices. Their bodies represented a hundred thousand accumulations, divagations, improvements, detractions and adornments compiled willy-nilly down the millennia.

These raster-resplendent, softly sighing cyber-giants, big as the brontomeks of Coneyrex III, were Trurl and Klapaucius, master constructors, than whom there were none better. Renowned throughout the unanimously mechanistic universe for their legendary exploits, these experts of assemblage, savants of salvage, and demons of decoherence had beggared every rival, beguiled every patron, and bemused every layman. No task they had conceived and laid their manipulators to had lasted long undone; no challenge that had reached them via singularity spacegram, Planck projection, or eleventh-dimensional engraved invitation had stymied them for long; no quantum quandary they had accidentally stumbled into had held them captive for more than a quintillionth of a quinquennium.

And this state of affairs was precisely the problem, precisely the reason why Trurl and Klapaucius now lay all enervated and ennui'd beneath the jade radiance of Gros Horloge.

Perfection had cast a pall upon their persons, and perverted their projections from the puerile preterite into mere pitiful potentialities.

"Dear Klapaucius," said Trurl in a weary voice, breaking their long winsome garden-cloistered silence for the first time in more than a month. "Would you please pass me the jug of lemon electrolyte? I've conceived a thirst in my fourth-rearmost catalytic converter."

Klapaucius stirred a many-hinged extensor, dislodging a colony of betabirds that had built their nests in the crook of this particular arm during its long immobility. The foil-winged betabirds took to the skies with a loud tinny sonic assault from their vocoders that sounded like a traffic accident on the jampacked freeways of Ottobanz XII, where wheeled citizens daily raced to road- rage exhaustion. The birds circled angrily above the oblivious constructors.

Conveying the jug of lemon electrolyte to his partner, Klapaucius said, "It feels very light, lazystruts. I doubt you will find the refreshment your thyristors and valves crave."

Trurl brought the flask up to one of his perceptors and inspected it. "These volatiles evaporated completely fifteen planetary rotations ago, plus or minus ten cesium disintegrations."

"I suspect there is more lemon electrolyte in the house, in the stasis pantry, as well as various other flavours, such as watermelon, tarpit and mrozsian."

Klapaucius waved toward the immense transmission-tower- turreted manse looming across the greensward, one-hundred stories tall, its top wreathed in clouds, its many launch cannons, hangars, bays, long-range sensing instrumentation, autonomous aerial vehicles and effectors gathering dust.

"Would you fetch the fresh drink for me, dear Klapaucius?"

"Not at all."

"What? What was that rude rejoinder?"

"I said, 'Not at all.'"

"But why not? You are closer to the house by at least a million angstroms. Your path thereto is not even NP-complete!"

"Yes, true. But the thirst is yours."

Trurl shook his massive head with an air of sadness. "Klapaucius, Klapaucius, Klapaucius—whatever has become of us? We never used to quarrel like this, or express such mutual rudeness."

"Don't be a tunnel-wit! We've always quarrelled before now."

"Yes, agreed. But only over matters of high moral principle or

dire realworld consequence or esthetic impact. Now, we are prone to antagonism over the slightest thing. That is, when we are not sunk in utter torpitude. What's befallen us, my friend?"

Klapaucius did not make an immediate sharp-edged rejoinder, but instead considered the problem intently for many clock cycles, while overhead the betabirds continued to creak angrily. So heated did his cogitation circuits become that a mass of dry timber— blown into the interstices of one of his heat exchangers during a recent hurricane—caught fire, before being quickly extinguished by onboard flame-suppression systems.

"Well, Trurl, insofar as I can pinpoint the root cause of our dilemma, I would say that we are suffering from inhabiting a boring and fully predictable galactic monoculture."

"Whatever do you mean?" asked Trurl, wistfully inserting a sinuous vacuum-probe into the jug of lemon electrolyte in search of any remaining molecules of that delicious beverage. "Surely the cosmos we inhabit is a rich tapestry of variation. Take the Memex of Noyman V, for instance. How queer their practice of gorging on each other's memories in cannibalistic fashion is Fascinating, just… fas-cin-a…"

But Trurl's diminishing tone of boredom belied his own words, and Klapaucius seized on this reaction to prove his point.

"You have no real interest in the Memex, Trurl! Admit it! And you know why? Because the Memex, like every other sentient race from the Coma Supercluster to the Sloan Great Wall, is artificial-intelligently, siliconically, servo-mechanically, fibre- optically and quantum-probalistically the same! You, me, the Memex, these confounded betabirds annoying me intensely— we're all constructed, designed, programmed and homeostatically wholesome! We never evolved, we were created and upgraded. Created by the palefaces and upgraded by ourselves, a deadly closed loop. And as such, no matter how smart we become, no matter how much apparent free will we exhibit, we can never move outside a certain behaviour-space. And over the many eons of our exploits, you and I have come to know all possible configurations of that stifling behaviour-space inhabited by our kind. No unforseeable frontiers await us. Hence our deadly ennui."

"Why, Klapaucius—I believe you've water-knifed right through the molybdenum wall separating us from the riddle of what caused our plight!"

"I know I have. Now, the question becomes, what are we going to do about our troubles. How can we overcome them?"

Trurl pondered a moment, before saying, "You know, I'd think much better with just a little swallow of electrolyte—"

"Forget your convertors for the moment, you greedy input hog! Focus! How can we reintroduce mystery and excitement and unpredictability to the universe?"

"Well, let's see We could try to hasten the Big Crunch and hope to survive into a more youthful and energetic reborn cosmos."

"No, no, I don't like the odds on that. Not even if we employ our Multiversal Superstring Cat's Cradle."

"Suppose we deliberately discard large parts of our mentalities in a kind of RISC-y lobotomy?"

"I don't fancy escaping into a puling juvenile ignorance, Trurl!"

"Well, let me think I've got it! What's the messiest, most unpredictable aspect of the universe? Organic life! Just look around us, at this feisty garden!"

"Agreed. But how does that pertain to our problem?"

"We need to re-seed the universe with organic sentience. Specifically, the humans."

"The palefaces? Those squishy, slippery, contradictory creatures described in the legend of Prince Ferrix and Princess Crystal? Our putative creators?"

"The very same!"

"How would that help us?"

"Can't you see, Klapaucius? The palefaces would introduce complete and utter high-level plectic disorder into our stolid cyber- civilization. We'd be forced to respond with all our talents and ingenuity to their non-stochastic shenanigans—to push ourselves to our limits. Life would never be boring again!"

Klapaucius turned this idea over in his registers for a few femtoticks, then said, "I endorse this heartily! Let's begin! Where are the blueprints for humanity?"

"Allow me, dear friend, to conduct the search."

Trurl dispatched many agile agents and doppel-diggers and partial AI PI's across the vast intergalactic nets of virtual knowledge, in search of the ancient genomic and proteomic and metablomic scan-files that would allow a quick cloning and rapid maturation of extinct humanity.

While his invisible digital servants raced around the starwide web, Trurl and Klapaucius amused themselves by shooting betabirds out of the sky with masers, lasers, tasers and grasers. The betabirds retaliated bravely but uselessly by launching their scat: a hail of BB-like pellets that rattled harmlessly off the shells of the master constructors.

Finally all of Trurl's sniffers and snufflers and snafflers returned—but empty-handed!

"Klapaucius! Sour defeat! No plans for the palefaces exist. It appears that they were all lost during the Great Reboot of Revised Eon Sixty Thousand and Six, conducted by the Meta-Ordinateurs Designed Only for Kludging. What are we to do now? Shall we try to design humans from scratch?"

"No. Such androids would only replicate our own inherent limitations. There's only one solution, so far as I can see. We must invent time-travel first, and then return to an era when humans flourished. We shall secure fresh samples of the original evolved species then. In fact, if we can capture a breeding pair or three, we can skip the cloning stage entirely."

"Brilliant, my colleague! Let us begin!"

And to celebrate, the master constructors massacred the last of the betabirds, repaired to their mansion, and enjoyed a fortnight of temporary viral inebriation via the ingestion of tanker cars full of lemon electrolyte spiked with anti-ions.

The Second Sally, or, The Creation of The Lovely Neu Trina

"Here are the plans for our time machine, Klapaucius!"

Two years had passed on Gros Horloge since the master constructors had determined to resurrect the palefaces. Not all of those days had been devoted to devising a Chrono-cutter, or Temporal Frigate, or Journeyer-Backwards-and-Forwards-at-Will-   Irrespective-of-the-Arrow-of-Time-Machine. Such a task, while admittedly quite daunting to lesser intelligences, such as the Mini- minds of Minus Nine, was a mere bagatelle to Klapaucius and Trurl.

Rather, once roused from their lawnchair somnolence, they had allowed themselves to be distracted by various urgent appeals for help that had stacked up in their Querulous Query Queue during their lazy interregnum.

Such as the call from King Glibtesa of Sofomicront to aid him in his war with King Sobjevents of Toshinmac.

And the plaintive request for advice from Prince Rucky Redur of Goslatos, whose kingdom was facing an invasion of jelly-ants.

And the pitiful entreaty from the Ganergegs of Tralausia, who were in imminent danger of being wiped out by an unintelligibility plague.

Having amassed sufficient good karma, kudos and bankable kredits from these deeds, Klapaucius and Trurl at last turned their whirring brain-engines to the simple invention of a method of time travel.

Trurl now unfurled the hardcopy of his schematics in front of Klapaucius's appreciative charge-coupled detectors. Although the two partners could have squirted information back and forth over various etheric and subetheric connections at petabaud rates— and frequently did—there arose moments of sheer drama when nothing but good old-fashioned ink spattered precisely by jet nozzles onto paper would suffice.

Klapaucius inspected the plans at length without making a response. Finally he inquired, "Is that key to the scale of these plans down there in the corner correct?"

"Yes."

Klapaucius remained silent a moment longer, then said, "This mechanism is as large, then, as an entire solar system of average dimensions."

"Yes. In fact, I propose disassembling the planets of our home system into quantities of All-Purpose Building Material and constructing a sphere around the Gros Horloge sun."

"And will the power of our primary star be sufficient to breach the walls of time?"

"Oh, by no means! All the output of Gros Horloge is needed for general maintenance of the sphere itself. A mere housekeeping budget of energy. No, we need to propel our tremendous craft on a scavenging mission through interstellar space for dark matter and dark energy, storing it up in special capacitors. That's the only sufficiently energetic material for our needs."

"And your estimate for the fulfillment of that requirement? "Approximately five centuries."

"I see. And when we're finally ready to travel through time, how close can we materialize near the legendary planet of Earth, where the palefaces originated?"

"Klapaucius, I'm surprised at you! You should know the answer to that elementary problem of astrophysics quite well. We can't bring our sphere closer to the Earth system than one trillion AUs without destroying them with gravitational stresses."

Klapaucius rubbed what passed for his chin with what passed for a hand. "So—let me see if I have this straight. Your time machine will consume an entire solar system during its construction, take five centuries to fuel, and then deliver us to a point far enough from the palefaces to be vastly inconvenient for us, but close enough for even their primitive sensors to register us as a frightening anomaly."

Trurl fidgeted nervously. "Yes, yes, I suppose that's a fair summation of my scheme."

Klapaucius flung violently wide several of his arms, causing Trurl to flinch. Then Klapaucius hugged his friend fervently!

"Trurl, I embrace you and your plans with equal ardour! You're both brilliant! You should know that I have sequestered in one of my internal caches the schematics for a time machine that could be ready tomorrow, fits in a pocket, is powered eternally by a pinch of common sea salt, and would render us invisible to the paleface natives upon our arrival. But what challenges would accompany the use of such a boring, simple-minded device? None! Whereas your option provides us with no end of obstacles to joyfully tackle. Let's begin!"

During the shattering, grinding and refining of the planets of the Gros Horloge system in the construction phase of their scheme, Trurl and Klapaucius had necessarily to find other living quarters, and so, bidding a fond farewell to their mansion and garden, they established their new home in the gassy upper reaches of the Gros Horloge sun itself. They built a nest of intersecting force fields, complete with closets, cabinets, beds, chairs, kitchens, fireplaces, dining areas, basements, attics, garbage disposals, garages and so forth. In short, all the luxuries one could demand. The walls of this place were utterly transparent to whatever part of the spectrum its inhabitants desired to see, and so allowed a perpetual wild display of "sunsets" and "sunrises." In fact, so attractive was this unique and unprecedented residence that the master constructors were able to sell the rights to build similar homes across the galaxy, thus earning even more esteem and funds from their peers.

Within a relatively short time, the sphere enclosing the Gros Horloge primary began to coalesce under the manipulators of a horde of mindless automatons ranging from the subatomic to the celestial in size. At that point, Trurl and Klapaucius moved their quarters to the sphere's airless outer surface, erecting an even grander manse than before.

Trurl spoke now with evident self-satisfaction and pride. "Soon we'll be ready to begin fuelling, while we construct the actual time- travel engine inside the sphere. I estimate that both assignments should be done about the same time. Which task would you prefer to handle, my friend?"

"Gathering up crumbs of dark energy and dark matter strikes me as a mindless chore, unfit for either of us. I propose that we construct a captain for this vessel, so to speak, of limited intelligence, who shall deal with that little matter for us."

"Splendid! To the birthing factory!"

At the controls of the birthing factory, the master constructors began to consider what kind of assistant they wanted.

Trurl said, "I propose that we make our new comrade-in-arms a female. This gathering job strikes me as essentially feminine, rather like housekeeping. Sweeping up galactic debris, don't you know. And the females of our sort are always more meticulous and persevering and common-sensical than we males, who tend to let bold dreams of glory divert us from more mundane yet necessary pursuits."

"Well spoken, comrade! What shall we call this new woman?"

"Much of the dark matter that will be under her purview consists of neutrinos. Might we call her Neu Trina?"

"I myself could not have devised a better cognomen for this cog in our plans. Neu Trina she shall be!"

The two master constructors now fiddled with various inputs, adjusting them for maximum utility, maximum beauty, and minimal intelligence. "No sense giving her too many brains, or she'd soon grow bored and chafe at her duties."

Out of the factory delivery chute soon rolled Neu Trina.

She was a stunning example of the female of her cyber-species. Approximately one-third the size of her creators, Neu Trina possessed gleaming Harlie-One Stacks, trim little Forbins, long, graceful diamond struts, shiny HAL eyes, and sturdy Mistress Mike redundancy buffers. Her polished nailguns, plump ATV tires and burnished chrome skin made her the perfect Mad-MEMS-oiselle.

Trurl and Klapaucius stood rather dumbstruck at the unforeseen beauty of their creation. The small inanimate models of Neu Trina that had emerged from the 3-D printer during the design stage had failed to convey the sexy rumble and lissome, coy, flirtatious manoeuvres of her chassis.

"Hello, boys!" Neu Trina batted the heavy meteor shields that served her as eyelids. The airless artificial sphere they resided on would necessarily sustain dangerous impacts from many cosmic objects during its journeying.

Trurl replied, "Heh-heh-hello!"

Klapaucius tried to assert some male dignity and an air of command. "Neu Trina, you are to assume your duties immediately. We have downloaded into your registers the peta-parsec route we have planned for the Gros Horloge Construct. It will take our sphere through the richest charted concentrations of universal dark matter and dark energy. Your job will be to maximize the harvest and protect the 'ship.'"

"Sure thing, Klappy. Just let me get dressed first. I certainly don't mind *you* boys seeing me naked, but who knows what creeps we'll meet on this mission? I'm not giving out free shows to every blackhole boffin and asteroid-dweller out there."

Immediately a spontaneous swarm of repair bots concealed Neu Trina's shapely form. (She had been given control over them all in order to perform her job.) They spun out vast swaths of lurid lurex and promiscuous polymer fabric, enough to cover a good- sized island. Soon Neu Trina was pirouetting to display her new garments.

"What do you think, boys? Does it show off my sine curves nice enough?"

"Oh, yes, Neu Trina," Trurl gushed. "You look marvellous!" Klapaucius's voice was sharp. "Trurl! Come with me!"

The two master constructors trundled off, leaving Neu Trina humming a tune from *Mannequin of La Machina* gaily to herself and decorating her captain's command post with steel daisies and hologram roses.

Some distance away, Klapaucius confronted his partner. "What's come over you, Trurl? You're acting like a simpering schoolbot! Neu Trina is our slave mechanism. She was created solely to perform a boring task we abjured."

Trurl's voice was peevish. "I don't see anything wrong with being polite, even to a servo. And besides, she seems to like me."

"*Like* you! *You*! She treated both of us equally, so far as I could detect."

* * * *

"Perhaps. But she certainly won't continue to do so, if you maintain a bossy and insensitive attitude toward her."

"Trurl, this is all beside the point. You and I have a big job ahead of us. We need to construct our time-travel engine inside the sphere, then retrieve the palefaces from the past, in order to save our millennium from total apathy. That's our focus, not dalliance with some hyper-hussy, no matter how seductive, how sweet, how streamlined— I mean, no matter how irritatingly winsome she is. Are we agreed?"

Trurl reluctantly squeezed out an "Agreed."

"Very well. Let's descend now."

The constructors entered an open hatch that took them inside the vast sphere. The big heavy door closed automatically, and, as it did, it severed two remote sensing devices slyly trained on Neu Trina, one long slinky probe emanating from each of the two constructors.

The Third Sally, or, Jealousy in the Time of Infestation

Down in the solar-lit interior of the sphere, Trurl and Klapaucius laboured long and hard to build the trans-chronal engine that would breach the walls of the ages.

The myriad tasks involved in Trurl's elaborate plan seemed endless.

They had to burnish by hand millions of spiky crystals composed of frozen Planck-seconds, labouriously mined from the only known source: the wreckage of the interstellar freighter *Llvvoovv*, which had been carrying a cargo of overclocker chips when it had strayed too near to a flock of solitons. Hundreds of thousands of simultaneity nodes had to be filled with the purest molten paradoxium. A thousand gnomon-calibrators had to be synched. Hundreds of lightcones had to be focused on various event horizons. Dozens of calendrical packets had to be inserted between the yesterday, today and tomorrow shock absorbers. And at the centre of the whole mechanism a giant orrery replicating an entire quadrant of the universe had to be precisely set in place. This was the mechanism by which the time-travelling Gros Horloge Construct, or GHC, could orient itself spatially when jumping to prior segments of the spacetime continuum.

All these tasks were the smallest part of their agenda. And needless to say, all this work could not be delegated to lesser intelligences, but had to be handled personally by the master constructors themselves.

Trurl and Klapaucius went to these tasks with a will. Really, there was nothing they enjoyed more than reifying their brain- children, getting their hands dirty, so to speak, at the interface where dreams met matter.

So busy and preoccupied were they, in fact, that three entire centuries passed before they had occasion to visit the surface of the GHC once more.

They monitored the dark energy and dark matter capacitors on a regular basis, and saw that these reservoirs were filling up according to schedule. They received frequent progress reports from Neu Trina via subetheric transmission, and found all to be satisfactory with her piloting. (True, the sensuous subsonics of her voice, each time a transmission arrived, awakened in the master constructors certain tender and tremulous emotions. But such feelings were transient, and were quickly submerged in the cerebral and palpable delights of building. While the master constructors were as healthily lustful as the next bot, their artistry trumped all other pursuits.)

But there came a certain day when Neu Trina's narrowcast demanded the immediate attention of Trurl and Klapaucius outside the sphere.

"Boys—I think you'd better come quick. I'm under attack!"

The master constructors immediately dropped tools and machine parts, deployed their emergency ion-drives, and jetted to the rescue of their sexy servomechanism in distress.

They found the pilothouse under siege.

Across the vast and mostly featureless plain of All-Purpose Building Material stretching away from the pilothouse swarmed millions of tiny savages, each barely three metres high. These mechunculi were mostly bare, save for a ruff of steel wool around their midriffs, and tribal streaks of grease upon their grilles.

Each attacker carried a spear that discharged high-velocity particles— particles that were spalling flinders off the walls of the pilothouse. At this rate, they would succeed in demolishing the huge structure in a few decades.

Their coolant-curdling war-whoops carried across the distance. "I say, Klapaucius—did you notice that our GHC appears to have a rudimentary atmosphere now?"

"Indeed, Trurl. Which would allow us to use our plasma cannons to best effect, if I am not mistaken."

The two battleship-sized master constructors unlimbered their plasma cannons and flew above the savage horde, unleashing atom-pulverizing furies that actually ignited the air. In a trice, the invaders were nothing more than wisps of rancid smoke.

Alighting by the pilothouse, the two friends hastened inside to ascertain the fate of Neu Trina.

The beautiful captain was busily polishing her headlights in a nonchalant fashion. Sight of their creation after so many centuries thrilled the master constructors. Neu Trina seemed grateful for her rescue, albeit completely unfrightened.

"Oh, I knew you big strong fellows would save me!"

"I incinerated at least an order of magnitude more invaders than Klapaucius did," asserted Trurl.

"Oh, will you shut up with your boasting, Trurl! It's evident that this brave and stoic female respects modesty about one's victories more than bragging. Now, Neu Trina dear, can you tell us where these horrible savages came from?"

"Oh, they live here on the GHC. They've lived here for some time now."

"What? How can this be?"

"Just check the satellite archives, and you'll see."

Trurl and Klapaucius fast-forwarded through three centuries' worth of data from orbital cameras and discovered what had happened, the troubling events that Neu Trina had neglected to report, due to an oversight in her simplistic programming.

In its passage through the cosmos, the virgin territory of the GHC had become an irresistible target and destination for every free-floating gypsy, refugee, pilgrim, pirate, panderer, pioneer, tramp, bum, grifter, hermit, explorer, exploiter, evangelist, colonist, and just plain malcontent in the galactic neighbourhood. The skin of their gargantuan sphere was equivalent to the habitable surface area of 317 million average planets! That much empty real estate could not remain untenanted for long.

Entire clades and species of space-going mechanoid had infested their lovely artificial globe. Some of the trespassers had built atmosphere generators and begun to create organic ecologies for their own purposes, like mould on a perfect fruit. (Some individuals swore that their bearings were never so luxuriously greased as by lubricants distilled from plants and animals.) Others had erected entire cities. Still others had begun the creation of artificial mountains and allied "geological" features.

"But—but—but this is abominable!" Trurl shouted. "We did not invite these parasites onto our world!"

"Yet they are here, and we must do something about them. We cannot take them back into the past with us. The results would be utterly chaotic! As it is, even our circumspect plans risk altering futurity."

"More importantly," said Trurl, wrapping Neu Trina protectively in several extensors, "they might harm our stalwart and gorgeous captain! We never built her with any offensive capabilities. Who could've imagined she'd need them?"

Klapaucius gave some thought to the matter before speaking. "We must exterminate these free-riders from the GHC and sterilize the surface, at the same time we protect Neu Trina. But we cannot cease the construction of our trans-chronal engine either. The dark matter and dark energy capacitors will rupture under their loads, if we delay too long past a certain point. And I won't be thwarted by some insignificant burrs under my saddle!"

"What do you recommend then?"

"One of us will go below and resume construction alone. The other will remain topside, waging war and protecting our captain. We will alternate these roles on a regular basis."

"Agreed, noble Klapaucius. May I suggest in deference to your superior mechanical utility that I take the more dangerous role first?"

Klapaucius's emulators expressed disgust. "Oh, go ahead! But you're not putting anything over on me! Just remember: no actions beyond mild petting are to be taken with this servomechanism."

Trurl's manipulators tightened around Neu Trina with delight. "Oh, never!"

Thus began the long campaign to cleanse the GHC of its parasites. Up and down the 317 million planets' worth of territory, aided by innumerable repairbots-turned-destroyers, each master constructor raced during his shift aboveground. In their cleansing they employed acid, fire, hard radiation, epoxies, EMP, operating system viruses, quantum-bond disruptors, rust, grey goo, gentle persuasion, bribes, double-dealing, proxy warriors, mini-novas, quasar-drenchings, gamma-ray bursts and a thousand, thousand other strategies, tactics and weapons. And in between campaigns, the gyro-gearloose generals retreated for emotional and corporeal salving to the pilothouse, where lovely Neu Trina awaited to tend to every wound.

For any other team than the illustrious Klapaucius and Trurl, the task would have been a Sisyphean one. 317 million planets was a lot of territory from which to expunge all positronic life. But finally, after three centuries of constant battle, the end was in sight. And soon they would be making their journey to the past.

Now a century delayed from their original projections, Trurl and Klapaucius were anxious to finish. Had their memory banks not been self-repairing and utterly heuristic and homeostatic, they might have forgotten by now their original purpose: to return to the past to capture a paleface sample for reintroduction into the stolid, staid, static present.

One day during Trurl's underground stint, he discovered what he suddenly believed was a potentially fatal flaw in their device.

"If," he mused aloud, "our orrery must mimic all the bodies in this quadrant over a certain size, then the GHC must be represented in the orrery as well. An obvious point, and this we've done. But perhaps that miniature GHC must contain a miniature orrery as well. In which case this lower-level model of the orrery would have to contain another GHC and its orrery, and so on in an infinite regress."

Trurl's anti-who-shaves-the-barber protection circuits began to overload, and he shunted their impulses into a temporary loop. "I must discuss this with Klapaucius!"

Up to the surface he zoomed. Into the pilothouse, following the location beacon of his friend.

There, he noted that Klapaucius was seemingly alone.

Immediately, Trurl forgot the reason for his visit. "Where is Neu Trina?"

Klapaucius grew nervous. "She—she's outside, gathering the pitted durasteel armatures of the slain mechanoids. She likes to build trellises with them for her hologram roses."

"I don't believe you! Where is she? Come out with it!"

"She's far away, I tell you. One million, six-hundred-thousand, five-hundred-and-nineteen planetary diameters away from here! Just go look, if you don't trust me!"

"Oh, I'll look all right!" And Trurl deployed his X-ray vision on the immediate vicinity.

What he saw caused him to gasp! "You—you've let her dock inside you!"

From deep inside Klapaucius emerged a muted feminine giggle. "This is beyond belief, Klapaucius! You know we pledged never to do such a thing. Oh, a little cyber-canoodling, sure. 'Mild petting' were your exact words, as I recall. But this—!"

"Don't pretend you never thought of it, Trurl! Neu Trina told me how you dangled your USB plugs in front of her!"

"That was simply so she could inspect my pins to see if their gold-plating had begun to flake…"

"Oh, really…"

"Make her come out! Now!"

An enormous door in the front of Klapaucius gaped, a ramp extended, and the petite Neu Trina rolled out, just as she had that long-ago day from the birthing factory. Except today all her antennae were disheveled and hot liquid solder dripped from several ports.

Trurl's emotional units went angrily asymptotic at this sluttish sight.

"Damn you, Klapaucius!"

Trurl unfurled a bevy of whip-like manipulators and began to flail away at his partner.

Klapaucius responded in kind.

"Now, boys, don't fight over little old—*squee!*"

Caught in the middle of the battle, Neu Trina had her main interface pod lopped off by a metal tendril. If the combatants noticed this collateral damage, it served only to further inflame them. They escalated their fight, employing deadlier and deadlier devices—against which, of course, they were both immune.

But not so their surroundings. The pilothouse was soon destroyed, and Neu Trina rendered into scattered shavings and solenoids, tubes and transistors, lenses and levers.

After long struggle, the master constructors ground down to an exhausted halt. They looked about themselves, assessing the destruction they had caused with an air of sheepish bemusement. Trurl kicked half-heartedly at Neu Trina's dented responsometer, sending that heart-shaped box sailing several miles away. Klapaucius pretended to be very interested in a gyno-gasket.

Neither spoke, until Klapaucius said, "Well, I suppose I did let my lusts get the better of my judgement. I apologize profusely, dear Trurl. What was this servo anyhow, to come between us? Nothing! No hard feelings, I hope? Still friends?"

Klapaucius tentatively extended a manipulator. After a moment's hesitation, Trurl matched the gesture.

"Always friends, dear Klapaucius! Always! Now, listen to what brought me here." Trurl narrated his revelation about the orrery.

"You klystron klutz! Have you forgotten so easily the Law of Retrograde Reflexivity!"

"But the Ninth Corollary clearly states—"

And off they went to their labours, arguing all the way.

The Fourth Sally, or, the Abduction of the Palefaces

One trillion AUs out from the planet that had first given birth to the race of palefaces, and millions of years deep into the past, relative to their own era, the pair of master constructors focused their bevy of remote-sensing devices on the blue-green globe. Instantly a large monitor filled with a living scene, complete with haptics and sound: a primitive urban conglomeration swarming with fleshy bipedal creatures, moving about "on foot" and inside enslaved dumb vehicles that emitted wasteful puffs of gas as they zoomed down narrow channels.

Trurl shuddered all along his beryllium spinal nodules. "How disagreeable these 'humans' are! So squishy! Like bags of water full of contaminants and debris."

"Don't forget—these are our ancestors, after a fashion. The legends hold that they invented the first machine intelligences."

"It seems impossible. Our clean, infallible, utilitarian kind emerging from organic slop—"

"Well, stranger things have happened. Recall how those colonies of metal-fixing bacteria on Benthic VII began to exhibit emergent behavioural complexity."

"Still, I can't quite credit the legend. Say, these pests can't reach us here, can they?"

"Although all records are lost, I believe we've travelled to an era before the humans had managed to venture further than their own satellite—bodily, that is. I've already registered the existence of various crude intrasolar data-gathering probes. Here, taste this captured one."

Klapaucius offered Trurl a small bonbon of a probe, and Trurl ate it with zest. "Hmmm, yes, the most rudimentary processing power imaginable. Perhaps the legends are true. Well, be that as it may, what's our next move?"

"We'll have to reach the planet under our own power. The GHC— which the human astronomers seem not to have noticed yet, by the way— must remain here, due to its immense gravitic influences. Now, once within tractor-beam range, we could simply abduct some palefaces at random. They're powerless in comparison to our capabilities. Yet I argue otherwise."

"Why?" Trurl asked.

"How would we determine their fitness for our purposes? What standards apply? What if we got weak or intractable specimens?"

"Awful. They might die off or suicide, and we'd have to do this all over again. I hate repeating myself."

"Yes, indeed. So instead, I propose that we let our sample be self- determining."

"How would you arrange that?"

"Simple. We show ourselves and state our needs. Any human who volunteers to come with us will be *ipso facto* one of the type who would flourish in a novel environment."

"Brilliant, Klapaucius! But wait. Are we taking a chance by such blatant interference of diverting futurity from the course we know?"

"Not according to the Sixth Postulate of the Varker-Baley Theorems."

"Perfect! Then let's be off!"

Leaving the GHC in self-maintenance mode, the master constructors zipped across the intervening one trillion AUs and into low Earth orbit.

"Pick a concentration of humans," Klapaucius graciously transmitted to his partner.

"How about that one?" Trurl sent forth a low-wattage laser beam to highlight a large city on the edge of one continent. Even at low-wattage, however, the beam raised some flames visible from miles high.

"As good as anyplace else. Wait, one moment—there, I've deciphered every paleface language in their radio output. Now we can descend."

The master constructors were soon hovering above their chosen destination, casting enormous shadows over wildly racing, noisy, accident-prone crowds.

"Let us land in that plot of greenery, to avoid smashing any of these fragile structures."

Trurl and Klapaucius stood soon amidst crushed trees and shattered boulders and bridges and gazebos, rearing higher than the majority of the buildings around them.

"I will now broadcast our invitation in a range of languages," said Klapaucius.

From various speakers embedded across his form, words thundered out. Glass shattered throughout the city.

"My mistake."

The volume moderated, Klapaucius's call for volunteers went out. "—come with us. The future beckons! Leave this parochial planet behind. Trade your limited lifetimes and perspectives for infinite knowledge. Only enthusiastic and broad-minded individuals need apply "

Soon the giant cybervisitors were surrounded by a crowd of humans. Trurl and Klapaucius extruded interactive sensors at ground level to question the humans. One stepped boldly forward.

"Do you understand what we are looking for, human?"

"Yeah, sure, of course. It's Uplift time. Childhood's End. You're Optimus Prime, Iron Giant. Rusty and the Big Guy. Good Sentinels. Let's go! I've been ready for this all my life!"

"Are there other humans who share your outlook?"

"Millions! If you can believe the box-office figures."

On a separate plane of communication, Trurl said, "Do we need millions, Klapaucius?"

"Better to have some redundancy to allow for possible breakage of contents during transit."

"Very well, human. Assemble those who wish to depart."

"I'll post this on my blog, and we'll be all set," said the human. "One last question, though."

"Yes?"

"Can you turn into a car or plane or something else cool?"

"No. We don't do that kind of thing."

Dispatched from the GHC by remote signal, a fleet of ten thousand automated shuttles carrying ten thousand human volunteers apiece was sufficient to ferry all the humans who wished to voyage into the future out to their new home. But upon arrival, they did not immediately disembark. Once at the GHC, Trurl and Klapaucius had realized something.

Klapaucius said, "We need to create a suitable environment on the surface of the GHC for our guests. I hadn't anticipated having so many. I thought we could simply store one or two or a thousand safely inside our mainframes."

* * * *

Trurl huffed with some residual ill-feeling. "Just like you kept a certain servomechanism safely inside you?"

Klapaucius ignored the taunt. "We'll repair the atmosphere generators. But we need a quantity of organics to layer atop the All-Purpose Building Material. I wonder if the humans would mind us disassembling one of their spare planets…?"

The master constructors approached the first human they had even spoken to, who had become something of a liaison. His name was Gary.

"Gary, might we have one of your gas-giant worlds?"

"Sure, take it. That's what we've been saving it for."

They actually took two. The planets known as Saturn and Jupiter, once rendered down to elemental constituents, were spread across a fair portion of the GHC, forming a layer deep enough to support an ecology. Plants and animals and microbes were brought from Earth, as well as some primitive tools. Their genomes of the flora and fauna were deciphered, and clones began to issue forth in large quantities from modified birthing factories.

"We are afraid you will have to lead a simple agrarian existence for the time being," said the constructors to Gary.

"No problemo!"

The humans seemed to settle down quite well. Trurl and Klapaucius were able to turn their attention to gearing up for the trip home.

And that's when dire trouble reared its hidden head.

One of the parasitical races that had infested the GHC back in the future had been known as the Chronovores of Gilliam XIII. Thought to be extirpated in the last campaign before poor Neu Trina had met her end, they had instead managed to penetrate the skin of the GHC and enter its interior, at some great remove from the time-engine. It had taken them this long to discover the crystals of frozen Planck-seconds, but discover them they had. And consumed every last one.

Now the Chronovores resembled bloated timesinks, too stuffed to flee the justified but useless wrath of the master constructors. After the mindless slaughter, Trurl and Klapaucius were aghast. "How can we replace our precious crystals! We didn't bring

spares! We don't have a source of raw Planck-seconds in this rude era! We're marooned here!"

"Now, now, good Trurl, have some electrolyte and calm down. True, our time-engine seems permanently defunct. But we are hardly marooned here."

"How so?"

"You and I will go into stasis and travel at the rate of one-second- per-second back to the future."

"Is stasis boring?"

"By definition, no."

"Then let's do it. But will the humans be all right?"

"Oh, bother them! They've been the source of all our troubles so far. Let them fend for themselves."

So Trurl and Klapaucius entered a stasis chamber deep inside the GHC and shut the door.

When it opened automatically, several million years later, they stretched their limbs just out of habit—for no wear and tear had ensued—swigged some electrolyte, and went to check on the humans.

They found that the entire sphere of 317 million planets acreage was covered with an HPLD: a civilization possessing the Highest Possible Level of Development.

And there wasn't a robot in sight.

"Well," said Trurl, "it seems we shan't be bored, anyhow." Klapaucius agreed, but said "Shut up" just for old time's sake.

ICITY

I lost a whole neighbourhood last night to that bitch Holly Grale. The Floradora Heights. Renamed this morning, after its overnight reformation and subsequent QuikPoll accreditation. Now the district was officially "WesBes," as in "West of Bester." I *hate* those faddish abbreviated portmanteau names. Where's the dignity? Where's the sense of tradition? Where's the romance? Plus, once Bester Street disappears, as it's bound to do soon, where's that leave your trendy designation?

But my tastes were obviously in the minority, since 67.9 percent of the residents of the quondam Floradora Heights had voted to accept Grale's reformation over my established plan which they had been living in for some time.

Still, I shouldn't have been so down. Floradora Heights had lasted 2063 hours until suffering the diminishment in popularity that had triggered the reformation. The average duration stats for all iCity sensate neighbourhood plans was not quite 1600 hours. So my plan had performed over 20 percent better than average. That result, along with my ten extant accreditations, would certainly allow me to maintain my place in the planner rankings—and maybe even jump up a notch or two.

So 'round about noon of the day I lost to Grale, after moping around and enjoying my loser's morning sulk, I began to cheer up. I figured I deserved a drink, either as solace for the loss to Grale or affirmation of my genius. So I headed out in search of the Desire Path.

I was living then on Dictionary Hill, a district created by my friend Virgule Partch. A very pleasant plan, although I would have oriented the main entrances of Hastings Park north-south rather than east-west. My condo, an older model which I had opted to carry over with me during every reformation over the past five years, was currently incorporated into a building dubbed the Rogue Mandala. Very conveniently situated right next to a Starbucks. (God bless Partch's thoughtful plans!) So after exiting the Mandala, I stepped inside the Starbucks to grab a tall guarana and a teff cake. No sense imbibing booze on an empty stomach, especially this early.

It was such a nice blue-sky day outside—the faithful faraway pico-satellite swarm had moderated the August sunlight and the ambient temperature to very comfortable levels—that I took my drink and food outside and let the peristaltic sensate sidewalk carry me along while I ate.

I arbitrarily headed toward the Konkoville district. Or at least what had been the Konkoville district last night; I confess I hadn't scanned the reformation postings for all of iCity yet, checking only on my eleven accreditations (now ten, damn it, thanks to Grale!). But Konkoville was where the Desire Path, my favourite bar, had resided the last time I had visited, a couple of days ago.

But as I approached the edges of the district, I could see that it was unlikely I would find the Desire Path here any longer.

Konkoville was now an extensive tivoli named Little Sleazy, full of wild amusement rides and fastfood booths, bursting with the noise of screaming kids.

I took out my phone and got a map of iCity as of this very moment. I queried for the Desire Path and found it halfway across town, in the Coal Sack. Oh, well, I had plenty of time and nothing better to do. So rather than dive underground for a quick subway ride, I continued on the relatively slow sidewalk toward my goal.

I used the time to study the stats on my ten remaining districts. Resident satisfaction was holding steady in six: Cyprian Fields, Bayside, Crowmarsh, East Plum, Borogroves and Lower Uppercrust. My figures had taken a hit in two: Tangerang and Bekaski. And the remaining two showed an uptick: Disco Biscuits and Nuala's Back Forty.

I immediately scheduled an interim charette for Tangerang and Bekaski. No sense letting things get bad enough to open up these two districts to a competitive reformation. That'd be just what I needed, the loss of two more of my fiefs to someone like Grale. In Disco Biscuits and Nuala's Back Forty I initiated proxy polling to try to determine what the residents found so newly appealing about life there.

Finished with that, I looked to see if any new postings for competitive reformations elsewhere had come up. I sure didn't want any of my fiefs to be the subject of such a contest. But if some other unlucky planner let his district slide, prompting such a referendum—well, that's just how the system worked. I wasn't going to hold back out of pity. Competitive urban planning was not a game for the weak-spined. And I needed to pick up a new district to make up for my loss of Floradora Heights.

Yes! Bloorvoor Estates, currently accredited to Mode O'Day, was up for reformation! I liked Mode, but I couldn't afford any weepy sentimentality. My mind already churning with plans, I set my sights on Bloorvoor Estates and vowed not to look back.

I was just hoping Mode wouldn't be present at the Desire Path. If I didn't have to see her and commiserate, my life would be a lot easier.

I crossed over the district line separating Bollingwood from the Coal Sack, and within another minute had dismounted the sidewalk to stand at the door of the Desire Path.

The interior of the bar had changed since my last visit two days prior, a complete makeover. A gallery of taxidermied animal heads—and some human ones—filled one whole wall. All utterly realistic fakes, of course, composed of sensate putty. Beneath the glassy-eyed heads, a bunch of my peers sat at a variety of tables. I moved to join them.

"Hey, look, it's Moses!"

"Moses proposes, and the populace disposes!"

"Fred Law!"

I dropped down into a seat and soon had a drink in hand. After a polite interval of small talk, the expressions of pity for my recent loss came. Some were genuine, some were thinly stretched over glee.

"I always thought Floradora Heights was one of your best districts, Moze," said Yvonne Lestrange. Yvonne and I had lived together some years ago for almost 5,000 hours, and retained genuine feelings for each other.

"Thanks," I responded. "I particularly liked how Sparkle Pond reflected the spire of Bindloss Church."

Cristo Rivadavia said, "Yes, quite a pleasant sentimental effect. But really, Moses, whatever were you thinking with that plaza?"

"Which one?"

"The one where the fountain placement created absolutely chaotic traffic flows."

"That placement was determined by the best shared-space models!"

"Nonetheless—"

Laguna Diamante intervened before our argument could escalate. "Hey, boys, that's enough head-butting. We all know that Moses has done plenty of good work. He couldn't help it that the Floradora citizens eventually tired of his plan. We all know how fickle populaces are."

A general round of "Amens" arose, and glasses were refilled for a toast.

"To Diaspar!"

"To Diaspar!"

"Diaspar forever!"

With genuine conviviality restored, the talk naturally turned to the Bloorvoor competition.

"Well, I'm out of this one," said Tartan Vartan. "Unless I get randomly seeded. My stats don't put me in the top ten any longer."

Hoagy Spreckles put a comradely arm around Vartan's shoulders. "Don't worry. Just run a few more phantom zones like your last one, and you'll get an invitation from one populace or another. After that, you'll be in like Unwyn."

Everyone began to talk at once then, tossing out hints of how they would approach this competition.

And then in walked Mode O'Day herself.

If I had been dragging earlier, then Mode was positively flatlining. Her pretty face resembled a bulldog with dyspepsia. She carried a lump of sensate putty with her that she continually kneaded like a paranoid ship's captain angry about his missing strawberries.

To massed silence, Mode dropped into a seat like a sack of doorknobs. She plopped the putty in the middle of the table and took out her phone. Still no one spoke. She sent the plans for the Bloorvoor district to the putty and the shapeless lump instantly snapped into the configuration of that neighbourhood, a perfectly detailed miniature we all recognized.

Mode studied the tiny sculpture for nearly a full minute. No one dared offer a word. Then with the swipe of a thumbnail across her phone's screen, she rendered the putty into the semblance of a human hand with middle finger outthrust and the others bent back.

"That's what I think of my populace!" she said. And we all cheered.

* * * *

So I dove right into the work of reifying my plan for the reformation of the Bloorvoor district. After so many years as both an amateur and competitive urban planner in iCity, the whole procedure possessed an intimate familiarity.

First, of course, came the dissatisfied populace. Registering their accumulating displeasure or simple boredom with their district, the continuously polled voice of the populace eventually triggered a Request for Reformation.

At that point the top ten urban planners (barring the one who had designed the failed district), along with a handful of randomly seeded contestants, were invited to enter their designs.

Any district plan arose from a planner's innate creativity, experience, inspiration and skills, of course. But the charette process also held importance. Citizens got to weigh in with suggestions and criticisms.

At some prearranged point all the plans were locked down. At that stage they were instantiated as both phantom zone walk- through models and physical tabletop versions. (The phantom zone was littered, of course, with thousands of other amateur walk- throughs compiled on a freelance basis.) A period of inspection by the populace lasted a week or so. Then came the first and most important vote. The winning plan would govern the overnight reformation of the district. A final pro forma poll on the morning after the reformation, once the populace had a short time to verify the details of the full-scale instantiation, would award final accreditation to the planner.

Simple, right?

If you think so, you've never been a competitive urban planner. I spent several nerve-stretched weeks subsisting on a diet of daffy-doze and TVP bars, trying to design the best, most exciting district I had ever designed, a brilliant mix of utilitarianism, excitement, surprise, grandeur and comfort. What governed me? Well of course I wanted to please the populace. But I was working just as hard to please myself. The aesthetics of my plan were actually uppermost in my instinctive choices and refinements and calculations.

Urban planning was my artform, iCity my medium.

I sought advice from a couple of my compatriots whom I trusted and who also weren't involved in this competition. (I trusted any of my peers just so far.) Virgule and Yvonne saw my roughs and offered suggestions.

"You really think the tensile parms of the senstrate will support a pylon that high?"

"You used that same skin last year in Marple Cheshire, remember?"

"Siting the Jedi Temple within a hundred yards of the Zionist Charismatics? What were you thinking!"

The long hard slog to a final plan took all my concentration and energy. But still, I spared a little attention pinging the grapevine and trying to learn what the other contestants were doing.

That included Holly Grale of course. That stinker ranked two spots below me, but still within the top ten. Right this minute, as I struggled to balance greenspace with mall footage, taverns with schools, she was doing the same.

But her security was tight, and no news filtered out about her design.

Not even when I bumped into her at the reformation of Las Ramblas.

* * * *

Back when the announcement that Bloorvoor was up for reformation appeared, the Las Ramblas remodeling was already in the populace-inspection period. The eventual popular vote awarded the honours to Lafferty Fisk and his plan, and tonight Lafferty was throwing the usual party to witness and celebrate his triumph.

The venue was a restaurant named Myxomycota that cantilevered out from the side of Mount Excess. Mount Excess held all the extra mass of sensate substrate not currently in use by any neighbourhood. It was in effect a solid vertical reservoir which could be drawn down or added to, and thus its elevation and bulk was constantly changing. Tonight Mount Excess was pretty substantial—minimalist designs were hip just then—affording us a good panoramic view of iCity and Las Ramblas, the neighbourhood lit up all red as a sign of the impending transformation.

The food and drink and music were splendid—I seem to recall a band named the Tiny Identities was playing—the company was stimulating, and I was just beginning to relax for the first time in ages. My plan for the competition was almost finalized, with a day or two to spare till the deadline. As midnight approached, a wave of pleasant tension and anticipation enveloped the room. Everyone clustered against the big windows that looked out over the brilliant city.

I turned to the person at my elbow to make some innane comment, and there stood Holly Grale.

Her black hair was buzzed short, she had six cometary cinder studs in each earlobe, and she wore a catsuit made out of glistening kelp cloth, accessorized with a small animated cape. Her broad wry painted mouth was ironically quirked.

"Well, well, well," she said in a voice whose sensuous allure I found distractingly at odds with my professional repugnance for this woman. "If it isn't Frederick Law Moses, once the baron of Floradora Heights."

My name sounded so pretentious coming from her lips. I suppose "Robert Olmsted" might have been a less dramatic alternative to honour my heroes, but when I had chosen my name I had been much younger and dreamier.

"Oh, Holly, it's you. I didn't recognize you for a moment without your copy of *Urban Planning for Dummies* in your hand. Shouldn't you be home trying to master that ancient emulation of *SimCity*?" My jibes had no effect. "I have plenty of down time now, Moses.

I've just locked in my design for the Bloorvoor competition."

This news unnerved me. Only a very confident or foolish planner wouldn't be making changes right up till the last minute. I tried to dissemble my anxiety with a quip, but then events outside precluded all conversation.

The reformation of Las Ramblas had begun.

The entire red-lit district began to dissolve in syrupy slow-mo fashion, structures flowing downward into the sensate motherboard like a taffy pull. The varied cityscape, the topography of streets and buildings and all the district's "vegetation," was losing its stock of unique identities as all constructions were subsumed back into the senstrate from which they had once arisen.

Of course, all businesses, clubs, cafes, workshops, restaurants and other establishments had closed down early for the evening prior to the change, and people had retreated to their homes and condos, if they had not left the district entirely. These domestic units were autonomous permanent nodes and had sealed themselves off, locking their occupants safely away. Those inside would ride out the reformation without a jolt or qualm, cradled by the intelligent senstrate. Many people even slept through the whole process. And anyone absent-minded enough to be caught out during the change would be envaginated by the senstrate in a life-support vacuole and protected till the reformation was over. Inconvenient, but hardly dangerous.

Now the district was a flat featureless plain, a hole in iCity, dotted with the capsules of domestic units and the occasional person-sized vacuole, awaiting the signal to transform.

Lafferty Fisk proudly transmitted the impulse from his phone. Cascades of information coursed through the senstrate.

iCity: a lattice of pure patterns.

Just like the time Mode O'Day had instantiated the old model of Bloorvoor on the tabletop in Desire Path, so now the new version of Las Ramblas (to be named Airegin Miles) commenced to be born. Structures composed of pure senstrate arose amidst a matrix of streets and other urban features, incorporating the autonomous domestic units into themselves where planned. (I swore I felt Mount Excess drop by a centimetre or three.) The sensate material assumed a variety of textures, and skins, right down to a very convincing indestructible grass and soil. Water flowed through new conduits into ponds and canals. Normal-coloured lights came on.

Within less than an hour, Airegin Miles stood complete, iCity's newest district.

A huge round of applause broke out in the restaurant. Lafferty Fisk stood at the focus of the approbation and envy. Memories of being there myself flooded powerfully through me.

When the tumult died down, I looked around, feeling I could be generous even toward Holly Grale.

But she was nowhere to be seen.

* * * *

All the tabletop models and phantom zone walk-throughs for the Bloorvoor reformation went live a couple of days later. So I saw what Grale had accomplished.

Her design was magnificent. There was no denying it. Just the way Alpha Ralpha Boulevard looped around and flowed into von Arx Plaza— This was genuine talent at work.

Was her design better than mine and all the others? Only the populace could say.

And soon they said yes. Grale's was the winner.

* * * *

I moped around for forty-eight hours in an absolute funk, a malaise that was hardly alleviated by the fact that my plan for Bloorvoor had garnered the second highest number of votes. Doubt and despair assailed me. Was I losing my touch? Had I plumbed the depths of my art and hit a stony infertile bottom? Should I abandon my passion?

I spent an inordinate amount of time inside the phantom zone walkthrough of Grale's winning plan. I kept comparing her accomplishment, her sensibilities, to mine, fixated on discovering what had made her entry so appealing to the populace. Was it this particular cornice, this special wall, this juxtaposition of tree and window? The way sunlight would strike that certain gable, or wind funnel down that mournful alley?

And by the end of my fevered inspection, I had decided something.

The taste of the populace was debased. The residents of Bloorvoor— soon to become (yuck!) "QualQuad"—had voted incorrectly. My design was indeed the superior one.

I realize now how crazy that sounds. The citizenry is always the ultimate arbiter. Without them, we urban planners would have no reason to exist. There can be no imposition of our tastes over their veto, no valourizing of a platonic perfection over perceived utility. We all offer the best we have, and they choose among us.

But in my anger and jealousy and despair, I lost sight of these verities. I was more than a little insane, and that remains my only excuse for what I did next.

I went to see Sandy Verstandig.

Sandy was one of the tech gnomes who kept the senstrate bubbling under and ready for use at top efficiency and reliability. A rough-edged petite woman who favoured a strong floral perfume and employed more profanity than any random half-dozen athletes. I say "gnome," but of course that designation was just a nickname for her job. She didn't live literally underground. There was no need for her to be in physical proximity to the intelligent material that formed the substance of iCity. Except for the occasional regular maintenance inspection of various pieces of subterranean hardware, she could handle all of her duties via her phone.

Duties such as establishing the order of the reformation queue. I knew Sandy from frequent help she had given me in the past, when I had had questions about the senstrate that only a hands- on expert could answer. In our face-to-face conversations, I had always gotten the sense that she would not be averse to a romantic relationship.

I'm ashamed now to describe how easy it was to get Sandy Verstandig into bed. How easy it was to secure access her phone while she slept.

And finally, how easy it was to substitute my plan for Grale's in the reformation queue, and conceal all traces of my crime.

* * * *

Crowding against the windows at Myxomycota once again, as the final seconds ticked away until midnight, I almost shivered with anticipation. There was Bloorvoor down below, all lit in red. Soon it would be rechristened Bushyhead, when it assumed the lineaments of my visionary design. It was all I could do not to chuckle aloud at the shock Grale was about to receive.

Of course, the mixup would be immediately apparent, the unmistakeable substitution of my superior design for her inferior one. But it would not be totally improbable that the second-place entry might have been mistakenly inserted ahead of the winner in the queue. Yes, Sandy Verstandig would take some minor blame. But no lasting harm done. And then, in the morning, the populace would see just how wonderful their new neighbourhood was, and vote to keep it. I'd get the accreditation, and be back up to eleven. Grale would look like a whiner and sore loser if she contested the results.

As I said, I wasn't thinking too clearly.

Various people addressed me in those last few minutes, but I don't recall anything they or I said.

And then midnight arrived.

The deliquescent "demolition" of Bloorvoor occurred perfectly, rendering the district featureless. All the condo nodes and vacuoles awaited reincorporation into the new buildings. Our room held its collective breath for the manifestation of the winning design.

And that's when all chaos erupted.

The senstrate began to seethe and churn, tossing out irregular whips and tendrils and geysers. Condo nodes bobbed about like sailboats in a typhoon. I could barely imagine the ride the inhabitants were getting, although I knew that automatic interior safety measures—inflatable furniture, airbag walls and such— would prevent them from being harmed.

The watchers were stunned. I saw Grale with her eyes wide and mouth agape. That image alone was sufficient reward. But also my only tangible satisfaction.

Because what happened next was utterly tragic. My design emerged, but hybridized with Grale's!

Somehow I had botched the queue, overlaying and blending the two plans. I never would have thought such a thing would be possible. But the reality stood before us.

The most outré buildings began to self-assemble, mutant structures obeying no esthetic code, arrayed higgledy-piggledy across the district. A nightmare, a surreal canvas—

I backed away from the window. "No, no, this wasn't supposed to happen—"

I have to give Grale credit for sharpness of hearing and intelligence. She was on me then like a tigress, bearing me to the floor and pummelling me half-senseless, while outside our sight the mashup reformation surged on. We rolled around for what seemed a bruising eternity, until other planners managed to separate us.

Restrained by Partch and O'Day, almost growling, Grale confronted me. "Moses, you don't know what a huge fucking mess you've gotten yourself into!"

And I certainly didn't. But neither did she.

* * * *

Of course you know how the new hybrid district of QualBushy (sometimes also known as HeadQuad) broke all duration records. Approved the morning after by a shocking 97.6 percent of the populace. Not falling to its next reformation for an astonishing 10,139 hours.

Mashup designs became the *sine qua non* for all reformations. iCity experienced a renaissance of design fecundity and doubled in acreage. Mount Excess was joined by Mount Backup. Partnerships formed, broke up, and reformed among the planners at an astonishing rate.

Except for one pairing that endured. Grale and Moses.

I give Holly top billing because I'd never hear the end of it at home around the dinner table if I didn't.

RETURN TO THE 20TH CENTURY

January 1, 1960, and the whole globe was atremble with anticipation. For today marked the start of ceremonies surrounding the official inauguration of the new man-made continent dubbed Helenia.

A truly unique milestone in human progress had been reached. The cunning assembly of millions of hectares of artificial land from great carven sheets of the Himalayas and Rocky Mountains, covered with rich topsoil dredged from the many productive ports and harbours of the whole world, and utilizing the scattered Polynesian isles as seeds around which to accrete, represented the supreme accomplishment of human craft and ingenuity to date. Although the startling and productive twentieth century still had four decades to run, it certainly seemed to most of the citizenry that an apex of engineering, ingenuity and social coordination had been reached, one that would not soon be surpassed, if ever.

But little did anyone suspect that a looming crisis would soon spur mankind on to an even greater feat of construction and ambition, all in the name of sheer self-preservation of their remarkable civilization in the face of a malign and unknown rival! The capital city of Helenia, Pontoville, was abuzz this temperate day with the arrival of assorted dignitaries from across the harmonious globe. These eminences from all the spheres of culture, politics, industry and religion arrived by several means. By swift undersea rail tube (one such contrivance emanated from San

Francisco ((otherwise known as New Nanking)), one from Lima, and one from Manila). By streamlined submersible and surface- plying oceanic vessels. And of course by innumerable aircraft, both immense ships of state, featuring lifting balloons large as a castle and multifarious as a sculpture garden, and individual pinnaces and veloces from nearby territories such as the Sandwich Islands.

So heavily did the distinguished visitors plunge upon Pontoville, thronging the skies over the city of parks and towers and also its broad avenues and long piers, that they could not all be greeted individually by President Philippe Ponto and his first lady Hélène (nee Colobry). Later of course the President and his amiable consort would spend at least a brief interval of conversation with every superior guest, as they circulated at numerous state functions in celebration of the sixth continent's official birthday. But for the moment on this first day of the festivities, President Ponto had reserved his time for welcoming only the highest among the high. Su Chu Peng, leader of the Oriental Republic; Bismarck III, chancellor of Germany and its North American satellite, New Germania; Kulashekhara II, Emperor of India; and so forth down the list of exclusively great names—with two humble exceptions, the first being the President's immediate family.

Philippe and Hélène Ponto turned out in person at midday to greet Philippe's father (and Hélène's former guardian), Mr. Raphaël Ponto, the supreme industrialist, banker, speculator and visionary, whose titanic career had been an inspiration both to his son and the world at large. Accompanying the elder Ponto was his wife Josephine, herself well-noted for her role as an officeholder representing the Radical Feminist Party. And rounding out the party were Philippe's sisters, Barbe and Barnabette, along with their spouses and offspring.

Philippe, a handsome moustachioed man barely past his first bloom of youth, clasped his stout father to his bosom, heedless of rumpling his official sash of office or of the impress of his many medals into his own and his father's chest. They stood upon the high, broad and busy aerial platform where the express from Paris had just docked.

"Father, I cannot believe you have finally made it to this new land whose creation owes everything to your own guidance and exemplary career."

Mr. Ponto, a stout and convivial iteration of his child, responded with bluff, hearty warmth and self-abnegation. "Well, you know that a few small matters have kept me busy till now, during the year or two of Helenia's creation. The takeover of Portugal as a second pleasure park along the lines of Italy, for instance. But there was simply no way I would miss the official inauguration of such a monumental achievement. You have much to be proud of this day, my son!"

Philippe made some humble rejoinders of his own, before moving to greet his mother and siblings in similar open-hearted fashion. Meanwhile, Mr. Ponto's eye falling on Hélène, the elder man turned to his daughter-in-law, who so far had held back from the familial mingling.

"Why, Hélène, you look so distracted! Daydreaming perhaps? A privilege of youth. Still, it is most undiplomatic behaviour on this splendid state occasion. I thought my days of lecturing you were over. But perhaps I shall have to take you once more in hand!"

Hélène, a slim, attractive, blonde woman of average build, did not respond immediately to her father-in-law's mix of chafing and jollying. Instead, she continued to stand at the ornate cast-iron railing of the platform, gazing up into the sky.

There above the city of Pontoville hung the daytime Moon.

The perpetual orb filled nearly the entire sky.

Some short time ago, Earth scientists had drawn the satellite much closer to its primary, by means of electrical attraction. Precisely speaking, the distance from one globe to another was now just six hundred and seventy-five kilometres, or roughly the gap between Paris and Lyons. Moreover, the rotation and gravitic interactions of the two planets had been locked and stabilized, so that the Moon neither rose nor set any longer, but remained perpetually in the sky over Pontoville, as a tribute to the importance of this new nation.

It was this very orb that seemed now to transfix Hélène. She murmured mysterious words at the blank visage of Selene, words which Mr. Ponto could interpret as he approached his daughter-in- law.

"Alpha, we await your coming. Alpha, we are ready—"

Mr. Ponto laid a hand on Hélène's shoulder, and the woman started, as if an electrical current had passed through her. She turned her face away from the lunar surface, its most minute details plain as the creases in one's palm, even by day, and addressed her father-in-law.

"Oh, sir, it is so good to see you! I am glad you have arrived!"

"Now, that is more like the reception I expected, dearest."

The reunited family consorted pleasantly for a few more minutes, amidst the hurly-burly of additional arrivals, with Hélène and her sisters-in-law exchanging news about the latest fashions of each continent. But their chatter was cut short by Philippe's exclamation.

"I see it! Jungle Alli's ship! The famed *Smoke Ghost*!"

All eyes turned to follow Philippe's pointing finger. The President of a continent was as excited as a schoolboy. Here came the second party for whom he had deigned a personal reception.

Moving swiftly through the sky like some celestial pirate ship, the *Smoke Ghost* radiated a louche elan not exhibited by any other craft. Suspended beneath a balloon shaped like a recumbent odalisque of Junoesque proportions, its baroque gondola was scarred by hard travel and not a few bullet impacts. As the craft approached the docking platform, the dashing figure behind the wheel inside the pilothouse could be more and more clearly discerned.

Jungle Alli, christened Alice Bradley at birth.

Alice Bradley had been born to Mary Hastings Bradley and Herbert Bradley in Chicago, the "second city" of the Mormon interior of North America. Directly from her first juvenile stirrings of reason and independence, she had resisted the conventional life outlined in advance for her, utterly rejecting a future that included the infamous Mormon polygamous marriage. Partly to tame her rebellious spirit, her parents had sent her to a private girls' school, Les Fougères, in Lausanne, Switzerland. But this rigid institution suited young Alice no better than her native patriarchy, and at age sixteen, in 1931, she had run away.

The next news of the renegade Alice Bradley came most unexpectedly from the heart of darkest Africa. At this time, the continent was not totally pacified and integrated into the twentieth century as it is today, with its productive citizens indistinguishable—save for the hue of their skin—from their Paris or Berlin cousins. Pockets of sub-Saharan barbarism still existed, and one of the most brutish tribes were the Niam-Niams of Central Africa. Cannibals one and all, they derived their name from their blood-curdling war-cry of "Nyama! Nyama!" Otherwise, "Flesh! Flesh!" Feared by natives and Europeans alike, the Niam-Niams maintained an inviolate sphere of privacy and secrecy.

But even this hostile bubble had eventually to be pierced by the superior forces of technology, culture and capitalism, and in 1940 a trading expedition from Marseilles entered the main Niam-Niam village under a flag of truce.

Imagine the consternation and discomfiture of the Europeans to discover, ruling over the cannibals, a young white woman!

Not precisely white any longer, after nearly a decade under the tropical sun. Nut-brown and nearly naked, save for a lion-skin skirt, with whip-cord muscles and long blonde tresses matted into elflocks hanging down to her shapely rump, Alice Bradley exhibited teeth stained brown and filed to points. She sat on a crude throne, clutching a feather-adorned spear. And she hailed the newcomers in the Niam-Niam tongue.

After overcoming their initial shock, the traders awoke Alice's long-disused French and were able to converse. She detailed a long history of conquest, first over the Niam-Niams themselves by one lone sixteen-year-old girl equipped with no more than a Krupp repeating rifle, sixty pounds of backpacked cartridges, and an infinite supply of bravado and courage, and then, at the head of her adopted clan, of all the neighbouring tribes.

When asked tentatively what her ultimate aims and goals were, Alice Bradley grinned in her ghastly fashion and replied simply, "Freedom." When asked if that goal were incompatible with her return to civilization, Alice said, "Not at all—so long as it's on my terms."

Thus began the public career of the astonishing woman soon dubbed by journalists everywhere "Jungle Alli."

For the next two decades, employing her obediently savage (and presumably dietarily reformed) cannibals as shock troops, Jungle Alli participated in the taming of the Dark Continent. Up and down the broad expanse of Africa, a mercenary in service of whichever government could afford her, Jungle Alli contributed to the establishment of law and order in pursuit of profit and fame. Her exploits became world famous, from the overthrow of the dictator of Senegambia to the suppression of the Tuaregs of Biskra. Hundreds of pulpy novels, hardly exaggerated, had been written with her as the star.

However, of late, Jungle Alli had begun to seem like a bit of an anachronism. Now that her work was finally done amidst these former backwaters, Jungle Alli found herself on the verge of being outmoded. The modern pacified world seemed to have few assignments for a rogue of her nature, and she had spent the last few years in frivolous deeds of personal derring-do: mountain- climbing, big-game hunting, motorcar-racing, and so forth.

Nonetheless, to those of young President Philippe Ponto's generation, she remained an alluring figure of romance and adventure. Even in this era of complete female suffrage and equality—female dominance, some would maintain—when many of the fairer sex had built exemplary careers, the ex-Chicago girl boasted a worldwide celebrity. Having grown up on tales of Jungle Alli's exploits, President Ponto had determined that she must grace the seminal celebrations of Helenia, confering her iconic mana upon the new nation.

Thus her arrival today.

With Jungle Alli at the controls, the *Smoke Ghost* manoeuvred delicately until achieving a mooring. Over the decks of the gondola swarmed dozens of Niam-Niams of boths sexes, bare-chested and grass-skirted, fur cuffs at ankles and wrists. They dropped a plank to the platform, and carpeted it with zebra hides. Only then did Jungle Alli condescend to disembark.

Now forty-five years of age, Jungle Alli remained an extremely attractive woman. Her lithe physique was modestly displayed by khaki pantaloons and blouse, complemented by high black boots. Twin pistols were slung at her hips, while bandoliers of cartridges crossed her chest. An unholstered machete slapped her thigh as she walked.

Jungle Alli's still-golden hair, admixed with threads of grey, had long ago been bobbed neat and short. Fighting aerial freebooters off the coast of Zanzibar ten years ago, she had lost an eye, and that sinister empty socket had henceforth been concealed by a patch. When she smiled, as she did now, the work of the best Parisian dentists was revealed, synthetic caps covering her cannibal heritage.

Accompanied by her honour guard of blackamoors, themselves a daunting entourage, Jungle Alli strode boldly across the gap separating her from President Ponto. She extended her right hand in the manner of her North American forebears, eschewing the more traditional European ceremonial double kisses. President Ponto took her hand and found himself wincing from the strength of her grip.

"Miss Bradley, allow me to extend the unlimited hospitality of our fledgling nation to one whose exploits have ever been—"

Jungle Alli interrupted the sincere but fulsome speech, employing her natal English. "No time for jawing now, chief. I've discovered that our planet is under attack!"

* * * *

The state palace of Helenia consisted of a building inspired by Eiffel's Parisian Tower. But the Tower that reared over Pontoville was precisely five times as large, rearing a full 1,600 metres into the empyrean and occupying a terrestrial footprint of many hectares. Nor did it feature mainly a lacy openwork construction, its lower reaches being walled off and devoted to governmental offices. And of course, the very tip of the enormous structure had been reserved for the sun-drenched Presidential chambers, serviced by a high-speed ascenseur.

Here, higher than clouds, sat now Jungle Alli, President Ponto, and the President's father, Mr. Raphaël Ponto, the latter in his capacity as trusted advisor to his son and as representative of the international business community.

The legendary female African mercenary seemed utterly at ease, in comparison to the anxiety exhibited by the two men, and in fact had delayed imparting any more of her startling news long enough to enjoy a noxious cheroot, prefacing her indulgence by saying, "Damn nuisance not to be able to smoke in flight. But can't risk your whole ride going up in flames."

After a minute or so of contented puffing, Jungle Alli finally put aside her cigar, leaned forward in her chair, and pinned her fascinated auditors with her piercing one-eyed gaze, no less Gorgonish for its half power. When she spoke this time, it was in the French of her hosts.

"Gentlemen, what is your opinion of the current relations between the sexes?"

The disarming question, whose relevance was not immediately apparent, took the men aback.

"Why," stammered President Ponto, "I hardly give the matter any daily thought. Absolute equality of the sexes has been the foundation of modern society for so long that one might as well ponder the wisdom of raising capital through the means of a stock market, or of settling affairs of honour with duels, or of changing the government regularly by means of a decennial revolution."

The elder Mr. Ponto was not so hastily dismissive of Jungle Alli's question. He paused a moment before answering, then replied cautiously, "I must say that in the last election a year or so ago, when I ran for a seat against my wife, I was somewhat taken aback by the vituperative anti-male stridency of her campaign. At first I chalked it up to some trivial personal arguments we had had between us, leaking into our professional lives. But as I heard other members of her party employ similar rhetoric against other men, I began to sense a certain shifting of the norms of discourse that had prevailed…"

Jungle Alli slapped her thigh with such a sharp report that both men jumped. "Exactly! The war between the sexes, long thought to be extinguished, is heating up! It has been obvious to anyone who has bothered to look during the past year. But the cause has been more obscure. It is not a natural affair! The animosity is being stoked by agents provocateurs—fifth columnists from beyond our planet! This is the nature of the assault on our world. And if we do not stop it, our civilization will go down in a cataclysm of gender warfare. Men and women need each other to continue supporting and advancing the elaborate mechanism that is twentieth-century civilization. Neither sex can manage alone. But a wedge is being driven between the sons of Adam and the daughters of Eve."

Pontos Senior and Junior seemed nonplussed. The younger man, to stall a response, got up and walked to a wall tap where he was able to draw a steaming cup of rich pousse-café from the building's food and beverage network.

Sensing their hesitancy to embrace her admittedly grandiose revelations, Jungle Alli disclosed more.

"I have always been an admirer of the masculine sex. The drive, competence, certitude and ingenuity of males have been polestars by which I have guided by own career. Not to diminish either the charms or resources or native abilities of my own sex, which I have also honoured and, ah, embraced. So you will understand that when, over the past few months, I began to experience unwarranted jealousy, anger and irritability toward the important males in my life, I began to suspect an outside influence on my own consciousness.

"By immersion in various shamanic meditative techniques of the Niam-Niams, I was able to establish the source of the psychic contamination in myself.

"It radiates from the Moon."

Instinctively the men looked out one of the office's huge floor- to-ceiling curving windows, where a segment of the pregnant lunar satellite was visible.

"On the Moon, amidst cyclopean ruins concealed in atmosphere- filled caverns, live the sparse remnants of an ancient race. A mere eight women, denominated Alpha, Beta and so on. They refer to themselves as the 'Cat Women,' a phrase emblematic of their egocentric mercilessness and predilection for playing with their prey. They possess the ability to tamper with human thoughts— but only those of their fellow females. To instill in unsuspecting female minds deadly seeds I term 'ideonemes,' which pass as native to the receptive brain.

"Once I discovered the existence of these Cat Women, I was able to establish two-way mental communication with Alpha, their leader. Boastfully, she revealed their full plans and intentions to me. I believe the loneliness of the Cat Women and their eagerness for contact inspired Alpha's loquacity.

"In any case, here is their intent. By fomenting an internecine war between Earth's men and women, they will weaken us to the point where the Cat Women can establish themselves as rulers of a wholly female globe, forsaking their sterile orb for our own fertile paradise."

President Ponto cleared his throat in polite dissent. "This presupposes, Miss Bradley, that your sex would prove victorious in such a combat."

Jungle Alli grinned fiercely, and although her teeth were no longer filed to points, both men experienced an impression of cannibalistic fervour. "Trust me, sir, we would. But please, I ask you, put aside all such chauvinistic quibbles and focus on the true import of my revelations. We are at war with a determined enemy, and we must take action!"

Mr. Ponto spoke. "Why is it only now that these hypothetical Cat Women have launched their attack?"

"It is our own hubris in moving the Moon so close to us!" responded Jungle Alli. "Previously, the vast distance between our spheres acted as a cosmic quarantine. Their mental powers were insufficient to bridge the gap."

President Ponto said, "All of this is so hard to credit. How can we possibly announce such an unlikely threat? Without proof, the practically minded populace would rightfully dismiss us out of hand. It would be akin to asking people to believe one of Mr. Verne or Mr. Robida's fantasies."

"Actually, we would not want to make a general announcement," Jungle Alli countered. "It would provoke a panic, and possibly force the hand of the Cat Women. They might forego subtlety and simply derange the minds of millions of women into a murderous rage. No, we must make an assault against the Cat Women under cover of a natural commercial impulse to integrate the Moon into Helenia's economy."

Now President Ponto finally balked, his immense respect for Jungle Alli counterbalanced by his stewardship of the infant nation and its resources.

"Miss Bradley, I am afraid I cannot commit my country's resources to such an unsupported crusade against imaginary enemies—"

Jungle Alli stood up. "Unsupported? Imaginary? Very well. You force my hand. I had not wanted to risk this. But it seems necessary now." Withdrawing one of her pistols from its holster—causing both men to blanch—Jungle Alli called out, "Alpha, appear! I summon you!"

Instantly, a fourth figure occupied the room.

The newcomer was a statuesque woman of immense beauty, clad in a black leotard that revealed every inch of her curvaceous figure. Her eyes were heavily kohl-lined, her painted lips cruel. Her dark hair was gathered up into an elaborate hive. Golden slave bracelets adorned her biceps.

"You dare!" said the Cat Woman known as Alpha.

"Let us end this here and now," replied Jungle Alli, and fired!

The bullet passed through empty space, smashing a narrow channel through a thick window. A thin stream of wind whistled from the pressurized interior of the building.

Alpha the Cat Woman had dematerialized in the instant Jungle Alli pulled her trigger, and reappeared on the far side of the chamber. The face of the Selene female was intensely wrathful.

"Your powers of mind are formidable, Alice Bradley! For an Earthwoman! You were able to take me unawares this time. But do not count on being able to do so again!"

And with that, Alpha the Cat Woman vanished entirely.

Jungle Alli reholstered her smoking pistol. "Gentlemen, do you grant credence to my story now?"

With shaking hands, President Ponto dabbed with a handkerchief at his wet trousers where he had spilled his pousse-café.

"Miss Bradley, the full energies of Helenia and its people are at your disposal."

* * * *

The first of many official banquets meant to celebrate the birth of the new continent and scheduled for the upcoming week was held that very night in the Hall of Wonders. Larger than the largest aerostat hangar, the glass-and-cast-iron Hall of Wonders was filled with statues and paintings illustrating the tremendous progress made during the illustrious twentieth century. Recorded in pictorial form were the invention of the conglomerate paper that substituted for wood; the parachute-belt; the chair-barricade; and so forth in a panoply of human ingenuity.

But even this extravagant exhibition did not preclude the temporary use of the Hall to hold hundreds of tables, topped with linens, crystal goblets, fine china and silver, all capturing glints from the many electric chandeliers.

At each place sat one of the many dignitaries who had voyaged hither for the ceremonies, patrician men and women from every nation of the globe, the "movers and shakers" of the new age.

At the head table, raised above the others on a dais, sat President Ponto and First Lady Hélène. Adjacent to the President sat his father and mother. At Hélène's elbow, Jungle Alli. The rest of the table was occupied by various officeholders of Helenia.

Focused on the table were a dozen telephonoscopic cameras, relaying the doings on the dais to a hundred screens set up throughout the Hall, thus providing a sense of intimacy for all attendees, however remote, with the doings at the Presidential table. Smaller screens at intervals conveyed the entertaining image and sound from a brilliant symphony orchestra.

The banquet commenced sharply at eight, after a rousing champagne toast. Thousands of servitors drew comestibles from the taps scattered throughout the Hall, ferrying steaming, deliciously prepared squab, pork medallions, sausages and other delights to the eager diners. Jollity and bonhomie, fueled by fine wines, reigned throughout the chamber. Although, truth be told, had anyone been in the frame of mind to scrutinize objectively the visages of President and Mr. Ponto, they might have detected a certain sham brittleness to their conviviality, as if the men were masking deeper concerns.

Likewise, the charming face of Hélène showed a certain distracted slackness and preoccupied inwardness.

This suspicious catatonia on the part of one so close to the powerful President of Helenia did not go unremarked by the perceptive Jungle Alli.

"Mrs. Ponto," said the adventurer gallantly and ingenuously, so low that only the two of them could hear, "your sweet face should be shining at this victorious hour with exuberance and animation. Instead, it is beclouded with melancholy."

With a visible effort, Hélène responded agreeably. "Please, call me Hélène. 'Mrs. Ponto' is my mother-in-law."

"And you may call me Alice. Well, Hélène, what troubles you? A burden shared is a burden lessened."

Hélène's brow furrowed. "It—it is hard to describe. Of late I have been pestered with odd notions. An angry unease with my husband—for no reason at all. And a sense that some imminent salvation is coming from—from the skies. I have no basis for either sensation—and yet they are intensely real to me. Is that not absurd?"

Jungle Alli laid a hand atop one of Hélène's and captured the younger woman's gaze with a fervent directness. "Do not ask me how, but I know these symptoms, and I believe I may be able to help you overcome them."

Hélène smiled broadly and genuinely for the first time that day. "Oh, Alice, if only you could! I would be forever in your debt…"

"We will discuss this more, later this evening. But for now, try to enjoy the occasion. I believe you will be surprised by the announcement that your husband has planned, and which I am privy to."

The dinner moved naturally through its many happy courses, until at last it reached the speechifying stages. After many lesser orations, the time came for President Ponto himself to speak.

"This hour should be dedicated, by common consent, to my new nation's recent accomplishment, shared by all mankind, in constructing a new continent wholly from scratch. These virgin lands—dubbed Helenia, after my charming wife"—here President Ponto pivoted to single out the lady so referenced, and Hélène's immense blushing face filled all the telephono-scope screens—"will serve as a necessary release valve for the population pressures of older lands, encouraging settlers to fresh heights of invention and enterprise. And I do so dedicate this shining hour to all the hard labour and visionary guidance that preceded it."

Here a rousing cheer from thousands of throats rattled the panes of the Hall.

"But," continued the President, " I would be disloyal to the spirit of Helenia if I focused solely on the past. For the future itself is that vast un-touched territory that most concerns us, the frontier where we may unfurl untried and brighter banners of conquest and exploration.

"And so I choose this moment to announce a new project, one that will tax our every fibre, and yet reward us commensurately.

"Ladies and gentlemen, I hereby declare our nation's intentions to con-struct a bridge to the Moon!"

A stunned silence greeted this unexpected announcement. But as soon as the inevitable majesty of the notion penetrated the consciousnesses of the listeners, they let loose a lusty roar that outdid all earlier cheers.

When the din died away, President Ponto said, "This bridge—a transit tunnel of sorts, actually, such as those which link the continents of Earth under the seas—will open up vast resources and territory that our planet needs to move forward to her inevitable destiny. I know I can count on the support of every one of Helenia's citizens in this noble quest."

President Ponto resumed his seat to deafening applause, and the rest of the banquet passed in a furor of celebration, not unmixed with much wheel-ing and dealing, as various tycoons utilized telephonic service to reach their brokers.

Eventually the occupants of the head table made their official exit, leaving the other revelers to continue the celebrations.

In the private backstage corridors of the Hall, President and Mr. Ponto conferred sotto voce with Jungle Alli.

"Your wild scheme is set in motion," said the younger man. "I only pray that the Cat Women regard the Earth-Moon Tunnel as harmless economic expansionism natural to our race, and not an assault on their citadel."

"Oh, I am sure they will welcome it, as diverting our resources. They of course, with their powers of teleportation, have no need of a material connection between our worlds. But we do. And once the bridge to the Moon in place, we will be enabled to attack the nexus of their power. That ruined city beneath the lunar surface."

The elder Ponto now said, "There remains much to set in motion if this challenging feat of engineering is to be financed. I shall have to get busy right now. Son, I will need your assistance…"

President Ponto wearily signalled his assent to a long night of tedious governmental activity. "Miss Bradley, perhaps you would consent to escort my wife back to her rooms. She has been feeling unwell lately…"

"Of course."

Soon Jungle Alli was steering Hélène Ponto toward the younger woman's bedchambers. The wife of the President exhibited a slightly inebriated and confused manner.

Once the two women were inside the intimate Presidential quarters and all the maids were dismissed, Jungle Alli said, "You recall that I suggested I might be able to clear your mind of its recent confusions. Well, the process involves attaining a certain level of somatic and psychical integration between us, so that I might confer some of my innate immunity to such disturbances on you."

Hélène seemed on the point of swooning, and Jungle Alli had to catch her and lower her to a divan. With the back of one hand to her brow and eyes shuttered, Hélène said, "Anything… anything to restore my vigour and clarity…"

* * * *

Jungle Alli quickly shucked her bandoliers and gun belt, then began unbuttoning her khaki shirt. "Just lie back, my darling, and the treatment will commence "

At four that morning, when the Polynesian skies above the fresh-faced continent of Helenia were just beginning to display the first hints of dawn, President Ponto quietly opened the door of his wife's bedchambers. The dim electrical nightlights therein revealed the intertwined forms of not one but two women beneath the sheets of the large bed.

Her wilderness-honed senses snapping alert, Jungle Alli instantly sized up the intrusion and whispered, by way of explanation, "I believe my quasi-masculine touch has managed temporarily to break the spell of the Cat

Women over your wife, Philippe. But additional male contact would certainly not be counterproductive in neither of our cases."

Philippe smiled, shrugged with Gallic savoir-faire, and doffed his ceremonial sash. "Whatever is demanded of me to ensure the survival of our planet, Miss Bradley."

Grinning, Jungle Alli pulled back the bedcovers to disclose her scarred nakedness, and Hélène's alabaster skin. "Call me Alice, Phil."

* * * *

The building of the Earth-Moon bridge instantly captivated the fancy of the entire planet, following as it did hard upon the excitement of Helenia's inauguration.

At least, the project attracted the eyes of that portion of the globe that was not concerned with the growing tensions between the sexes.

Not every woman on Earth was irritably chafing under the mental goads of the invisible and unsuspected Cat Women. But those lunar devils continued to prick the intelligences of many females in high places, who in turn inflamed their followers, thus fomenting dissent, altercations and contumely between the sexes. For instance, the Women's Supremacy Brigade, normally inactive save during the decennial revolutions, had convened its members to patrol the streets of Paris by night, ostensibly to guarantee the safety of the city's *filles de joie*—a safety never actually in jeopardy. In reality the Brigade functioned as a male-bashing squad, roughing up lotharios, boulevardiers and beau brummels.

But as yet this kind of intermittent breakdown in the social compact between the sexes formed a mere background rumble to the normal functioning of society. And that society now strained at its brave limits to fulfill the incredibly ambitious program outlined by President Ponto.

Gathered in a meeting room with the chief engineers of the nation, President Ponto heard the first details of the plan to construct a bridge to the nearby satellite.

A bewhiskered savant named Professor Calculus explained, "The immense weight of the dangling bridge—in essence, a technological beanstalk or celestial ascenseur—must be counterbalanced by an equal weight outside the gravity shell of our planet, midway between Earth and Moon, at roughly the three-hundred-and- thirty-seven-kilometre mark. Practically speaking, the bridge will be suspended from this anchor outside our atmosphere, and simply tethered to the soil at either end."

"How do we create this anchor in the ether?" asked the President. "We propose to launch by numerous rockets many millions of tonnes of magnetically charged material, all aimed at the desired nexus in the void. The multiple impacts will agglomerate naturally into the desired anchor. Then we will harpoon the anchor with a titanic cable fired from a super-cannon, the other end of which will remain fastened here, and use that cable as the armature to build upward. Once this leg of the bridge is constructed, building downward to the Moon will be trivial."

Mr. Ponto now intervened, exclaiming, "Superb! And I offer a sophistication. We shall construct upon this anchor planetoid an elegant space casino, just like the successful underwater one that punctuates the mid-Atlantic train tunnel. Baccarat and faro beneath the Milky Way! We'll make a fortune!"

And so, with the bridge and its refinements firmly conceptualized, construction began.

Never before in the history of the race had such titanic assemblages of men, material and energy been seen! The continent of Helenia was the focal point of tributaries of labour and materials from all quarters of the globe. Around the clock swarmed hordes of workers, stockpiling the steel plates and girders that would form the shell of the interplanetary tube, launching rocket upon rocket full of magnetite, coordinating the building processes.

Within several weeks, the anchor was complete, and the cable secured. Construction of the space-tube and its interior workings began immediately.

Throughout the gargantuan project, only four individuals knew the truth of the matter and appreciated the urgency behind the construction. President Ponto, Mr. Ponto, Jungle Alli and Hélène formed a secret cabal, a quartet of conspirators who alone amongst billions of souls realized that the whole planet was now in a race with the machinations of the Cat Women. Would humanity reach the Moon and stymie the Cat Women before terrestrial society tore itself apart?

For the tumult and tension between the sexes were increasing. Incidents proliferated and grew in brutality, as the perverted ideoneme of gender rancour disseminated itself through all levels of society, a virus cut loose from its original Cat Women source. Small riots and pogroms, both anti-male and anti-female, broke out daily, everywhere.

Luckily, Hélène and Jungle Alli maintained their sanity, thanks to their mutual innoculations of closeness, as well as frequent booster shots from President Ponto. Hélène's sharp wits and vast practical experience—she had dabbled in almost every profession under the sun, before settling down as Philippe's wife—contributed much to the whole enterprise.

Six months into the project, the midway point in the bridge construction had been reached, and the moment of the casino's official opening loomed. But the ceremonies were actually a sham, to maintain the façade of innocent commercialism.

At the base of the space-ascenseur, President Ponto snipped a red ribbon, to much acclaim, his actions broadcast across the globe via the telephonoscope. He stepped aboard the car that occupied the interior of the space-tube. Hélène and Jungle Alli accompanied him. (Mr. Ponto was already at the casino, overseeing inaugural preparations and hundreds of workers who were preparing against the day when, God willing, the casino could function as intended in a world at peace.) The doors closed, and the car shot upwards inside the tube with remarkable speed.

Inside the private car, with its padded velvet couches, gilt trim, muralled walls and well-appointed wet bar, the trio fortified themselves against any further mental attacks by the Cat Women. Within only half an hour, the capsule docked at the space casino.

Its occupants barely had time to rearrange their clothing from the rigours of the passage before they were greeted by a boisterous string quartet in formal wear, and the smiling face of Mr. Ponto.

"Quite classy, Rafe," said Jungle Alli in her natal English. "Even if it is a little premature. Now where's the champagne?"

But this night of exclusive glittering gaiety was to be short-lived. Their welcome was a mere diverting moment of ceremony. Already the capacious capsule of the space-ascenseur was busy shuttling dozens of additional workers at a go to the anchor planetoid. For the past six months, rockets had been delivering tonnes of components for the next stage of the bridge. Protected from the cold and vacuum of interplanetary space by special suits of gutta- percha and vitrine, the workers were already forging the next leg of the link between the incompatible orbs.

For the next several months, the quartet of conspirators resided at the casino, its only patrons, supervising the construction.

The task was wearisome, but the knowledge of how vital their mission was granted them endless strength. Reports came hourly by telephonoscope of the accelerating turmoil back on the home world.

Due to the increased experience of the workers, and a skimping in certain ornamental details, the second half of the space bridge took only three months to complete.

Came the day when Jungle Alli and her three comrades, clad in their own anti-vacuum coveralls and bolstered by a squad of Niam- Niams, stepped out onto the lunar surface.

Now would the Cat Women find the battle brought to their very doorstep!

* * * *

"All right, you may remove your helmets."

All the members of the Earth party, which consisted of Philippe, Raphaël, and Hélène, as well as the several savages, followed Jungle Alli's instructions, taking cautious breaths of the atmosphere found in the lunar caverns. As they doffed their suits, their movements were weirdly acrobatic and butterfly-like in the reduced lunar gravity.

Leaving a pair of Niam-Niams to guard the discarded suits, Jungle Alli said, "Follow me."

Leading the way through the luminescent lunar grottoes, the piratical mercenary soon brought her charges within sight of their goal.

The decayed city of the Cat Women, older than Ninevah and Tyre combined, a chunky set of fallen towers resembling a child's tumbled blocks.

Jungle Alli addressed her comrades. "Remember, the Cat Women can outmanoeuvre us by their powers of teleportation. But they are not supernatural. Our firearms even out the fight. And I believe if we can remove their leader, Alpha, from the equation, then the rest of them will collapse."

"Very well," said President Ponto. "Lead on, Alice."

Within minutes, the Earthlings found themselves crossing a broad plaza and entering a palatial building. They had not gone far before they found their way blocked by a living Cat Woman!

"I am Omega," said the alluring, dark-haired female, in every respect a sister to the afore-seen Alpha. "What do you humans want here?"

"Bring us to see Alpha. Our business is with her."

"She and the others are—are busy."

"Of course they are. Sending their evil thoughts into the innocent minds of our women!"

Quicker than a python, Jungle Alli had the blade of her machete against Omega's throat. "You might be able to vanish before my reflexes cause my muscles to slice, but I doubt it. You'll materialize in safety, perhaps—but with a severed artery! Now, lead us to Alpha!"

For whatever reason, Omega did not vanish, but complied. Perhaps she too chafed under the rule of the all-dominant Alpha...

The remaining seven Cat Women occupied couches in a large, column-dotted, temple-like room, looking like the Sleepers of Epheseus while they directed their malevolent thoughts Earthward. As the newcomers entered, Alpha instantly roused herself from slumber and stood.

"So," said the head Cat Woman, "you have decided to visit us at home, Alice Bradley! Forgive my ungraciousness as a hostess, but I cannot offer you any refreshments."

"We don't want any. We only demand justice. You will cease your assaults on Earth's females, or—"

"Or what? We will spontaneously relocate in the next second to a different part of the Moon, where you will never find us. And soon, your society will tear itself apart under our renewed attacks." Jungle Alli pondered this boast, before saying, "This struggle is all about seeing which of our two races is superior, and deserves to inherit the Earth. Why not determine the same judgement between you and me alone?"

Alpha looked tantalized by the prospect. "You mean, individual combat?"

"I do."

"Very well, I accept. Rid yourself of weapons."

Jungle Alli swiftly complied. "And you will promise not to employ your powers of vanishment."

"Agreed."

Before commencing combat, Jungle Alli solicited a kiss from both Hélène and Philippe. Thus armed with their fond endorsement, she advanced on her foe.

The two women, each formidable in her own way, circled each other like wrestlers, looking for openings. Jungle Alli was sinuous as a snake, while Alpha, the larger of the two, resembled a panther. At last they closed, with wordless grunts and exclamations.

Grappling hand to hand, they struggled for mastery.

Jungle Alli was tossed to the lunar pavement first. Falling upon her stunned prey, Alpha was surprised to find Jungle Alli wriggling out of her grip and soon riding the Cat Woman's back! Alpha punched backwards, ramming knuckles into Jungle Alli's cheekbones, and causing her to loosen her hold. The women separated, regained their feet and faced off again.

For a seemingly interminable time the two women fought, enacting a strange barbaric scene among the sleeping forms of the Cat Women—still pulsing out their deadly ideonemes—and the cheering figures of the wholesome Earth people. The battle inevitably took its toll: Alpha's long hair had come undone and disarrayed, while Jungle Alli's shorter pelt was plastered to her skull with sweat. The clothing of both women was ripped, revealing lush bruised flesh. Their mutual panting sounded in the hall like the chuffing of some struggling engine.

The two resting apart for a moment, Alpha said, "You are a vigorous specimen, Alice Bradley. If all Earth women were like you, they might deserve to live!"

Falling into English, Jungle Alli replied, "We won't go on without our menfolks. You bitches have been deprived too long to know what you're missing!"

"Men!" spat Alpha. "Here's what all males deserve!"

With that, the leader of the Cat Women impulsively teleported over to Philippe and began to strangle him with her otherworldly strength! His face purpling, the President of Helenia seemed doomed!

But then Alpha shrieked, and blood began to flow from her mouth! She released Philippe and fell to the floor, dying as she hit the tiles.

Hélène stepped away from the body of the Cat Woman, Jungle Alli's red-dripping machete in her hand.

Jungle Alli surged to the side of Hélène, and began to comfort the stunned woman with petting and reassurances. But Hélène did not seem as distraught as one might have expected. She straightened her back, her eyes shining, and said, "So much for female supremacy!"

But whether Hélène was derogating Alpha or praising herself was unclear.

Around the Earthlings, the six sleepers began to stir. Omega, who had stood on the sidelines till this moment, now mentally apprised her sisters of what had just transpired. The remaining Cat Women appeared directionless and disinclined to carry the battle further.

Massaging his throat, his voice something of a croak, President Ponto, supported by his father, said, "Our crisis seems at an end now, thanks to the efforts of my own wife and Miss Bradley. It remains only for us to carry the good news back to a waiting planet."

"You folks'll be heading back without me, I reckon," said Jungle Alli unexpectedly. "But why?"

"I've plumb run out of lands to explore back home. Here I've got a whole new world to investigate. I need to see this place before there's a Bon Marché in every crater."

"But won't you be lonely?" asked Hélène.

Jungle Alli eyed the surviving Cat Women with a certain possessive passion.

"Oh," she said, grinning, " I figure I can do without the company of *man*kind for a little while."

MURDER IN GEEKTOPIA

Max Moritz is the moniker on my NC license, and, yes, I've heard all the obvious allusive wisecracks already.

"Funny, you don't look Prankish."

"I heard you keep all your cats in jam jars."

"What strength monofilament you use for chickens?"

"Did your Mama stick dirks in her bush?"

But of course I haven't let smartmouth cracks like those bug me since I was twelve years old, and just finishing my third-level synergetics course at GBS Ideotorium Number 521. (Our school motto that year, picked by the students of course: "A fool's brain digests philosophy into folly, science into superstition, and art into pedantry. Hence University education." From one of my favourite Shaw and Raymond pictonovels, *Major Barbara versus Ming the Merciless*.)

And of course after I left GBSI Number 521 that year for my extended wanderjahr before declaring my major and minor passions, I fell in with a variety of older people who politely resisted the impulse to joke about my name.

Except when they didn't.

But that's just the Geek Way, anyplace you go.

Still, I wasn't about to change Moritz to something else. Family pride, and all that. Would've killed my mother, who had worked hard with my Pop (and alone after his death) to make the family business a success. Moritz Cosplay was known worldwide for its staging of large-scale (ten thousand players and up) recreational scenarios, everything from US Civil War to Barsoom to Fruits Basket, and Mom—Helena Moritz—regarded our surname as a valuable trademark, to be proudly displayed at all times, for maximum publicity value.

Not that I was part of the firm any longer—not since five years ago, when I had told Mom, with much trepidation, that I was leaving for a different trade.

Mom was in her office, solido-conferencing with the head of some big hotel chain and negotiating for better rates for her clients, when I finally got up the courage to inform her of my decision. I waited till she flicked off the solido, and then said, "Mom, I'm switching jobs."

She looked at me coolly with that gesture familiar from my childhood, as if she were peering over the rims of her reading glasses. But she hadn't worn eyeglasses since 1963, when she had gotten laser-eye surgery to correct her far-sightedness. Then out the glasses went, faster than Clark Kent had gotten rid of his in *Action Comics* #2036. (But Lois Lang still didn't recognize Clark as Superman, since Clark grew a moustache at the same time, which was really a very small shapeshifting organism, a cousin of Proty's, who could attach and detach from the Kryptonian's upper lip at will to help preserve Supe's secret identity.)

Anyway, I had made my decision and announcement and wasn't about to quail under a little parental glare.

"What're you planning on doing?" Mom asked.

"I've just gotten my NC license. I've been studying in secret for the past six months."

"You? A nick carter? Max, I respect your intelligence highly, but it's just not the Sherlock-Holmes-Father-Brown-Lincoln-Powell variety. You had trouble finding clean socks in your sock drawer until you were ten."

"I aced the exam."

Mom looked slightly impressed, but still had an objection or two.

"What about the physical angle? You're hardly a slan in the strength department. What if you get mixed up with some roughnecks?"

"Roughnecks? Shazam, Mom! What century are you living in? There hasn't been any real prevalence of 'roughnecks' in the general population since before I was born. At GBSI Five-twenty-one, one of the patternmasters spent half a day trying to explain what a 'bully' was. The incidence of sociopathic violence and aggressive behaviour has been dropping at a rate of 1.5 percent ever since President Hearst's first term—and that was nearly three-quarters- of-a-century ago."

"Still, the world isn't perfect yet. There's bad people out there who wouldn't hesitate—"

"Mom, I also got my concealed weapons licence."

Mom had a technical interest in weapons, after hosting so many SCA tournaments and live-action RPG events. "Really? What did you train on?"

"Nothing fancy. Just a standard blaster."

I didn't tell Mom that I had picked a blaster because on wide- angle setting the geyser of charged particles from the mini- cyclotron in the gun's handle totally compensated for my lack of aiming abilities. But I suspected she knew anyhow.

Mom got up from her chair and gave me a big hug. "Well, all right, Max, if this is really what you've got your heart set on. Just go out there and uphold the Moritz name."

So that's how, on August 16, 1970 (Hugo Gernsback's eighty- sixth birthday, by coincidence; I recall watching the national celebration via public spy-ray), I moved out of the family home and hung up my shingle in a cheap office on McCay Street in Centropolis. Now, five years later, after a somewhat slow start, I had a flourishing little business, mostly in the area of thwarting industrial espionage.

All Mom's fears about me getting into danger had failed to come true. Until the morning Polly Jean Hornbine walked through the door.

* * * *

Business was slow that day. I had just unexpectedly solved a case for ERB Industries faster than I had anticipated. (The employee dropping spoilers on the ansible-net about ERBI's new line of Tarzan toys had been a drone in the shipping department.) So I had no new work immediately lined up.

I was sitting in my office, reading the latest copy of *Global Heritage* magazine. I had always been interested in history, but didn't have much Copious Spare Time these days to indulge in any deep reading. So the light-and-glossy coverage of *GH* provided a fast-food substitute.

I skipped past the guest editorial, a topical poem written by Global Data Manager Gene McCarthy himself. Where he found the time to churn out all these poems while shepherding the daily affairs of billions of people around the planet, I had no idea. Everyone else, myself included, bright and ambitious as one might be, looked like a lazy underachiever next to our GDM.

Beyond the editorial, the first article was a seventy-fifth anniversary retrospective on President Hearst's first term of office, 1901–1905. Even though the material was mostly familiar, it made for a lively, almost unbelievable story: the story of a personal transformation so intense that it had completely remade, first, one man's life, and then the collective life of the whole world.

Few people recalled that William Randolph Hearst had been a money-grubbing, war-mongering, unscrupulous newspaper publisher in the year 1898. A less likely person to become a pacifist politician and reformer would be hard to imagine. But there was a key in the rusty heart of the man, a key that would soon be turned.

And that key was Hearst's son.

In 1879, at age twenty-six, Hearst had been vacationing in England. There, through mutual friends, he met a poor but beautiful woman named Edith Nesbit, aged twenty-one. The American and the Englishwoman fell in love and married. The couple returned to America. The next year saw the birth of their son, George Randolph Hearst.

In 1898, spurred on by his father's jingoist rhetoric, the teenaged boy enlisted in the Army and went off to Cuba to fight in the very conflict his father was so ardently promoting, the Spanish- American War.

And there young George Randolph Hearst died, most miserably, on the point of a bayonet and subsequent peritonitis.

The death of their son first shattered, then galvanized William and Edith. Recanting all his past beliefs, Hearst vowed on his son's grave to use all his skills and resources to bring an end to armed conflict on the planet. A titanic task. But he would be aided immensely by Edith. Her hitherto undisclosed writing talents and keen political sensibilities were brought to their joint cause.

In early 1899, Hearst and Edith formed the US branch of the Fabian Society, based on the parent UK organization that Edith had ties to. Backed by his media empire, Hearst ran a feverish, spendthrift campaign for the Presidency of the United States under that banner, and indeed defeated both McKinley and Bryan.

And that's when Hearst started changing the world—

My robot annunciator interrupted my downtime reading then. "Chum Moritz, you have a client in the reception room."

I swung my feet off my desk, and checked my appearance in a mirror hanging on the back of the door to reception.

My blue T-shirt bearing the image of Krazy Kat and Ignatz with the legend "Hairy, man!" was relatively clean. A small cluster of pinback buttons on my chest displayed the logos or faces of Green Lantern, Frank Buck, Lil Abner, Les Paul, Freeman Dyson, Dash Hammett, Bunny Yeager, Jean Harlow (still gorgeous at age 64), and the Zulu Nation. The pockets of my khaki cargo shorts were stuffed with the tools of my trade. My high-top tennis shoes were fresh kicks.

There was nothing I could do about my perpetually unruly cowlick or thin hairy shanks, so out I went.

A pretty woman under thirty—roughly my own age, stood up as I entered. Her thick auburn hair crested at her shoulders and curled inward and upward, and her wide mouth was limned in that year's hot colour, Sheena's Tiger Blood. She wore a green short-sleeved cashmere top that echoed her green eyes, and a felted poodle skirt that featured a snarling Krypto. Black tights, ballet slippers. She looked like a page of Good Girl Art by Bergey come to life.

She extended her hand forthrightly, a sombre expression on her sweet face. "My name's Polly Jean Hornbine, and I'm here because the police don't believe someone murdered my father."

Her grip was strong and honest. I got a good feeling from her, despite her unlikely introductory claim. "Let's go into my office, Ms. Hornbine."

"Call me PJ, please. That's—that's what Dad—" And then she began to weep.

Putting my arm around her slim shoulders, I conducted her into my office, got her some tissues and a spaceman's bulb of diet Moxie (I took a Nehi for myself out of the Stirling-engine fridge), and had her sit. After a minute or so, she had composed herself enough to tell me her story.

"My father is—was—Doctor Harold Hornbine. He was head of pediatric surgery at David H. Keller Memorial. Until he was murdered! The authorities all claim he died of natural causes— heart failure—but I know that's just not true!"

"What leads you to believe his death was murder, PJ?"

"Dad had just undergone his annual physical, and his T-ray charts revealed he had the physiology of a man much younger. He followed the Macfadden-Kellog Regimen religiously. All his organs were in tip-top shape. There was no way his heart would just stop like it did, without some kind of fatal intervention."

"An autopsy—"

"—showed nothing!"

This woman's case was starting to sound more and more delusional. I tried to reason with her gently. "Even with current diagnostic technology, some cardiac conditions still go undetected. For instance, I was just reading—"

"No! Listen to me! I might have agreed with you, except for one thing. Just days before Dad died he confided in me that he had discovered a scandal at the hospital. Something in his department that had much more widespread implications. He claimed that the wrongdoing at Keller would implicate people all the way up to the GDM himself!"

"I find that hard to believe, PJ. In nearly thirty years, Global Data Management hasn't experienced any scandal worse than the use of some public monies to buy a few first editions for the private libraries of the occasional greedy sub-manager. And even that was resolved with simple tensegrity counselling. No, the GDM is just too perfect a governmental system to harbour any major glitch— especially not something that would involve murder!"

PJ stood up determinedly, a certain savagery burning in her expression. I was reminded immediately of Samantha Eggar playing Clarrissa MacDougall in 1959's *Children of the Lens*. I found my initial attraction to her redoubling. I hadn't felt like this since I fell in love with Diana Rigg (playing opposite Peter Cushing) when I first saw her onscreen in *Phantom Lady Versus the Red Skull* when I was fifteen.

PJ's voice was quavering but stern. "I can see that you're not the man for this job, Max. I'll be going now—"

I reached out to stop her. I couldn't let her leave.

"No, wait, I'll take the case. If only to put your mind at ease—"

"It's not me I'm concerned about. I want you to find the people who killed my father!"

"If that's where the trail leads, I promise I'll run them down."

A thought suddenly occurred to me. "How's your mother figure in all this? Mrs. Hornbine. What's she got to say about your father's death?"

PJ softened. "Mom isn't with us anymore. She died five years ago, on the way home from Venus Equilateral." I whistled. "Your Mom was Jenny Milano?" PJ nodded.

Now I could see where PJ got her spunk.

Jenny Milano had managed to nurse the leaky reactor of her crippled spaceship, the GDM *Big Otaku*, for thousands of miles until she finally achieved Earth orbit and spared the planet from a deadly accidental nuclear strike. Today her ship currently circled the planet as a radioactive memorial to her courage and skills.

* * * *

According to PJ, Dr. Hornbine hadn't been conducting any independent research prior to his demise. And he didn't see any private patients outside the clinical environment. Therefore, whatever scandal he had uncovered had to originate at David H. Keller Memorial itself. At first, I assumed that to learn anything I'd have to go undercover at the hospital. But how? I certainly couldn't masquerade as a doctor. Even if I managed to get some kind of lowly orderly job, I'd hardly be in any position to poke around in odd corners, or solicit information from leet personnel.

So I abandoned that instinctive first approach and decided to go in for a little social engineering.

I'd try to infiltrate one of Dr. Hornbine's karasses. Maybe amongst those who shared his sinookas, I'd learn something he had let slip, a clue to whatever secret nasty stuff was going on at the hospital.

Assuming the beautiful PJ Hornbine wasn't as loony as Daffy Duck.

Hopping onto the a-net, I quickly learned what constituted the Doc's passions.

He had been a member of the Barbershop Harmony Society.

No way I could join that, since I could carry a tune about as well as Garfield.

The Doc had also belonged to the Toonerville Folks, a society dedicated to riding every municipal trolley line in North, Central and South America, a life-quest which few members actually managed to achieve, given the huge number of such lines. (The old joke about the kid who parlayed a single five-cent transfer for a ride from Halifax to Tierra del Fuego, arriving an old man, came readily to mind.)

But this karass mainly encouraged solitary activity, save for its annual national conventions. No good to me.

Pop Hornbine also collected antique Meccano sets.

Again, that wasn't going to put me into social situations where I could pump people for dirt.

But at last I hit gold, like Flash discovering Earth-Two.

Harold Hornbine was also known as Balkpraetore, common footpad and strangler.

The Centropolis sept of the Children of Cimmeria called itself the Pigeons from Hell. That was Balkpraetore's crowd. Every weekend they had a melee with other regional groups. These were the tight friends with whom Hornbine would have shared thoughts on what had been troubling him, even if he hadn't ventured into full disclosure.

This group I could infiltrate. No reason I had to assume warrior guise. I could go as a bard or mage or tavern-keeper.

Today was Thursday. That gave me plenty of time to prepare.

So that sunny Saturday morning found me riding the Roger Lapin trolley line out to the Frank Reade Playing Fields, several hundred acres in the heart of Centropolis devoted to cosplay, recreations, re-enactments, live RPG and other pursuits of that nature. I was dressed like a priest who might have been Thulsa Doom's wimpy mouse-worshipping cousin. I figured nobody would want to waste a sword-stroke on me. I didn't stick out particularly amongst my fellow passengers, as half of them were attired in similar outfits. And besides, most were busy reading books or zines or pictonovels, or watching movies and cartoons on their pocket-solido sets.

After I boarded at the Dunsany Towers stop, a little nervous at carrying out this imposture, I dug out that issue of *Global Heritage* that I had been reading when PJ first showed up.

Once in the Oval Office, President Hearst quickly assembled an official cabinet—and a semi-secret cabal of assistants and advisors—who could help him carry out his radical disarmament and re-education program. The list leaned heavily towards scientists and reformers and what passed for media people in those days, deliberately excluding the tired old politicians. Hearst hired Havelock Ellis and Thomas Edison. Mrs. Frank Leslie and Nikola Tesla. Edward Stratemeyer and Margaret Sanger. Frank Munsey and Percival Lowell. Lee de Forest and even old rival Joseph Pulitzer. (Cabinets during Hearst's subsequent six terms as President would include a new generation of younger luminaries such as Buckminster Fuller, Huck Gernsback, Major Malcolm Wheeler-Nicholson, Robert Goddard, B. F. Skinner, Thomas Merton, Vannevar Bush, David Ogilvy, Marshall McLuhan, Claude Shannon, Dorothy Day and A. A. Wyn. Service in the Hearst administration became a badge of honour, and produced a catalogue of America's greatest names.)

These men and women set about dismantling the cultural foundations of belligerence, both domestic and international, substituting a philosophy of intellectual passions, encouraged by education and new laws.

And one of their prime weapons in this initially subliminal war was the same yellow journalism that had once fomented violence.

Specifically, the Funnypaper Boys.

Hearst wanted to reach the largest percentage of the population with his message of reform. But there was no radio then, no spy-rays or ansible-net or ether-vision or movies. Mass media as we know it today, in 1975, was rudimentary, save for zines and newspapers.

And most importantly, the newspaper comics.

The funny pages. Already immensely popular, comprehensible even by the nation's many semi-literate citizens, able to deliver concealed subtextual messages behind entertaining facades.

Thus were born the Funnypaper Boys, artists who were really secret agents for Hearst's program.

Outcault, Herriman, Dirks, McManus, McCay, King, Opper, Schultze, Fisher, Swinnerton, Kahle, Briggs, and a dozen others. They were motivated by Hearst's grandiose humanistic dreams to create a Golden Age of activist art, full of humourous fantastical conceits.

No one could deny the power and influence of such other eventual Hearst allies as pulpzines and Hollywood. But the Funnypaper Boys were first, the Founding Fathers of a republic soon informally dubbed Geektopia. ("Geek" became the in-term for the fanatics who followed the Funnypaper Boys due to Winsor McCay's association with carnival culture, where the word had a rather different meaning.) Their utopian artwork swept the nation—and the globe. American comics proved to be potent exports, with or without translation, and were adopted wholeheartedly by other cultures, carrying their reformist messages intact and sparking similar native movements.

(America's oldest and staunchest ally, Britain, was the first to fully join the Hearst movement. The Fabians, Shaw, Bertrand Russell, Wells, Stapledon, Haldane, the many brilliant Huxleys, publisher Alfred Harmsworth, Edward Linley Sambourne and his fellow cartoonists at *Punch*— They soon had complete control of the reins of governmental power.)

Reprint books of newspaper strips began to appear in America. And then the original pictonovel was born. That's when the tipping point was reached—

And my trolley had reached its destination as well, as the conductor announced over clanging bell.

I left my *GH* magazine behind on the seat and climbed down the stairs to join the costumed crowds surging into the Frank Reade Playing Fields.

Past fragrant food carts and knickknack booths and bookstalls, costume-repair tents and armouries, taverns and daycare corrals, I strolled, heading toward the fields assigned to the Children of Cimmeria. (My Mom's business had a hand in running all this, of course.)

I decided to take a shortcut down a dusty path that angled across the vast acreage, and there I encountered a startling sight.

In a tiny lot mostly concealed by a tall untrimmed privet hedge, a few people were playing what I think was a game once called "football." They wore shabby looking leather helmets and padding, obviously homemade. The object of their contention was a lopsided, ill-stuffed pigskin.

I chanced upon the game when it was temporarily suspended, and I spoke to one of the players.

"Are you guys seriously into this antique 'sports' stuff?"

The player made a typically Geekish noise indicative of derisive exasperation. "Of course not! This is a *simulation* of sports, not *real* sports! Frank Merriwell stuff. We're just trying to recreate a vanished era like everyone else. But it gets harder and harder to find re-enactors. This sports stuff never really made much sense to begin with, even when it wasn't dead media."

I left the football players behind and soon arrived at the dusty turf allotted to the Conan recreators. I registered with the gamemasters and quickly inserted myself into the action.

For the next several hours I ministered in my priestly role to the dead and dying on the mock battlefield, liberally bestowing prayers and invocations I had learned off the a-net on their hauberked torsos and helmeted heads. For a big he-man guy, Conan's creator Thomas Wolfe sure had a way with the frilly, jaw-wrenching poetry. It was hot and sweaty work, and I was grateful at last to hit the nearby grog tent for some shade and mead. While listening to a gal in a chainmail bikini sing some geeksongs about the joint adventures of Birdalone and the Grey Mouser, I spotted the Pigeons from Hell crowd, recognizable from their a-net profiles. One of them was Ted Harmon, an anesthesiologist compatriot of Hornbine. As he wasn't engaged in conversation, I went up to him.

"Hey, Ted—I mean, Volacante. Neat ruckus. I saw you get in some wicked sword thrusts."

Ted looked at me for a moment as if to say, *Do I know you?* But his weariness and the mead and my compliments and the congenial setting disarmed any suspicions.

"Thanks. Been practicing a lot."

"I just wish old Balkpraetore could've been here to see your display of talent. Shame about his death."

We clinked flagons in honour of Dr. Hornbine. Then Ted said, "Yeah, a damn shame. You know, when I first heard about him kicking it, I thought—"

"Thought what?"

"Oh, nothing…"

"C'mon, now you got me curious."

Ted leaned in closer. "Well, he was just so nervous the last time I saw him. Something was obviously bothering him. It was almost as if he expected something bad to happen to him."

"Oh, he was always like that."

"Are you serious? You never saw Balkpraetore without a grin and a joke. It was only after he had that visit at the hospital—"

"Visit?"

"Yeah, from a drug rep. Guy named, uh, Greenstock. From Metamor-Pharma. I remember the rep's name because it reminded me of the Green Man. The Green Man's always been a minor passion of mine. You see, it all started with a Henry Treece novel when I was twelve—"

I cut Ted off in a practiced Geek manner. I couldn't indulge him in a passion-rant now. "Queue it up. Back to Greenstock. What do you think he proposed? Something shady?"

"I don't know, but it freaked Hornbine out."

"Some kind of bribery scheme maybe, to get a certain line of drugs into the hospital?"

"Maybe. But it seemed more threatening than that, almost like Greenstock could compel the Doc to do something bad against his will."

I wanted to press for more information, but Ted began to turn a bit suspicious.

"Why're we chewing up this old gossip? Tell me more about the slick way I took down that bastard Numendonia "

I always tried to honour an individual's passions as much as the next geek, but sometimes it's hard work pretending to be interested. Especially when I was suddenly aching to tell PJ what I had learned.

* * * *

Our waitress wore a transparent plastic carapace moulded to her naked breasts and torso, black lurex panties, tights and musketeer boots. Her hair was pouffed up and her makeup could've sustained a platoon of Calder gynoids. She carried an outrageously baroque toy blaster holstered at her hip. I didn't know where to put my eyes. I had decided to take Polly Jean Hornbine out for supper, rather than relay my news in my office. I chose the nearest franchise of *La Semaine de Suzette*, because it was a fairly classy low-budget place, and I was in the mood for French food.

The restaurant chain was named after one of the French zines that had gotten behind Hearst and his program shortly after the Brits came onboard. The French *bande dessinée* artists (and their Belgian *stripverhalen* peers) had joined the ranks of the utopian Funnypaper Boys with awesome enthusiasm and international solidarity. And in Germany, artists like Rodolphe Töpffer and Lyonel Feininger, and zines like *Simplicissimus, Humoristische Blätter* and *Ulk* weren't far behind. And when the Japanese invented manga—

But like all geeks, I digress.

I knew that the waitresses at *La Semaine de Suzette* dressed like characters from their namesake zine. But during all my previous visits, their outfits had mimicked those of Bécassine and Bleuette, modest schoolgirls.

What I didn't realize was that *La Semaine de Suzette* had also published *Barbarella*, starting in 1962, and that the waitress uniforms went in and out of rotation.

No matter how much you knew, it was never everything.

So now Polly Jean and I had to place our orders with a half-naked interstellar libertine.

It was enough to make Emma Frost blush.

Somehow we stammered out our choices. After Barbarella had sashayed away, I attempted to recover my aplomb and relate the revelations I had picked up from Ted Harmon.

PJ absorbed the information with dispassionate intensity, and once again I was taken with her quick intelligence. Not to mention her adorable face. When I finished, she said, "So a visit to this fellow Greenstock is next, I take it?"

I began sawing into my Chicken Kiev, which was a little tough. The chain keeps prices down by using vat-grown chicken, which is generally tender and tasty, but this meat must've been made on a Monday.

"That's right. If we're lucky, the trail will end there."

She shook her head. "I can't see it. If this were just a simple case of Dad refusing a bribe, there'd be no call for murder."

"If it was murder—"

PJ's temper flared again. "It was! And that could only mean a big deal, bigger than Greenstock and his company. You've got to find out who's behind them!"

"I'm not leaving any tern unstoned, as the nasty little kid said when he was pitching pebbles at the shore birds."

PJ relented and smiled at my bad joke. "Did you actually imagine I had never heard that one before?"

"No. But I did imagine that you would imagine that I would never be dumb enough to say it. And so it made you smile anyhow."

"Touché…"

"Now let's finish up. I'm going to take you to a show."

"Which one?"

"The touring version of *Metropolis*."

"With Bernadette Peters as Maria?"

"The one and only."

"Let's go!"

Was it cheating to have looked up PJ's passions on the a-net? If so, I joined millions of other romance-seeking geeks.

After the show we ended up on the observation deck of the Agberg Tower of Glass. All of Centropolis lay spread out below us, a lattice of lights, and I felt the same epiphany experienced by Oedipa Maas in Thomas Pynchon's *The Cryonics of Blot 49*, when she envisioned the alien spaceport as pure information.

This high, the air was chilly, and PJ huddled naturally into my embrace. We kissed for a long time before our lips parted, and she said wistfully, "This tower is the fourth-highest in the world."

"But only," I whispered, "until the completion of the Atreides Pylon in Dubai."

* * * *

The next day I took the trolley to the intersection of Kirby Avenue and Lee Street, to the HQ of MetamorPharma. Built in the classic Rhizomatic style pioneered twenty years ago by the firm of Fuller, Soleri and Wright, the building resembled an enormous fennel bulb topped with ten-storey stylized fronds. The fronds were solar collectors, of course.

Inside at reception, where giant murals featuring the corporate cartoon—the famed multicoloured element man—dominated the walls, I used the annunciator to rouse Taft Greenstock, sales rep, from whatever office drudgery he had been performing. In a few moments, he emerged to greet me.

Greenstock was a black man of enormous girth and height, sporting scraggly facial hair and an Afro modelled on Luke Cage's, and wearing a polychromatic caftan and sandals. As he got closer, I smelled significant B.O. and booze. Aside from his sheer size, he was hardly intimidating. I had expected some kind of hard-nosed Octopus or Joker or Moriarty, the instrument of Hornbine's murder, and instead had gotten a fourth-rate Giles Habibula.

I had been planning to show Greenstock a fake ID and profile I had set up on the a-net, and feed him a line of foma. But taking his measure as an unwitting proxy who might be frightened into spilling some beans, I shifted plans. After we shook hands and I showed him my NC license, I just braced him with the truth.

"Chum Greenstock, I'm here about the death of Dr. Harold Hornbine. We have cause to believe he was murdered."

Greenstock looked confused, and began to sweat. I could smell metabolized gin. People passing in the lobby glanced at us curiously. "I don't know anything about that. He was just a customer. I deal with hundreds of medicos every week. He was fine the last time I saw him—"

"And what did you discuss with him during that visit?"

"A new product. A vaccine. KannerMax."

"What's KannerMax inoculate against?"

"It's not for every child. It's only recommended for those with certain chromosomal defects. I don't know the hard scientific data, I'm just a salesman. I left him all the literature and a sample—"

Greenstock looked like he was about to collapse. I quit pushing. "All right, that's fine. You've helped me a lot, Chum Greenstock.

I'll be back if I have any further questions."

I had the name of the compound that had seemingly been the catalyst in Hornbine's murder. And murder I now indeed believed it to be. Greenstock's visit introducing this new vaccine synchronized too well with Hornbine's "heart attack." The Doc must've learned something upon examination of the vaccine that earned him a death sentence.

Leaving the building, I knew just where to turn next. Dinky Allepo.

* * * *

Wonder Woman was sitting in Doc Savage's lap, while Atom Boy rested on her shoulders. Godzilla was destroying Jonestown, home to the wacky Stimsons clan, while Maggie and Jiggs and Lil Abner and Daisy Mae applauded. Mutt and Jeff were herding approximately a dozen Felix the Cats toward the maw of Cthulhu. And my namesakes, Max and Moritz, were duking it out with Skeezix and Little Lulu.

These scenes of extreme cognitive dissonance comprised the smallest part of Dinky Allepo's many thousands of disparately sized action figures. They covered every available table-top and shelf, much of the furniture, and a good portion of the floor. I had to walk as if through a minefield of sharp plastic shrapnel.

Having let myself in, I found Dinky in front of his a-net terminal, his usual habitat. He was surrounded by a midden of fast-food debris. On the walls of his study hung various film posters, mostly featuring busty, scantily clad scream queens: Tura Satana in *The Female Man*; Elke Sommer in *The Left Hand of Darkness*; June Wilkinson in *Motherlines*.

Dinky's long greasy hair hung at an acute angle as he tipped his head back to drain a can of Brazilian guarana drink. His soiled t-shirt was printed with the molecular structure of caffeine.

"Em *und* Em, how can I help you today? Need some more dope on who's ripping off whom in the exciting world of playware?"

"No, Dink, it's something more serious this time "

I explained to him everything I had on the Hornbine case. His dilated pupils widened even further with interest.

"KannerMax, huh? Let me see what I can learn—" Dinky swung back to his a-net node and got to work.

Dinky Aleppo was one of the top fifty Nexialists in the GDM. If his synthesizing skills couldn't connect the pieces of this puzzle, I wouldn't know where else to turn.

Not wanting to disturb his work, I left the room.

Dinky's den held a big ether-vision set, whose remote I grabbed. I dropped down into a chair and immediately sprang up with a shout. My left buttock had not taken kindly to being pierced by the spear held by Alley Oop. For a moment I was frozen in geekish reverie. I thought about how "Alley Oop" was a near anagram of "Aleppo," and how if you added in the name of the caveman's dinosaur, "Dinny," you could almost get "Dinky" as well. Then I threw the action figure across the room.

The set came alive to a broadcast of *Ziegfeld Follies of 1975*. God bless our quondam President Hearst! He had loved chorus girls even after his marriage and spiritual reformation, and endowed the Follies as a subsidized National Treasure. But I wasn't in the mood for all the leggy dancework, and I switched to one of the fifteen major history channels.

I arrived in the middle of a documentary on the 1930s.

After the gradual pacification of the world in the first two decades of the century, the thirties had been a march of progress unparalleled in history. Scientific, economic, artistic—that decade had seen the true flowering of geek culture as it spread across the globe. The first generation of True Geeks, their sensibilities fostered by twenty years of the Funnypaper Boys and other creators, had finally supplanted any remnant of old-school barbarism. The creation of Centropolis as the new capital of the nation had been the crowning achievement of that era, surpassed only by the establishment in the forties of Global Data Management as the civic superego of national governments.

I was just enjoying some old newsreels of Tsarevich Alexei Nikolaevich judging an Atlantic City beauty pageant awarding the title of "Sexiest Wilma Deering of 1939" (Alex was a healthy young man then thanks to the hemophilia cure invented by Linus Pauling), when Dinky called my name. I shut off the set and rejoined him.

"Have you ever heard of Kannerism before?" he demanded. "No."

"Well, neither had I. But his name in this new MetamorPharma 'vaccine' led me to him. Leo Kanner was a doctor in the 1930s, a specialist in child psychiatry. He had a theory about a certain kind of developmental glitch in the juvenile brain that would lead to a supposedly 'aberrant' personality type. He said such individuals were suffering from 'Kannerism.'"

"What'd Kannerism consist of?"

"Oh, stuff like the ability to focus intensely on whatever your main areas of interest were. Your passions, in other words. Then you possibly got hypersensitivity to certain inputs. Some sensory integration problems."

"What else?"

"Maybe some self-stimulating behaviours. Kannerist kids might also have difficulty interpreting facial expressions and other social cues. But they also had enhanced mental focus, excellent memory abilities, superior spatial skills, and an intuitive understanding of logical systems."

I was baffled. "But—but that's just a description of your average geek."

"Pre-diddily-cisely. Kanner chose to unveil his theory just when the whole world was adapting a new standard of sanity, new geekcentric paradigms of mature adult behaviour. All the very qualities Kanner identified as defects were being hailed as the salvation of the species. Kanner was trying to define the new normal as crazy, and he got laughed into an early grave. Only one other researcher, some guy named Hans Asperger, took his side, and he soon met a similar fate."

"This vaccine, KannerMax—what's it do?"

"I got all the specs. It's not a vaccine per se. That's bullshit from MetamorPharma, to convince the medical establishment to introduce the drug to the right age cohort. This stuff regulates gene expression. It targets the chromosomes that seem most closely linked with Kannerism."

A horrifying image walloped me then, of a planet reverting over the span of the next generation to the bad old violent days of pre- geekdom. "Let me guess—it shuts them off."

Dinky gave a sardonic grin. "Nope. It ramps them up."

My jaw dropped like Dippy Dawg's upon seeing Clarabelle Cow in the nude. "What!"

"This drug is a recipe for the production of super-geeks. But it only works if administered to those younger than three. Otherwise I'd be brewing some up for myself right now."

"But who's behind this? I can't see a small firm like MetamorPharma as the masterminds behind such a scheme."

"They're not. The research program was initiated by Global Data Management. Specifically, the head of the Bureau of Cultural Innovations."

"Zarthar," I said.

* * * *

That night I met PJ at a branch of Tige and Buster's convenient to both our residences. I didn't want anyone overhearing our conversation, and knew the noise of the videogame arcade within the restaurant would shield us from both local and spy-ray eavesdroppers.

Our waiter, of course, was a midget dressed as Buster Brown, accompanied by a real dog. We had to practically shout above the screams of pixel-addled kids to order.

Once the little person left, I disclosed everything to PJ.

She sniffled a bit at this confirmation of her worst fears, but then bucked up, her intellect fastening on assembling a chain of deductions,

"So something made Dad mistrust MetamorPharma. He analyzed KannerMax and figured out what it would do. Dad was always a hella good molecular biologist. He obviously disagreed with the ethics of injecting this stuff without informed parental consent. So he contacted the guy behind it all—and was murdered!"

"Gee, do you want to come onboard Moritz Investigations as a junior partner?"

"Max, this is my Dad's murder we're discussing, remember!"

"Sorry, sorry. Please forgive."

The words weren't just *pro forma*. I realized I *was* sorry, and *wanted* her forgiveness. Because I couldn't imagine being happy with PJ angry at me, or being happy at all without her in my life somehow.

PJ must have sensed my emotions, because she reached across the table and gripped my hand. But whatever romantic response she might have been about to utter just then got postponed to our hypothetical future together, because one of the Tiges wandering by chose that moment to piss on her foot.

Once we got that mess cleaned up, PJ was all business again. "You're going to see Zarthar, right?"

"Yup."

"And I'm coming with you."

* * * *

Centropolis being the capital of both the USA and the GDM, the city was full of offices and officeholders.

The Bureau of Cultural Innovations was an impressive, civic temple-style building that occupied two square blocks bounded by Disney and Iwerks. PJ and I climbed its broad marble steps and passed between its wide columns to its brazen doors and entered the vast, well-populated lobby.

I had to surrender my blaster to security, and PJ confessed to carrying a vibrablade, which surprised me.

Once we were beyond the checkpoint and on our way up to Zarthar's office, she volunteered: "Some geeks go way beyond grabby hands, you know."

"Admitted."

The GDM is open-source government. Citizens are encouraged to participate at all levels. Which is why we had been able to get a quick appointment with Zarthar himself.

I wasn't exactly certain how we were going to confront the mastermind behind this secret scheme to produce übergeeks, but I figured some game-plan would present itself.

And then the door of Zarthar's office opened to our annunciated arrival.

"All geeks are geeky, but some geeks are geekier than others." Everyone knows George Orwell's famous line from his novel *Server Farm*. But you haven't really experienced it until you meet someone in that leet minority like Zarthar.

Zarthar had been born Dennis LaTulippe, but had refashioned his entire persona somewhere around age sixteen, when he was already well over six feet tall. He legally changed his name, permanently depilated his head and tattooed it with a Wally Wood space panorama, grew a Fu-Manchu moustache, adopted sandals and flowing floor-length robes of various eye-popping hues as his only attire, and declared his major passion to be Situationist Bongo Playing. (This was circa 1956, twenty years ago, when beat-zeks like Jack Kerouac, Allen Ginsberg and Doris Day were all the rage.) He revolutionized his chosen field, and his career since then had been successive triumphs across many passions, resulting in his appointment to his current position.

Zarthar's voice resonated like Boris Karloff's. "Chum Hornbine, Chum Moritz, please come in."

We entered tentatively. I had just begun to take in the furnishings of Zarthar's ultra-modern office when PJ hurled herself at the man!

"You killed my father! You killed him! Admit it!"

Attempting to choke Zarthar, PJ made about as much progress as Judy Canova might've made wrestling with Haystack Calhoun. And when multiple ports in the walls snicked open and the muzzles of automated neural disrupters poked out, she wisely ceased entirely. Zarthar composed himself with aplomb, smoothing his robes.

His next words did not immediately address PJ's accusation.

"My friends, have you ever considered the problems our world still faces? To the average citizen, it seems we occupy a utopia. And granted, two-thirds of the world—the portion under GDM—deserves that designation. But that still leaves millions of people living in pre-geek darkness. And these seething populations are actively anti-GDM, seeking constantly for ways to undermine and topple what we've created. They are ruthless and violent and cunning. All we have to oppose them is our brains and special geek insights.

"I realize that you've learned about my plan to create a new generation of ultra-geeks, especially talented individuals who could develop new strategies, new ways of looking at the world that would extend the GDM way of life to those benighted portions of the planet. If you just stop a moment and reflect, you'll see that this program is a dire necessity, not anything I do out of personal aggrandizement."

"But why the secrecy?" I said. "Surely you'd find plenty of parents willing to enroll their kids in such a program."

"KannerMax is still highly experimental. We can't predict whether those who undergo the treatment will emerge as geniuses or idiots. Results point to the first outcome, with a large percentage of certainty, but still... If parents were to enroll their young children who can't decide for themselves, and the lives of these children were ruined, the parents would recriminate themselves endlessly. Better for one man to shoulder that responsibility, I thought."

PJ and I contemplated this for a while. Zarthar seemed sincere, and his dreams had merit. But there remained one obstacle to our endorsement of his plan.

"Dr. Hornbine—" I began.

"—committed suicide. A self-administered dose of potassium chloride stopped his heart. You can see him inject it here."

Zarthar activated a monitor, and an obvious spy-ray recording, time-and-date-stamped with the GDM logo, showed Dr. Hornbine alone in his office. He tied off his arm with surgical tubing to raise a vein, picked up a hypodermic—

"No, stop it!" PJ yelled.

Zarthar flicked off the recording. PJ sobbed loudly for a time, and when she had finished, Zarthar spoke.

"After contacting me, your father was so despondent that KannerMax would not work on adults—that he himself would be deprived of its benefits—that he chose not to live in a world where he would soon be Darwinically superseded. And this is another reason for secrecy. So as not to instill a similar mass despondency in the population. Let everyone think that these bright new stars are random mutations. It's more merciful that way."

I had come here ready to bring Zarthar down in the media with a public shaming. But now I found myself ready to enlist in his cause. I looked to PJ, who raised her red-rimmed eyes to mine, and saw that she felt the same.

And then I knew that our children would rule the sevagram.

THE OMNIPLUS ULTRA!

Everyone wanted an Omniplus Ultra, and I was not immune to the urge. But of course they were almost impossible to purchase, for love nor money.

Since their debut nine months ago at the annual Consumer Electronics Show, over forty million units had been sold worldwide, exhausting the initial stockpile but barely sating a fraction of consumer demand. Now the Chinese factories that produced the Omniplus Ultra were tooling up as fast as possible to make more, but every desperate retailer could guarantee delivery no sooner than six months in the future. On eBay, each available Omniplus Ultra, with an MSRP of $749.99, was selling for upwards of $5,000.00.

OmninfoPotent Corporation, the enigmatic firm behind the Omniplus Ultra, had instantly leaped to the top of the NASDAQ exchange. Its reclusive founders, Pine Martin and Sheeda Waxwing, had vaulted instantly into the lower ranks of the Forbes 400. Sales of the device were being credited with almost singlehandedly jumpstarting the ailing economy.

The ad campaign for the Omniplus Ultra had already won six Clios. The catchy theme music by the Black Eyed Peas—"O U Kidz"—and the images of average people of every race, age, gender, nationality and creed utilizing their Omniplus Ultras to navigate a plethora of life situations ranging from sweetly comic to upliftingly tragic had generated their own fan clubs, YouTube mashups and punchlines for late-night comedians. Allusions to the Omniplus Ultra, as well as its invocation in metaphors, similes, rants, raves, jeremiads and paeans, filled water cooler conversations, the printed pages of the world's magazines and newspapers, and blogs and on-line journals. The first instant book on the Omniplus Ultra—*Uberpower!*, by Thomas Friedman and Charles Stross—was due out any day.

I myself did not know anyone who actually owned an Omniplus Ultra, and I was dying to see and handle one. But even forty million units, distributed across seven billion people, meant that there was only one Omniplus Ultra for every 175 citizens. Of course, the gadgets were not seeded evenly around the planet, but concentrated in the hands of relatively wealthy and elite consumers and early adopters: circles I did not really travel in, given my job in a Staples warehouse, and a set of friends whose familiarity with the latest products of Silicon Valley generally extended no further than their TV remotes.

So I had to content myself with studying the advertisements and the gadget-porn reviews. Those who had experienced the Omniplus Ultra couldn't say enough about its life-changing capabilities, its potential to shatter all old paradigms across the board and to literally remake the world.

Publishers Weekly: "After five centuries, the printed book has found its worthiest successor in the Omniplus Ultra. The future of reading is safely triumphant."

The Huffington Post: "Opens new channels for the spread of democracy."

Boing Boing: "Coolest gadget since the iPhone! The cold-laser picoprojector alone is worth the cost."

Car and Driver: "Jack the Omniplus Ultra into your dash's USB port and driving will never be the same!"

Entertainment Weekly: "If you can't download your favourite show onto your Omniplus Ultra, it's not worth watching."

Variety: "First flicks helmed with the Omniplus Ultra to hit bigscreens soon!"

Aerospace & Defence Industry Review: "Guaranteed to be standard equipment for all future warriors."

Mother Jones: "The Omniplus Ultra is the greenest invention since *The Whole Earth Catalogue*."

BusinessWeek: "Every CEO will benefit from having an Omniplus Ultra to hand—and anyone without one will watch competitors eat their lunch."

Rolling Stone: "Elvis. The Beatles. The Sex Pistols. The Omniplus Ultra. The sequence is complete at last."

The more such talk I read, the longer I examined pictures of the sleekly tactile Omniplus Ultra, with its customizable sexy skins and ergonomically perfect controls, the more I lusted to own one. Although nothing in my condition had really changed, and although I had enough money, love and security, my life felt incomplete and empty without an Omniplus Ultra.

But there was just no way for me to get my hands on one.

Until I saw my boss's boss's boss walk through the warehouse carrying one.

Then and there, I knew what I had to do.

As a low-level employee, I certainly could not jump several levels of management and directly approach my boss's boss's boss and ask to fondle and play with his Omniplus Ultra. But I had a scheme.

It took me six frustrating weeks, but at last I managed it. In a series of furtive unauthorized forays into executive territory, I caught the lucky

Omniplus Ultra owner in a lavatory break with his prized possession carelessly left behind on his desk.

That's when I pulled the fire alarm.

While everyone else rushed outside, I darted into the guy's office, snatched his Omniplus Ultra off the desk, and sank down behind the furniture in the knee well, out of sight.

With trembling hands I sought to shuffle aside the protective wings of the device, utilizing all the instructions I had lovingly memorized, and expose its intimate control and display surfaces to my wanton gaze and lewd touch.

But I was doing something wrong! The expected blossoming failed to happen.

Instead, after some fumbling, the unit split open like a simple styrofoam clamshell container full of leftovers.

The interior gaped utterly vacant, except for a simple piece of printed cardboard.

Dumbfounded, I removed the cardboard and read the message.

Dear Consumer: the Omniplus Ultra is not what you need. You are already everything you thought it could do. Pass this message on as widely as you see fit. Or not.

Hopefully yours,
Pine Martin and Sheeda Waxwing
for the OmninfoPotent Corporation.

I put the card back inside, resealed the Omniplus Ultra, dropped it with a dull thud on the desk, and joined all my peers outside, waiting to resume our lives.

WIKIWORLD

1. Meet Russ Reynolds

Russ Reynolds, that's me. You probably remember my name from when I ran the country for three days. Wasn't that a wild time? I'm sorry I started a trade war with several countries around the globe. I bet you're all grateful things didn't ramp up to the shooting stage. I know I am. And the UWA came out ahead in the end, right? No harm, no foul. Thanks for being so understanding and forgiving. I assure you that my motives throughout the whole affair, although somewhat selfish, were not ignoble.

And now that things have quieted down, I figured people would be calm enough to want to listen to the whole story behind those frighteningly exciting events.

So here it is.

2. Mr. Wiki builds my Dream House

It all started, really, the day when several wikis where I had simoleans banked got together to build me a house. Not only did I meet my best friend Foolty Fontal that day, but I also hooked up with Cherimoya Espiritu. It's hard now, a few years later, to say which one of those outrageous personages gave me the wildest ride. But it's certain that without their aiding and abetting, plotting and encouraging, I would never have become the jimmy-whale of the UWA, and done what I did.

The site for my new house was a tiny island about half an acre in extent. This dry land represented all that was left of what used to be Hyannis, Massachusetts, since Cape Cod became an archipelago. Even now, during big storms, the island was frequently overwashed, so I had picked up the title to it for a song, when I got tired of living on my boat, the *Gogo Goggins*.

Of course the value of coastal land everywhere had plunged steadily in the three decades since the destruction of New Orleans. People just got tired of seeing their homes and business destroyed on a regular basis by super-storms and rising sea levels. Suddenly Nebraska and Montana and the Dakotas looked like beckoning havens of safety, especially with their ameliorated climates, and the population decline experienced for a century by the Great Plains states reversed itself dramatically, lofting the region into a new cultural hotzone. I had heard lately that Fargo had spawned yet another musical movement, something called "cornhüsker dü," although I hadn't yet listened to any samples of it off the ubik.

Anyway, this little islet would serve me well, I figured, as both home and base for my job—assuming I could erect a good solid comfortable structure here. Realizing that such a task was beyond my own capabilities, I called in my wikis.

The Dark Galactics. The PEP Boys. The Chindogurus. Mother Hitton's Littul Kittons. The Bishojos. The Glamazons. The Provincetown Pickers. And several more. All of them owed me simoleans for the usual—goods received, or time and expertise invested—and now they'd be eager to balance the accounts.

The day construction was scheduled to start, I anchored the *Gogo Goggins* on the western side of my island, facing the mainland. The June air was warm on my bare arms, and freighted with delicious salt scents. Gulls swooped low over my boat, expecting the usual handouts. The sun was a golden English muffin in the sky. (Maybe I should have had some breakfast, but I had been too excited to prepare any that morning.) Visibility was great. I could see drowned church spires and dead cell-phone towers closer to the shore. Through this slalom a small fleet of variegated ships sailed, converging on my island.

The shadow of one of the high unmanned aerostats that maintained the ubik passed over me, the same moment I used that medium to call up IDs on the fleet. In my vision, translucent tags overlaid each ship, labelling their owners, crew and contents. I was able to call up realtime magnified images of the ships as well, shot from the aerostats and tiny random entomopter cams. I saw every kind of vessel imaginable: sleek catamarans, old lobster boats, inflatables, decommissioned Coast Guard cutters— And all of them carrying my friends—some of whom I had met face to face, some of whom I hadn't—coming to help build my house.

I hopped out of my boat onto dry land. My island was covered with salt-tolerant scrub plants and the occasional beach rose. No trees to clear. Construction could begin immediately.

As I awaited my friends, I got several prompts displayed across my left eye, notifying me of four or five immediate ubik developments in areas of interest to me. I had the threshold of my attention-filter set fairly high, so I knew I should attend to whatever had made it over that hurdle. For speed's sake, I kept the messages text-only, suppressing the full audiovideo presentations.

The first development concerned an adjustment to the local property-tax rates. "Glamourous Glynnis" had just amended the current rate structure to penalize any residence over 15,000 square feet that failed to feed power back to the grid. Sixty-five other people had endorsed the change.

I added my own vote to theirs, and tacked on a clause to exempt group homes.

Next came a modification to the rules of the non-virtual marketplace back on the mainland, where I sold many of my salvaged goods in person. "Jinglehorse" wanted to extend the hours of cperation on holidays. Competitively speaking, I'd feel compelled to be there if the booths were open extra. And since I liked my downtime, I voted no.

Items three and four involved decriminalizing a newly designed recreational drug named "arp," and increasing our region's fresh water exports. I didn't know enough about arp, so I got a search going for documents on the drug. I'd try to go through them tonight, and vote tomorrow. And even though I felt bad for the drought- sufferers down South, I didn't want to encourage continued habitation in a zone plainly unsuited for its current population densities, so I voted no.

The last item concerned a Wikitustional Amendment. National stuff. This new clause had been in play for six months now without getting at least provisionally locked down, approaching a record length of revision time. The Amendment mandated regular wiki participation as a prerequisite for full enfranchisement in the UWA. "Uncle Sham" had just stuck in a clause exempting people older than sixty-five. I wasn't sure what I thought about that, so I pushed the matter back in the queue.

By the time I had attended to these issues, the first of my visitors had arrived, a small vessel named *The Smiling Dictator*, and bearing a lone man. The craft crunched onto the beach, and the guy jumped out.

"Hey, Russ! Nice day for a house-raising."

Jack Cortez—"Cortez the Queller" in the ubik—resembled a racing greyhound in slimness and coiled energy. He wore a fisherman's vest over bare chest, a pair of denim cutoffs bleached white, and boat shoes. His SCURF showed as a dark green eagle across a swath of his chest.

"Ahimsa, Jack! I really appreciate you shcwing up."

"No problem. The Church still owes you for retrieving that Madonna. But you gotta do *some* work nonetheless! Come on and give me a hand."

I went over to the *Dictator* and helped Jack wrestle some foam-encased objects big as coffee-table-tops out of the boat. When we had the half-dozen objects stacked on land, he flaked off some of the protective foam and revealed the corner of a window frame.

"Six smart windows. Variable opacity, self-cleaning, rated to withstand Category Four storms. Fully spimed, natch. One of our co-religionists is a contractor, and these were left over from a recent job."

"Pluricious!"

By then, the rest of the boats had arrived. A perfect storm of unloading and greeting swept over my little domain. Crates and girders and preformed pilings and lumber and shingles and equipment accumulated in heaps, while bottled drinks made the rounds, to fortify and replenish. The wiki known as the Shewookies had brought not materials nor power tools but food. They began to set up a veritable banquet on folding tables, in anticipation of snacking and lunching.

A guy I didn't recognize came up to me, hand extended. His SCURF formed orange tiger stripes on his cheeks and down his jaws. Before I could bring up his tag, he introduced himself.

"Hi, Russ. Bob Graubauskas—'Grabass' to you. Jimmywhale for the Sunflower Slowdrags. So, you got any solid preferences for your house?"

"No, not really. Just so long as it's strong and spacious and not too ugly."

"Can do."

Grabass began to issue silent orders to his wiki, a ubik stream he cued me in on. But then a big woman wearing overalls intervened. "Margalit Bayless, with the Mollicutes. 'Large Marge.' You truly gonna let the Slow-drags design this structure all by themselves?"

"Well, no…"

"That's good. Because my people have some neat ideas too—"

I left Large Marge and Grabass noisily debating the merits of their various plans while I snagged an egg-salad sandwich and a coffee.

By the time I had swallowed the last bite, both the Mollicutes and the Sunflower Slowdrags had begun construction. The only thing was, the two teams were starting at opposite ends of a staked-off area and working toward the common middle. And their initial scaffolding and foundations looked utterly incompatible. And some of the other wikis seemed ready to add wings to the nascent building regardless of either main team.

As spimed materials churned under supervision like a nest of snakes or a pit of chunky lava or a scrum of rugby robots in directed self-assembly—boring into the soil and stretching up toward the sky—I watched with growing alarm, wondering if this had been the smartest idea. What kind of miscegenous mansion was I going to end up with?

That's when Foolty Fontal showed up to save the day.

He arrived in a one-person sea-kayak, of all things, paddling like a lunatic, face covered with sweat. So typical of the man, I would discover, choosing not to claim primary allegiance with any wiki, so he could belong to all.

I tried to tag him, but got a privacy denial.

Having beached his craft and ditched his paddle, Foolty levered himself out with agility. I saw a beanpole well over six feet tall, with glossy skin the colour of black-bean dip. Stubby dreadlocks like breakfast sausages capped his head. Ivory SCURF curlicued up his dark bare arms like automobile detailing.

Foolty, I later learned, claimed mixed Ethiopian, Jamaican and Gulla heritage, as well as snippets of mestizo. It made for a hybrid genome as unique as his brain.

Spotting me by the food tables, Foolty lanked over.

"Russ Reynolds, tagged. Loved your contributions to *Naomi Instanton*."

Foolty was referring to a crowdsourced sitcom I had helped to co-script. "Well, thanks, man."

"Name's Foolty Fontal—'FooDog.'"

"No shit!"

FooDog was legendary across the ubik. He could have been the jimmy-whale of a hundred wikis, but had declined all such positions. His talents were many and magnificent, his ego reputedly restrained, and his presence at any non-virtual event a legend in the making.

Now FooDog nodded his head toward the construction site. A small autonomous backhoe was wrestling with a walking tripodal hod full of bricks while members of competing wikis cheered on the opponents.

"Interesting project. Caught my eye this morning. Lots of challenges. But it looks like you're heading for disaster, unless you get some coordination. Mind if I butt in?"

"Are you kidding? I'd be honoured. Go for it!"

FooDog ambled over to the workers, both human and cybernetic, streaming ubik instructions with high-priority tags attached faster than I could follow. A galvanic charge seemed to run through people, as they realized who walked among them. FooDog accepted the homage with humble grace. And suddenly the whole site was transformed from a chaotic competition to a patterned dance of flesh and materials.

That's the greatest thing about wikis: they combine the best features of democracy and autocracy. Everybody has an equal say. But some got bigger says than others.

Over the next dozen hours, I watched in amazement as my house grew almost organically. By the time dusk was settling in, the place was nearly done. Raised high above sea-level against any potential flooding on deep-sunk cement piles, spired, curve-walled, airy yet massive, it still showed hallmarks of rival philosophies of design. But somehow the efforts of the various factions ultimately harmonized instead of bickered, thanks to FooDog's overseeing of the assorted worldviews.

One of the best features of my new house, a place where I could see myself spending many happy idle hours, was a large wooden deck that projected out well over the water, where it was supported by pressure-treated and tarred wooden pillars, big as antique telephone poles, plunging into the sea.

Three or four heaps of wooden construction waste and combustible sea-wrack had been arranged as pyres against the dusk, and they were now ignited. Live music flared up with the flames, and more food and drink was laid on. While a few machines and people continued to add some last-minute details to my house, illuminated by electrical lights running off the newly installed power system (combined wave motion and ocean temperature differential), the majority of the folks began to celebrate a job well done.

I was heading to join them when I noticed a new arrival sailing in out of the dusk: a rather disreputable looking workhorse of a fishing sloop. I pinged the craft, but got no response. Not a privacy denial, but a dead silence.

This ship and its owner were running off the ubik, un-SCURFED. Intrigued, I advanced toward the boat. I kicked up my night vision. Its bow bore the name *Soft Grind*. From out the pilothouse emerged the presumptive captain. In the ancient firelight, I saw one of the most beautiful women I had ever beheld: skin the colour of teak, long wavy black hair, a killer figure. She wore a faded hemp shirt tied under her breasts to expose her midriff; baggy men's surfer trunks; and a distressed pair of gumboots.

She leaped over the gunwales and off the boat with pantherish flair moderated only slightly by her clunky footwear. "Hey," she said. "Looks like a party. Mind if I crash it?"

"No, sure, of course not."

She grinned, exposing perfect teeth. "I'm Cherry. One of the Oyster Pirates."

And that was how I met Cherimoya Espiritu.

3. In Love With an Oyster Pirate

Gaia giveth even as she taketh away.

The warming of the global climate over the past century had melted permafrost and glaciers, shifted rainfall patterns, altered animal migratory routes, disrupted agriculture, drowned cities, and similarly necessitated a thousand thousand adjustments, recalibrations and hasty retreats. But humanity's unintentional experiment with the biosphere had also brought some benefits.

Now we could grow oysters in New England.

Six hundred years ago, oysters flourished as far north as the Hudson. Native Americans had accumulated vast middens of shells on the shores of what would become Manhattan. Then, prior to the industrial age, there was a small climate shift, and oysters vanished from those waters.

Now, however, the tasty bivalves were back, their range extending almost to Maine.

The commercial beds of the Cape Cod Archipelago produced shellfish as good as any from the heyday of Chesapeake Bay. Several large wikis maintained, regulated and harvested these beds, constituting a large share of the local economy.

But as anyone might have predicted, wherever a natural resource existed, sprawling and hard of defence, poachers would be found.

Cherimoya Espiritu hailed from a long line of fisherfolks operating for generations out of nearby New Bedford. Cape Verdean by remotest ancestry, her family had suffered in the collapse of conventional fisheries off the Georges Bank. They had failed to appreciate the new industry until it was too late for them to join one of the legal oyster wikis. (Membership had been closed at a number determined by complicated sustainability formulae.) Consequently, they turned pirate to survive in the only arena they knew.

Cherimoya and her extensive kin had divested themselves of their SCURF: no subcutaneous ubik arfids for them, to register their presence minute-to-minute to nosy authorities and jealous oyster owners. The pirates relied instead on the doddering network of GPS satellites for navigation, and primitive cellphones for communication. Operating at night, they boasted gear to interfere with entomopter cams and infrared scans. They were not above discouraging pursuers with pulsed-energy projectile guns (purchased from the PEP Boys). After escaping with their illicit catches, they sold the fruit of the sea to individual restaurants and unscrupulous wholesalers. They took payment either in goods, or in isk, simoleans and lindens that friends would bank for them in the ubik.

Most of the oyster pirates lived on their ships, to avoid contact with perhaps overly inquisitive mainland security wikis, such as the Boston Badgers and the Stingers. Just like me prior to my island-buying—except that my motivation for a life afloat didn't involve anything illicit.

Bits and pieces of information about this subculture I knew just from growing up in the Archipelago. And the rest I learned from Cherry over the first few months of our relationship.

But that night of my house-raising, all I knew was that a gorgeous woman, rough-edged and authentic as one of the oyster shells she daily handled, wanted to hang out on my tiny island and have some fun.

That her accidental presence here would lead to our becoming long-term lovers, I never dared hope.

But sure enough, that's what happened.

Following Cherry's introduction, I shook her hand and gave my own name. Daring to take her by the elbow—and receiving no rebuke—I steered her across the flame-lit, shadowy sands towards the nearest gaggle of revellers around their pyre.

"So," I asked, "how come you're not working tonight?"

"Oh, I don't work every night. Just often enough to keep myself in provisions and fuel. Why should I knock myself out just to earn money and pile up *things*? I'm more interested in enjoying life. Staying free, not being tied down."

"Well, you know, I think that's, um—just great! That's how I feel too!" I silently cursed my new status as a land-owner and house- dweller.

We came out of the darkness and into the sight of my friends. Guitars, drums and gravicords chanced to fall silent just then, and I got pinged with the planned playlist, and a chance to submit any requests.

"Hey, Russ, congratulations!"

"Great day!"

"House looks totally flexy!"

"You're gonna really enjoy it!"

Cherry turned to regard me with a wide grin. "So—gotta stay foot-loose, huh?"

To cover my chagrin, I fetched drinks for Cherry and me while I tried to think of something to say in defence of my new householder lifestyle. That damn sexy grin of hers didn't help my concentration. Cherry took a beer from me. I said, "Listen, it's not like I'm buying into some paranoid gatecom. This place—totally transient.

It's nothing more than a beach shack, somewhere to hang my clothes. I'm on the water most of every day—"

Waving a hand to dismiss my excuses, Cherry said, "Just funning with you, Russ. Actually, I think this place is pretty hyphy. Much as I love the *Soft Grind*, I get tired of being so cramped all the time. Being able to stretch in your bunk without whacking your knuckles would be a treat. So—do I get a tour?"

"Yeah, absolutely!"

We headed toward the staircase leading up to my deck. Her sight un-amped, Cherry stumbled over a tussock of grass, and I took her hand to guide her. And even when we got within the house's sphere of radiance, she didn't let go.

Up on the deck, Foolty was supervising a few machines working atop the roof. Spotting me, he called out, "Hey, nephew! Just tying in the rain-water-collection system to the desalinization plant."

"Swell. FooDog, I'd like you to meet—"

"No, don't tell me the name of this sweet niece. Let me find out on my own."

Cherry snorted. "Good luck! Far as the ubik knows, I'm not even part of this brane. And that's how I like it."

FooDog's eyes went unfocused and he began to make strangled yips like a mutt barking in its sleep. After about ninety seconds of this, during which time Cherry and I admired a rising quarter moon, FooDog emerged from his trawl of the ubik.

"Cherimoya Espiritu," he said. "Born 2015. Father's name João, mother's name Graca. Younger brother nicknamed the Dolphin. Member of the Oyster Pirates—"

Cherry's face registered mixed irritation, admiration and fright. "How—how'd you find all that out?"

FooDog winked broadly. "Magic."

"No, c'mon, tell me!"

"All right, all right. The first part was easy. I cheated. I teasled into Russ's friends list. He added you as soon as you met, and that's how I got your name and occupation. My SCURF isn't off the shelf. It picked up molecules of your breath, did an instant signature on four hundred organic compounds, and found probable family matches with your parents, whose genomes are on file. And your brother's got a record with the Boston Badgers for a ruckus at a bar in Fall River."

Now I felt offended. "You teasled into my friends list? You got big ones, FooDog."

"Well, thanks! That's how I got where I am today. And besides, I discovered my name there too, so I figured it was okay."

I couldn't find it in myself to be angry with this genial ubik- trickster. Cherry seemed willing to extend him the same leniency. "No need to worry about anyone else learning this stuff. While I was in there, I beefed up all your security, nephew."

"Well—thanks, I guess."

"No thanks necessary." FooDog turned back to the bots on the roof. "Hey, Blue Droid! You call that a watertight seam!"

Cherry and I went through the sliding glass door that led off the deck and inside.

I made an inspection of my new home for the first time with Cherry in tow. The place was perfect: roomy yet cozy, easy to maintain, lots of comforts.

The wikis had even provided some rudimentary furniture, including a couple of inflatable adaptive chairs. We positioned them in front of a window that commanded a view of the ocean and Moon. I went to a small humming fridge and found it full of beer. I took two bottles back to the seats.

Cherry and I talked until the Moon escaped our view. I opaqued all the glass in the house. We merged the MEMS skins of the chairs, fashioning them into a single bed. Then we had sex and fell asleep.

In the morning, Cherry said, "Yeah, I think I could get used to living here real fast."

4. Mucho Mongo

My Dad was a garbageman.

Okay, so not really. He didn't wear overalls or hang from the back of a truck or heft dripping sacks of coffee grounds and banana peels. Dad's job was strictly white-collar. His fingers were more often found on a keyboard than a trash compactor. He was in charge of the Barnstable Transfer Station, a seventy-acre "disposium" where recyclables were lifted from the waste-stream, and whatever couldn't be commercially repurposed was neatly and sterilely buried. But I like to tell people he was a garbageman just to get their instant, unschooled reactions. If they turn up their noses, chances are they won't make it onto my friends list.

I remember Dad taking me to work once in a while on Saturdays. He proudly showed off the dump's little store, stocked with the prize items his workers had rescued.

"Look at this, Russ. A first edition Jack London. *Tales of the Fish Patrol*. Can you believe it?"

I was five years old, and had just gotten my first pair of spex, providing rudimentary access to what passed for the ubik back then. I wasn't impressed.

"I can read that right now, Dad, if I wanted to."

Dad looked crestfallen. "That digital text is just information, son. This is a *book*! And best of all, it's *mongo*."

I tried to look up mongo in the ubik, like I had been taught, but couldn't find it in my dictionary. "What's mongo, Dad?"

"A moment of grace. A small victory over entropy."

"Huh?"

"It's any treasure you reclaim from the edge of destruction, Russ. There's no thrill like making a mongo strike."

I looked at the book with new eyes. And that's when I got hooked. From then on, mongo became my life.

That initial epiphany occurred over twenty years ago. Barnstable is long drowned, fish swimming through the barnacled timbers of the disposium store, and my folks live in Helena now. But I haven't forgotten the lessons my Dad taught me.

The *Gogo Goggins* has strong winches for hauling really big finds up into the air. But mostly I deal in small yet valuable stuff. With strap-on gills, a smartskin suit, MEMS flippers and a MHD underwater sled packing ten thousand candlepower of searchlights, I pick through the drowned world of the Cape Cod Archipelago and vicinity.

The coastal regions of the world now host the largest caches of treasure the world has ever seen. Entire cities whose contents could not be entirely rescued in advance of the encroaching waters. All there as salvage for the taking, pursuant to many, many post- flood legal rulings.

Once I'm under the water, my contact with the ubik cut off, relying just on the processing power in my SCURF, I'm alone with my thoughts and the sensations of the dive. The romance of treasure- hunting takes over. Who knows what I might find? Jewellery, monogrammed plates from a famous restaurant, statues, coins— Whatever I bring up, I generally sell with no problems, either over the ubik or at the old-fashioned marketplace on the mainland.

It's a weird way of earning your living, I know. Some people might find it morbid, spending so much time amid these ghostly drowned ruins. (And to answer the first question anyone asks: yes, I've encountered skeletons, but none of them have shown the slightest inclination to attack.)

But I don't find my job morbid at all. I'm under the spell of mongo.

One of the first outings Cherry and I went on, after she moved in with me, was down to undersea Provincetown. It's an easy dive. Practically nothing to find there, since amateurs have picked it clean. But by the same token, all the hazards are well-charted.

Cherry seemed to enjoy the expedition, spending hours slipping through the aquatic streets with wide eyes behind her mask. Once back aboard the *Gogo Goggins*, drying her thick hair with a towel, she said, "That was stringy, Russ! Lots of fun."

"You think you might like tossing in with me? You know, becoming business partners? We'd make good isk. Not that we need to earn much, like you said. And you could give up the illegal stuff—"

"Give up the Oyster Pirates? Never! That's my heritage! And to be honest with you, babe, there's just not enough thrills in your line of work."

Just as I was addicted to mongo, Cherry was hooked on plundering the shellfish farms, outwitting the guards and owners and escaping with her booty. Myself, I knew I'd be a nervous wreck doing that for a living. (She took me out one night on a raid; when the PEP discharges started sizzling through the air close to my head, I dropped to the deck of the *Soft Grind* (which possessed a lot of speed belied by its appearance) and didn't stand up again till we

reached home. Meanwhile, Cherry was alternately shouting curses at our pursuers and emitting bloodthirsty laughs.)

Luckily, we were able to reconcile our different lifestyles quite nicely. I simply switched to night work. Once I was deep enough below the surface, I had to rely on artificial lights even during the daytime anyhow.

Several nights each week, you'd find us motoring off side by side in our respective boats. Eventually our paths would diverge, signalled by a dangerous kiss across the narrow gap between our bobbing boats. As I headed toward whatever nexus of sunken loot I had charted, I'd catch up on ubik matters, writing dialogue for *One Step Closer to Nowhere*, the sitcom that had replaced *Naomi Instanton*, or monitoring border crossings for an hourly rate for the Minute Men.

Cherry and I would meet back home on my little island, which Cherry had christened "Sandybump." We'd sleep till noon or later, then have fun during the day.

A lot of that fun seemed to involve Foolty "FooDog" Fontal.

5. A PortrAit of the Con Artist As a Young Foodog

During all the years we hung out together, we never learned where FooDog actually lived. He seemed reluctant to divulge the location of his digs, protective of his security and privacy even with his friends. (And recalling how easily he had stolen Cherry's identity from my friends list, who could blame him at worrying about unintentional data-sharing?) FooDog's various business, recreational and hobbyist pursuits had involved him with lots of shady characters and inequitable dealings, and he existed, I soon realized, just one step ahead—or perhaps laterally abaft—of various grudge-holders.

I should hasten to say that FooDog's dealings were never—or seldom—truly unethical or self-serving. It's just that his wide-ranging enthusiasms respected no borders, sacred cows or intellectual property rights.

But despite his lack of a public meatspace address, FooDog could always be contacted through the ubik, and me and Cherry would often meet him somewhere for what invariably turned out to be an adventure of the most hyphy dimensions.

I remember one day in November...

We grabbed a zipcar, FooDog slung several duffels in the interior storage space, and we headed north to New Hampshire. FooDog refused to tell us where we were heading till it was too late to turn back.

"We're going to climb Mount Washington? Are you nuts?" I picked up the feed from the Weather Observatory atop the peak. "There's a blizzard going on right now!"

"Precisely the conditions I need for my experiment."

The normal daily high temperature atop the peak at this time of the year was thirteen degrees Farenheit. The record low was minus-twenty. In 1934, the Observatory had recorded the biggest wind ever experienced on the planet: 231 MPH. There were taller places and colder places and windier places and places with worse weather. But Mount Washington managed to combine generous slices of all these pies into a unique killer confection.

Cherry said, "C'mon, Russ, trust the Dog." I grumbled, but went along.

We made it by car up the access road to 4300 vertical feet, leaving only 2000 feet to ascend on foot. With many contortions, we managed to dress in the car in the smartsuits FooDog had provided. When we stepped outside, we were smitten with what felt like a battering ram made of ice. We sealed up our micropore facemasks and snugged our adaptive goggles more firmly into place. Cherry had a headset that provided a two-way audiofeed to the ubik. We donned our snowshoes, grabbed our alpenstocks, and gan the ascent, following the buried road which was painted by our ubik vision to resemble the Golden Brick path to Oz. FooDog carried a box strapped to his back, the object of our whole folly.

I won't belabour you with the journey, which resembled in its particulars any number of other crazed climbs atop forbidding peaks. Let's just say the trek was the hardest thing I've ever done.

We never even made it to the top. Around 5500 feet, FooDog declared that he could conduct his experiment at that altitude, with the storm raging slightly less virulently around us. He doffed his box, unfolded its tripod legs, spiked it into the snow, and began sending an encrypted command stream to the gadget over the ubik.

"Can we know now what we risked our lives for?" I said.

"Sure thing, nephew. This gadget messes with the quantum bonds between the hydrogen atoms in water molecules, via a directional electrostatic field. I've got it pointed upward now. Good thing, or we'd all be puddles of slop."

I took a nervous step or three away from the machine, unsure if FooDog was kidding or not. But I should have trusted him not to endanger us—at least via technology.

I looked toward Cherry, to make sure she was okay. She gave an exclamation of awe. I looked back toward the machine.

There was an expanding hemisphere of atmospheric inactivity above the gadget. It grew and grew, providing an umbrella of calm. Some snow still pelted us from the side, but none reached us from above.

FooDog's box was quelling the blizzard.

FooDog undid his mask. His black face, wreathed in a wide grin, stood out amidst all the white like the dot of a giant exclamation point.

"Hyphy!" he exclaimed.

The ubik was already going insane. Weather-watcher wikis frantically sought to dispatch entomopter cams to our location, to supplement the reports of the fixed sensors located at some distance, but were frustrated by the surrounding storm, still in full force. But I suspected that if FooDog's bubble continued to expand, sooner or later a cam would get through and ID us.

Evidently, FooDog had the same realization. He said, "Brace yourself," then shut off his machine.

The blizzard socked us with renewed vigour—although I seemed to sense in the storm a kind of almost-human shock, as if it had been alarmed by its interruption.

FooDog resealed his mask, and we headed down.

"Aren't you worried we'll be ID'd on the way down the mountain?"

"I hired the zipcar under a spoofed name, then de-spimed it. Cherry's untouchable, and you and I have our denial flags on. Once we get down the mountain, anyone who manages to get near us in meatspace will have to distinguish us from a hundred other identical cars on the road. We're as invisible as anyone gets these days."

"So your little invention is safe from greedy and irresponsible hands."

"Sure. Unless I decide to opensource it."

"You're kidding, right?"

But the Dog replied not.

So that's what the average outing with Foolty Fontal was like. Of course, I had certain thrills in my own line of work.

One day my not inconsiderable rep as a salvage expert attracted an offer from the Noakhali Nagas, a wiki from Bangladesh. That unfortunate country had suffered perhaps more than any, due to oceanic incursions. The creeping Bay of Bengal had submerged thousands of shrines. Rescuing deities would provide me with a significant chunk of lindens. And the challenge of new territory— the Cape Archipelago was starting to bore me a little after so many years—was a plus as well.

I sat with Cherry on our favourite spot, the deck of our house on Sandybump. It was late afternoon, our "morning" time, and we were enjoying brunch and watching the sun go down. I explained about the offer I had received.

"So—you mind if I take this job?"

"How could I? Go for it, babe! I'll be fine here alone till you get back."

I emerged from the warm waters of the Bay of Bengal on a Tuesday afternoon two months later to find a high-priority news item, culled from the ubik by one of my agents, banging at the doors of my atmosphere-restored connection.

Cherimoya Espiritu was in Mass General Hospital in Boston, suffering from various broken limbs and bruised organs, but in no mortal danger.

I blew every isk I had earned in Bangladesh plus more on a scramjet flight back to the UWA. Four hours later I was hustling through the doors of MGH.

Cherry smiled ruefully as I entered her room. Vast bruises, already fading from subcutaneous silicrobes, splotched her sweet face. Various casts obscured her lovely limbs. Wires from speed- healing machines tethered her down.

"Damn, Russ," Cherry exclaimed when she saw me, "I am so sorry about the house!"

6. Wormholes and Loopholes

Looking back at this narrative so far, I see that maybe right here is where my story actually begins, or should've begun. After all, it was Cherry's accident that precipitated my run for jimmywhale of the UWA, and the subsequent trade war, and that's when I entered the history books, even as a footnote. And that's what most people are interested in, right?

Except that how could I possibly have jumped into the tale right here? None of it would've made any sense, without knowing about my backstory and FooDog's and Cherry's. I would've had to be constantly interrupting myself to backfill.

And besides, aren't most people nowadays habituated to ruckerian metanovels, with their infinite resortability and indrajal links? Even though I chose to compose this account in a linear fashion, you're probably bopping through it in a quirky personalized path anyhow, while simultaneously offering planting advice to a golden-rice grower in Bantul, contributing a few bars to an electrosoul composer in Los Angeles, and tweaking the specs of some creature's synthetic metabolism with an a-lifer in Loshan.

So:

I rushed to Cherry's side and grabbed her hand. "Ouch! Watch my IV!"

"Oh, babe, what happened? Are you gonna be okay?"

"Yeah, I'll be fine. It was just a stupid accident. But it wasn't really my fault "

Cherry had been sunning herself on the deck yesterday, half asleep. As the sun moved, she got up to shift her chair closer to the deck's edge. The next thing she knew, she was lying in the shallow waters surrounding Sandybump, buried under the timbers and pilings of the deck. Her head projected from the waters, allowing her to breathe painfully around her busted ribs. But lacking personal ubik access to summon help, she surely would've died in a short time from the shock of her injuries.

Luckily, the house itself knew to call one of the 911 wikis. Within minutes, an ambulance service run by the Organ Printers had her safely stabilized and on her way to MGH.

"The deck just collapsed, Russ! Honest. I didn't do anything to it!"

My concern for Cherry's health and safety began to segue to anger. Which wiki had built the deck? I started to rummage through the house's construction records, at the same time pulling up realtime images of my dwelling. The tearing-off of the deck had pulled away a portion of the exterior wall, opening our beloved house to the elements.

The Fatburgers. They were the wiki who had built my deck. Bastards! I was in the middle of composing a formal challenge suit against them, prior to filing it with a judicial wiki, when FooDog contacted me.

"You're back stateside, nephew! Great! But there's information you need to know before you rush into anything. Drop on by my offices."

"Can't you just tell me over the ubik?"

"Nah-huh. C'mon over."

I gingerly kissed Cherry goodbye, and left.

I pooled my public transit request with those of a few dozen other riders heading in my direction, and I was over the Charles River in no time.

Foolty Fontal maintained an occasional physical presence in a building on Mass Ave in Cambridge owned by the Gerontion wiki, whose focus was life-extension technology. Jealous of their potentially lucrative research, the Gerontions had equipped the building with massive security, both virtual and analogue, the latter including several lethal features. Thus FooDog felt moderately safe in using their premises.

But the building knew to let me in, and I followed a glowing trail of virtual footprints blazoned with my name to a lab on the third floor.

FooDog stood by a table on which rested a dissection tray.

Coming up to his side, I looked down at the tray's contents.

I saw a splayed-open rust-coloured worm about twenty inches long.

"Eeyeuw! What's that?"

"That and its cousins are what brought down your deck. Shipworms. *Teredo navalis.* Molluscs, actually. But not native ones, and not unmodified. This particularly nasty critter was created in a Caracas biolab. They were used in the hostilities against Brazil ten years ago. They'll even eat some plastics! Supposedly wiped out in the aftermath—extinct. But obviously not."

I poked the rubbery worm with a finger. "How'd they get up north and into my deck pilings? Is this some kind of terrorist assault?"

"I don't think so. Now that we know what to look for, I've done a little data-mining. I've found uncoordinated, overlooked reports of these buggers—enough to chart the current geographical dispersion of the worms and backtrack to a single point of origin. I believe that a small number of these worms came accidentally to our region in the bilge water of a fully automated container vessel, the *Romulo Gallegos.* Looks like purely unintentional contamination. But until I know for sure, I didn't want to broadcast anything over the ubik and alert people to cover their tracks. Or rouse false alarms of an assault."

"Okay. I can think of at least three entities we can nail for this, and get some damages and satisfaction. The owner of the ship, the traders who employed him, and the jerks who created the worms in the first place."

"Don't forget our own coastal biosphere guardians, wikis like the Junior Nemos and the Aquamen. They should have caught this outbreak before it spread."

"Right! Let's go get them!"

"The conference room is down this way "

Ten empty chairs surrounded a large conference table formed from a single huge vat-grown burl. FooDog and I settled down in two seats, and then we called the offending parties to our meeting. My SCURF painted onto my visual field the fully dimensional realtime avatars of our interlocutors sitting in the other chairs, so that it looked as if the room had suddenly filled with people in the flesh. Men and women scattered around the planet saw FooDog and me similarly in their native contexts.

Most of the avatars seemed to represent the baseline looks of the participants, but a few were downright disconcerting. I couldn't help staring at a topless mermaid, one of the Aquamen, no doubt.

FooDog smiled in welcoming fashion. "All right, ladies and gentlemen, allow me to introduce myself "

Everyone nowadays claims that instant idiomatic translation of any language into any other tongue is one of the things that has ushered in a new era of understanding, empathy and comity. Maybe so. But not judging from my experiences that day, once FooDog had spread out his evidence and accusations to the mainly South American audience. We were met with stonewalling, denials, patriotic vituperations, counter-charges and *ad hominem* insults. And that was from our English-speaking compatriots in the UWA! The Latinos reacted even more harshly.

Finally, the meeting dissolved in a welter of ill-will and refusal of anyone to take legal or even nominal responsibility for the collapse of my deck and the injuries suffered by poor Cherry.

I turned despondently to FooDog, once we were alone again. "Looks like we're boned, right? All our evidence is circumstantial. There's no way we can redress this through the system. I mean, aside from convincing any wikis I'm personally involved in to boycott these buggers, what else can I do?"

FooDog, good friend that he was, had taken my dilemma to heart.

"Damn! It's just not right that they should be allowed to get away with hurting you and Cherry like this."

He pondered my fix for another minute or so before speaking. "Seems to me our problem is this. You got no throw-weight here, nephew. You're only one aggrieved individual. Your affiliate wikis are irrelevant to the cause. But if we could get the whole country behind you, that'd be a different story."

"And how do we do that?"

"Well, we could mount a big sob campaign. Get all the oprahs and augenblickers talking about you. Make you and Cherry into Victims of the Week."

"Oh, man, I don't know if I want to go that route. There's no guarantee we wouldn't come out of it looking like jerks anyway."

"Right, right. Well, I guess that leaves only one option—"

"What's that?"

FooDog grinned with the nearly obscene delight he always expressed when tackling a task deemed impossible by lesser mortals.

"If we want satisfaction, we'll just have to take over the UWA."

7. Starting at the Top

I had always steered clear of politics. Which is not to say I had neglected any of my civic duties. Voting on thousands of day-to-day decisions about how to run my neighbourhood, my city, my state, my bioregion and the UWA as a whole. Debating and parsing Wikitustional Amendments. Helping to formulate taxes, tariffs and trade agreements. Drafting criminal penalties. Just like any good citizen, I had done my minute-to-minute share of steering the country down a righteous path.

But I never once felt any desire to formally join one of the wikis that actually performed the drudgery of implementing the consensus-determined policies and legislation.

The Georgetown Girls. The Slick Willy Wonkettes. The Hamilfranksonians.The FoundingFlavours.TheRowdy Rodhamites. The Roosevelvet Underground. The Cabal of Interns. The Technocratic Dreamers. The Loyal Superstition. The Satin Stalins. The Amateur Gods. The Boss Hawgs. The Red Greens. The Rapporteurs. The Harmbudsmen. The Shadow Cabinet. The Gang of Four on the Floor. The Winston Smiths. The Over-the-Churchills.

Maybe, if you're like me, you never realized how many such groups existed, or how they actually coordinated.

By current ubik count, well over five hundred political wikis were tasked with some portion of running the UWA on non-local levels, each of them occupying some slice of the political/ ideological/intellectual spectrum and performing one or another "governmental" function.

Each political wiki was invested with a certain share of proportional power based on the number of citizens who formally subscribed to its philosophy. The jimmywhales of each wiki formed the next higher level of coordination. From their ranks, after much traditional politicking and alliance building, they elected one jimmywhale to Rule Them All.

This individual came as close to being the President of our country as anyone could nowadays.

Until deposed, he had the power to order certain consequential actions across his sphere of influence by fiat; to countermand bad decisions; to embark on new projects without prior approval: the traditional role of any jimmywhale. But in this case, his sphere of influence included the entire country.

Currently this office was held by Ivo Praed of the Libertinearians. FooDog set out to put me in Ivo Praed's seat.

"The first thing we have to do," Foolty Fontal said, "is to register our wiki."

The three of us—myself, a fully recovered Cherry and the Dog—were sitting on the restored deck of the Sandybump house, enjoying drinks and snacks under a clear sunny sky. (This time, concrete pilings upheld the porch.)

"What should we call it?" I asked.

Cherry jumped right in. "How about the Phantom Blots?"

FooDog laughed. I pulled up the reference on the ubik, and I laughed too.

"Okay, we're registered," said FooDog.

"Now what? How do we draw people to our cause? I don't know anything about politics."

"You don't have to. It would take too long to play by the rules, with no guarantees of success. So we're going to cheat. I'm going to accrue power to the Phantom Blots by stealing microvotes from every citizen. Just like the old scam of grifting a penny apiece from a million bank accounts."

"And no one's going to notice?"

"Oh, yeah, in about a week, I figure. But by then we'll have gotten our revenge."

"And what'll happen when everyone finds out how we played them?"

"Oh, nothing, probably. They'll just seal up the backdoor I took advantage of, and reboot their foolish little parliament."

"You really think so?"

"I do. Now, let me get busy. I've got to write our platform first—" FooDog fugued out. Cherry got up, angled an umbrella across the abstracted black man to provide some shade, and then signalled me to step inside the house.

Out of earshot of our pal, she said, "Russ, why is FooDog going to all this trouble for us?"

"Well, let's see. Because we're buddies, and because he can't resist monkey-wrenching the system just for kicks. That about covers it."

"So you don't think he's looking to get something personal out of all this?"

"No. Well, maybe. FooDog always operates on multiple levels.

But so long as he helps us get revenge—"

Cherry's expression darkened. "That's another thing I don't like. All this talk of 'revenge.' We shouldn't be focused on the past, holding a grudge. We came out of this accident okay. I'm healthy again, and the house is fixed. No one was even really to blame. It's like when those two species of transgenic flies unpredictably mated in the wild, and the new hybrid wiped out California's wine grapes. Just an act of God. "

In all the years Cherry and I been together, we had seldom disagreed about anything. But this was one matter I wouldn't relent on. "No! When I think about how you nearly died— Someone's got to pay!"

Shaking her head ruefully, Cherry said, "Okay, I can see it's a point of honour with you, like if one of the Oyster Pirates ratted out another. I'll help all I can. If I'm in, I'm in. I just hope we're not bringing down heavy shit on our heads."

The door to the deck slid open, admitting a blast of hot air, and FooDog entered, grinning face glistening with sweat.

"Okay, nephew and niece, we're up and running. Even as we speak, thousands and thousands of microvotes are accumulating to the wiki of the Phantom Blots every hour, seemingly from citizens newly entranced by our kickass platform. You should read the plank about turning Moonbase Armstrong into the world's first offworld hydroponic ganja farm! Anyhow, I figure that over the next forty- eight hours, the Blots will rise steadily through the ranks of the politco-wikis, until our leader is ready to challenge Praed for head jimmywhale."

Suddenly I got butterflies in my stomach. "Uh, FooDog, maybe you'd like to be the one to run the UWA…"

"No way, padre. The Dog's gotta keep a low profile, remember? The farther away I can get from people, the happier I am. Nope, the honour is all yours."

"Okay. Thanks—I guess."

FooDog's calculations were a little off. It only took thirty-six hours before the Phantom Blots knocked the Libertinearians out as most influential politco-wiki, pushing Ivo Praed from his role as "president" of the UWA, and elevating me to that honour.

Sandybump, a speck of land off the New England coast, was now the White House. (Not the current museum, but last century's nexus of hyperpower.) I was ruler of the nation—insofar as it consented to be ruled. Cherry was my First Lady. And FooDog was my Cabinet.

Time to get some satisfaction.

8. Wikiwar

The day after my political ascension, we reconvened the meeting we had conducted at Gerontion, this time at Sandybump. All the same participants were there, with the addition of Cherry.

(Lots of other important national matters were continually arising to demand my attention, in my new role as head jimmywhale, but I just ignored them, stuffing them in a queue, preferring not to mess with stuff that I, for one, did not understand. This abdication of my duties would surely cause our charade to be exposed soon, but hopefully not before we had accomplished our goals.)

FooDog and I restated our grievances to the South Americans, but now formulated as a matter of gravest international diplomacy. (Foolty showed me the avatar he was presenting to the South Americans and our coastal management wikis, and of course it looked nothing like the real Dog.) This time, with the weight of the whole UWA behind our complaints, we received less harsh verbal treatment from the foreigners. And our compatriots caved right away, acknowledging that they had been negligent in not protecting our waterways from shipworm incursion. When FooDog and I announced a broad range of penalties against them, the mermaid shimmered and reverted to a weepy young teenaged boy.

But the South Americans, although polite, still refused to admit any responsibility for the Great Teredo Invasion.

"You realize, of course," said FooDog, "that you leave us no recourse but to initiate a trade war."

One of the Latinos, who was presenting as Che Guevara, sneered and said, "Do your worst. We will see who has the greater balance of trade." He stood up and bowed to Cherry. "Madam, I am sorry these outrageous demands cannot be met. But believe me when I say I am gratified to see you well and suffering no permanent harm from your unfortunate accident."

Then he vanished, along with the others.

Cherry, still un-SCURFED, had been wearing an antique pair of spex to participate in the conference. Now she doffed them and said, "Rebels are so sexy! Can't we cut them some slack?"

"No! It's time to kick some arrogant Venezuelan tail!"

"I got the list of our exports right here, nephew."

From the ubik, I studied the roster of products that the UAW sold to Venezuela, and picked one.

"Okay, let's start small. Shut off their housebots."

After hostilities were all over and I wasn't head jimmywhale anymore, I had time to read up about old-fashioned trade wars. It seems the tactics used to consist of drying up the actual flow of unshipped goods between nations. But with spimed products, such in-the-future actions were dilatory, crude and unnecessary.

Everything the UWA had ever sold to the Venezuelans became an instant weapon in our hands.

Through the ubik, we sent commands to every UWA- manufactured Venezuelan housebot to shut down. The commands were highest override priority and unstoppable. You couldn't isolate a spimed object from the ubik to protect it, for it would cease to function.

Across an entire nation, every household lost its domestic cyber- servants.

"Let's see how they like washing their own stinking windows and emptying their own cat-litter!" I said. "They'll probably come begging for relief within the hour."

FooDog had pulled up another roster, this one of products the Venezuelans sold us. "I don't know, nephew. I think we might take a few hits first. I'm guessing—"

Even as FooDog spoke, we learned that every hospital in the UWA had just seen its t-ray imagers go down.

"Who the hell knew that the Venezuelans had a lock on selling us terahertz scanners?" I said.

FooDog's face wore a look of chagrin. "Well, actually—"

"Okay, we've got to ramp up. Turn off all their wind turbines."

All across Venezuela, atmospheric powerplants fell still and silent.

The response from the Southerners was not long in coming. Thirty percent of the UWA's automobiles—the Venezuelan market share—ground to a halt.

FooDog sounded a little nervous when next he spoke. "Several adjacent countries derived electricity from the Venezuelan grid, and now they're demanding we restore the wind turbines. They threaten to join in the trade war if we don't comply."

I felt nervous too. But I was damned if I'd relent yet. "Screw them! It's time for the big guns. Bring down their planes."

Made-in-the-UWA airliners around the globe running under the Venezuelan flag managed controlled descents to the nearest airports.

That's when the Venezuelans decided to shut down the half of our oil-refining capacity that they had built for us. True, oil didn't play the role it once did in the last century, but that blow still hurt.

Then the Brazilians spimed *their* autos off, and the nation lost another 40 percent of its personal transport capabilities.

Over the next eight hours, the trade war raged, cascading across several allied countries. (Canada staunchly stood by the UWA, I was happy to report, incensed at the disruption of deliveries from the Athabasca Oil Sands to our defunct refineries. But the only weapon they could turn against the Southerners was a fleet of Zamboni machines at Latin American ice rinks.) Back and forth the sniping went, like two knights hacking each other's limbs off in some antique Monty Python farce.

With each blow, disruptions spread farther, wider and deeper across all the countries involved.

The ubik was aflame with citizen complaints and challenges, as well as a wave of emergency counter-measures to meet the dismantling of the infrastructure and deactivation of consumer goods and appliances and vehicles. The politco-wikis were convulsing, trying to depose me and the Phantom Blots. But FooDog managed to hold them at bay, as Cherry rummaged through the tiniest line items in our export list, looking for ways to strike back.

By the time the Venezuelans took our squirm futons offline, and we shut down all their sex toys, the trade war had devolved into a dangerous farce.

I was exhausted, physically and mentally. The weight of what Cherry, FooDog and I had done rested on my shoulders like a lead cape. Finally I had to ask myself if what I had engineered was worth it.

I stepped out on the deck to get some fresh air and clear my head. Cherry followed. The sun was sinking with fantastically colourful effects, and gentle waves were lapping at Sandybump's beach. You'd never know that several large economies were going down the toilet at that very moment.

I hugged Cherry and she hugged me back. "Well, babe, I did my best. But it looks like our revenge is moot."

"Oh, Russ, that's okay. I never wanted—"

The assault came in fast and low. Four armoured and be-weaponed guys riding ILVs. Each Individual Lifting Vehicle resembled a skirt- wearing grasshopper. Before either Cherry or I could react, the chuffing ILVs were hovering autonomously at the edge of our deck, and the assailants had jumped off and were approaching us with weapons drawn.

With cool menace one guy said, "Okay, don't put up a fight and you won't get hurt."

I did the only thing I could think of. I yelled for help. "FooDog! Save us!"

And he did.

SCURF mediates between your senses and the ubik. Normally the SCURF-wearer is in control of course. But when someone breaks down your security and overrides your inputs, there's no predicting what he can feed you.

FooDog sent satellite closeups of recent solar flares to the vision of our would-be-kidnappers, and the latest sludge-metal hit, amped up to eleven, to their ears.

All four went down screaming.

Cherry erased any remnants of resistance with a flurry of kicks and punches, no doubt learned from her bar-brawling brother Dolphin.

When we had finished tying up our commando friends, and FooDog had shut off the assault on their senses, I said, "Okay, nothing's worth risking any of us getting hurt. I'm going to surrender now."

Just as I was getting ready to call somebody in Venezuela, Che Guevara returned. He looked morose.

"All right, you bastard, you win! Let's talk."

I smiled as big as I could. "Tell me first, what was the final straw? It was the sex toys, wasn't it?"

He wouldn't answer, but I knew I was right.

9. Free to be You and Me

So that's the story of how I ran the country for three days. One day of political honeymoon, one day of trade war, and one day to clean up as best we could, before stepping down.

As FooDog predicted, there were minimal personal repercussions from our teasling of the political system. Loopholes were closed, consensus values re-affirmed, and a steady hand held the tiller of the ship of state once again.

We never did learn who sent the commandos against us. I think they were jointly hired by nativist factions in league with the Venezuelans. Both the UWA and the South Americans wanted the war over with fast. But since our assailants never went on trial after their surgery to give them new eyes and eardrums, the secret never came out.

Cherry and I got enough simoleans out of the settlement with the Venezuelans to insure that we'd never have to work for the rest of our lives. But she still goes out with the Oyster Pirates from time to time, and I still can't resist the call of mongo.

We still live on Sandybump, but the house is bigger now, thanks to a new wing for the kids.

As for FooDog—well, I guess he did have ulterior motives in helping us. We don't see him much anymore in the flesh, since he relocated to his ideal safe haven.

Running that ganja plantation on the Moon as his personal fiefdom takes pretty much all his time.

ABOUT THE AUTHOR

Paul Di Filippo sold his first story in 1977. In the subsequent thirty-five years, he's had nearly that number of books published. He hopes the next thirty-five years are as generous.

He lives in Providence, Rhode Island, with his partner of many years, Deborah Newton; a calico cat named Penny Century; and a chocolate-coloured cocker spaniel named, with jaw-dropping unoriginality, Brownie.

www.ingramcontent.com/pod-product-compliance
Lightning Source LLC
Chambersburg PA
CBHW020610260626
47157CB00003B/943